Josiah Stubb:
The Siege of Louisbourg

C W Lovatt

A Wild Wolf Publication

Published by Wild Wolf Publishing in 2014

Copyright © 2014 C W Lovatt

First print

ISBN: 978-1-907954-37-5

Also available in e-book

www.wildwolfpublishing.com

Further works by the author

The Adventures of Charlie Smithers (2013)

Wild Wolf's Twisted Tails (2013)

For the mad woman at
246-23rd Street

Acknowledgements

There are a great many people I would like to thank for helping get Josiah Stubb off the ground. Some names I know, most I don't. First there is the helpful staff at Parks Canada, both at Louisbourg, and again at Signal Hill in St. John's. Then there are the long-suffering actors and actresses at the Fortress who play their unassuming roles for the tourists, day in and day out, yet knowledgeably answer all sorts of questions about the period and their surroundings. Then there is Linda Kennedy and her staff at the Point Of View Suites where we stayed while in Louisbourg; everyone very helpfully and enthusiastically offered suggestions every morning at breakfast, and offered their congratulations every evening when we returned, tired and elated, from another day of discovery. At St. John's, thanks go out to the helpful staff and archivists at the library of Memorial University, who put us on the path to Gerald Penney Associates, a little jewel of an archeological consulting firm we learned a wealth of knowledge from. They, in turn, pointed us in the direction of St. John's' beautiful glass and granite museum, named with typical Newfoundland candour, "The Rooms." I would also like to thank Deb Clark Gillihan for reading the manuscript, and for offering me her views. Then there is that great team at Wild Wolf Publications for managing to put all this into some sort of order, in a last minute flurry of activity. And, of course, as always my greatest asset, Amber Clark, for digging up research material, and without whose patience and guidance this book would never have seen the light of day. Thank you all.

Preface

Most Canadians first learn about the Battle of the Plains of Abraham while they are still in school, and I was no exception. Relatively speaking, we were told a great deal about that campaign, while the campaign that took place the previous year (the one that made this one possible) is mere skin and bones.

Yes, we were told that the Fortress of Louisbourg cost a fortune to build (over 30,000,000 *livres*, a monstrous amount at the time,) and that Louis XV is said to have sourly quipped that, for such a price, he ought to be able to see the peaks of its buildings from his palace in Versailles. And yes, we were also told that it became known as "The Gibraltar of North America," and was deemed impregnable by its military contemporaries. But with this planted firmly in our young minds – of a fortress so grand and impregnable that it defied the imagination – our grade school history teachers then went on to tell us that it was attacked twice…and taken twice - once in 1745 during the War of the Austrian Succession (and returned to the French via the Treaty of Aix-la-Chapelle,) and again in 1758, at the time of this story. Even at that tender age, the first question to spring to mind was "How?" If this bastion of French pride was everything that we were told it was (and it was, as I would see for myself decades later) *how* was it taken? I did ask at the time, but my teacher did not know either, and quickly turned the subject elsewhere before I could pester her any further.

So I suppose that the first tiny seed was planted way back then, sometime in the mid 1960's: one day I would find the answer, and then I would let everyone else know. So here we are, all these years, and a different century, later; that day has finally arrived.

However, make no mistake, this book was not written with grade schoolers in mind (insofar as I ever have anyone in mind when I write.) I think that some subliminal part of me wrote it for all the other kids of my day, who are all grown now, as I have grown, and can take a good story with an edge. For, as much as I am a history buff, I found out long ago that I absorb far more by reading a well-researched work of fiction than I ever did from a textbook. As a writer of fiction, the story is always the main thing; if any of the historical details stick, then it is all to the good.

Having said that, although telling the tale of young Josiah Stubb was my first concern, my intention with this book is to describe what happened at Louisbourg, in the summer of 1758, as diligently as possible. Here you will find how the conclusion we know today very nearly did not come about at all: when Wolfe (then only a brigadier, the most junior of three) had his nose bloodied for him on the 8th of June, the day of the landing, and would have retreated, had it not been for the courage of his junior officers, and a great deal of luck, but also how he then quickly turned defeat into victory. Then there is the story of desperate raid and counter-raid – of how, by varying degrees, the British attempted to drive their attack home, and how the French strove to delay the progress of their ancient enemy until the onslaught of winter, which would certainly have seen the lifting of the siege. Having found his land legs, you will also see how Wolfe continued to keep the French off-balance, by virtue of impetuous courage and energy, while his more experienced contemporaries dawdled along with methods tried and true, which, left to their own devices, in all likelihood, would have failed.

Also, I would like to mention that, while Josiah's regiment, the 51st did exist at the time, it was not at the siege, so in essence I made it part of the story's fiction. Why? Because the regiment that it is based upon, the 40th (made up of garrison companies in Newfoundland and Nova Scotia - putting it conveniently in St. John's during Josiah's youth,) *was* at the siege, and although the grenadier company *was* with Wolfe at the landing, and again at Lighthouse Point, it was not at all of the actions described, all of which did actually happen – some accurately recorded, some with a bit of guesswork and license. So rather than being historically inaccurate, I decided to invent an entirely new regiment that did manage to insinuate itself into all the salient points as they happened. Ain't fiction grand?

In closing, I would like to point out that, for a fiction writer, a great deal of research went into this project: book after book of historical accounts, maps poured over, reams of notes, visiting libraries and museums, and even a working vacation taken to the reconstructed fortress, before moving on to St. John's, to get a nuance of where the story took place. Perhaps inevitably, a great deal of help was enlisted along the way, all for the sake of accuracy. It being my opinion that, if they are going to take themselves seriously, writers of historical fiction owe it to themselves not to dishonour the past by getting their facts wrong. If there are any errors, the fault is entirely my own.

CWL

Table Of Contents

Prologue

(The hour: just past midnight, the eighth of June, the year: 1758 – the place is on the waters just off of the southeastern tip of Cape Breton Island...or as it is known by its present occupants, Ile Royale)

It was the dead of night, but a beehive of activity was taking place throughout the fleet. A sober procedure of well-trained crews hoisting ship's boats to their davits, at the command, lowering away, one by one, into the tumbling sea; hundreds upon hundreds of them, the squeal of so many ropes running through such a multitude of blocks piercing the quiet, overruling the low creaking of the ships themselves, as they roll majestically on the ocean swells.

Sails furled, riding at anchor on a lee shore, against a quarter moon their masts are revealed in stark contrast through the dim light of the eastern sky, like a ghostly forest of denuded trees, hulls outlined in shadow. There are nigh on two hundred of them, transports mostly, but the ponderous weight of warships is also present. The massive ninety-gun *Namur* is here; so too are the *Royal William* and *Princess Amelia*, both of eighty guns each; two carry admirals' flags, the *Princess Amelia* a commodore's. Forty men of war, twenty of them ships of the line, each capable of facing the best that the French can throw at them. A mighty armada in its own right, they could sail to the furthest reaches of the known world with impunity, and in fact had done so; for their homeports are far away, countless leagues over a distant horizon, in Portsmouth and Spithead.

Some few miles to the west, the French fortress of Louisbourg is cloaked in darkness, land and sky indivisible, quiet as though sleeping – a ruse that everyone, from the lowliest sailor to the grandest admiral, desires to believe, but in their heart of hearts, none dare.

At the appointed hour, from the frigates comes the sound of muffled drums beating to quarters, and a flurry of activity as topmen swarm up the ratlines and let go sails, each instantly

13

billowing in the stiffening wind. Bowsprits prod the darkness as these graceful vessels slip their moorings, and begin to make way from their stations on the wings, where they had stood as sentinels, like sheep dogs overlooking their flocks. *Squirrel* and *Sutherland* make for White Point, guarding the entrance to Gabarus Bay; *Gramont, Diana,* and *Shannon* set course for Flat Point, a jut of land halfway down the length of the bay itself, where it is known that the defenders are well provided with heavy batteries; and *Kennington* and the snow, *Halifax,* steer toward the most important goal of all – Fresh Water Cove. Once on station, each drops anchor to provide a steady platform for their guns, with a spring trailing from the cable to the stern, giving them the capability of bringing their broadsides to bear with all due speed, wherever the need is greatest.

Aboard the transports, the order is given, and the troops begin to file on deck from the holds, up over the sides, and down to where the boats wait with their crews of weathered tars. There is a minimum of noise, for all has been well rehearsed many times in the month preceding. Hours pass, miraculously without incident in the nearly non-existent light. The seas, although not heavy, are far from calm, and quite easily could be fatal to the uninitiated. Yet thousands of men have descended safely: the first assault wave, even their artillery – a few light six-pounders – have been hoisted over the side and lowered gently into the boats. It is a task that would daunt any navy in the broadest daylight and in the gentlest of seas, but there is no confusion here, merely men with a job to do, and a determination to do it well.

When all is ready, as the frigates begin to let loose their broadsides at the shore, one by one the first flotillas of boats begin to leave the shelter of their mother ships. Soon they are passing through the picket-line of men-of-war, after which, as if by magic, they coalesce into their separate divisions: White under Whitmore head for White Point, Blue under Lawrence to Flat Point, and finally Wolfe's Red Division, the attack division, steer the greatest distance, toward Fresh Water Cove.

So far all has gone well, in spite of the hazards; for these manoeuvres have been well rehearsed many times, and many times in darkness as total as it is now.

Leaving the safety of the fleet behind them, urged on by the hoarse whispers of their petty officers, tars at the oars pull toward the shore. At the planning table, every known hazard has been identified and, in theory, overcome.

Now, at long last, the moment to put the theory to the test has arrived.

Chapter One

Under a graying sky, *Kennington* and *Halifax* continued popping away with their broadsides, the blasts echoing off the shore, reaching us flat and muted in the early morning wind. We watched them with a measure of hope, as the tongues of flame stab, again and again, in the uncertain light, each of us praying with forlorn anxiety that the navy would actually manage to hit something for a change.

On board our barge, I watched as its prow heaved in the violent swell, for some reason reminding me of Fat Sally's chemise.

Odd how the mind works: here I was sailing into the teeth of the French defences along with the rest of my mates, and also like the rest of my mates, feeling green as grass while our stomachs heaved right along with the boats – partly in fear, but mostly due to those blasted waters off the coast. Odd that I should think of her now, or think of her at all, really, but her chemise did tend to heave up and down quite a bit, especially when the lads were on the town with a few coins to spare; and although not wooden in any way, shape or form, it had to be admitted that Fat Sally was quite as ponderous as a ship of the line, let alone a barge.

Yes, it was odd, but like I said, I was afraid, and I've heard from many of the older hands that it's only natural to think of your mother at a time like this.

I might have dwelled on in quite a bit more depth, but just then my thoughts were interrupted by the sound of retching coming from behind me, shortly followed by the wet splatter of vomit in the scuppers.

Sergeant Bell, a viper at the best of times, must have had an even greater craving for the hair of the dog this morning than was usual. It was causing him to feel especially liverish for he snapped, "Right, Todsmuir! I'll have the skin off your back for that!"

"Let be, Sergeant," I overheard Captain Beaumont murmur before raising his voice so that everyone could hear, "It won't be long now, lads!"

When this failed to raise any cheers – we were all that miserable – he added, "Think of it, men! Good solid ground before you, just as God intended for an honest land soldier!"

That drew a titter, but only just. All of us had been called many things since accepting the King's shilling, but never before had we been referred to as 'honest'. On second thought, it was probably the land itself that he was referring to, not us. Yes, that was much more likely.

Sitting amidships on one of the barge's splintery thwarts, with my musket clutched between my knees, I was sandwiched so tightly between my best friend, Daniel Hawthorne on my right, and Benjamin Stockingsdale, the company's pervert, on my left that I was scarcely able to twiddle my fingertips. I felt helpless as a newborn kitten, tossed about on the briny sea as the tars strained at their oars, pulling us ever closer to our destiny. I had to admit that the land appeared honest from over a mile away. It looked solid and reassuring to my lubberly eye, but I knew that it was misleading. There was nothing reassuring about where we were going, nothing at all.

Yet we had been seventeen long days in the transports – ten of them at sea, ever since we sailed from Halifax near the end of May, rolling around in those leaky old tubs, pressed together, tight as sardines, sicker than dogs to a man. We were heartily fed up with it all. Though we knew that the looming shore was, in fact, bristling with cannon and thousands of the enemy bent on our destruction, and we were rightfully apprehensive of that fact, I believe that it was universally preferable that we get on with the job, and leave those much-loathed ships behind us.

It had to be just past five o'clock in the morning, on the eighth of June. A massive flotilla of boats from our armada of one hundred and fifty transports and forty men of war was pulling toward the shores of Gabarus Bay, just two leagues down the coast from the French fortress of Louisbourg: by all accounts, the most formidable stronghold on the North American seaboard.

Louisbourg had to be taken; that had been the word going through barracks since time out of mind. French warships and privateers based there had always been preying on our merchant fleet in times of trouble, and trouble was more the norm these days than ever before. But it wasn't just the threat to Britain's commerce that gave it such importance; the fortress was a symbol of the arrogant pride of France, and it was our duty to bring it to its knees.

There were more than twelve thousand of us: regular line soldiers, mostly, with the addition of the Royal Navy's compliment of marines, and a few companies of Rangers. These last were part of the light infantry - a new creation, but already possessed with a reputation for being wild and undisciplined, of little use on the line during a set-piece battle, but it was said that they waged war on an equal footing with the tactics of the Canadiens and their Indian allies. Those savage foes had seriously hampered our armies on more than one occasion in the past. It was hoped that here the Rangers would prove an effective counter measure for what was to come.

The lads in my own regiment, the 51st, were loath to admit to an inferiority to anyone with regard to Indian fighting. Since long before my birth, when the regiment was first formed from garrison troops from the colonies of Nova Scotia and New Foundland, our chief opponents had been the local natives. It was against these people that we had learned our trade through bitter experience, having over the decades the graves in our cemeteries to prove it. Yet, though fighting in the way of the New World had become our bread and butter, we continued to drill as regular line troops, for the French and *their* regulars were always just over the horizon; so at last, when the call came for this latest attempt to humble our old enemy once and for all, we were ready.

Meanwhile Todsmuir had begun to retch again, and was soon joined by others sitting next to him. Inevitably, this was accompanied by more vomit, the sounds of half-digested salt pork being regurgitated, urging others to follow suit. When the time came for Stockingsdale to turn green and lean forward, voiding his stomach between his knees, splattering his gaiters, and liberally decorating my own, I knew that I would not be far behind. Sure enough, when the odor reached my nostrils, the world began to spin and my stomach to roil, and I could actually feel my face turning even greener than it already was. Then I was leaning forward like everyone else, heaving the contents of my stomach onto my boots, miserably wishing that I was dead..

By the very erect nature of Sergeant Bell, standing in the prow with his back to us, I thought he was struggling to contain his passion to wade in with a rope's end, to punish our unsoldierly behaviour, but then he, too, was leaning over the gunwale, feeding the fish with his own offering, while his knees buckled, leaving him draped over the side like a discarded doll.

At last our captain followed suit over the other bow. He was largely an unknown quantity to us in the ranks, having joined the regiment from England scarcely a month before we had set sail for this godforsaken place. Not openly given to drink, like most of our officers, he seemed a likeable sort, and competent at his trade, if he could be judged during our training back in Halifax. So far there had been nothing to contradict that assessment, for even now, caught in the grips of seasickness, he was bravely muttering words of encouragement to us all between retchings, while the tars made little effort to hide their contempt.

In fact, I did hear the bo'sun mutter something from his place at the tiller, something about 'bloody sojers,' and wondered aloud about who was going to clean up the ''orrible mess'.

He was ignored to a man, for there seemed no dignified response, until Daniel, who had thus far proven immune to our malaise, opined in a loud voice that certain sailors, who shall remain unnamed, should shut their bloody gobs, and get on with their work.

The bo'sun squawked like a stuck goose, loudly demanding 'that man's name!' and was greeted with angry muttering from our ranks.

"Silence! God damn your eyes!"

Captain Beaumont had managed to regain his feet, and while still white as a sheet, held himself erect as an example to us all. His own anger was fighting a battle of wills with his desire to simply remain inert until the boat reached the shore.

He drew his sword, and swaying uncertainly, jabbed it landward to our destination. "So you show fight, do you?" he said, addressing the boat as a whole, "Well, my lads, you'll have your bellyful, of that I can promise you! Today we fight for England! Today we are brothers! There!" he cried, jabbing with his sword, "There is your enemy!"

He looked such a vision of wrath that there was no alternative but to burst out laughing.

"Oh that's rich!" someone cried between gasps, "To think of the swabbies and ourselves as brothers! Oh my! Oh my!"

I even heard the bo'sun chuckle in agreement, "That'll be the bloody day I call a lobster back *my* brother!"

Captain Beaumont's fury looked to achieve mountainous proportions. Sergeant Bell, having been shamed to his feet by his superior, looked so much like a moth-eaten terrier, awaiting the command to dart in and nip a convenient heel, that we laughed all the harder.

To be sure, ours was not a normal reaction in an army that has been taught to fear and respect their officers, if not love them, but we all sensed that Beaumont was very different from any that we had previously known. Whatever the reason for his having been sent to a regiment, long accustomed to being saddled with flawed superiors, it had not been for lack of amiability, and our laughter was merely a manifestation of the affection we returned.

Sure enough, our captain's face grew as dark as a storm cloud, but when he saw that we'd meant no harm, that we were laughing at a joke, however unintended, he allowed his better nature to gain the forefront of his feelings. Soon the frown had disappeared altogether, to be replaced by a shrug and a sheepish smile, leaving that viper, Bell, confused and uncertain – at which we laughed even more.

"Right, then," Beaumont, judging our mood to a tee, put a hand in his pocket and drew out a coin. "Bo'sun! I see that the boat to our right – excuse me – to *starboard*, carrying those awful fellows from the 35th, is pulling ahead. This sovereign shall go to you and your fine crew if you can reverse the situation!"

At which we all sent up a cheer, and with sickness and squabbles now forgotten, those of us who were not busy urging on the tars, or shouting taunts across the water to the boys of the 35th, were glaring at the shore, growling like dogs, thirsting to be at the French.

It lasted but a short while, of course, before a terse signal from the squadron commander's craft in the van ordered us to maintain station, but the purpose had been served. We were a different lot now than from moments before.

The captain's smile broadened, and he tossed the coin to the bo'sun, who caught it in an expert hand, before causing it to disappear inside his shirt.

"If duty had not intervened," he told him solemnly, "I am certain that you would have succeeded." Which drew another laugh and a cheer. Thanks to our captain's leadership, we were settled and of a mind. Woe betide the enemy when we came to grips!

By now we had halved the distance to the shore, and been ordered to maintain silence. With the sun rising at our backs, enough light was available to show us our destination, which was far from reassuring.

Much of the Gabarus Bay littoral was nothing but steep cliffs and boulder-ridden beaches upon which, even now, we could see the white caps of huge waves smashing themselves with such violence that many a manly bowel loosened at the sight. There must be some mistake! Surely Admiral Boscawen had not meant for us to attempt a landing here? But the tars pulled on relentlessly, the petty officer at the tiller calmly issuing orders for the boat to maintain the pace.

I turned to Daniel, all my earlier confidence having leaked away into my boots. "What do you make of that then, Dan?"

Daniel leaned over and spat carefully between his knees. "Another day another cock-up, Josiah," he said, as if not the least surprised, "Surely, you didn't expect to live forever?"

Well no I hadn't, but neither had I planned on being crushed and drowned by the shores of the back of beyond at the tender age of nineteen. I gestured toward the raging surf, "The boats will be smashed to kindling if we try to go in there!"

Daniel's laughter was bitter, though soft, "Aye, you'll earn your pay today, Josiah, never fear!"

"Silence in the ranks!" Bell's hissed whisper, intended to be severe, reminded me of the whistle of steam from a boiling kettle. His eyes, usually so piggish and small, now seemed unnaturally large for his head, and his mouth kept contorting so that the curled and waxed ends of his moustaches were constantly being bent at the most unlikely of angles. His sanction had not been directed solely toward Daniel and myself, however; as we had drawn nearer and the illumination increased, uneasy murmurs could be heard throughout the boat.

I heard a low keening coming from my immediate left, and thought that Stockingsdale was struggling in the throws of fear, but when I checked, saw with disgust that he was doing it in his own unique way.

Somewhere along the line, he had secretively undone the buttons of his flies, inserted his right hand, and was now busily occupied with the workings thereof.

I must have gasped because he looked at me, and without slackening the pace, managed a slow, wicked grin, revealing several yellowing and crooked teeth, where there were any teeth at all.

"We're all dead men, Joss," he whispered in an unsteady voice, indicating with his well-stubbled chin the tumultuous surf, the roar of which could now be heard quite plainly, "but I'm having it off one more time before I go, damned if I'm not! My advice is for you to do the same!"

I felt my eyes roll, and in my disgust, must have leaned away from the brute. This, in turn, drew Daniel's attention, for I could not lean away from Stockingsdale without leaning into my friend. He summed up the situation at a glance, and gave a low, derisive snort followed by a whispered, "Aye, that's the way, Ben" he chortled, "There's the French, and here's you coming at them with your hand on your knob. Like as not when we hit the beach you'll forget your musket, so when the order comes to fix bayonets, you needs must run them through with yon pox-ridden blade instead!"

The very thought must have been sufficient for his intentions, for the depraved fool's eyes began to lose focus, and his face reddened to match his coat. I could stand to bear witness to the revolting scene no further, and hoping for a less horrendous place to rest my eyes, glanced to Daniel. He returned my consternated gape with a grin and a wink, whispering, "Takes all sorts, Josiah!" A statement which I found impossible to controvert.

Meanwhile, it would seem that all other eyes were fixed upon the shore, for no other comment was made on Stockingsdale's shocking behaviour, which was a great pity. I had no doubt that a taste of the cat would have done him a world of good!

Then my mind was wrested from this comforting thought when I saw Captain Beaumont's outstretched arm pointing to a specific tract of land; he was leaning toward Sergeant Bell, his tall mitre bobbing back and forth in his excitement.

By now the sun had risen sufficiently, that if I craned my neck, I could see a cove with a crescent of sandy beach, perhaps four hundred yards in length - very pretty in the morning sun.

This had to be where the landing was intended, for here the surf was more subdued, protected by the headlands, and even more importantly, appeared to be free of boulders. Indeed, this would seem to be the case, for word began circulating back to us - overheard snippets of the animated conversation between Captain Beaumont and Sergeant Bell – that this was Fresh Water Cove. I studied it with mixed feelings; for although not a master tactician by any means, I did not need to be to realize that such a small beach would allow little room for manoeuvre, and that we would be going in on a full frontal assault.

Daniel cursed under his breath, sending another stream of spittle to mingle with the vomit in the scuppers. "That bloody well figures," he said, "put all those high mucky-mucks in the same room together, and the best they can come up with is to attack head-on!"

I shared his sentiment, of course, but at the same time had to admit that the nature of the island's natural defences seemed to allow for very little else. If we were going to attack, it had to be here, regardless of what *Monsieur* decided to throw at us. The lot of the common soldier and the Fortunes of War were always at odds that way.

So thinking, I watched while the leading boats put their rudders over, setting their bows directly toward the beach.

Our boat was complete silence now, but for the lapping of the water and the creak of the oars in their locks. To a man, we held our breath, frozen with tension, watching the shore as we continued to edge cautiously forward. All of us knew that the French were not fools: if we saw the advantages of landing here, it was certain that they realized it, too; and as the sun rose higher, we were given proof.

What at first might have been mistaken as a narrow belt of grassland verging on the beach, was now revealed to be a forest of branches from felled trees blocking access to the heights beyond. Any attacking force must needs wade through

24

this obstacle first before hoping to come to grips with the foe. The assault would be slowed to a crawl and all cohesion lost for a few critical moments when it was most needed; while those caught in that maze of limbs would be helplessly exposed to the fire of the enemy.

Yet as we drew nearer, there was still no sign of *Monsieur*, only a terrible silence, like the calm before a storm, setting our nerves on edge - each of us wondering if, even now, some Frenchman had us locked in his sights.

A signal went up from our general's boat, and the bo'sun ordered his tars to pull for the shore. We gripped our muskets ever harder, and began to prepare ourselves for the assault. We had practiced this moment for the past month in Halifax Harbour and felt confident that we were up to the job. We were grenadiers after all, the elite of the army, and the reason why our company had been detached from the 51st to serve in the Red Division under General Wolfe for the main attack while the remainder of our regiment were with General Whitmore, engaged in a feint off White point. Still, it was one thing to feel confident on a peaceful, sunny afternoon, secure behind the guns of our garrison, and quite another to be just off the enemy's coast, with every moment fraught with tension and the fear of imminent death or dismemberment. That is when you look at the fellows next to you (yes, even Stockingsdale) and hope that, when the moment comes, you will possess the fortitude to stand side-by-side with them in the line and face the enemy, unflinching, while he unleashes hell at you.

Silently, ever more closely, we approached the gentle sands of the beach, until we were within pistol-shot - so close in fact that I felt a brief welling of hope rise in my breast that we had achieved complete surprise.

So of course that was the moment when calamity rained down all around us with a vengeance.

It began in the form of sheets of smoke and flame erupting from the tops of the low cliffs, some few yards in from the beach, closely followed by the roar of great guns, and the staccato popping of musketry; and we were being deluged in a maelstrom of hot metal, splashing about the boats like torrential rain, or sending up giant geysers, bracketing us in walls of seawater twice the height of a man. Judging by the crumpling forms of red-coated figures, at least some of that metal had found a mark, scything into the closely packed boats like a plague, discomfortingly like a judgment from Heaven.

We sat in our boats, too stunned to move; for although resistance had been expected, the fury of the onslaught had been so terrible that, in an instant, it drove our spirits from our breasts and reason from our minds.

In the deafening silence that followed, while we sat bobbing on the waves, gazing stupidly about ourselves, there came a long drum roll, and with a vast, Gallic cry echoing off the headlands, the French colours were up, waving their defiance in the wind.

This spurred our fellows into action, but all cohesion was gone; some, sensing that a landing was impossible, began to come about, while others, in the midst of all that chaos, resumed their struggle for the shore, only to be caught in another salvo.

All was a confusion of smoke from spent powder until we could no longer see the beach, though it was a scant few yards away. Meanwhile, crashing volleys of musketry continued to ring out, leaving scarcely a boat of our leading wave unscathed. Even over the deafening thunder of the cannonade, we could hear the screams of the wounded, rendering us helpless with rage.

Growling incoherent oaths, the tars pulled ever harder before the bo'sun could prevail upon them to cease, it being uncertain how to proceed. At which point Private Snead, a veteran of many years, could contain himself no longer. Leaping to his feet, he shook his fist at the enemy, roaring an oath, before swinging back to the rest of us, laughing like a man who has taken leave of his senses.

"That's the way, boys!" he cried, "This is what we came halfway round the world to conquer! Who among us wouldn't travel halfway to hell just to come to grips with this moment?"

With his eyes blazing, perhaps as much from strong drink as from excitement, he pressed on, "In his dotage, who among us wishes to tell his grandchildren that, when the time came, his spirit failed!" Then whirling on the sailors resting on their oars he shouted, "Come on you swabbies! Let's get at them Frog bastards! Come on, I say!"

Furious, Sergeant Bell roared a belated, "Silence, that man!" at the top of his lungs, but words were never more wasted; for at that moment an incoming round from a six-pounder seared over our heads, but, alas, not over Private Snead's. It took him from the lower jaw upward, leaving his tongue wagging still, with frothing gouts of blood to add colour to his argument.

For a long moment the corpse continued standing, its harangue even more incoherent than ever; then slowly, it pitched forward onto its erstwhile companions. It is sad to say, that they did not receive it with affection, but held it at bay as best they might, grimaces of disgust on every face, while the dead man's arms flapped and coiled - the spouting blood augmenting the crimson of their uniforms in an everlasting remembrance.

"Oh, poor fellow!" Captain Beaumont murmured, producing another round of laughter from us all.

There are some who might think it callous, but death was not new to us, nor we to it. In our view, Snead had got off easy – a clean death in a moment of glory, instead of, for instance, being left to die by inches, alone in the wilderness, without a scalp – or to be brought low by a debilitating and inglorious disease. Too many of us had gone that way, men who were just as good, if not better, than he. So no, Snead had his moment, and we would not begrudge him it, because all of us knew that our own turn might be just around the next corner. When it came, all that could be hoped for was a clean slate and the respect of our mates. For there was not a man among us who questioned, that when Death laughed at you, all that you could do was to look him in the eye, and laugh right back.

Now, with Snead dismissed from our minds, all eyes returned to the battle – or the impending massacre, more like. No one could doubt, with more and more shot and shell coming at us every second, that we were in a bad situation. *Monsieur* had seized the upper hand, and by the incoming rounds that continued to pepper us in our floundering boats, he meant to keep it. Not a man of us could fight back, not a man of us could find cover. All that was left was to glare our defiance, and die.

Given that this was our only choice, still, our indignation knew no bounds when, amidst the smoke from the cannon and musketry, we saw the signal to retreat raised from our general's barge. Every one of us knew that to continue the attack was futile, yet we resented retreat bitterly. For with the tumultuous seas, and the scarcity of time, even we lowly soldiers were aware that this was our single opportunity. By forsaking it, we were staring at defeat yet again.

I watched as a naval officer in the boat next to ours suddenly spun away from the tiller with a ball in his arm, and a seaman scramble aft to take his place; but my mind was incapable of accepting that it, and all the other horrors taking place all around us were real. Instead it seemed to be a dream, or rather a nightmare, that was playing out in front of my eyes, and had little to do with myself. Such is the way my mind continued to work while sitting helpless, awaiting my own turn to be cut down. Negating the present, instead it reflected on the long journey the world had travelled to get us to this sorry pass.

Although Britain and France had officially declared war in 1756, it had already been raging in the New World for two long years before then, and ever since events had been going badly for us.

Starting with Washington's repulse at Great Meadows in 1754, then General Braddock's debacle on the Monongahela River the following year, and the fall of Fort Oswego the year after that, combined with the loss of Minorca across the Atlantic, the situation was already sufficiently desperate by the previous year, when we heard of the fall of Fort William Henry along with the atrocities suffered by our folk after the surrender. The thirst for revenge had been high but remained unappeased. Our attempt at Louisbourg the previous summer, under Lord Loudon, had to be abandoned due to that worthy's so badly mishandling affairs that it had resulted in his recall to England in disgrace.

For our part, we in the ranks were glad to see him go. Yet Loudon was but one in a long list of incompetent generals sent to us by Whitehall – it being the worst kept secret anywhere that the Cavendish government was corrupt and prone to patronage, to the point where we had lost faith in all of them, if not in ourselves. In fact, in all that time there had been only two victories of note: one in far off India, at a place called Plassey (at around the same time Loudon was making such a mess of things); and the other two years before that and much closer to home, at Fort Beauséjour, the French fort guarding the approaches to what was left of their colony of Acadia.

I had taken part in that campaign, although it hadn't amounted to much – just a short charge with the bayonet to chase the rascals back inside their walls, and a brief bombardment before the white flag came up. It was the part that came after that I didn't care for – none of us did.

You see, the Acadians were in a peculiar situation: they don't care for the British, to be sure, but neither had they much confidence in their own government in Versailles, claiming that it had abandoned them. The fact that events bore out those claims must have come as the coldest of comfort.

The conquest of Acadia had begun much earlier, during the War of the Austrian Succession with the fall of Port Royal. This regained control of all the land of our former colony of Nova Scotia up to the Missaquash River, and was not returned with the coming of peace, leaving the inhabitants with a sense of anger and betrayal. But rather than return to France (a foreign country to the vast majority), most chose to stay on their land and try to make a go of it among the hated British.

At the time, no one on our side could see any reason why they shouldn't, but now with the recommencement of hostilities, and with us holding all of Acadia and its large French speaking population, there was a fear in London that this might lead to an insurrection, although not many of us in the occupying force thought so. We could see that, by and large, they wanted to be left alone to live in peace, and those living in the previously conquered area (what had become the British colony of Annapolis Royal) claimed neutrality when war was declared; but it was their misfortune to live in an area that guarded the mouth of the St. Lawrence River, and that was, therefore, deemed strategically important. In fact, some ass in London felt that it was so important that when, predictably, still clinging to their neutrality, the silly fools refused to swear allegiance to King George, it was thought best to get rid of them altogether. The result was that they were uprooted from homes their families had lived in for centuries, packed aboard ships, and sent off in their thousands back to France, a land very few had ever before seen.

It was a dirty job, rounding up families and burning their homes. The worst part was that we in the 51st had been garrison troops at Fort Lawrence across the river from Beauséjour, some even intermingling with the local population during the peaceful years. Some, officers included, had even married into their families. So when the order came, it was doubly distasteful, in that they were sending away their own wives' relations.

As for myself, it was hard to watch Marie and Josette being forced into the boats. My dislike for a Frenchman is as hereditary as the rest, almost to the point of being instinctive, but a French *woman*, on the other hand, is a petticoat of a different colour. They were as pretty and bold as a man could ask for, and knew enough about the carnal act to excite even the most somnolent of fellows. So it was hard lines watching them being shipped off like that. Yet in Bernadette's case, with her swollen belly and angry brothers on the lookout for me in

30

all the lower taverns, I have to admit that the expulsion did have its uses.

Once upon a time I had not been so cold-hearted. Once upon a time I had believed in love, and a girl's laughter and flower petals sprinkled across naked breasts.

"I love you, Josiah," she had said, "and I shall love you forever and ever."

I was not that same man in Acadia; nor am I now. I had since learned that love is a luxury reserved for the fortunate. Alas, that is not me, therefore I take my revenge wherever I find the means.

But all that is by-the-by, and has little to do with the current subject. What I mean to say is, that when all is said and done, although I do not much care for a Frenchman, I respect him – it would be foolish not to. I daresay that is the universal opinion in the entire British army. But while I do not like him, I would not have shipped them off like that, given a choice and most likely, if the situation had been reversed, he would not have done it to me, neither. So while Beauséjour could be claimed as a victory of sorts, it has left a bad taste in our mouths ever since, and, indeed, only succeeded in driving those who were left into the ranks of the enemy after all.

All that was in the past, however, and things were different now, or so we hoped. Last year the Cavendish government had been voted out and William Pitt voted in as Lord Privy Seal. With him had come a new philosophy on how to wage war, and a new attitude to see that it was done. The vile practice of patronage had been tossed onto the midden heap at last, and senior officers were being appointed on ability alone.

Although Major General Amherst was largely unknown to us, we were better acquainted with our brigade commander, General Wolfe. Back in Halifax, he had drilled us until we dropped, and had become known as a tyrant with a passion for discipline and detail. Under his command, we worked harder than we ever had before; but this was largely recognized to be the trait of a general who left as little to chance as possible –

one, in fact, who planned on winning - a notion that, for once, coincided with our own desires. So, by the time we embarked for Louisbourg, we knew that, although victory was far from assured, given such leadership, the odds in our favour had greatly increased.

But now, crammed aboard the landing barge, our boots steeped in vomit, along with Snead's blood and brains, we stared with disbelief at the signal from the brigadier ordering the retreat.

I turned to Daniel, whispering, "What's this then, Dan? Retreat? Lord knows when we'll get another chance!"

Daniel pulled a face, indicating the French cannonade, and the death-trap on the beach, with a disgusted twitch of his chin, "Call that a chance, Josiah?" By now all the boats were in the process of coming about, and the French, sensing victory, had redoubled the intensity of their fire to some effect. "A snowball would have a better chance in Hell than we would going in there. No, my son," he offered me a crooked grin, while a sailor cursed when his oarlock was shot away, "it's back to the ships for the likes of us, and we can continue puking our guts out while the toffs try to figure out where the next debacle's going to be."

Of course he was right, but that didn't make it any easier to accept, so I contented myself with a muttered, "Going in is almost preferable to that."

He laughed aloud, which drew one of Sergeant Bell's bleary-eyed glares. Daniel returned it with a glare of his own, for it was well known that there was no love lost between them. Presently, Bell decided to take a greater interest in the plight of the rest of the boats while the bo'sun began to bring ours about.

My friend dismissed our sergeant with a final derisive stare before returning to our conversation as if it had never been interrupted. All the while the furious firing continued.

"You're a rum one, aren't you, Joss? Gnashing at the bit to sell your precious hide for King and Country, are you? Well, never mind, old thing, you'll get your chance. The way things

32

are going, you and I will be old men, or more likely mouldering in our graves in some forgotten backwater, long before this war's over."

"Oh ta, I'm sure!" I told him, pulling a face of my own.

Another round from a six-pounder plowed alongside, drenching everyone with seawater.

Daniel spat out a mouthful, and grinned. "You bloody colonials are all alike – none of you are happy unless you're taking a bullet for the old country!"

"Not bloody likely!" I swore over the din of the cannonade, "I simply want to get on with it, is all! What we do not do today will have to be done tomorrow, or the day after, or the day after that. The war is not going to go away, so we might as well face it head-on, is all I am saying!"

"Well, you may be right about that, mate," Daniel allowed, "and I want to see the end as much as you, but it doesn't seem likely to happen today."

I think that is when I heard the shout that proved just how wrong a man could be.

Chapter Two

"What's that?" Captain Beaumont cupped a hand to his ear, straining to listen, "I can't comprehend a word the fellow is saying."

The officer in the boat to our left – pink-faced Ensign Greenly, heir to a baronetcy, or so the story went – was gesticulating with excitement, squeaking out something at the top of his lungs, while jabbing a finger landward.

"Can't say, sir," Sergeant Bell made a great show of attempting to listen, at the same time doing his utmost not to breathe rum fumes into our captain's face, but after a very few seconds, he gave up with a sad shake of his head. "It's the young ones, sir, they forget to stay calm, if you don't mind my saying so, sir. They forget everything that their wise old sergeant ever taught 'em at the first flash of gunpowder. Why I…"

"Quiet, Sergeant! I am attempting to listen!"

"Of course, sir! Very sorry, sir! Mum's the word, sir!"

"Sergeant!"

"Right, sir! Quiet as a mouse, that's me, sir!"

Ignoring him, Beaumont turned to us, casting his eye on every face while he considered; finally his gaze fell upon me.

"Stubb."

"Sir?"

"You have good ears, don't you?"

"It's all this wilderness fighting, sir," Bell continued, explaining reflectively, while he unbuckled his canteen and helped himself to a healthy draft, "crouched behind a tree for hours on end, without ever saying a word, waiting for the enemy to walk into the ambush. That's what I mean, sir, training, pure and simple."

Following my captain's example, I too ignored the sergeant, and replied, "I should think that it's adequate, sir."

"Of course there's rocks, too, sir."

In spite of himself, Beaumont's attention was pried from the other boat, and was compelled to ask, "What was that, Sergeant?"

"Rocks, sir," Bell pointed out with ponderous sagacity. "There's some quite good rocks to hide behind, as well as trees. It takes a soldier's eye…"

Dismissing him more firmly this time, the captain returned his attention to me. "Get up here, Stubb! Quick man; I want to know why that young whipper-snapper is in such a taking!"

"…to see the lay of the land, in a manner of speaking, sir. Years of service, that's what's needed…"

I stood at the gunwale, cupping a hand to my ear, while Captain Beaumont impatiently clapped his own hand over Bell's mouth, cutting him short with a muffled squawk. Leaning out as far as I dared, I strained to listen, sweating with concentration.

High and thin, over the sounds of the sea and the roar of cannon, I heard Greenly shout, "A landing! A landing!" and followed to where he was gesticulating so wildly.

The right end of the cove terminated at an unimposing shoulder, scarcely worth noticing, but it was to this point that three of our boats had drifted, without a doubt while trying to evade the murderous barrage, and it was to these that Greenly was indicating. It was the matter of a second to see that some of those people were also waving, trying to attract our attention, while others were leaping from the boats to the shore.

"Christ!" I swore without thinking, and again with little thought to the impropriety, grasped the captain by the shoulder, and pointed. "It's a landing, sir! Some of our lads have made it in!"

Without heed to the liberty I had taken, Beaumont released Bell and snapped open his telescope, training it to the spot where I was pointing.

After a brief moment, he exclaimed, "There's no sign they've been spotted! My god! They must be out of sight!" He

35

snapped his telescope shut again, and without taking his eyes off of the spot, ordered, "Signal the brigadier! Tell him we've found the chink in their armour after all!" then turning to the bo'sun, he pointed, "Get us in there, lively now!" A savage grin of elation was twisting over his face. "There will be some hot work before we've earned our breakfast, lads, but I believe that oysters, or some other such French cuisine shall be on the menu!" at which we all gave up a great cheer, and urged the tars on to their utmost.

As our boat was near the extreme right of the Red Division's line, we were able to cut in toward our goal, under the cover of smoke from the enemy's spent powder, without much change in course or without drawing undue attention to ourselves. The French were still preoccupied with the easy pickings from our attempt to withdraw, and appeared to have no time for what would look like a straggling vessel trying to escape the line of fire – which was true by all accounts. We were heartily vexed at constantly being shot at without the capability of fighting back. Now that the tables appeared about to be turned, we found our spirits much revived, and our lust for revenge all the stronger.

As we rounded the point and closed with the shore, we saw that it was as rocky and inhospitable as the majority of this wretched coast, but as we drew nearer, we saw that there was the barest of spaces cleft into the rock, just large enough for one or two boats and that was all. A lieutenant from the 35th stepped out from the shadows just as we docked, his orange facings flashing in the morning light, while he cautioned everyone to silence. "Quiet!" he whispered in a hoarse rasp that could have been heard in London, even over the surf, "*Monsieur* lies just beyond the rise!" pointing at the rising mound of the shoulder scant yards inland. He motioned for us to follow as soon as we stepped ashore, lucky enough to do so without wetting our feet. "This way, but for Christ's sake be careful, or we'll bring the entire frog-eating army down on our heads!" So saying, he led the way up the fairly steep slope. After pausing long enough to fix bayonets, as was the general order upon landing, we followed as quietly as we could, careful to keep our equipment from rattling against the rocks. While in progress I noticed a sinister watchtower hovering over us at the top of the summit. It was not difficult to imagine Gallic eyes narrowing over leveled muskets poking through the embrasures, mouths sneering in triumph as fingers tightened on the triggers. I braced myself, expecting the impact of a bullet at any moment, but none ever came. The darkened embrasures remained silent, and I knew that, by some miracle, the French had not bothered to occupy this bastion. If they had thought to man it with so much as a platoon of invalids it would have been our undoing.

Upon reaching the crest of the ridge, we found a narrow belt of trees with others of the 35th - no more than a few dozen - already there, lying on their stomachs, intent on keeping their heads below the horizon. Many had taken out their cleaning kits and were attempting to dry their muskets – an onerous chore at any time, but doubly so in such an awkward position, and even more so by the razor-sharp bayonet locked onto the end of the muzzle. As we took our places by their side, and I took out my own cleaning utensils, I heard a voice whisper nearby, "Who do we have here, Mr. Brown?"

"A boatload of those fine fellows from the 51st, Mr. Hopkins," the other wheezed excitedly.

"Excellent!" the first replied, "Now where the devil is Grant? That young pup is never around when I need him."

"I'm here, sir," a youth's voice piped in a wounded tone, "At your elbow."

"Bless my soul, so you are!" the first riposted, "Good lad; now, d'you suppose you could fetch their officer for me?"

"He already has, lieutenant," Captain Beaumont whispered beside me as I busily wiped the moisture from my musket with my neckerchief, taking special care around the firing mechanism and touchhole.

Taking note of our mitres, Hopkins whispered approval, "Ah! Grenadiers! This will do nicely, sir! We'll soon have need of your muscle, I reckon."

Beaumont asked, "What's the situation, then?"

"Shhh! Quiet, sir, I beg of you," Hopkins told him, "The French are just beyond the trees!"

My captain's voice was steady when he said, "Show me."

I watched the two officers inch through the undergrowth, and thought to follow suit. I finished ramming a dry patch down the barrel, hopefully sponging up any excess moisture; then gently, ever so quietly, placing my hands with care, I managed to pull myself forward until reaching a point where it was possible to see the ground beyond...and very nearly cried out with shock! By the stifled sound of Beaumont's gasp I wasn't the only one, either!

They said afterward that the enemy were fifty yards away, but it seemed more like five. They were artillerymen, servicing a battery of two six-pounders, and one monster of twenty. Even as I watched, a mustachioed sergeant put his match to the bloody thing, and it went off with such a tremendous bang that we were showered with leaves and small branches torn loose by the concussion.

The round must have been telling, for the gunners took the time to squeal with Froggish delight before returning their attention to the working of the gun. All of them had their backs to us, apparently unaware of our presence. It was a tempting target, and I was quivering to be at them. It would seem that Lieutenant Brown was likewise affected, for he had crept forward to join the other officers, and now whistled out in that hoarse whisper, "Shall we go for them, sir?"

Captain Beaumont shook his head, "We dare not risk it. Where there is artillery the infantry is sure to be close at hand." As if to confirm this, a ragged volley of musketry burst just out of our line of sight, yet sufficiently near that we could see the glimmer of the muzzle flashes. "We have our toehold here, yet risk losing all if action is commenced precipitately."

There was silence, and then Brown asked, "Beg pardon, sir?"

"He says that we should wait for reinforcements to come up," Hopkins told him, "Otherwise we'll be up to our necks in it if we don't."

"Ah, yes, '*precipitately*', sir! My thoughts exactly, sir!"

Beaumont continued, "It is, however, incumbent upon us to remain secreted in these woods for as long as possible, until our numbers be sufficiently augmented. Stealth, gentlemen, is of the essence. We must issue orders to the men, forbidding the loading of their weapons. I need not remind you what a calamity it would be should one accidentally discharge."

After both lieutenants murmured their agreement (in Brown's case, somewhat uncertainly), Beaumont cast his eye about until he spotted me.

"Ah, there you are, Stubb. You heard?"

"Yes sir," I replied.

"Any questions?"

"No, sir."

Whereupon, he told me, "The lieutenants and I shall go back to see about bringing up the reinforcements. Keep a sharp eye on our friends yonder, will you?"

"Of course, sir."

"Good lad," he said, then after a short pause whispered, "and take good care that none of them see you, understand?"

"Yes, sir!"

With that, all three retreated deeper into the undergrowth, and were soon lost from sight.

Notwithstanding that the enemy were within easy hailing distance, now that the prospect of immediate action lessened, my tension began to ease along with it. It was hard watching the Frogs so near, servicing those menacing guns, and to be unable to act; but I suppose that every soldier can be philosophical about such occasions. Now that I was out of the line of fire, the temptation to blot them momentarily from my mind would not be denied, and I could not help my thoughts returning to Sally.

         *   *   *

I remember that it was the twenty-first day of December, the occasion of my thirteenth birthday back in St. John's, when we were still living in the old single-roomed, clapboard shack, clinging precariously to the rocks under the walls of Fort William on Maggoty Cove. I was sitting on the hearth, close to our meager fire, with my slate on my lap, trying to stay warm while engrossed in my studies. Sally had just finished making payment to my tutor, Mr. Bellsworth, moments earlier, and while he was doing up the buttons on his flies preparatory to departing, he admonished me to study more diligently at my prepositions. Then, with a swirl of flakes coming in from the open door, and my mother's warm farewell from behind the curtained alcove that passed as the bedroom, he was gone, back to his wife and family on the Upper Path and, I assumed, to indulge in the warmth and pleasantries of a domestic Yuletide.

After a minute, Sally emerged from behind the curtain, pulling at the voluminous hems of her dress before coming over to the fire, her cheeks and chins well-flushed. Then, with a flourish, she produced a stick of sugar candy from behind her back, and offered it to me along with an affectionate, motherly smile.

"Now then," she cooed lovingly, as was her habit whenever addressing me, "'oo's been a good lad, eh?"

I set my slate aside and accepted the candy with a relish. Sugar came from the far-off West Indies, and was more precious than gold! I had tasted it on only one previous occasion, when I had been able to steal a very small piece from a victualer's store in the harbour.

"Thank you Sally!" I said warmly, the sweetness settling over my taste buds. "You are the best mother ever!"

"Ow!" she simpered, jowls quivering with delight, "yore such a lovely boy! I can't 'elp but loves ye wiff all me 'eart, an that's a fact!" So saying, she bent down, fondling my head while giving me one of her great, slobbering wet kisses on the cheek. She smelled of lye and tobacco...and perhaps something else that reminded me of Mr. Bellsworth, for no reason that I could fathom.

We sat and talked of my studies for some minutes, her hand caressing my curls while I sucked on the candy. She was a great one for an education, was Fat Sally: she said that it would make me a man of the world one day. Of course I had heard her own story long ago, about how she never had the opportunity for learning, and that she'd had to get by the best that she could with only what the good Lord had given her. "It's not that I'm complaining, dearie," she'd told me once, "not everyone can have the advantages, can they? It's just that I would like something better for my sweet little lad, that's all." So I took great care, working as hard as I was able, and was encouraged when Mr. Bellsworth said that I showed promise. Sally had been so overjoyed that, after he'd gone, she'd let it slip that she had given him the house special, free of charge, as a way of expressing her gratitude. I remember being surprised about that, and although I had no idea what the house special entailed, it drove home how important my studies were to her. For kind-hearted to a fault, and simple as far as the academic world was concerned, my mother was astute when it came to business, seldom giving away goods for nothing in return.

Now, sitting by the fire, she reached into her pocket and pulled out her pipe and pouch. She filled the bowl with tobacco, lighting it with a glowing ember from the fire; then, puffing contentedly, she smiled at me, though her eyes had a faraway look, as if contemplating something mysterious.

I sat, waiting patiently, for I knew that this was my mother's way of broaching subjects of importance, using the time to organize her thoughts into words; but just when she put her pipe aside, and leveled her gaze at me (a sure sign that she was about to begin) there came a loud knock at the door.

"Oh bloody 'ell!" she swore, her thoughts interrupted. "Who could it be at this hour, and on a Saturday, too?"

She rose to see who it was while I remained seated, noting to myself that the subject of which she wished to speak must be very important indeed. For the hour could be no later than seven in the evening, and Saturdays had always been one of her more lucrative days. For her composure to slip to such a degree was very rare.

She stopped at the door, one hand on its rough-hewn planks, the other on the latch.

"Who's there?" she called, I am sure in an angrier tone than was intended.

A man's voice, thickened with grog, came to us from the outside. "It's me, Sally! It's Ben!"

"Lord save us!" she muttered, more ill-tempered than ever, before allowing her voice to rise, "Mr. Stockingsdale is it? What do *you* want?"

"I want *you*, Sally!" he said, accompanying his words with a great groan of longing, "I's filled with such a need that I's bound to burst if you don't let me in!"

Sally yelled through the planks, "Go away! This is a place of business, not a charity!"

"But I've money!" Benjamin cried, "The dice were with me tonight!"

"Yore putting me on, Mr. Stockingsdale!" she retorted with a derisive snort. "The only thing in your pocket is your hand, and it's not money it's got hold of, but your knob!"

"Aye, it does!" a passionate moan filtered through to us, "but there's summat in t'other, honest there is!"

Sally frowned, turning an ear to the door while speculating. "Do you swear?"

"On my mother's grave!"

I almost laughed aloud at the thought that the memory of Ben Stockingsdale's mother was something to be held as sacred, but as I said, Sally was a kind-hearted soul, and believed strongly in the virtues of parenthood.

Still wary, however, she unlatched the door and opened it a crack. "Show me then."

A grimy hand, poking out of the cuff of a threadbare uniform, darted through the opening, palm extended. Sally rummaged through its contents with one of her sausage-like fingers, her lips whispering as she calculated the total.

After no more than a few seconds, she cried, "There's naught 'ere but 'arf a shilling!"

"Please, Sally!" Benjamin's voice was louder now that the door was ajar. I saw a boot inserted into the crack between it and the jamb. "I's in the werriest degree of pain! I swear!" he wheedled, "My balls is turnin' blue from the pressure!"

There was the lengthiest of pauses, and then, finally, cursing herself for a fool, Sally swept the coppers into her own hand before swinging the door wide, allowing Stockingsdale to stumble inside, sporting a degraded smile. True to his word, one hand was inserted in his pocket, the coarse wool rippling manically as he clutched at himself.

"Oh Sally!" he cried, lurching toward her, attempting to embrace her with his unemployed arm, but she held him off easily.

"Not in front of the boy," she told him with a warning nod in my direction, "I run a respectable business 'ere, I do!"

Benjamin's head wobbled toward me, still grinning blearily, his hair matted and soiled. "It's young Josiah, is it? Compliments of the evening to you, lad!"

I returned the greeting. Then, dismissing me, he returned his attention to my mother. Abandoning his attempt to embrace her, he now began pawing ineffectually at her bosom. "My god, Sally," he cried, "you may be fat as a sow, but yore all woman, you are!"

"Right," she sighed, and taking hold of the offending hand, swung him around with terrifying force, releasing him with practiced ease, allowing his trajectory to catapult him onto the bed. He landed on the mattress with a crash and a flurry of burlap from the curtains. With markedly more decorum, Sally followed, rolling up her sleeves, pausing at the entrance to give me a warm smile. "Don't worry, luv. I won't be but two shakes of a lamb's tail. 'Arf a shilling don't go far these days."

43

With that she disappeared inside. From behind the curtain, I heard Benjamin cry, "Oh Sally! Sally darlin'!" then there was a short pause followed by a squawk of rapturous delight…that was cut short almost before it began.

A few more seconds passed, then Sally said, "Right then, off with you."

Groggy now, and yet somehow affronted, Benjamin asked, "Wot, is that all?"

"Yes, Mr. Stockingsdale, that is all," my mother patiently replied, yet with mettle in her voice that few dared challenge. "Yore relaxed now, aren't you, and yore balls ain't blue no more, are they? So that's all of my time you'll be having for the moment, and I'll bid you a good evening."

Muttering, Benjamin emerged a short time later, appearing to me sad and crestfallen. He bade me a brief farewell, and with a last soulful look at the curtained enclosure, left our cabin, pulling the door quietly shut behind him.

The curtains parted and my mother stepped back into the room, rolling down her sleeves and adjusting her massive bosom within her bodice. Then, apparently without another thought to Benjamin Stockingsdale, she reclaimed her place by my side and took to a speculative toying with my curls once again.

Smiling, I continued to wait patiently.

It was not long, however, before she began.

"Oh Josiah," she sighed, still caressing my hair, her smile somehow wistful, "Yore thirteen now, almost a man. Where 'ave all the years gone, that's wot I'd like to know?"

I knew that the question was rhetorical, so held my peace, still waiting.

"I'm very pleased at 'ow yore lessons 'ave been coming along," she told me. "Mr. Bellsworth 'as proved quite capable in that regard, wouldn't you say?"

I offered her a nod, but again it was not required, for she was wending her way through a maze, and would reach the center in her own good time.

"Almost a man," she repeated, this time reflectively, as though more to herself than to me. "Soon you'll be grown and out the door."

I stirred uncomfortably, for I could not imagine such a thing. Outside of what I'd read in books, our little cabin on the outskirts of St. John's was all the world that I knew, and could not imagine a desire to know more.

As if reading my mind, she continued, "I've done my very best to raise you to be a man of the world, I 'ave. The best ej-oo-ca-shun that money can buy, leastwise in these parts: books, numbers, ciphering, all that lot; I've done my very best so you'll be ready when the time comes." Her words were filled with a fierce pride - Sally, of course, was illiterate. "The world can be such a marvelous place for the young and adventurous," then her face darkened, "but it can be bloody 'orrible, too, if you don't mind yore step!"

Wide-eyed, I asked her, "What do you mean, Sally?"

Instead of replying directly, she said, "You'll be a man of talent, I can see that already, I can; but there's more to life than talent, isn't there? You must also be clever, but even that ain't enough, is it? Not when it comes to affairs of the 'eart."

Mystified, I asked, "Affairs of the heart?"

"Love," she explained woodenly, as though a veil had fallen over her face, betraying dark emotion.

I squirmed more uncomfortably than ever. "Love?"

"There are those out there wot would steal yore 'eart." I could not doubt that she was speaking from experience. "And use it against you when you least expect it. That is love, my son, and it is wicked and terrible!"

Still mystified, I told her, "But mother, I love you. Is that wicked?"

Then she was clasping me to her bosom, drowning me in the scent of her soap. "Never!" she cried, "That is the love between a mother and 'er son, and is the most precious thing in all the world!" She continued holding me close, and I could feel the heat of her tears as they tumbled to my brow. Then, almost savagely, she pulled me away, holding me at the length of her arms. "The love I speak of," she told me, "is that which 'appens between a woman and a man, and will break the 'eart of the unwary!" She spoke with such passion that I could only sit and stare, wide-eyed with fear. When she saw the affect her words had produced, she brought herself under control, yet her face remained a mask of anguish. "My boy! My dear, sweet boy! Yore as innocent now as the day you was born!"

"Sally," I told her, imploring, "I do not know what you mean!"

"I know you don't. I know." She seemed lost in introspection while she stared at me, as though I was naked in front of the world; then with her eyes beginning to glaze and to become even more unreadable, she allowed herself a languorous grin, and added, "But never mind, dearie, for I shall teach you, won't I? When you've learned everything I know, there's naught that those wicked sluts an' 'ores can touch you!"

I thought about this for a minute, my head aching from the concentration. "But you're a slut, Sally," I told her, "and a whore. Everyone says."

"Ah yes," she replied sagely, "but there's sluts an' there's sluts, aren't there? *An'* there's 'ores an' then there's 'ores. Now, you trust your dear old mum, don't you?"

"Of course," I replied without hesitation, "you know I do."

"Very well then," she told me, " As wise as 'e is about book learnin', there's certain things about the world that Mr. Bellsworth knows very little," she gave me a baleful eye, "I'm 'ere to tell you! Why, with yore looks and a bit of tutelage – tender years notwithstanding - you could surpass him in a fortnight. Combine that with *everything* I 'ave to teach, *an'* the package 'tween yore legs," her eyes drooped lazily down to my groin, causing a mysterious excitement in me, heretofore unknown, "you could 'ave the world at yore feet, you could!"

I thought it a very nice thing to have the world at my feet, and told her so.

"Then you just trust yore dear old mum." While speaking, she reached out, and with a practiced hand, began to gently massage an area of my body that, for some mysterious reason, had become excited. "An' leave everything up to me."

"Sally," I asked, gasping for breath, the fire seeming suddenly to be burning much brighter, sucking the very air from my lungs, "whatever are you doing?"

"Why, I'm about to give you yore birthday present, aren't I?" she told me, the folds of flesh and kindness on her face now tempered with a certain huskiness in her voice, matching an expression of greed. "One day you'll look back an' see that it was the most important gift a lad could ever receive!"

The buttons of my flies seemed to have come undone of their own volition. Her hand snaked into the opening, taking hold of me.

"Gor blimey!" Now it was Sally's turn to gasp, her eyes opening wide, the glazed expression gone as if by magic. She inserted both hands into my breeches, taking hold, while rasping out a throaty chuckle. "I always knew there was *potential*," she said, eyes twinkling. "I couldn't 'elp but notice you was larger than normal for a boy, but this," she crowed merrily, "this surpasses all belief, it does!"

I continued with my struggle to breathe, yet a strange excitement was coming over me, an anticipation of what was to come, even though I had very little idea what that might be.

"Gammon then," Sally cried, although she was not really speaking to me, "let's 'ave you out so we can take a look!"

She managed the extrication after some little trouble; then sat back and regarded it while her face fairly glowed with pleasure.

"Ow, yore an 'andsome, devil, you are!" she cooed as though speaking to an infant. "Yes, very handsome, indeed!" Her hands continued to fondle me, as if unable to resist the temptation.

47

My gasping was becoming quite audible now, while, in answer to her attention, I was becoming ever more rigid, the discomfort balanced with that still mysterious anticipation.

My mother's voice was husky when she said, "Just look at you! Why, yore the most beautiful thing in all the world!" and again, as if unable to control herself, she plunged forward, mouth ajar, her eyes glittering with greed.

"Sally!" I cried, but that was as far as I got before the warmth of her mouth fueled a different fire, this one from low in my belly. Before I knew what was happening to me, the room began to spin, and I lay back, dizzy, while the heat channeled deeper into my body. Then, while my mother continued to minister her attention, it surged to the surface, erupting with what felt like the force of a volcano. I think I shouted something, but could not be sure what it was. The room was spinning wildly now; it sounded as though Sally was in some danger of choking, and still it continued, again and again, until I was completely spent at last.

I lay shaking like a leaf, feeling somehow close to tears. Presently Sally's face swam into view, wiping her lips with the back of one hand, before smiling down at me - for the first time in my life, a smile I was unable to return.

Finally, I was able to order my thoughts sufficiently to speak.

"Sally?"

"Yes, dearie?" she asked, propping herself up on one ponderous elbow.

"This," my head lolled side to side as if still dizzy – in truth, this continued to be the case, "this *thing* that just happened…"

"Yes, my son?" She smiled, cuddling me close with one massive slab of an arm, until I was, once more, overwhelmed in her reassuring scent.

"Is that what you have been doing behind the curtain, all this time, with all those men?"

*   *   *

The roar of the guns had dwindled into muted insignificance while past and present traded places. I mused on that particular era of my education, when my mother had stolen my innocence. For me, life had taken on an entirely new meaning, and would never be the same from that moment on.

Unbidden and unwelcome, I was suddenly exposed to the heartache of Elizabeth's beautiful face swimming into my thoughts, but it was gone before I could react – to be replaced by that of Captain Broadstreet, glowering with fury. This last was so disagreeable that it was almost with a sense of relief that I finally noticed the French soldier gaping at me, not ten yards away.

Chapter Three

I suppose that I must have gaped back at him – it seems more than likely. So taken by surprise was I that any other reaction could scarcely be imagined.

The first thing I wondered was: how long had he been standing there - musket at port arms, tricorne slightly off kilter, and a perfect 'O' where his mouth should have been? The second thing I wondered, before dismissing it as so much useless speculation, was how could I have been so foolish as to allow him to see me?

It immediately came to mind that my wool-gathering had placed me at a distinct disadvantage, at the same time making me achingly aware that, due to Captain Beaumont's orders, my musket was not loaded. His on the other hand probably was. Even if he did not shoot me on the spot, if he chose to charge instead, I was by no means certain that I could gain my feet before he was upon me.

This must have gone through his mind as well, although perhaps not so quickly. I could tell by looking at his face that he was calculating the odds, and that he was finding it ponderous to do so. Eventually, I could see his eyes flicker from side to side, and I knew that he was thinking, that where there was one of the detested redcoats, there was bound to be more nearby, and did he want to take a chance on his skewering this one only to be skewered in turn by one of his comrades lurking in the undergrowth – who was, perhaps even now, leveling his own musket and sighting down the barrel at his chest?

It must have been this last thought that sprung him into action, for with cries of "*Aidez moi! Les Anglais sont ici!*" he turned and ran back to his lines, at last rendering my own limbs capable of movement. Therefore, dashing to the rear, I hailed the first officer I saw, which happened to be Lieutenant Brown.

He admonished me to silence with a finger to his lips and his eyes bulging like an owl's in a way I might have found comical at any other time.

"Quiet lad!" he rasped in that same coarse whisper, like coal rumbling down a chute, "There's Frogs not a hundred yards away!"

Containing myself with difficulty, I replied, "Yes sir, I know," then, allowing myself a short breath, admitted, "One of them spotted me only a second ago!"

Brown's eyes grew even larger, and then he swore and stomped a foot before lending me a baleful eye. I thought that he might strike me, or at the very least place me under arrest, right then and there, but instead he took a deep breath and bellowed the stand-to at the top of his lungs. Seconds later officers and men came thundering up through the trees.

Captain Beaumont was amongst the foremost, loose strands of hair draping down the side of his face. He glanced at me, then asked the Lieutenant, "Sighted us, have they?"

"Yes sir," Brown said with a disgusted look in my direction.

If he was dismayed, Beaumont showed no sign. Instead he said, "Very well," before turning to Sergeant Bell, who in turn was doing his utmost to burn holes through me with one of his patented glares. "Have the men form up at the edge of the wood, but keep them well covered. There is little use in offering the enemy a target any more than we must."

"Sir!"

"Oh, and Sergeant," Beaumont called just as Bell turned to go, with one last sneer in my direction.

"Sir?"

"Give the order to load."

There was a fierce gleam in the red-streaked maize of the sergeant's eyes when he answered, "Yes sir!" and stalked off, his mitre swaying precariously when he stumbled over nothing save his own two feet, from what I could see.

That part of his duty seen to, Beaumont watched him go with some misgivings before turning to me. "I'll deal with you later," he promised in a voice hard as flint. "Now fall in with the others."

I joined my mates just inside the treeline, burning with shame and fretful of what the future might hold because of my indiscretion.

Then came the order, "Load your weapons!"

Without conscious thought, I placed the hammer at half cock, and took a cartridge from my cartouche. Then, biting off the end, I poured a pinch of powder into the frisson pan before snapping it shut, after which I upended the musket, and poured the remainder down the barrel. Next went the ball and cartridge paper, seated securely in place with the ramrod. Now loaded, praying that I had succeeded in drying my piece sufficiently, I stood to attention at shoulder arms, the signal that I was ready for the next command.

I stole glances to right and left, noting my comrades in close proximity. Daniel grinned and offered a wink. I attempted to return it, but feared that my effort was a feeble one. On my other side, Stockingsdale gripped his musket in white-knuckled hands, keening softly to himself, seemingly unaware that he was doing so.

Casting my eye further down the line, I saw that in addition to the dozen from our own regiment, there was close to equal numbers from the 35th, and perhaps twice as many Rangers - scarcely fifty souls to maintain our hold on our pathetically small beachhead. However, even as I contemplated on how few we were, there was a commotion behind me and I risked a quick glance to see grenadiers from the 63rd struggling up the slope, along with a boatload from the 60th – both lights and grenadiers, appearing drab and unimpressive in their faceless tunics beside the magnificence of the highlanders, with their white facings, swaying kilts and bearskin mitres – notwithstanding that all were thoroughly sodden from an imperfect landing. For now the boats were coming in greater numbers, forcing the majority of the men to disembark in the water and wade to shore, carrying their muskets and cartridge boxes over their heads. Reinforcements were arriving as quickly as such a small docking would allow, and I was able to take some comfort while turning my eyes away. It would seem that word had gotten out to these few boats, at least, and more were seen crowding in every minute, attempting to deliver their human cargo as quickly as they were able.

Then someone cried out, and it was impossible not to risk a second glance down the slope. Now the boats were thick upon the landing with the swell unabating. I recognized one filled with grenadiers with the buff facings of our own regiment attempting to disembark, and saw Lieutenant Forsyth leading his men over the gunwales, sword in hand, with the water up to his chest, waving for them to follow. Then a sudden swell picked up the whaler and carried it over him. Even as I watched, the boat struck the rocks with such force that it stove in the bow and several of our fellows were tumbled over the sides, onto the rocks and were severely dealt with by the waves. The boat was smashed into the shore, again and again, until it was little more than a collection of broken sticks. Finally it sank altogether, forcing the tars to give up their oars and take to the water. This they did with much reluctance, for there was little hope that any of them could swim. In any case the waves picked them up, one by one, and smashed them senseless onto the rocks, before pulling them back out to sea, where they were soon swallowed by the undertow. I never did discover if any from that boat survived the ordeal; if any did, it was certain that Lieutenant Forsyth was not of that number.

Shaken now, I turned back to my front and hoped mightily that such a terrible scene would not be repeated.

Meanwhile, *Monsieur,* having been alerted by my carelessness, had sent a small party of Indians and Canadiens to deal with us. Spread out in skirmishing order, scarcely fifty in number, all told: it was a force hopelessly inadequate for the task.

There was some worry as to whether the French artillery would be turned our way, for they were more than capable of doing us much mischief, but they were more concerned in the sealing of their victory by dealing with our main force, still within range, rather than a few dozen stragglers, and had made the mistake of leaving us to their infantry to deal with.

The skirmishers came up to us most cautiously, for they had no way of knowing how few were our numbers. If they had charged immediately, when our strength was roughly equal to their own, and we with our wet muskets unable to reply to their fire, there was every chance they would have succeeded; but not knowing, they contented themselves with peppering the wood with their musketry from a distance, hoping to keep us contained until their main strength was at liberty to come up and finish the business. It was a fateful decision.

From immediately behind me I heard Captain Beaumont cry, "Take cover!"

Stepping lively, I placed myself behind the bole of a tree – a poor specimen, on this windswept shore - sensing my comrades doing the same along the length of our single, oh-so-thinly-stretched line. Peering around the emaciated trunk, I could see the front ranks of the enemy quite clearly, scarcely a hundred yards off, firing independently, and closing on our wood with the utmost caution.

Still from behind me, Captain Beaumont's voice rang clear, "Steady lads! Let them close!"

Little by little the enemy shortened the distance, filling the air with their savage howls, doing their utmost to weaken our courage while giving strength to their own. The distance between us had been halved when Captain Beaumont finally gave the command, "Make ready!"

I thumbed back the hammer to full cock, praying that my attempt to prepare my weapon had been sufficient. There was the metallic clicking all along the line as others did the same.

"Present!"

I rolled my shoulder around the tree, leveling my piece at the loose ranks spread out some dozens of yards away.

"Fire!"

I pulled the trigger; the wedge of flint clamped in the hammer struck the frisson, showering sparks onto the powder in the pan. There was a jet of smoke at my cheek a split-second before the flame shot through the touchhole and into the powder of the main charge. There followed a sharp bark, and I was relieved to feel the crash of the butt against my shoulder. Then an even greater cloud of smoke erupted from the muzzle, hurling the heavy lead ball - three quarters of an inch in diameter - over the distance between our forces.

Although our volley was only sporadic at best, as several muskets predictably misfired, the thick fog from spent gunpowder obscured the field, not allowing me to see if my shot had been accurate. Instead I leapt back behind the tree, my right hand already fumbling in the cartouche for another cartridge, anticipating the order to reload.

"Reload!"

The procedure was repeated, and soon, with a quick tamp, I pulled the ramrod from the barrel and shot it home in its sleeve, before slamming the musket to my shoulder. All around me those whose weapons had misfired were frantically going about the laborious business of removing the faulty charges and making speedy reparations, at the same time doing their utmost to remain under cover.

Beaumont's voice was calm, as though unconcerned, as if we were still at drill on the parade square back in Halifax, instead of fighting for our lives while we clung to our modest patch of ground in the very heart of enemy territory.

"Make ready!"

Again our little wood was filled with the sound of hammers ratcheting to full cock.

"Present!"

Once more I stepped out from the shadow of the tree, leveling my piece at the breast of the nearest Frenchman.

"Fire!"

More muskets fired this time, we prayed, with some effect.

The order to reload was given, then closely followed with, "Fire at will!" giving those amongst our number, with a faster ability, the freedom to pour as much shot into the French in as little time as we were able, without waiting for the word of command.

It was here that the constant musket drill began to pay dividends. We toiled without thinking, capable of going through the intricate steps like mindless machines, some of us capable of sending off as many as four rounds in a minute. In our haste, even the task of aiming was suspended – the lack of visibility making it an impossibility in any case – but merely pointed our weapons in the general direction of our antagonists, and pulled the trigger before repeating the process, over and over again.

I had become a thing incensed; forgotten now were thoughts of Sally and the negligence of my duty. There was only the relentless process of loading, one step after the other, as quickly as possible, and firing into the smoke and confusion, all the while possessed of a savage desire to inflict death upon my enemy. For of course, at the bottom of my savagery was a primordial fear fanning the flames of my rage, because I was all too well aware that the enemy was equally desirous of inflicting death upon me.

Close on that thought, I saw Todsmuir spin and go down, a bullet shattering his shoulder. Hard evidence that the enemy were succeeding in expending a few cartridges of their own.

The remainder of us continued a galling fire, stretched nerves stretched even further; for we knew that it was a race between *Monsieur's* completing the defeat of our initial attack and our accumulating sufficient numbers before launching our offensive. If the former were to happen first, and those great guns were turned our way before the main strength of their infantry came to deal with us, we were – as Stockingsdale had proclaimed earlier - "all dead men". Indeed, kept in ignorance of the fate of the main attack as we were, but fearing that it must be a disaster, we could only return fire as best we might, with our efforts fueled by despair.

How long this deadlock lasted I cannot say – with the French unwilling to come in, and ourselves lacking the strength to go out after him – for the other fog of war had come to envelope me, where my world had shrunk into little more than firing my weapon into the smoke and confusion as fast as I was able, each time expecting a bullet to find me the same way that one had found poor Todsmuir; yet we continued to stand our ground, Stockingsdale on my left and Daniel on my right, doing what little damage we could, while endeavoring that it should not be done to us in return. This was our world, shrieking death and savage elation, all built on a cornerstone of fear. We resolved to face the enemy, to fight until struck down; in any case there was little else we could do.

Then, eventually, I was aware of someone else sharing the shelter of my tree, and with Stockingsdale another, and I began to realize that the reinforcements were coming up at last!

My fellow, a grizzled creature with a long scar angling down one side of his face, disappearing into weathered wrinkles and graying side-whiskers, grinned and winked at me. To my battle-dazed mind he seemed horrifically sinister.

"Hogging all the fun, are ye?" he asked, then spun around, quick as lightning, and fired into the smoke. I fancied that I heard a yelp of pain pierce through the tumult.

Spinning back with all due alacrity, he immediately began to reload, easily outpacing myself. I had been constantly firing my weapon for some time now, and my four rounds a minute had been reduced to three, and then still further to two, as spent grains of gunpowder continued to foul the barrel, making it increasingly arduous to load after every discharge. My new friend, on the other hand, was fresh, and his musket clean.

I took precious seconds to note that fellows dressed in the same plain green jacket were continually reinforcing us, and understood that it was the Rangers who were coming to our aid. This was confirmed a moment later, when I saw the imposing form of Major Scott striding up through the trees, return Captain Beaumont's relieved salute, and then grasp his hand as though greeting an old friend.

I was very much heartened when I re-entered the fray – firing and reloading as fast as my tired arms and mind could manage. A very popular officer in the army, Scott had been given command of the new light infantry companies, recruited especially to counter the tactics of the Indians and Canadiens, who had such telling effect against Braddock in '55. Most of these men were accomplished woodsmen from our colonies to the south, all of them noted for their prowess with a musket, an asset to be very much appreciated at the moment.

Gradually, as our numbers grew and the French muskets fouled, our fire had gained ascendancy over that of the enemy, although the odd still form amongst us gave proof that he was still very much in the fight. Yet our meager toe-hold must have become a general landing place by now, for I could see the uniforms of other regiments come to join us, and even the fresh uniforms (as of yet ungrimed by conflict) of our own grenadiers from the 51st, stately and proud, striding like gods through the chaos to take their place in the firing line. Of a certainty what our numbers now were I could not say, but we were far more than the first paltry few that had come ashore in what seemed an eternity ago (although I was to find out later that it was less than a quarter of an hour) and I knew that the time to strike was fast approaching. When I saw General Wolfe - unobtrusive in his common soldier's coat - conversing with Scott and the other officers freshly arrived, I was certain of it.

Sure enough the cease fire was shouted up and down the line, followed instantly by the order to reload. Then Captain Beaumont was out in front of us, just out of the tree line, his mitre gone. Spent powder smudged his face, accenting the whiteness of his teeth through his savage grin. He was gripping his musket in one hand, while frantically waving his sword to the right and left with the other.

"Form line!" he shouted, and we leapt to do as we were ordered, the urgency in his voice spurring us on. Through the smoke could be heard the sound of ramrods seating bullets into French muskets as they prepared for yet another volley. There wasn't a moment to lose.

We formed a line so ragged, that had he been present, it would have caused our Regimental Sergeant Major to burst into tears. Yet with time being of the essence, Beaumont merely raised his sword and cried, "Make ready!" then, "Present!" so hard on its heels that it sounded like a single command. A split second later, he threw himself to the ground, beneath our row of leveled weapons, and shouted, "Fire!"

Our volley was as ragged as our line - somewhat less than half of our number having loaded on time for the command. In truth, there were a few who had been so pressed, that either there had not been the opportunity, or in the excitement they forgot to remove their ramrods before pulling the trigger. They could be seen darting through the air like so many javelins.

Now Beaumont was on his feet again, waving his sword, this time at the enemy.

"Come on!" he cried, and we raised a cheer and dashed after him, the filtered sun glinting off the deadly points of our bayonets as the rest of our line advanced with us.

By this point *Monsieur* was tired and must already be very close to breaking under our incessant fire. Now, with our ragged volley roaring out its challenge, and then with the sight of us emerging from the smoke - doubtless, our faces as streaked with sweat and spent powder as Beaumont's – with our bayonets leveled at their breasts, the French did not stand, but gave way as soon as they saw our mitres. Unfortunate for some, this was not soon enough, for they were caught unprepared, and were hurled aside or skewered where they stood. The rest turned tail and ran.

I suppose that our charge was a pitiful thing - ragged and not at all in unison for its full impact to be felt – but our blood was up, and the pure speed and savagery with which we burst out of those clouds of powder smoke was as much an assault on their minds as their persons, so that by the time we closed with them they were already caught up in the grip of their fear.

All was exhilaration and confusion as we swept into them. There was a vision of a Frenchman directly in front of me, kneeling, caught in the act of ramming his cartridge home, but staring, transfixed at the sight of us, unable to move. I remember the red facings on his coat, and that he had a day's stubble for a beard, and that I hated him more than I had ever hated anyone – this man, with whom I had never shared a word in my life. One moment he was there, the next there was a tug at the point of my bayonet, and he was nothing more than a voice screaming in my wake.

I saw another of the enemy turn to run, and watched his eyes open wide when Stockingsdale plunged his bayonet into his spine up to the lock ring; and another, when he turned to fight, only to be felled when Daniel delivered a savage kick to his groin, before clubbing his head with the butt of his musket. Then all was fleeing Frenchmen, and we pursuing hard on their heels over the broken ground.

The battery was the next position that we took – our charge having come so sudden that the gunners managed to escape with only their lives, without any thought to spiking their cannon to deny us their use. We swept past without pause, every man wanting to exact as high a toll in blood as possible. We were afraid, and our pride demanded that *Monsieur* be even more afraid, or that he should die.

Then it was Major Scott out in front of us, waving his sword to the right, toward an entrenchment where the last of the fleeing enemy had taken refuge. Snarling like dogs, our stride barely checked as we wheeled about to take them in flank and rear.

As we neared, I saw that all was confusion. These troops had been preoccupied with repulsing our frontal assault, and must have been elated at their easy victory. Now, with the unwelcome sight of us in their rear, cutting off their line of retreat, elation turned to panic in the blink of an eye.

To his credit, one of their officers did attempt to have his men make a stand, but their ranks were in chaos from the fellows we had already routed streaming into them for safety, and only a shot or two came our way. Then we were jumping into their trench at one end even as they were leaping out at the other. We were cheering like madmen, rolling them out of their position as easily as could be imagined. A momentum had been started, and once started, could be stopped only with the greatest difficulty. A Marlborough might have stopped them, or a Wolfe, but Monsieur had neither with him that day, so their entire line collapsed from end to end, and we could see them abandoning their positions with all due haste, just as had the gunners at the battery, most fleeing with only their personal accoutrements – many with not even that – unwilling to tarry long enough to take away any of their supplies.

Once the retreat had become general, there were those who were able to keep their heads and attempt to form a rearguard large enough to keep us at bay while their comrades made good their escape. But our pressure was relentless, and with by now superior numbers, the conclusion foregone.

At such a pace, even over the worst ground imaginable, it was not long before the walls of the fortress itself came into view. At that very moment I saw a puff of smoke billow from its ramparts, followed within seconds by a little black dot appearing in the sky, growing larger as it drew ever nearer. It landed some distance in front of us, in a shower of flying clods, then skipped - ricocheted off a rock - and flew over our heads, roaring like a tempest as it passed.

With the absence of any of our drummers to sound the recall, Captain Beaumont was before us once more, waving his sword to draw attention to himself. "Back!" he cried, "Back I say!" and in a calmer tone added, "That is sufficient, lads! You have done well, but there is nothing to be gained by holding our ground!"

Heeding our captain, we backed away with our face to the enemy, shouting our insults as we abandoned the field. When it was judged that we were sufficiently out of range of

61

the enemy's cannon, a halt was called, and we were given leave to lie down and rest.

It was not that we did not understand that the correct decision had been made to call a halt. Louisbourg, with its many bastions, was one of the most formidable fortresses in the New World, and deemed by many to be impregnable. Infantry could not take that mighty cornerstone of arrogant pride alone; heavy artillery and weeks, if not months of endless pounding were required to batter down the walls before we could come at them. Still, after all of this day's endeavour, we had come close - so agonizingly close - to our objective, but in the end, had to stand and watch, helpless, while the last French soldier entered the city and the gates slammed shut in our face.

Yet, despite our disappointment, it had to be acknowledged that the first bold step had been achieved, and in so little time, with so few casualties, that it was difficult to believe. In fact, as more and more of the army came ashore, word came to us that the greatest loss of life had occurred, not during our charge, nor during the firefight amongst the trees, but at the landing, when boats were overturned by the heavy surf while attempting to debark. It was there that some dozens of our comrades had been smashed senseless on the boulder-ridden shore and drowned. I recalled Lieutenant Forsyth, and those who had the misfortune of having been in the same boat with him at the time, and I found myself shuddering at the thought of such a fate

It seemed a miracle, especially when I harkened back to when we made land and saw the tower looming above us, so dark and deserted. Had it been manned, a single company might have held the entire position with ease. Even so, once our presence was known (I felt myself flush with shame) we could not have withheld a determined effort to drive us back into the sea; but such had not been the case. Had the enemy shown willing to come at us in close quarters, we would have had no choice but to surrender, or to die. Yet battle is forever a confusing affair with much resting on small, seemingly insignificant intangibles, and it would appear that this one had been no exception. To drive the point home even further, it must be noted that however far this single small victory would take us, it all began with an accidental landing of a few dozen soldiers, and a failure by the enemy's commander to interpret the situation as it unfolded. Had he but waited to open fire until the van of our force had landed on that tree-strewn beach, our losses would have been too great to contemplate. As it was it had been a near run thing with only the clear heads of a handful of junior officers to thank for it not having turned into a catastrophe.

Much of the future remained undisclosed, and for a certainty nothing was a preordained conclusion, but barring a disaster of enormous proportion, or monumental stupidity by those in command, the results of today's success bore one strong inclination of some significance – Louisbourg would fall.

Perhaps it would not happen soon, but now that our forces were coming ashore in overwhelming numbers, forcing a state of siege on the enemy, there was a strong inclination to suspect that the conclusion was all but foregone. No fortress, however strong, had ever outlasted a siege, barring the timely arrival of a relieving force; but given that the Royal Navy had bottled up the mouth of the harbour, no such force was likely to come without a major naval engagement; and the risks of such an engagement were so meager as to be virtually nil. Following Osborn's success at Cartagena earlier this year, King Louis' fleets were now blockaded in the ports of Brest and Toulon. There was still the overland route from Quebec, of course, but even that had been compromised when we took Beauséjour back in '55; so, once we were ashore, any betting man would find it a hard go finding odds favourable to the French. It would not be easy – it never is – but the reducing of fortresses has become a science over the years, the major requirements being the strength of our arms, and the sweat off our backs, and that we had in abundance.

Still, there were many things that could go wrong. As I said, an act of monumental stupidity or a natural disaster –

both of which had proven possibilities in the past, such as, Braddock on the Monongahela as an example of the former, or the hurricane that was inflicted upon our fleet the year previous as one for the latter. Much was still in the fickle hands of the gods of war, but if we were led with honest capability, success was strongly in our favour.

However all that lay somewhere in the future. For a simple soldier, who existed mainly in the present, it was enough to know that he was alive.

After wood was gathered, and a small fire lit, Daniel unclipped his water bottle, and holding it up as he would a tankard, said, "Here's to you, Joss," and drank deeply before offering it to me. I accepted it and returned the gesture before raising it to my lips. The rum burned like fire, and did nothing to quench the thirst I now felt once the excitement of battle had worn off. So I returned the bottle and took out my own. The water was fresh from a nearby stream, the first I'd tasted in weeks. I took a deep swallow and felt much refreshed. I offered it to Daniel. He hesitated, then nodded, stopping the cork on his own bottle. "Aye, you're right," he said, reaching over, "all that cartridge chewing leaves a man's mouth dry as a desert." He took another long swallow, and allowed that it hit the spot. "Best go easy on the grog anyway," he reasoned, "there's no way of knowing when more might come our way."

I gestured to the fortress, its ramparts just visible in the distance, "I wonder what they will have in there?" It might not be martial, nor was it attendant to duty in any recognized form, but the desire to sample the enemy's strong drink was as good an incentive to storm the walls as any.

Daniel pulled a face. "Something pissy, and something French," he said, at which we both laughed.

The fire now burning nicely, I nestled a pot, scavenged from the spoils left by the enemy, amongst the coals, before filling it with the remnants of my canteen.

All around us loaves and wedges of cheese were produced from pockets as we took our breakfast. We had not been allowed our packs to save space in the boats, so carried our necessaries in that fashion. We ate but sparingly, the officers having cautioned that it might take days for our supplies to arrive from the ships.

As the water heated, I chewed thoughtfully, and took the opportunity to contemplate the fortress across two miles of open ground, with the spire of its clock tower jutting above the horizon, and a low, dark line slightly visible over top of its protecting glacis - indicating the walls themselves. If the ground we held was any indication, what lay between us and our goal was fen and peat bog, generously laced with ponds and solid rock, with here and there higher undulations passing as hills. As likely as I had said that it would fall, Louisbourg was as far from an easy nut to crack as could be.

Situated on a low peninsula on the western end of a natural harbour, this was a fortress to be reckoned with. Outside of one or two unimpressive knolls, there was very little natural cover for an attacking force to take advantage of, but must approach in the traditional, time-consuming manner of parallel and sap, dug laboriously by hand over a period of many weeks if not months, and I was to find that no ground was less suited for the purpose. Even then, assuming these trenches could be dug, a final assault would be required, up the long exposed incline of the glacis before having to deal with an eight foot drop into the fosse - all the while exposed to the withering fire, before ever even coming to face the challenge of her stone walls - twenty feet high and as many thick - with its great bastions ensuring that our approach would be swept with a deadly enfilade. There were the King's and Queen's Bastions in the centre, then the two smaller demi-bastions on the wings - the Princess to the south protecting the coast, and the Dauphin covering the northern approaches along the Barachois inlet; and with two more – the Brouillon and the Maramas - to resist anyone foolish enough to try a landing along the inhospitable shores of Rochefort Point. It was enough to quail even the stoutest heart.

Nothing but a proper siege – with great guns neutralizing the enemy's fire, while others battered a breach in her walls -

could ever hope to reduce something so formidable; and even then, the price was sure to be high.

I finished my meal with these discomfiting thoughts occupying my mind. Then, with the water now boiling, I unclipped my mug from my belt, and dipped it into the kettle, sprinkling in tealeaves from my pockets. All around others were doing the same. Setting the mug aside to cool, I rummaged further until I found my cleaning kit.

Daniel swallowed a last morsel of the coarse, regulation bread, before gesturing with his own mug, first to my kit, and then toward the fortress, much as I had; the speculation was, in its way, the same.

"Reckon you won't need that for a while," he said, picking at his teeth with a grimy thumbnail, "it'll all be pick and shovel from hereon in."

I took my musket across my knee, and with a punch and small hammer removed the barrel pins. "I expect you are right," I agreed, setting the stock carefully to one side before inserting the barrel - breech first - into the kettle. "However, I cannot say that I fancy the notion."

I left the hot water to soften the powder grains encrusted around the touchhole, before taking up the ramrod. Screwing a worm onto the end, I fastened a coarse piece of linen to it and rammed it down the muzzle, feeling the resistance gradually lessen as the water-soaked rag cleaned the barrel from end to end.

Dan offered a guffaw. "Remind me to tell Bell," he said, laughing at his own wit, "He can inform the captain that digging trenches doesn't at all agree with poor Private Stubb…here, what's wrong with you, then?"

He had meant it as a joke, of course, but his mentioning the captain caused me to forget all about the difficulties we faced taking the fortress, reminding me instead of my earlier blunder back at the wood where we had landed, causing my spirits to plummet like a rock, making it impossible to hide my distress.

Concerned now, my friend prodded me to speak, and soon I was telling him the story. At last, when I was finished, he let out a low whistle, all of his former levity forgotten.

"This could be trouble, Josiah," he told me as if I did not already know, before adding something else of which I was all too aware, "It could mean the firing squad!"

"Ta very much," I told him. I thought the irony that my life was in peril as much from an English bullet as from one that was French very rich.

After drying the barrel, I fastened an oily rag to the worm, and rammed it more forcefully than was necessary into the muzzle, preserving the inside from rust; then I yanked it out and began using it to buffet the outside as well.

Daniel had enough sense to see that he was not being helpful. "I'm sorry, Joss, it's just that this ain't like you at all."

"I know," I said miserably.

"What were you thinking to let him get that close?"

I glanced up quickly, then just as quickly back down again, concentrating inordinately on my work.

"Sally," I told him.

"Sally?" He frowned, "What, you mean *Fat* Sally?"

I nodded, more miserable than ever.

"Christ!" he muttered, then changed tack, mellowing his tone with reason, "I know that she's your mother and all, Josiah, but for god's sake, man, what of your duty?"

Growing weary of my friend giving voice to the obvious, I said, "If you have a point to make, Daniel, then please do so. Otherwise I wish to hear nothing further on the subject."

He caught himself a second time, and looked away. "I'm sorry, that was stupid of me."

"Yes, it was," I agreed.

"But," he asked, shaking off the awkwardness, "what will you do?"

I shrugged, replacing the barrel in the stock, before tapping the pins firmly back into place.

After a moment's unease on both our parts, I sensed him in a contemplative pause an instant before leaning forward

67

to be sure he had my attention. "Josiah," he said in a low voice, heavy with portent, causing my eyes to rise to meet his, "you could run."

Once more I shrugged, "To where? This place is swarming with our people now. I would be tracked down and caught in no time at all."

After checking to make sure no one was eavesdropping, he hunkered even closer, gesturing with his eyes, not daring to point with his arm.

"There," he said, indicating the fortress, "you could run there!"

Dumbfounded, I stared at him, wondering if he had taken leave of his senses. "Are you mad?" I asked, and continued, lowering my voice when I noticed heads beginning to turn our way, "Are you seriously suggesting that I desert to the enemy? To the *French*? I would rather swim in blood!"

Daniel attempted to stare me down, but after a moment, he flushed and looked away. "It was just a thought."

"Well stop it!" I hissed, "Your thinking is giving me a headache!"

I do not know how much longer this conversation would have gone on, but it was curtailed at any rate, when Sergeant Bell hove into sight with two of his cronies, Jeffers and Harris, in tow.

I could tell at a glance that they meant business. Jeffers and Harris were marching in step, carrying their muskets at shoulder arms with bayonets fixed. Bell was two paces ahead with his hangar sloped against one shoulder. He appeared sober for once. All three looked grim as the devil.

Sighing, I tested the flint's seat in the hammer before cocking it and pulling the trigger. Satisfied with the sparks flashing from the frisson, I put my musket aside, feeling uncertain as to whether I would ever see it again. Then there was nothing for it but to stand and face them, all the while willing my knees not to tremble.

Daniel looked up when I rose, and saw the sergeant and his escort approaching. He glanced uncertainly at me, then got to his feet as well, his musket held significantly at port arms, ready for instant use.

"Put that down, you daft bugger!" I growled from the corner of my mouth, "There is nothing to be gained if you get yourself into trouble as well!"

But he remained motionless, his lower jaw jutting obstinately. "Bell'll have it in for you," he said, "just to get to me."

While everyone disliked the sergeant, some hated him more than most, Daniel included in that number. Bell, on the other hand, made no secret of his detestation for my friend, and had vowed to have the skin off his back on more than one occasion.

"Don't flatter yourself!" I told him, "Besides, it's not bloody well up to Bell, now is it? Now, ground that musket you fool, or you will be giving him just the excuse he needs to put you under the cat!"

Bell spotted me as soon as I stood. His bloodshot eyes widened with surprise, and he stopped so suddenly that Jeffers and Harris had to look lively not to run into him. Then, with the points of his moustache twitching like an irritated cat, he came on, looking more like an inebriated dustman than ever.

Daniel hesitated, then set his musket aside, spitting from the corner of his mouth to show his disgust.

Bell came to a halt in front of me, Jeffers and Harris quivering to attention behind him.

"Private Stubb!" He jacked up and down on his toes, like a man who is containing himself with the greatest difficulty.

"As you see, Sergeant," I replied, grateful that my voice was steady.

"Silence!" he screamed, jutting his face up into mine – I was the taller by four inches, a fact that annoyed him to no end. "You will silence that insolent mouth, do you hear!"

I thought to reply, but decided against it. Instead, I looked him full in the face, and tried to imagine that the stale rum fumes on his breath were not quite so overwhelming.

"What do you think you're looking at, you horrible man!"

I brought myself to attention, raising my eyes to stare at the badge on his mitre. "The little hairs quivering in your nostrils, Sergeant!" I replied as I would have on parade, that is to say at the top of my voice, and was rewarded with one or two badly stifled guffaws from some of the fellows close by, who were watching with interest.

That earned me another tirade that lasted until I looked him full in the face again, whereupon, mindful of his twitching nose hairs, he stopped and barked, "You are to accompany me at once!"

From my side, Daniel asked, "Is he being arrested, Sergeant?"

Up until that moment Bell had ignored my friend; now he turned, ever so slowly, and glared his hatred. "You will speak when you are spoken to, Private Hawthorne. Is that understood?"

Daniel, who at a full six feet was an inch taller than I, looked down his nose at Bell, staring his contempt.

Bell took a step closer, hoisting himself up onto his toes again. "Right," he murmured in a voice too low for anyone but my friend and myself to overhear, "I'm watching you, Hawthorne; one day you'll go too far!"

Daniel did not deign to reply, but hovered where he stood, malice exuding from every pore, his hands clenching and unclenching into fists.

This did not go unnoticed by Bell, for without taking his eyes off Daniel, he said quietly, "Harris."

From where he stood at attention a pace behind Bell, mindful of the eyes of the rest of the company upon him, Harris stiffened even further, like a bird dog on the verge of pointing out a bevy of quail. "Sergeant!"

"Private Stubb is to accompany us. If Private Hawthorne, or anyone else, makes a move to interfere," Bell allowed himself a brief pause to dart a threatening glare all around, "you will shoot them on the spot; is that clear?"

Harris, the arse-kissing bastard, slung his musket from shoulder to port arms, resting his thumb on the hammer. Pig eyes gleaming above that ferret nose, a slow, evil grin spread across his day's growth of stubble when he looked directly at Daniel and said, "With pleasure, Sergeant!"

This was met with some menacing growls from the bystanders. So I could see that there was nothing else for it. Of course there never had been from the beginning.

I told Bell, "I am at your disposal, Sergeant."

Bell swiveled his glare back to me, considered for a moment, then sneered, "Very well, Stubb," before jerking his head back to where Jeffers and Harris stood waiting. "Fall in."

I felt the eyes of my comrades on my back, and went without any further ado, although not so troubled as I might have been. Wherever they were taking me, and for whatever purpose, I had reason to hope. For one important fact stood out from all the mystery - Bell had avoided answering Daniel's question, which I am sure he would not have done, had the situation been at all different from what it was.

Contrary to appearances, it would seem that I was not under arrest after all.

Chapter Four

Long ago, I discovered that the best way to endure being sodomized was to send my mind elsewhere. It was Sally that taught me, as she had taught me all things to do with fornication.

"Try to relax, dearie," she'd told me, just prior to my first occasion with Mr. Bellsworth, "Think of something nice and you'll do fine, I'm sure."

This had been shortly after my thirteenth birthday, after the night when my second education had begun.

The intervening weeks had not been spent in idleness, for her teaching had been quite intense, primarily because the great fishing fleets had yet to arrive, and the ship carrying the garrison's wages was not due until spring; therefore there was little custom to be had for the present. So, until the time returned when the streets were once more alive with the bustle of commerce, my mother had devoted herself to showing me the various ways that a man might lie with a woman.

"Cor luv a duck! Don't stop, Josiah! Please! Don't stop!" her great head was swaying from side to side, caught in the throws of delirium, "Ah! Yes! There it is! There's a good lad! Yes! A...very...good...lad...*indeed*! Yes! Yes! Oh! *Y-e-e-e-e-s-s-s-s-s*!!"

Moments after, we lay side-by-side, gasping in recuperation. I remember hoping that I would be allowed to rest - for this had been my fourth lesson in three hours, and fatigue was upon me.

At length, she was able to muster enough energy for a mighty heave that positioned her onto her side, at the same time threatening to jar the framework of the bed from its moorings. She lay there, gazing fondly upon me, perspiration plastering her hair to her jowls, and one massive slab of breast curling into the hairs of an equally sweating armpit.

"'Oo's bin a good lad, then, eh?" She leaned over, slobbering a kiss on my lips, plying her liver of a tongue on my own, and once more began to grope down into my nether region, attempting to manipulate what had become unmanipulative.

I had been studying adjectives, of late, and had discovered one that suited my mother quite well – insatiable. Yet even as I considered it, I realized that this was a condition she reserved only for myself; for with customers, Sally was usually as brief as was humanly possible, saving only those rare occurrences when a client should come to the door willing to part with three shillings or more.

She continued to palpate with expert fingers, with that same hungry look in her eye – the same hungry look that was causing me to feel more and more unease as time went on - yet though I tried my best to please her, it was not possible to respond.

Unwilling to admit defeat, Sally now changed tack, slobbering her kisses on my chin, then my neck, then my under-developed chest, before descending, but I had to beg her to leave off.

She did stop, although with a reluctance that I found disquieting. Instead, heaving herself up once more to my side, her hands would not remain still, but began caressing the sweat-dampened curls on my brow. She smiled as sweetly as she ever had, yet the hunger never quite left her eyes, but merely became veiled with affection, and remained lurking in the background.

"'Ow," she breathed tobacco and rum, "I do so love you, my son!"

"I love you too, mother," I replied, though not returning her smile; for I was somehow reminded of the time when she had lectured on the evils of love, although I knew that it could not pertain to her. Fat Sally was my mother, and a mother's affection was the only true thing in the world; that she had also taught me.

We continued to lie there, in silence now, although Sally's mind continued to work while mine began to doze. Finally she sighed, a huge gust of woeful breath.

I shook myself awake and asked her what was wrong.

"Nothing, dearie," she continued to twine her fingers through my hair, her eyes now askance, "it's just that…"

"Just that what?" I asked.

"Well, it's just that times is 'ard these days, aren't they, wot with no money for the sojers and all, *an'* the fleet not due 'til the ice breaks. *Then* there's that Connelly bitch wot's set up shop in the Cribbies over on River'ead, too – the bog-trotting sow - although wot anyone sees in her is beyond me. Thin as a rail, she is, *an'* poxed from head to toe, I shouldn't wonder."

Sally was referring to Abigail Connelly, who, but for an unsightly birthmark on one side of her face, I had thought rather pretty. She had arrived on a boat from Ireland the previous year to be with her husband – a private in Fort William's garrison - only to find that he had died from cholera a short time earlier. Those first few months had been hard for Mrs. Connelly. With her husband deceased, and therefore denied lodgings, she had been turned out to fare as best she could on her own. Even the local reverend, staunch Church of England that he was, would have little to do with the despised papists. In the end, facing starvation and the oncoming winter, Abigail's choices had been few and far between. Consequently she had taken lodgings in the Irish community on Riverhead Road and set up shop, as Sally had mentioned. Winsome and lusty as she was (and only slightly flawed), apparently Abigail had begun making inroads on Sally's monopoly, and Sally did not like it one little bit. I did not think that there was any truth to what she had said about her being poxed, either, but recognized it as merely the product of my mother's wishful thinking.

"Wot's needed is something different – something that will attract a new class of gentleman." She was speaking in that same old way, as when I cipher through a mathematical equation and already know the answer but am required to show how I had arrived at such a conclusion. Whatever it was, Sally already knew the answer; she was just showing me how it had been achieved.

For my part, I could not imagine what she was thinking. Gentlemen had seldom been part of her custom, new class or old, but I remained silent, and allowed my desire for sleep to lull me away. So tired was I, in fact, that I was only half aware when she said, "Let's give something a try then, shall we?" and rolled me gently onto my stomach, with a blanket bunched under my loins.

I must have slept, for I awoke to the drowsy feeling of warm grease being smeared over my buttocks, but before I could react, there was the heat of Sally's breath in my ear, whispering, "Dear Josiah, you know that your mother loves you, don't you?"

"Yes, Sally," I managed to murmur, "of course I do."

"And you trust her, don't you?"

Again I answered to the affirmative. I did trust her, without question; she was my mother.

"And you understand that our business requires something novel to offer our clientele?"

I was too tired to notice that Sally's business had become 'our' business, and 'our' clientele, so managed some sort of reply without further thought.

"Then it's time for your education to continue in another vein," she whispered, and so saying, demonstrated by gently, but firmly, beginning to force the tip of her finger into my backside.

My mother was a strong woman, and had the bulk to back it up, but although I was still in my tender years back then, and somewhat undernourished besides, she was no match for me at that particular moment; for I was out from beneath her and off the bed like a whippet!

"Sally!" I cried, my eyes must have been saucers, "What on earth..."

"It's our means of making ends meet, isn't it?" she replied with just a hint of impatience.

"But..."

"But nothing, Josiah!" she was suddenly shouting, her jowls quivering with anger, "'Aven't I always done wot's best for you, with never a single thought for myself, eh? 'Aven't I!"

I stood by the bed, clutching my arms to my chest, shivering for all I was worth, doing my best not to notice how the wind whistled through the chinks in the clapboard siding. Earlier, over our meal of stale cheese and mouldy bread, Sally had announced that there was an insufficiency of wood for the fire. That had been but mildly disconcerting at the time, for when Sally exerted herself, she could generate heat like she was made of hot coals instead of flesh and bone. But now, bereft of both clothing and the warmth of her proximity, I immediately felt the frost on my skin, and began hopping from one foot to the other in an attempt to generate what little heat I could of my own.

Meanwhile, Sally's sudden burst of anger had not waned.

"An ingrate, that's wot you are!" she cried, her face flushed and red, "Why just a mealy little ingrate! 'Oo's been working their fingers to the bone, heh? Day after day – night after bleedin' night, 'oo's given you everything you 'ave, that's wot I'd like to know, 'oo?"

"You have," I acknowledged through chattering teeth.

"Too right!" she cried, "And 'oo's loved you like a mother all these years, and kept you safe from the wickedness of the world, hey? Tell me that, you ungrateful wretch!"

"But Sally," I pointed out, "you *are* my mother!"

Her eyes momentarily widened, as though caught by surprise, but then she looked askance and continued with scarcely a pause.

"Right, my lad," she started to roll up her sleeves, the way that she will when intending serious business, but stopped when she realized that she was wearing none. Instead, she glowered at me and said, "That will be quite enough of your sass!"

Naked as I was, I daren't make a run for it – she would be upon me before I could pull one leg of my breeches past my knee, and then I'd be for it! Something, maybe the angry look in her eye, told me that what happened after that would make those other few times, when she had deemed it necessary to resort to corporal punishment, mild by comparison.

So again, I hastened to respond that it was she who had made such heroic sacrifices on my behalf.

Nor was it a lie, and on top of that, the chill in the cabin's single room, along with our less than adequate meal, had driven home how desperate our straights had become, in a way that Sally's frustration never could.

Then abruptly as it had come, the anger left her face, in its stead leaving her woefully crestfallen.

"Dear Josiah," she said, with a tear beginning to peep through a fold of flesh, "all I 'ave to teach you is my trade. And now that the years...well...I'm not the girl I used to be, am I? And competition is grim at my age." Another tear ventured out to join the first, wrenching at my heart-strings.

"Mother!" I cried, taking an unconscious step toward the bed, "You must not weep!"

"I can't 'elp it, can I?" she snuffled, a pure picture of misery. "I've done all I can to put food on the table, an'...an'..." she wailed, "I've failed so miserably!"

She held herself in check, but only with an effort that was most visible even to my tender years. It was clear to me, that if we were to survive the winter, my heretofore insulated world would have to change. It took but a matter of seconds for me to reach a decision.

"You are right," I told her, venturing another step closer, "it is time that I did more." I had almost said that it was time that I took on the role of a man, but it did not seem appropriate, under the circumstances.

Now Sally began to cry in earnest - the first time I had ever seen her so – in great, porcine sobs that I could not resist. When she held out her arms, I went into them, willingly.

That must be understood – that I went willingly, although never with any joy.

*   *   *

Sergeant Bell led the way to a settler's cabin (the former owner presumably now safe behind the fortress walls) brushed by the sentry on duty, and knocked respectfully at the door.

"Come!"

We entered with my escort on either side, filling the single small room.

Captain Beaumont was sitting at the rough-hewn table, going over reports and returns. He finished reading the one in front of him, then took up a goose quill from the table, dipped it into a bottle of ink, and signed his name at the bottom before laying it aside and taking up another from the pile at his elbow.

"Ah, Sergeant," he said, glancing up, "a good day. Yes, all told, a very good day, indeed."

"Yessir!"

"Casualties at the landing were high," he admitted, "the loss of Lieutenant Forsyth is irreplaceable."

Bell bowed his head and did his best to look solemn. He and I had both known the Lieutenant back in St. John's, and while the sergeant's opinion was his own affair, mine was that few heads ever came thicker than Forsyth's. Forever reluctant to do anything without orders, this new idea of independent thinking encouraged in our junior officers had been wasted on him, and quite possibly, if he had survived, would have succeeded in getting even more of us killed; so I was not unduly saddened at his passing, but more so for those who had been in the boat with him at the landing.

After an appropriate time of reflection had passed, Beaumont broke the solemnity by saying, "But from that point on there were only three casualties out of the entire company, and no deaths, although the surgeon does not hold out much hope for poor Todsmuir."

"Bullet wounds, sir," Bell shook his head sadly, "nasty things."

"He expects infection will carry him off."

"Mixture of gunpowder and rum, sir," the sergeant offered with a certain air of sagacity, "dose 'im up with that. Works every time...leastwise sometimes it does, sir. It's what

78

we used in the old days." Bell obviously considered that what had served in the past would serve equally well in the present, an argument that was difficult to counter. The mortality rate of the sick and wounded was as high as it had ever been.

Whether or not the captain had an opinion of Bell's version of medical science, he did not share it with the room at large. Instead, looking up at last, his eyes set upon me and then quickly away. Unsmiling, he almost whispered, "Ah yes, Stubb." Then taking up the quill again and signing another form, he took the next from the pile, and began to read, saying, "That will be all, Sergeant."

Bell hesitated; obviously he had hoped to be present when my punishment was pronounced.

"Regulations state, sir, that when in company of an officer, a prisoner..."

"Yes, Sergeant, thank you," Beaumont did not look up, and after the shortest of pauses said, "leave us, please."

Bell shuffled from foot to foot, so reluctant was he to absent himself. Then, doing little to hide his frustration, he abruptly spun a smart about-face, glancing a look of dark hostility my way before heading for the door. Once it was ajar, he stopped and did a hesitant half-turn.

"Prisoner's escort, too, sir?"

Still refusing to look up, Beaumont replied, "Private Stubb is not under arrest, Sergeant...at the moment." He left it hanging, momentarily, for my benefit, I thought, and then finished with, "So yes, escort too, if you please, and Sergeant..."

Bell stopped again, waiting, "Sir?"

"We are not to be disturbed, is that clear?"

Bell looked from me to the captain, clearly mystified, as was I, myself.

"Very good, sir," and then he was gone.

After both sergeant and escort had left, and the door shut firmly behind them, Beaumont put his quill aside, looking up at last, his handsome face studying me with tired, expressionless eyes.

As I stood at attention before him, attempting to fix my own eyes on a point against the opposite wall, appropriately obeisant, I found it virtually impossible to keep them from darting down to regard my superior as he was regarding me, in an attempt to guess at my future.

For the first time I noticed that the state of his uniform had scarcely changed since the battle. His face itself was clean and evidently newly rid of signs of the recent contest, but his mitre seemed not to have been recovered as yet, nor was his coat brushed of ground-in powder and dirt. Indeed, during the uncomfortable pause, I could not help noticing a sprig of spruce had become lodged in his epaulette, doubtless acquired during the fighting in the wood.

Beaumont studied me for a moment longer, then apparently seized by a surge of restless energy, sprang to his feet and strode over to the single window. He stood there with his back to me, gazing out, which must have been quite a chore, for it was glazed over with oiled paper, and not at all transparent.

He continued like this for quite some time, occasionally rising up on his toes, and then down again, reminding me uncomfortably of Sergeant Bell; but in the sergeant's case it had been malice propelling him up and down. If I did not know any better, with Captain Beaumont I would have said that it was nerves.

Finally, still without turning, he said, "You fought well today, Stubb."

His words might have hit me like a charge of grapeshot, so struck was I! My mouth must have been hanging open, for whatever I had expected from this encounter, by no means was this compliment ever foreseen to play any part!

Finally, I opened my mouth – to speak this time – then shut it again to clear my throat before making a second attempt.

"Thank you, sir."

He made no indication that he had heard me, but continued standing at the window with his nose to the oiled paper, tweaking himself, up and down, on his toes.

Instead, he came at the subject (whatever it was) from a totally different angle.

"They tell me that you are educated."

Still gaping at the back of his head, I managed to stammer, "Not formally, sir."

"By whom then?"

"Why, by Mr. Bellsworth, sir, back in St. John's…and what I was able to pick up on my own of course, sir…from books," I finished lamely.

The head at the window jerked up and down, exactly twice, like a puppet in the hands of an unpromising novice.

"Bellsworth," he mused, as though trying to recall, "I have heard the name bantered around. Educated at Cambridge, they say, although they also say that he leans too much toward strong drink, and the company of lewd women."

I thought of Mr. Bellsworth with my mother behind the curtain, the bed rocking off the wall like the beating of a drum, and me studying Homer by the fire. Whoever 'they' were, I thought, their information was accurate, up to this point; but if the captain was grilling me for information regarding my tutor's morals - or lack of them, as the case may be – I was hesitant to oblige him, so maintained my silence.

The captain's intentions continued to mystify me when he asked, "You know your numbers?"

"Tolerably well, sir."

"And you can write?"

"Why, yes sir."

Without turning to face me, Beaumont inclined his head. "Show me; put your name to the back of one of the forms."

After a brief hesitation, I took up the quill, and dipping it into the bottle of ink, did as ordered. Then bringing the sheet of paper over to where he had taken station at the window, I held it up for him to see.

He studied it for a moment.

"You have a fine hand."

A lifetime of dealing with Fat Sally while she gradually wended her way to the subject had taught me that it would be arrived at all the sooner by my speaking only when spoken to. Indeed, incongruent though it might seem, at the moment there was a similarity growing between the two. But before I could properly come to grips with this thought, Beaumont changed tack again.

"What books have you read?"

I fancied that I was making a habit out of gaping at him. "Sir?"

"What books?" he snapped, perhaps a trifle impatiently; or was the impatience merely an extension of nerves?

I frowned, going back over the years, "I started out with Defoe when I was younger, sir."

"Robinson Crusoe?" He seemed to pick up interest, as though this were a pleasant distraction.

"Yes sir."

"Of course," the head nodded, approvingly this time, "the perfect book for a child." Then he abruptly broke from reverie and demanded, "What else?"

"Well, there's Don Quixote..."

Obviously surprised, the captain spun around. "Cervantes? In Spanish?"

"Why, no sir. I don't speak it."

The handsome brows knitted, "Then where?"

"Smollett made a translation, sir, a few years ago."

Beaumont actually smiled, and in his eyes I fancied that I saw a dawning of respect. "Smollett, eh? I might have known, the scamp!" Then he floored me with, "Perhaps you might lend it to me some time?"

"Why, of course, sir. I'd be honoured!"

But he brushed this aside, and asked, "Any more?"

"Well..." I ventured reluctantly, not sure how this would be received, "there's Fielding, sir."

"Ah! 'Tom Jones'!"

"And others, sir," I told him, beginning to feel more at ease.

"Fielding," Beaumont chuckled, "a great wit!"

"I thought so, too, sir."

"A bit racy though, wouldn't you say?"

"Perhaps a little raw, sir."

Then Beaumont seemed to change tack, yet again.

"What about Amory, or James Hervey?"

And again I hesitated. "Mr. Bellsworth once loaned me a copy of one of Amory's, the one about the ladies of Great Britain…"

"'*Memoirs of Several Ladies of Great Britain*'? Do you mean that one?"

"The very same, sir."

"And?"

I hung my head, ashamed.

Yet Beaumont's voice was kind enough, and somehow amused, when he asked, "Too serious, perhaps?" I nodded, and he managed a soft laugh, "As it was for Mr. Bellsworth, too, I am sure." Then with scarcely a pause for breath, he made an effort to come closer to the point.

"Dereliction of duty is a serious offence at any time. During time of war it carries the death penalty; are you aware of that?

The room had become very still when I replied, in a voice scarcely above a whisper, "Yes, sir." Any ease that I had felt vanished on the instant.

Captain Beaumont nodded, though he would not meet my eye.

"You are also aware that, at *present*," he let the word hang, as he had earlier, "you have not been placed under arrest?"

Now his eyes did dart up to meet mine, so I carefully inclined my head to show him that I was so aware.

Then as if he feared that what I saw of him might not be to his liking, he returned to the window, this time with his hands behind his back.

"Able at mathematics," he said, as if reciting from a list, "schooled in your letters, and judging from your vocabulary – which is quite extraordinary for an enlisted man, and a colonial besides – you have excelled in your efforts. Intelligent and brave, with a physique that qualifies you as a grenadier, the army's elite." One might have thought that he would have mentioned this with some sense of pride, for he, too, was a grenadier, but he spoke as if mentioning the fact in passing. "You are a valuable man, Stubb," his voice became reflective when he unconsciously repeated, "yes, a very valuable man." But then as suddenly as it had come, the moment passed as he pried himself away from whatever conundrum had forced its way into his thoughts. "I should not doubt that you have a promising career before you. In time a sergeant's stripes, certainly, possibly even Regimental Sergeant-Major; or if the Fates are with you, possibly even commissioned from the ranks; such things are not unheard of, you know?"

What the captain was referring to was, given an instance of noticeable bravery, combined with a significant number of officer's names on the butcher's bill after an engagement, a field commission might be awarded, and given a small miracle, made permanent. The odds were dead-set against such an occurrence but as Beaumont had said, not entirely unheard of.

Still, I was not such a fool as to think that he was spinning dreams for my own personal amusement, so was prepared when he added, "It would be a pity for all that promise to end in front of a firing squad before this day's sun has set."

He paused, waiting, I think for me to respond, possibly even hoping that it should be I, somehow, who would broach the elusive subject. However when this failed to materialize, he turned to a new line of questioning, all the while twining his oration around me, as a snake might its prey.

"Who gave you the books?"

The question caught me dumbfounded. "Why, Mr. Bellsworth, sir."

"Out of the goodness of his heart?"

Even given the tension of the moment, I had to allow the ghost of a smile to breach my defences, "Hardly that, sir."

"Yet books are expensive; who bought them? Was it you, yourself?"

Too late, I saw the line of his questions and could only answer, "No, sir, not all of them."

Now he turned from the window, regarding me through eyes veiled with excitement. "Then who?"

My tongue felt as if it were made of wood when I answered, "My mother, sir."

"Your *mother*?" The heat from his gaze was searing into me, burning in its intensity.

"Yes, sir."

"Not your father?"

I said, "No, sir," looking him full in the eye.

Yet he evaded my challenge, instead continuing with his cursed questions.

"Did your mother inherit money, perchance?"

"No, sir," and suddenly tired of playing, I added, "as you well know."

Without any indication that he had heard me, Beaumont continued on, the fever still burning within him.

"Your mother is Sally Stubb, is this not true?"

I fought not to strike him, "You know it is, sir."

"Known by the lower sorts as '*Fat Sally*', a lady of – how should I say – *questionable* morals?"

I responded with words as brittle as ice. "The very same, sir."

"In fact, she is a common whore; is that not so?"

I allowed that it was, as she would herself, had she been present.

"So you are, in fact, a whoreson?" He phrased it as a question, not a statement, yet rhetorical, his sneer too prominent to be genuine. I held my peace. So far, '*they*' had been accurate with their facts. It was too much to hope, that with Beaumont coming ever closer to the bull's eye, he would miss it altogether.

85

Having left his question hanging, the captain mused along on a train of thought. "An educated son of a whore," he seemed to be attempting disdain, but sounded nervously amused, "who, by all accounts, has been taken with a fancy that he might better his lot in the world, perhaps even come to rise above his station one day. A whoreson with a great deal of ambition by any standard," he attempted another sneer, but his obvious excitement was too great to carry it off, as he finished his musing with, "I wonder what a fellow like that might do – how low he might be willing to debase himself in order to rise so high?"

The answer to that, as I am sure he well knew, was that I would have done anything. Ignorance had been the wall needing to be scaled, and books the ladder with which that had been achieved, in some measure to the point of surpassing my tutor. Money had been the necessity - at first to fend off starvation, but later to acquire knowledge, and a winsome boy, well-schooled in the arts of whoredom, might command a significant price for his services, given a select clientele. Beaumont already possessed this information, of that I was certain; it remained to be seen how he planned to use it.

"The truth is that you, yourself, are a whore; is this not so?" The captain's eyes seemed glazed with fever, perspiration causing his face to shine, and excitement his hands to tremble.

This time it was I who could not hold his gaze, yet I responded with vehemence. "No, sir!" I told him, clinging to a finely wrought line. I was not that boy anymore; I had succeeded in escaping from his skin – or so I strove to believe.

"Oh, but you are!" the captain insisted, before dashing my fantasy to the wind. "Once a whore, always a whore. Didn't you know that, Stubb? Didn't anyone tell you? Didn't you realize, that for all of your high blown aspirations, that is all you will ever be?"

"No!"

As violent as my denial was, Beaumont brushed past it with ease.

"All that is left undecided," he told me, in a voice that was far from steady, "is what the price shall be!"

And there it was.

I tried to hide my revulsion, but the statement had come so swiftly that I fear I had little success. It was now obvious what Beaumont wanted, and it struck me far deeper than I would ever have thought possible.

Captain Beaumont? I must admit that I never would have suspected. His good humour and easygoing ways were well-regarded by the lads – by *myself,* until this moment. Always a cheerful smile and a word for everyone, already he knew every man in the company by name, and we loved him for it. But especially, big and strapping, sandy-haired and handsome as he was, it had become common to see him with the hand of any one of the prettier, more genteel ladies from the garrison on his arm, and we lads used to speculate – half-joking, many of us in awe – which one would be next. That it had all been a carefully wrought disguise to hide the fact that he was a sodomite, not one of us would have ever guessed, even though it had been my experience that these were the very kind that had always appeared at Sally's door, usually during the darkest of nights, with that haunted look in their eye, because they had heard rumours of the pretty boy and his skill, and felt compelled to come and experience it for themselves.

All that aside, had I known any of this earlier, it was doubtful that the outcome would have been different. I was trapped, and we both knew it – ever since I had allowed my mind to wander at the edge of the wood.

Beaumont came up behind me, whispering in my ear, while slipping my tunic from my shoulders. "Cheer up," he said, "it's not as bad as all that." He reached around and unbuttoned my breeches, his voice continuing to shake with excitement. "Or would you rather face a firing squad after all?"

I was numb with shock, yet even after all of my efforts to leave that part of my life in the past, I was not such a fool as to think there was an alternative; and as bad as that was, even in my confused frame of mind, it seemed a small enough price to pay for my life. After all, Beaumont would not be the first, not by any means. Sally had taught me all too well. It had become a function, that was all, in fact not any more disagreeable than many other parts of army service, and if I were being honest with myself, less disagreeable than most. The fact that I had thought those days behind me did not signify. As I had said, I was trapped.

So, looking carefully away, I hooked my thumbs into the waistband of my breeches, and pushed them to the floor. Then I bent over the table, concentrating, steeling myself not to recoil at his touch. I heard Beaumont undoing his own buttons – it is possible, especially when every moment is spent praying never to hear that sound again – then I felt him close in behind me, followed immediately by an insistent push. There was that old, familiar, unpleasant sensation, and I willed myself not to cry out in anguish. By the time he had begun in earnest, my mind was far away.

Out of urgency, I sent it where it would go of its own volition, and even in the extremity of my situation, realized some dismay when I found that it still went unerringly to Elizabeth.

I was lying with her in our glade once again. I could feel the warmth of the sun on my shoulders while basking in the beauty of her smile, and the glory of her milk-white body, her skin smooth as silk.

"I love you, Josiah, and I shall love you forever and ever," she told me through warm, glowing eyes, and then giggled while I sprinkled flower petals across her breasts.

When she looked at me that way all things were possible. It was as though Sally's prophecy had come true, and the world was at my feet – a world of such beauty and promise that I had heretofore failed to suspect that it could possibly exist. Then, suddenly quite serious, she took my face in her hands, gazing ever deeper into my eyes, and for the hundredth time within the hour, I fell in love with her all over again. "Nothing will ever come between us, I swear it!" So saying, she pulled me down to her lips, and everything was the sweetness of her kiss. I dwelled there with her, her arms and legs wrapped around my body while the heat of her breath filled my ear.

Eventually a distant awareness informed me of the captain's hands clenching into my shoulders, and I sensed the ordeal coming to an end. I came back to myself in time to hear Beaumont say in a harsh whisper, "Get out!"

I collected my uniform with some difficulty, for my mind was still at sea, and by now the room quite dark. At last respectable, or as close as I would ever be again, I was able to make my way to the door in silence, leaving the captain facing the window as before.

The night air was cool and sweet, yet my skin crawled at its touch, as though it were infested with vermin. I decided to make my way to the stream, wincing at the dull familiar ache low down on my inside. The need to bathe had seldom been so strong in me.

Just before the door latched shut, I heard a sound coming from inside the cabin. Shaken from my own thoughts, I paused to listen, perplexed by what it might be. Yes, there it was again, unmistakable - the great, choking sounds of a man sobbing.

Chapter Five

The following days were spent clearing ground for the camp and its defences, all of which would not have been possible but for the supplies we had captured when the French line had so precipitately collapsed on the day of our landing. The much-anticipated supplies from the fleet had thus far failed to arrive, as the seas had once more risen, making it impossible for boats to come ashore. The bread and cheese from our pockets had long since been consumed, making Captain Beaumont's jest about eating French cuisine prophetic as, along with guns and ammunition, the enemy's field rations were also numbered amongst the booty taken.

Following the episode with Beaumont, when I finally made my way back to our lines, I found Daniel awake, anxious for my return. In truth, he was by no means alone, for although it was past the first week in June, the nights here were cold and the wind ever strong and present. For those of us unfortunate enough not to have commandeered a blanket from captured French stores, sleep was a rare commodity as our own blankets were still aboard the transports. The long and the short of it was that when I at last felt able to stumble my way through the dark to my friend's side, there were plenty of the lads still awake to help me find my way.

He rose to greet me, but I collapsed on the ground at his feet, curled into a ball, my arms hugging my chest with my back to him. He called out to me, his voice filled with concern, but instead of answering, I pretended sleep. There were no words inside of me, and if there were, there was little that I could tell him in any event. As close as he was to me, I could not speak to Daniel about what had happened; I could not speak to anyone. All I could do was lie on the cold hard ground, nursing my sorrow, and glean what little comfort could be had by his presence.

As foretold, I slept very little that night. Whenever my eyes closed, all I could see was Beaumont's excited sneer, taunting me, confirming what I had not dared to allow my mind to dwell on. I was a whoreson, there was never any doubt of that, and I had been a whore as well; but as hard as I tried, all my attempts to lock that part of my past away had come back to haunt me with a vengeance. So as the night rolled on into morning, and I battled the conflicting emotions within me, one thought stood out above all others: someone had betrayed my secret.

I should not have been surprised, although I was, deeply so. After all, betrayal was not uncommon in the gutter; in fact it was more common than one might imagine, without a code of knaves that is so often spoken of. Starvation is always just around the corner when living in poverty, and one did what was necessary to survive. The fact that Sally had invested so heavily in my education may have been a testament to a mother's love for her son, but it was more an investment into her own future than anything else. Nothing was for nothing; that was one of my first lessons, and I had learned it well. Close behind it was an understanding that information was power over others, and if you used that power wisely, you could rise above them by putting them beneath your heel. Valuable lessons both, but not so valuable as understanding that what you had learned, others could as well. The question was: who had been aware of my past, and was most likely to profit by it?

The first part was easily answered. All that remained to discover the second was to ask him.

It was an hour before reveille when I checked to see if Daniel was asleep. He was, but in the grey light of dawn I could see his eyes twitching behind his lids like mice under a blanket, a sure sign that his rest was not an easy one. I crept away from his side with all the stealth of which I was capable.

As luck would have it I found Stockingsdale within the minute. I knelt down beside him without any difficulty, for his reputation preceded him, and most evenings was given as wide a berth as possible by all others in our company. I took great care not to make a sound when I slid my bayonet from its scabbard and held it to his throat.

"Good morning, Benjamin," I whispered pleasantly, although there was murder in my heart.

His body went rigid, and I knew that he was awake.

"Who's there," he whispered back, and then scarcely without pause asked, "Is that you, Josiah?"

"Been expecting me, have you?" I growled, giving the bayonet a twist.

"Not in so many words," he allowed, his voice strangulated by the pressure, "but I knew it was only a matter of time before you put two and two together."

"What do you mean?"

This was not the pathetic claim to innocence that I had envisioned, and so, took me off my guard. To compensate, I gave the bayonet another twist, knowing full well that another ounce of pressure would see the end of him.

There was a gasp, and then the loathsome man's choked whisper from the pressure of the needle's tip on his throat, as he replied, "I mean that I've known you all your life, Josiah. I've watched you grow, and I know you for a bright spark."

Still none the wiser, but with an uneasy feeling stirring in the bottom of my stomach, I demanded that he explain himself. Incredibly, I felt him chuckle, silent judderings of mirth, vibrating down the bayonet's shaft.

"I mean your ma asked me to look out for you is all."

"My mother?" I asked, before stupidly adding, "*Sally*?"

"The very same," he replied, as the needle's point withdrew ever so slightly.

I demanded, "And what has she to do with what happened last night, damn you?" I willed the bayonet closer, but it failed to obey.

"Only in an incidental and indirect manner," Stockingsdale allowed, although still chuckling.

"You'd better start making sense, Benjamin, or I swear..."

"Sally asked me to look out for you – she begged me to," his eyes were dull silver in the duller light, "and so I did."

"You *betrayed* me!" I accused savagely, "You went to the captain!"

"Oh, aye, I did that," Stockingsdale gently eased the tip of my bayonet further from his throat. I did not resist. "And didn't I overhear Bell talking to Jeffers, saying you was for it? And didn't I also know certain things about the captain and his proclivities? If you been a soldier as long as I have, you learn to keep your nose to the ground, boy."

"The ground?" I sneered, "You mean the gutter!"

"If you prefer," he admitted, then added with an edge, "but it's the same gutter you come from, Josiah. The only difference between us is I like it there."

Perverted and disgusting though Stockingsdale might be, his curious sense of honesty – or honour – was enough to confuse anyone.

"So you went to Bell requesting a word with the captain – about me."

"About nothing," Benjamin replied with a haughtiness that should have seemed ridiculous, coming from such a depraved creature. "There's things I could say about our sweet-tempered sergeant that would cause ears to prickle, I'll warrant, and a hint to him along those lines was enough to get me in to see the captain."

"So you told him about me, about my past!"

"I *hinted,*" he repeated, this time with emphasis, as though it made all the difference in the world, "sometimes heavy, sometimes light, with just a tease thrown in that I knew something about a certain officer what had peculiar tastes along certain lines, that's all. Could be I put it in such a light as he would see it would be a service to His Majesty, to overlook what was really but a small indiscretion in order to retain a lad of such promise."

"You convinced him that it was his duty to bugger me!"

"I convinced him of nothing," he replied blandly, "Beaumont was capable of that all on his own; but who could say I was wrong if I did, eh? Your bloody stupidity could've been the death of us all, you young pup! Some punishment was in order, and that's what you got, ain't it?"

"But..."

"You're alive, Josiah," Stockingsdale interrupted, suddenly impatient, "and I wouldn't take too hard a line against Beaumont for what happened, neither. He's a decent sort, for an officer. If you had been anything other than what you are, he would have respected that, and had you before a drumhead court martial, and decently shot before sunset." Then, with a note of finality, he added, "Now, let be!"

I did not want to, nor could I have if I tried. I was tormented by what had been done to me – forced back into my past after so much effort had been made to leave it behind. Yet I had to realize that there was little to be gained from trying to express those feelings to Stockingsdale. If the tables had been turned, he would have gone willingly – probably would have turned a handsome profit - and counted himself lucky in the bargain.

Yet I could not let it stand as it was, so I asked, "Why did you do this?"

Stockingsdale looked surprised, "Why I told you: your mother asked it of me!"

"But why?" I persisted, "What do you stand to gain?"

Here Benjamin's surprise gradually coalesced into a knowing grin. "Your ma mayn't be the prettiest piece back home, and mayhap her best years're behind her, not to mention her behind itself – wide as a battleship it is, but cor, Josiah," and he moaned ecstatically, "she's all the woman I need, an' it don't hurt my chances none if she were to be grateful to one Benjamin Stockingsdale, Esquire, now do it?"

I was staggered, of course, at the very thought of this evil old reprobate having aspirations of becoming my stepfather, and shuddered accordingly. Then I was also equally staggered that my mother could still possess enough charm to appeal to anyone, even if it were no one better than this man, who had fewer morals than a pig!

94

I glared at him, making no effort to hide my disgust - both for his effrontery and his reasoning - but it was useless to attempt to quail Stockingsdale with something so meaningless to him as disgust. Therefore, with nothing further to add but a last grunt of dissatisfaction, I pulled away and crept back to Daniel, without it ever occurring to me that I might have thanked the old fool, or that, in this case at least, my past had been my salvation.

I found Daniel awake and stretching, rubbing his shoulders, trying to generate some warmth into his limbs. He offered a nod when he saw me, and smiled, yet asked no questions. He had sensed that I was reluctant to speak of the previous night's proceedings, and respected my wishes; however, he did place a hand on my shoulder, and said, still smiling, "If you ever need an ear..."

I forced a smile of my own - even managed a laugh – and told him that there was nothing to be concerned about: Beaumont had given me righteous hell, and that had been the end of it, which was not, strictly speaking, a lie. Daniel's smile never quite reached his eyes, as I'm sure, neither did my own, but he accepted my story with a shrug, and mercifully left it alone.

That had been three days earlier, and now we were busy helping the artillery with one of the few six-pounders that had come ashore on the day of the landing. We were attempting to manhandle the brute over the boggy ground so that it might be situated as an added protection of our encampment.

The artillery sergeant shouted, "Heave!" just before flinging himself against one of the gun carriage wheels. The rest of us, perhaps a dozen all told, did likewise, with the spectacular result of getting the wheels to do a half-turn before the entire accursed contraption sank up to its axle in the mud, where it sat, leering, daring us to do our worst.

"Leave the bloody thing!" Daniel advised with some feeling. We had been toiling all morning, and thus far, after a generous investment in perspiration, not to mention aching backs, had succeeded in reaching a point some few hundred yards from where we had started.

The sergeant regarded my friend with distinct agitation. One might have thought that his mother had just been referred to as a slut. I understand, that in most circles, this is regarded as an egregious insult.

"None of that!" he barked, still with a jaundiced eye toward Daniel. "Until the navy decides to get off their backsides and get into the war we'll need every piece of ordnance that we've got!"

The rest of us considered the giant breakers thundering onto the shore behind him, trembling the very ground beneath our feet, and sending towering geysers high into the air. By comparison, those treacherous waves experienced on the day we landed seemed tame and inconsequential. Anyone could see that it would be suicide to attempt to reach land in such a heavy sea; yet evidently, the sergeant was no great lover of the navy, and had no wish to appreciate their difficulties when his own were so demanding.

"Right, you lads," the sergeant gestured toward his own men, "in you go," indicating the swamp enclosing their mired gun. However, he did not include any of us detailed from the 51st in the order. A likeable fellow at heart - save only where his beloved six-pounder was concerned - the sergeant was clearly hoping that our efforts would be voluntary.

The artillerymen hesitated, glancing from one to the other – shrugging and being shrugged at in turn. Eventually they shed themselves of their blue coats, and leapt, one after the other, into the mud, sinking to within inches of the tops of their gaiters.

Daniel, ever hostile to authority, started to laugh, which caused many red faces and muttered curses among the sweating artillerymen. The laughter stopped short however, when I shed my own coat, and leapt in after them. There followed an elongated pause riddled with disbelief so acidic that I felt it burning holes in my back; then, muttering some low curses of his own, he stepped gingerly in after me, and in due course was followed by others of our detail.

"What are you about, then, eh?" he asked in a low whisper, clearly annoyed.

"Why, not a thing," I told him with a bitter laugh, "not a sweet blessed thing. I am simply doing my utmost for king and country, just as any soldier in His Majesty's service ought to, yourself included."

Now it was my turn to be regarded with a jaundiced eye, which I managed to ignore by grabbing hold of a spoke and heaving for all I was worth.

Daniel's voice was heavy in my ear as he took hold of the next spoke behind me. "Something has changed in you, Joss," he said, "and I'm not sure that I care for it!"

"That is life for you," I told him with an equally bitter laugh, "there is no telling where you are going to be after the dice has been cast."

"There, you see?" clearly my answer had done little to mollify him, "That's exactly what I mean: I haven't got the foggiest notion what you're talking about."

I laughed again, more bitter than ever, "Nor do I!"

He clucked his tongue disapprovingly, "You're speaking in riddles, you are!"

"Let it be, can't you!" I snapped with more anger than intended, yet it was beyond my ability to apologize. So I compounded the wrong by adding, "Leave me alone!"

The offended silence that answered told me that my wish was being granted. The despair I felt upon throwing myself against the gun carriage wheel had little to do with freeing the cannon from the Cape Breton gumbo.

My bitterness had put me at odds with the world, even Daniel, but with no one more than myself. Everything, all that I had done to place myself on that long, arduous road toward respectability – my education, my attempt at hiding from the past, burying myself in the anonymity of the army, my bid to become a man of the world - had received a serious blow, perhaps even one that was mortal. I was a whore, born of a whore, and so I would remain in the eyes of everyone who had known me before, and of those that they chose to tell. The question remained if the will still existed not to see the same thing in my own eyes.

Perhaps there was an even greater question: was such an unlikely goal even attainable? I had been reminded of my station, in a way that struck home just how deep was my folly for ever having attempted such a change in the first place. My past held me subject to the mercy of an unmerciful world at any time, or any place, that it might choose to rear its ugly head. It held up a dark lantern so that I might see all of the inescapable days of my future, thereby overwhelming me in waves of bitterness and anger.

I could have wept with the thought of my aspirations for respectability, for therein lay the key to any sort of happiness still open.

The mere mention of the word, *'happiness'*, sent my mind back to unbidden memories of Elizabeth and that day on our meadow: her eyes - cornflower blue – her flaxen hair and ivory teeth, the sweetness of her laughter mingling with the drone of honeybees on the warm summer air. I had tasted perfection, and once having tasted it, must set it aside, and try to forget. I had possessed her, and realizing how impossible it would be for such wondrous moments to be repeated, caused a sudden surge of anguish to course through my body, in turn causing the gun to judder a quarter turn forward.

"That's it, lads!" the sergeant cheered, fairly leaping up and down in his excitement, "Bend to with a will! She's coming, I swear it!" Then, changing his focus from our pathetic selves to his charge, he leapt to the front, facing us, and coaxed, "Come on, dearie! Who's the good little girl, eh? Come on, sweetness; come to papa, there's my darling!"

His shouting gradually echoed away into an inconsequential drone as my mind sought release from both torment and drudgery. As during the episode with Beaumont, now, too, it chose not to remain in the unbearable present, but instead would not be denied, no matter how hard I tried to forget a regret-filled past - bitter dregs of memory of a bitter life, but for one cherished pearl that shall forever be welcome…the moment when I first set eyes on her.

*   *   *

At the height of the season St. John's was a bustling town. Men mostly, for although large, the population was in the main transient, as the great fishing fleets came and went; yet it offered a rich commerce for Sally and myself, as urges of the body do not rest when absent from the ports of home.

I had just finished meeting with the captain of a fishing schooner, in from the Grand Banks heavy-laden, and with a will to treat himself over his good fortune. I trust that I had not disappointed his expectations, for he offered a handsome gratuity over and above our agreed upon price. I remember that he and everything around him stank of codfish.

Three years had passed since Sally first had me sodomized, with half an eye to the future, and the other half to her own insatiable appetite.

So it was with my mother: she often had a purpose hidden behind the one in plain sight. Indeed, I was less sure whether my being violated was a step toward introducing me into a trade of my own, or was simply an extension of her craving. Whatever her intension, Sally seldom failed to avail herself of the results.

As for myself, I could not claim to enjoy any part of my new life. It was a strange world that my mother was introducing me into. As I continued to mature, I was to find that I had no idea of how truly bizarre that world could be.

I was now well into my sixteenth year: still boyish in appearance, yet beginning to show a fledgling promise of manhood. Unusually tall and broad of shoulder to begin with, my unceasing efforts to please my mother essentially ensured that my expertise only increased as my childhood was left behind. With this in mind, perhaps it was inevitable that I eventually procured a regular clientele of my own, with virtually every setting of the sun.

99

It might be gathered that I had not been idle during those intervening years, and it might also be gleaned that Sally and I had prospered in some measure. We had moved from our little cabin on Maggotty Cove, and taken rooms across the length of the King's Beach in Darkuses, close to Rotten Row, but also close to the naval yards, where we both might expect some custom. The eccentricity of the names notwithstanding, it was by far a more respectable area, allowing us better to entertain a more refined (and wealthy) class of people. I say *people*, and not *men*, because, as word got out through the lower circles of the town, an increasing number of my clients were women.

By far and away, the majority of the settlement's income was wrested from the sea. The perils of such an occupation, combined with the thriving of the cod fishery, virtually assured any amount of widows, with any amount of wealth. Uniformly old to be sure, withered beyond any recognition of beauty, but still endowed with the fires of passion, they were willing to part with that wealth just as freely as would a man. Indeed, they revelled in my burgeoning manliness, as well as the consequence of my education, just as exuberantly as would any other. Afterward, they were always seen to the door wearing smiles that seemed to suggest that they deemed the trade from marriage to widowhood a fair one.

I did not, as a rule, conduct business at a client's place of residence. There were many pitfalls in my profession, and putting one's self into an unknown situation was potentially hazardous. Enemies abounded, both for those whose tastes I appealed to, and for myself for catering to them. Within our rooms the ancient blunderbuss that Sally had taken on trade, from a customer down on his luck, offered some measure of protection. Outside of them I was fair game for whatever villains should wish to do me harm. However, when a knock came at the door the previous afternoon, revealing a simple fisherman with cap in hand, I immediately recognized the fellow as one of the crew of a favoured client. So when the invitation was extended - to visit his master later that evening aboard his ship – I had agreed without a qualm. I knew him for a good sort at heart, easily pleased, and known to be lavishly generous whilst in his cups. Upon being informed that he had begun celebrating his good fortune well before his ship had reached harbour, I could not resist a knowing smile, and shared a wink with the sailor, for such folk are altogether more amiable to certain attitudes than most landsmen.

I bade him wait while I went to change into something more suitable for the occasion. I knew my man: a rugged sailor and a *bonvivant,* one of the few of my regular male clients who had no liking for boyish beauty or elegant foppery. Instead, his generous nature preferred to think of me as a man such as himself, and with an inclination such as his own. So it was no trouble at all to choose the black leather breeches that fit like a second skin, and a plain white linen shirt. With the addition of knee-high boots, a black silk cape, and a broad-brimmed hat, also in black, I was the very picture of a man of mystery, and therefore irresistible to the hopelessly inebriated.

I was not such a fool as to venture forth unarmed, for it is always best to plan for any eventuality; so I slipped a dagger into my boot, and we set out into the darkness together.

The seaman had brought a lantern with him, so we had no hardship making our way down Parson Garden's steep decline to the Lower Path, then over to Yellowbelly Brook, and from there down to the wharf. We found the quay with a minimum of stumbling about, and I was soon standing on the deck of the *Mariposa*, struggling with an urge to hold my nose against the stench, and being ushered into the captain's cabin by my grinning escort.

The deck beams were low, making it impossible to stand erect. There was a lantern on a hook swaying gently with the tide, casting as many shadows as rays. They revealed the captain on a cot by a portal, which was mercifully open. He did not stand to greet me, but rather smiled, patting the mattress beside him. I made my way to where he was sitting, somewhat marring my mystique by hunching over so as not to smash my head on the heavy timbers of the ceiling.

We spoke for a while, but the conversation did not carry. He talked of fish, talked with a relish, slurred though his words had now become, I tried to weave threads of philosophy into the fabric, but with little success, as I had to leave off at intervals to make a quick gasp for air by the portal, which he found vastly amusing.

He offered me a glass, and filled it with a barely palatable Madeira, for it had not travelled well; but I sipped from it regularly, willing my palate to conform. On nights such as this wine was my devoted companion.

As the time passed and the conversation trailed, he asked if I were chilled. I took the hint and removed my hat and cloak, gingerly setting them on the deck where the dirt was less prominent.

He studied me for a while, and I watched as the lust grew in him the way I had seen it grow countless times in others. He leaned forward to kiss me; I turned my head away, reminding him of my rule. He hid his disappointment well, yet his smile was sad on the tail of his apology.

To forestall the gloom taking hold, I asked him to help with my boots, laughing when I told him how thoughtless it had been for me to wear something so clumsy. He smiled too, yet when he got down on his knees and took hold of the heel, he assured me that they were exactly what he had hoped for. The first came off with a minimum of struggle, and as a reward, I allowed him to kiss my foot, hiding my revulsion with generous sips from my glass. The second came off as easily, and I concentrated on the Madeira burning in my stomach so that I might not feel anything else.

He worked his way up to my groin, and tarried there. I allowed it for a short while before stopping him with both hands to the side of his face, making the excuse that I had not come for my own pleasure. He smiled and winked, gratified by the compliment. It was conquest he sought after all.

He rose up and clasped me to his chest, attempting another kiss, but I held up an admonishing finger between our lips and smiled, slowly shaking my head. This time the smile was not returned, but my shirt was whipped over my head, and I suffered his lips on my neck, the bristles of his beard rasping against tender flesh, scouring a rash that would be visible come morning. By now his need was overwhelming, and I was tossed onto his cot as roughly as if I were a sack of grain. As he reached for me, my eyes sought out the leather purse on the table, fat with coin…and there they remained.

The sun was well risen upon waking to the sound of a gun firing a signal from the battery off South Head. I stole quietly from the cramped quarters of the cot, untangling myself from the captain's limbs, my stomach and mouth sour from the wine. His eyes opened while I was struggling into my boots, and we shared a smile. He indicated the purse on the table. I picked it up and handed it to him so that he might count out the coins; but he shook his head, bidding me keep it. The purse was heavy.

I thanked him warmly, and he did the same to me, saying that he was sure to call on me again. We both laughed when I answered, that if he expected another engagement aboard his ship, a good scrubbing might be in order. Then I left him stretching luxuriously, while I closed the door quietly behind me.

I have not seen him since.

The day was warm so I draped my cloak loosely over one shoulder, and returned the friendly waves of farewell from one or two of the crew before stepping down the gangplank onto the wharf, mindful that they were watching me, so I was careful not to appear too lubberly while descending.

I had intended on going directly home, for the weight of the purse on my belt was a constant reminder that the wharf was an uncertain place, even in the light of day, and Sally would fret until she knew that I was safe and sound; but half a mile up the harbour I noticed a sizeable crowd gathering along the King's Pier. Reminded of the gun firing its salute, I stared up at Flagstaff (which even then some were beginning to refer to as Signal Hill) and saw from a mile away the little bits of red flying from the mast, and realized that something of importance was at play. Therefore, being as curious as the next person, I first checked that my purse was well hidden, and that the dagger was in my boot, before proceeding to join the onlookers.

As I drew nearer, I could hear the crowd murmuring excitedly among themselves while being kept away from the landing by a double file of marines, standing at attention, looking smart in their red coats. Over the entire assembly gulls and cormorants wheeled and soared above their heads, their cries adding to the din, as if even they were giving some consequence to the occasion.

I remained puzzled as to what that occasion might be until, looking out into harbour, I saw a great man-of-war coasting past Chain Rock with a commodore's broad pennant flying from the mizzen-top, and I realized that this must be the reason for all the fuss – the governor's fleet had arrived.

Such was an annual occurrence, for the navy commanded in St. John's, the commodore filling the role as governor of all things, civil and military. Yet the North Atlantic in winter was no place for even the sturdiest hull, so the fleet returned to England late in the season, and back to our shores the following spring, bringing with them provisions and all the officials of government. Of course, the occasion of their arrival was always met with interest, for those disembarking from the ships would hold sway over much of our lives during the ensuing months, and it was only natural to indulge our animal curiosity by trying to gauge their worth when they landed. Some would be fearful, others speculative, all of them studying the faces and the bearing of each individual when he first set foot on land, judging how he would use them, or be used by them, as the case may be.

The great ship dropped anchor with a mighty splash just as I arrived and found a space at the crowd's edge. Shortly we could see a boat being swung to the davits and lowered onto the water, presently filling with seamen to man the oars. Then, to the sound of a bo'sun's piercing whistle, we saw a slight, blue-coated figure –adorned in the gold braid of his rank -

descend from the warship's side to take his place in the stern sheets. Immediately the oars were lowered, and the tars began to pull for the shore. It was but a matter of minutes before they arrived at the wharf, discharging him, and the crowd let out a great cheer as the marine band began to play. Amidst the roll of drums and the crashing of cymbals, he doffed his hat to the union flag fluttering in the wind, and returned the salute of the garrison commander before stepping forward to be introduced to some of the town's leading citizens, who were even now arriving as quickly as you could imagine.

Judging by his thin, humourless features, I guessed that the future might not be as bright as one might hope, for he seemed a pious sort with a stern nose for duty that spelled hard times for those of my trade. Still, there were ways around authority: Sally would see to it. So if the future did not hold the best of times for us, we would be able to get by without too much bother, and profit in the bargain.

Meanwhile more boats were coming in and depositing their passengers with further ado: more naval officers, who would hold some station within the new governor's administration. All were given some form of applause from the crowd who, attempting to gauge by rank the extent of each figure's importance, had to guess just how loud that applause should be.

Finally, after perhaps an hour from beginning to end, a last boat arrived, discharging a post captain this time. He was as tall as the commodore, but broader at the shoulders, with a freshly wrought scar down the length of his cheek, and a uniform coat displaying an empty sleeve. When he stopped to salute the flag, the townsfolk looked on respectfully, yet did not attempt to hide their fascination for his wounds. It was thus that the very last person to come ashore was largely ignored, for all eyes save my own were glued to the heroic figure of her father.

She was a tall girl of close to my years, Saxon-haired as was her sire, yet fine-boned where his were strong and inclined to be lean. There could be no doubt that they shared the same blood, however: it was in the clear blue of their eyes, and the fullness of their mouths, and perhaps, too, it was in the pride of their bearing. I had never seen anyone more beautiful.

I am afraid that I stared, forgetting all of the breeding that Bellsworth had attempted to instill in me over the years. She was exquisite, by far and away the finest creature ever to grace our humble shore, and I felt such a sudden yearning for her that it was quite impossible for me to look away. I marveled at her. I worshipped her, and while all others gazed with such open admiration upon her father, I longed to possess her!

Finding herself momentarily ignored in this strange, foreign little town a world away from all that was familiar, her eyes began to play over the crowd, studying them as curiously as they had all the others before her. It was not hard to imagine her wondering how she would get along, and what impact her father's decision for her to join him at his new appointment would have on her life.

It was then that our eyes met – hers dazzlingly beautiful, wide with surprise - and mine undoubtedly as foolish as only a provincial buffoon's could be. I thought that I must melt under such brilliance and forgot to breathe. Then a blush rose to her cheeks, and I felt ashamed for my boorishness having embarrassed her. She glanced quickly down and away, her lips slightly parted as though she, too, was struggling for breath. I felt wretched and unhappy; and for the first time in my life, totally unworthy, yet still I could not look away – not even if it were to save my soul.

Her blush had reddened her cheeks so thoroughly that it had spread to her forehead and what little I could see of her neck before it disappeared into the high collar of her gown. It seemed to consume her, burning her up in flames of confusion, and just when I thought that I could feel no worse…she smiled.

Chapter Six

The morning fog was thick, and a good thing, too; the road followed the shore around the harbour, and we must be well within range of the French cannon.

There were more than twelve hundred of us: three battalions plus four companies of grenadiers. It was rumoured that our destination was the high ground at the far end of the harbour over two miles away, to the lighthouse at the end of the point.

It was not a good road; the forest verged too close onto its edge for one thing, and would allow us little time to react should a war party of Indians suddenly burst from its shadows. So it was a relief to see, here and there, the green coats of rangers amongst the undergrowth, guarding our flank from ambush.

"Reckon there'll be a battle, Joss?" Daniel asked me, but I merely shrugged a reply, for I was still consumed with bitterness, even though it was now four days since the episode with Beaumont.

The seas had still not settled, and though impossible to bring stores and provisions in from the fleet as yet, it was decided that Lighthouse Point must be taken in anticipation of the time that they could. A battery was to be placed there to harass the town and the ships of the French fleet anchored in the harbour, but most importantly the Island Battery guarding the harbour's mouth would come within range. Should that stronghold be silenced, *Monsieur* had only his own few ships to protect him from the massive broadsides of our own fleet.

"Well *I* think there'll be a battle," Daniel continued with some conviction, ignoring the fact that I had not spoken, "Can't see the point of so many of us being involved, otherwise." He did not seem afraid; I doubt that he knew the meaning of the word; yet it was all one to him that the air had been full of smoke for the past hour, carried down to us on a rare east wind. Through the fog could be seen the far-off glimmer as the French set fire to the position, obviously preparing to abandon it.

"They're bound to have a battery set up there," he pointed out. "The ground's far too favourable not to."

And *Monsieur* was far too outnumbered to be able to afford to hold it, I thought impatiently.

"Taking a battery," Daniel mused, "bloody work, that." When I still did not deign to reply, he continued, "Canister, grape, they'll probably cut us down in bloody swaths!"

I could not refrain from studying him with a critical eye.

He smiled, and nodded cheerfully, "Test the mettle of a man, that will!"

"You're daft," I told him, unable to restrain myself.

"Aye, Joss," he laughed, "daft as a bugger, that's me!"

And then I was laughing too.

"I shall lay odds that they are going to shoot away your essentials!"

"Long odds," Daniel observed, still giggling, "long essentials, too, now that you mention it." Then we were both giggling together like children, stifling it as best we might, while leaning into one another to keep ourselves from falling down laughing.

"Silence in the ranks!" Sergeant Bell growled softly, eyes front, as he continued strutting along like a peacock.

Daniel paused to deliver a glare of the purest impudence. Bell must have felt it, for the side of his face began to turn crimson.

Turning away from the despised sergeant, Daniel leaned into me, and whispered, "Know what I think?"

"No, Dan," I smiled, "what do you think?"

"I think, that if there's a god, then if anybody's pecker gets shot off," he gestured with his head, "then it's going to be his."

I followed the gesture, and knew that he intended for me to see Bell, but the sergeant was marching alongside our captain, and all my new-found levity immediately drained away.

Beaumont was not quite staggering, but his face was pinched and grey as he visibly struggled to maintain his posture. I had seen others like that, whether struggling in the grips of fever or after days spent without sleep. Grim satisfaction filled me, for I had never known such hatred!

There was a burr of wings, and I saw a kestrel burst out of the fog, only to disappear again on the instant; and I found myself wondering what it would be like to enjoy such freedom.

But I shook the thought away with an angry gesture. I was not free, nor had I ever been! Survival had usurped my past, and now my past held sway over the present. Freedom was a foreign word on a foreign tongue, and dangerous to contemplate.

I could not restrain the sudden, savage twist in my heart, however, for I remembered that there had been a time when everything seemed possible.

*   *   *

"Come on, luvie!" Sally exhorted, shrilling at the top of her lungs, "Do what's right for Mama!"

In truth, I had done my utmost, and was for the first time untouched by her exhortations. At last I rolled off the mound of her stomach, landing hard on the mattress, unable to resist making the comparison between Sally and the captain's daughter – for such was the way Elizabeth was known to me at the time. It had been a mere matter of days since I had first gazed upon her down at the pier, but already she occupied the forefront of my thoughts, and the longer she dwelled there, I was forced to take stock of my own life more clearly, and realize that, somehow, certain bonds must at last be broken.

Deprived of her pleasure, Sally never missed a beat, but dove down to resuscitate me, but I pushed her away.

"'Ere," she said, wounded, "wot's wrong with you, then?"

I could find no words to reply, but lay resolute on my back, and would not speak.

"Somethink's bothering you, isn't there?" Sally asked, attempting to kiss me, but I turned my face to the wall. After another hurt pause, she asked, "Don't you want to get on with your tutorial?"

I had long since relinquished the belief that the continuation of our intercourse had anything to do with education, so maintained my silence.

Finding herself spurned, Sally's temper began to emerge.

"Ow, you've become 'igh an' mighty, 'aven't you, my son!" she cried, suddenly bitter, "Too good for yore dear old ma!"

"No, Sally," I admitted, finding the words for this much, at least, "not too good, just too young, and too much…your *son!*"

She reared back at that, jowls quivering with indignation.

"Too much my son, is it? Well just answer me this, mister 'igh an' mighty: 'oo loves you more than anyone else in this world, eh? Answer me that, if you can!"

"You do, Sally," I answered miserably, although there was no surrender in my voice.

"An' 'oo answers for yore wishes, an' does all that she can for yore creature comfort?"

Wearily I replied, "You do." but said no more.

I could feel her sensing victory when she said, "Too right! An' when yore poor old mum asks for just a little gratification in return, what does she get?"

"What she deserves!" I had not meant for it to come out so hard, but once uttered, the words could never be taken back, so I continued on the course that I had set. "You have injured me, Mother!"

Sally's jowls slapped at both cheeks before she managed to reply, "Ow! Poppycock an' twaddle! I've done naught but look after yore best interest, I 'ave!"

At which I at last leveled my gaze and said, "Thank you, but now I prefer to go forward on my own."

At which she screeched, and cried, with tear-filled eyes, "Ow Josiah! 'Ooo taught you to be so 'eartless?"

I could not help myself from replying, "Why, you did Mother."

Now the tears began to fall in earnest, while, I must confess, eliciting little sympathy from me. For whenever I looked upon her - at her fat, jowly face that all but obscured her eyes, at the bags of her breasts making a perfect match to the bag of her stomach, to the huge, unkempt whole of her, I could not help making the comparison to the slender, willowy form of the captain's daughter and that golden moment when I was allowed to witness the brilliance of her eyes. Such guileless radiance, I was sure, could hide very little of the true nature of such a perfect creature – such a one as I had never known, nor had ever dreamed existed in this world. I had looked upon her and was lost. She had looked upon me…and *smiled*!

"Ungrateful wretch!" Sally accused, dabbing at her eyes with a corner of the bed sheet. I felt a twinge of sympathy at the simple grace of her sorrow, the effect being spoiled, however, when she took the sheet and blew her nose into it. "How can you do this to yore poor old mum, that's wot I'd like to know!" Suddenly she rose upon her knees in a fit of towering rage, every inch of her quivering like an overflowing bowl of pudding. "You are ungrateful, as ungrateful can be! An' cruel an' 'eartless, besides!"

The very picture of her was so utterly revolting that it did finally pierce my sense of shame. I rose up on my own knees and put my arms around her to offer comfort. Sobbing aloud now, she flung hers around me, and clung with such fierce possessiveness that I had to fight to pull away.

"I am not ungrateful, I assure you," I told her. "I owe you everything, Sally; but this…" I gestured around us, at the bed and soiled sheets, "This must end."

Her anger evaporated as suddenly as it had come, while her face collapsed into silent tears. She turned her head away from me, cheek to shoulder, strands of sweaty hair obscuring the rest. She spoke quietly, as in a daze, as if already past hope. "There's someone else, isn't there?"

I thought of the shining perfection of the captain's daughter, yet possessed just enough wisdom to know that such an aspiration, once put into words, would appear as folly itself. But at the same time I could not deny that she had smitten me, so in the end said nothing.

However, saying nothing was as good a confirmation that there was another as it would have been had I voiced it aloud; for Sally was suddenly fierce once more – fierce and imploring. "Ow my son!" she cried, grasping my shoulders, "Can't you see? This is the love – the *wicked* love – that I tried so 'ard to save you from!" So saying, her eyes seemed to reflect inwardly, and her voice faltered.

Gently, I extricated myself from her grasp and left the bed. I could not find words; something so pure and wonderful, so delicate and fragile, as what I was feeling defied them. Yet if there was one conviction in this world which I held with absolute certainty, it was that, this time, my mother was wrong.

I turned away and took up my breeches, pulling them on as I rose from the bed. Just as I was buttoning up, I happened to glance at Sally. She wore an expression so nakedly woe-filled that I confess that I felt a temporary weakening of my resolve, but then the vision of my desire swam before my eyes, the wonder of her smile as it slowly curled onto her beautiful lips, and I found the strength to turn away. Indeed, it was such an abrupt motion that I was not blind to the gesture - that I was not reluctantly turning away from my mother, but, foolish though it might be, turning whole-heartedly toward something else, something infinitely more wonderful, and suddenly it was impossible to keep my heart from soaring!

Perhaps it was this strange new sensation carrying me that caused the room to feel close, for I felt a strong need to be out into the air for no better reason than it was the same air that she breathed, the same sky that she was under, and at that moment I could not think of anything more wonderful!

I performed a hasty ablution at the basin on the side table, before reaching for my hat and coat.

There was a thread of panic in her voice when Sally asked, "Where are you going?"

I laconically replied, "Out," while making my way to the door.

"Yore going to *her*, aren't you?"

In a sense I was; anywhere but here would be closer to her, but again, these were sentiments that were too complicated for me to articulate. So I contented myself with a shrug, and reached for the latch.

"Ow! Wot's to become of me, then?"

I stopped at the threshold and turned. I believe that I was alarmed to hear her panic so nakedly obvious. Whatever Sally had been, and had done to me, I could not escape the fact that she was still my mother.

She remained on the bed where I had left her. Except now she was sagging in on herself like a bag of flour, or several bags, if you like. Tears oozed from her eyes, and streamed onto her cheeks to be lost in the folds of flesh, while a thread of mucous streamed from one nostril, and remained so, for she was too forlorn to attend it. The entire vision was so unutterably pathetic that I could not find it in my heart to leave her so.

"What do you mean, Sally?" I still stood on the threshold, with my hand at the latch. As much as I cared for my mother, I could still hear the day calling to me, and I longed to be away.

With eyes puffed even more than was normal, she snuffled, and wiped at her nose with her hand, smearing mucous up and down her forearm.

"Well, I'm not a spring chicken anymore, now am I?" and the thought caused her to renew her wailing, "An' all the lads I was ever able to attract to my bed at the best of times was always the poorest sort! Why, even Mr. Bellsworth prefers you to me, doesn't he? Don't say 'e don't, 'cause I know 'e does!"

I did not contradict her, but the rum had been having its way with Bellsworth lately, and I had long since learned all that he had to teach. My mother was a hard businesswoman, and perhaps I had learned that from her, too; for as much as I owed the old sod, he had been paid in full, and he could no longer afford the price that I charged. Aye, it was a hard world, but I was only practicing what I had been taught.

Still, there was Sally, old and fat, and just about as dejected as it was possible for a person to be; and here was I, young and alive, and overwhelmed with this feeling that I was on the verge of some grand adventure. But first I had to try to make amends, even if they would only be partially pleasing to her.

"Why Sally," I told her as gently as possible, "you shall have these rooms for as long as you like."

She snuffled some more, then hiccoughed, "B-but what about you? Won't you stay here with me, then?"

I smiled and went to her, tenderly taking her by the hand. I shook my head, for it was time for me to go out into the world on my own.

Of course when I told her, this brought on another wail and a fresh course of tears; then she said, "But I don't get on as well as I used to, do I? Why, there's my lumbago wot's making it 'arder an' arder for me to get out of bed between customers, then there's my gout wot's been giving me the dickens lately, too; not to mention the rheumatism – it 'urts like the devil, I don't mind telling you! So oo's to help me around the place if yore not here, answer me that?"

"You shall have a maid," I told her, again without thought; for my high spirits were already tugging at the ties that bound me, and I had little patience for something so sensible as thinking.

Sally's eyes widened with surprise before the weight of the surrounding flesh forced them closed again.

"Ow la!" she snorted contemptuously, "Yore 'avin' me on! Fancy the likes of me with a maid!" But I could tell that she had taken an interest in the idea.

"No, Mother, I have never been more serious," I said, and on a note of inspiration added, "Perhaps Mrs. Dawe might help."

For a wonder, this caused Sally to forget her woe long enough to look thoughtful.

"Do you really think she might 'elp?" she asked in a tiny voice, hardly above a whisper, yet for the first time carrying a nuance of something that was not entirely woe-filled.

I found myself warming to the idea. "I shall send a message at once, asking if she will see me."

Isabelle Dawe was one of the wealthier ladies of the settlement, recently widowed from one of the local magistrates, who, it was said, had met his untimely (and unlamented) end as a result of an act of revenge when the Irish had rioted the previous year. Ever since, she had draped herself in the black garb of mourning, outwardly maintaining the demeanor of one who is torn by grief, piously refusing even to acknowledge the body of the man accused of the murder for as many months that it had hung in display up on Gibbet Hill. More to the point, however, soon after that unfortunate affair, she had also become one of my more regular customers. For contrary to appearances, there was not a saintly bone in Mrs. Dawe's body, although it must be said that she had always been generous to me after our encounters. So I had reason to believe that she would be willing to assist in finding Sally a maid, perhaps even part with one of her own. It was not out of the question, after all; she did have rather an abundance of them.

I could tell that Sally was taken with the idea more and more. "Well," she said, pulling thoughtfully at her bottom lip, "if you really think so…"

I kissed her cheek, and repeated, "I shall go at once," before making a second attempt toward the door.

"You never told me 'oo she is," her voice was light, as if she were merely making conversation, "this other woman of yores." Yet I could sense the undercurrent of bitterness.

I stopped, but did not turn around.

"I suppose she must be beautiful…and young?"

I longed to tell her, "Yes!" To speak of her would bring her to life, it would give me the greatest happiness; but my throat was too constricted with emotion.

"She can't be anything like me," she added, subtly more bitter still, "not like yore mother."

For a moment my happiness was swept away by an icy chill.

"Go to her, then!" It was not necessary to look at her to see the sneer.

I launched out the door, but not in time to prevent myself from hearing the low, feral hiss.

"The *bitch*!"

*   *   *

"Have you taken leave of your *senses*, man?" Mrs. Dawe then swore a streak so blue that I can scarcely repeat it.

"I assure you, ma'am," I told her, although I was not entirely sure that such was the case at all, "that I have not."

I had accosted a street urchin along the Lower Path down by Jobs Cove, and given him a carefully folded message, along with a shiny new penny, and sent him up to the front door of the large, ochre-painted mansion that was Dawe Hall – the home of the last of the Dawes – and watched from a safe distance as the proceedings unveiled.

The young snerp had taken the penny, and swore an oath only slightly less vulgar than had Mrs. Dawe herself, before setting off at a sprint. Once arrived, finding himself too slight of stature to reach the brass doorknocker, undaunted he proceeded to pound on the panels with his tiny fists, as though beating upon the surface of a drum.

It was but a short while before the door swung open and a manservant appeared, looking like the wrath of God, and with his own fists clenched, glared both up and down the street. However, upon finding no one in his line of vision, he became confused and uncertain, until he chanced to look down and beheld the young juggins' impudent scowl, holding up his grimy little hand, undeniably with a folded sheet of paper within it.

116

The man's confusion increased tenfold when he read the name on the cover, and even more still when the urchin presented him with the penny.

Words cannot describe the look of venal greed that crept onto his face as, once more, he looked up and down the street before pocketing the coin. Then bidding the brat wait at the door, he gingerly took the note between thumb and forefinger before disappearing inside. He was back within the minute with another note for the boy, then shooed him away with whisking motions of his hands.

The guttersnipe snatched the message and dashed off, but not before delivering to the servant a rude gesture and mouthing something that I could not make out. Then he was scampering back across the street and around the corner to where I was hidden.

"Give over!" he demanded, holding out one hand while clutching the piece of paper to his emaciated little chest with the other.

Carefully, I counted out two new pennies, even shinier than the first, into his horny little hand, and just managed to grab the note before he disappeared in a puff of pure triumph and shocking blasphemy.

Once alone, I unfolded the paper and read what was inside. It consisted of four words.

'*Fifteen minutes. Back door.*"

Twenty minutes later, I was sitting at Mrs. Dawe's kitchen table, and defending myself against accusations of stupidity and/or madness.

She leveled a gaze at me with such severity that I could not help but think of the number of servants upon whom such a look had been delivered, just prior to finding themselves out on Queer Street. Still, I did not flinch, and after a while, unflinching herself, she said, "You have a nerve, fellow, for showing your face at my door. Have you forgotten I've a reputation to uphold?"

"I bid you be at ease, Isabelle," I told her, purposefully using her Christian name to remind her of happier times, "I was not observed."

Mrs. Dawe sliced the air with the razor-sharp ridge of her nose, glaring at me down its length. Isabelle was not ordinarily a fool, nor gladly suffered those who were. Yet I knew that she had a weakness for me.

True to form, soon enough the sternness collapsed, and her face was a mixture of misery and happiness when she asked, "Oh why have you come here, Josiah? What will people think?"

"They will think what you tell them to think," I replied testily; for it was one thing to know oneself as a pariah, but quite another to be constantly reminded of it.

She tossed this aside with a dismissive gesture – undoubtedly she had already reached the same conclusion on her own – then swooped down, enfolding me in an embrace. I was given a brief odor of French perfume before she was swooping away again, to the far corner of the room, where she stood, trembling, with her back to me.

Finally she cried, "What do you want, you...*miscreant*!" Before I could reply, she continued, "It's money, isn't it? Blackmail! Admit it!"

More confounded than ever, I declared, "I admit to nothing of the kind!"

"Then you've come to ravish me! In my own kitchen!" She heaved a warm sigh, "You despicable cur!"

I managed a chuckle, and said, "Hardly that!"

To which she turned, and with sagging shoulders and a melancholy smile, admitted, "No, hardly that."

So I told her why I had come, and though the grey bun on her head bobbed every so often when a telling point surfaced, she heard me out in silence.

When I was finished, she said, "So, that fat old troll and you are quits, is that it?"

To which, carefully, I replied, "My mother and I have agreed that it is time for me to go out on my own."

118

"But naturally," her lip curled, "you want to see to her comfort?"

"Naturally," I said evenly.

Suddenly she rounded on me. "Tell me Josiah, who is she?"

Taken completely by surprise, I could but stammer, "Who is who?"

She leveled a gaze of fond reproach. "Do you take me for a fool? Wherever there is anything of consequence, there is *always* a woman!"

I continued to stammer, my mouth agape like a landed cod, until I noticed her bittersweet smile.

She said, "Damn you, Josiah!"

I found myself smiling in return, and could only shrug.

Then she swooped down upon me once more, and coddling my face in her wrinkled old hands, demanded, "You will be careful, will you not?"

I assured her that I would, although I had little understanding as to her meaning.

She remained embracing me, so I allowed my head to rest for the moment against the brittle bones of her chest.

"So," she mused, more to herself than to me, "the world continues to turn, and little Josiah is ready to leave the nest." Then she held me at arms length, and continued, "So now you're looking for someone to help your mother in her dotage."

I was on the verge of protesting that Sally was far from her dotage, as anyone willing to go half an hour with her in a bedroom would attest, but I well knew Mrs. Dawe and her need for a pound of flesh, so held my tongue.

"Hmm," she mused, fingering her lip, "Perhaps there is someone, although I had to give her notice some time ago."

"Oh?"

"She's Irish," Mrs. Dawe pointed out with a shudder, perhaps remembering the circumstances of her late husband's demise.

"Yes?"

119

"And she's *Catholic*," an even deeper shudder.

"Oh dear!"

"And she drinks like a fish, as you might well expect."

Solemnly I informed her, "Isabelle, she sounds like perfection."

At which point she released me, then with a secretive smile went over to the door, and turning the key, offered a grin, quite lewd for someone of such advanced years.

"Very well, then," she said, beginning to unlace her bodice, "that's been taken care of. I've done my part; wouldn't you agree that it's time to reward my services?"

*   *   *

Tess O'Donnell turned out to be everything that Isabelle had promised: an Irish Colleen of indeterminate years, a devout follower of the papist church and a drunkard. What Mrs. Dawe did not tell me, however, was that before anything could be done for my mother, it was necessary to gain Miss O'Donnell's release from the Yellow House, which was the term used by the settlement for our gaol.

"Are you *quite* sure this is the...ah...*person* you want?" the bailiff's assistant asked outside the cell door. "I do not mean to speculate," he assured me, "but it does seem rather a lot of money for what, at best, can only be described as a dubious return."

A conscientious man in his way, the assistant was referring to the indenturing of prisoners, and the price of their release. In this case, it would seem that he thought it a poor bargain, and felt obliged to inform me as such.

From the shadows on the other side of the bars could be heard a woman, her voice roughened from years of tobacco and strong spirits, giving a lusty rendition to *Whiskey in the Jar*.

I did hesitate – I would have been a fool not to – but Isabelle had seemed quite certain that this girl was the perfect choice for Sally, and perhaps had hinted that none other of sufficient training could be found who would be willing to accept the position at any rate. So, placing a greater than usual trust in her judgment, I voiced my desire to enter the cell so that I might have a look at her.

The good man rolled his eyes, and muttering something about a fool and his money, took out his key and unlocked the heavy, iron-bound door. It swung inward with a protesting squeal of rusting hinges.

The air was close and foul inside, for there was no window, and by the look of it, the straw should have been changed ages ago. As the gaoler entered, leading the way, his lantern pushed back the shadows, revealing a bucket rusting in a corner. It was from there that the most nauseating of the odors seemed to be coming, and I took care to stay as far away from it as possible.

"I should have warned you to bring a posy," he apologized, holding his own handkerchief to his nose. "It gets bad in here during the summer months."

I could not refrain a glare, and voicing the opinion that the place was little better than a pigsty.

"Oh aye," he agreed with a shrug, "but straw costs money, and there is little enough of that to feed the poor wretches let alone provide clean bedding," here he paused before appending, "leastways that is what the bailiff claims."

It was the same old story: a case of a corrupt official skimming the cream from the budget to line his own pockets, while those charged to his care subsisted little better than mistreated animals. I swallowed my anger with some difficulty, for I realized that it would serve little purpose, and got down to the business at hand.

The cell was a large single common room housing both men and women, and judging by the small, ragged bundle I could see curled against the far wall, children as well.

The gaoler cast his lantern about, here and there, at times pausing to lower it to the filthy straw to study a fitful, sleeping face - without exception, every one pinched with deprivation - before moving on. All the while, the raucous voice of the singing woman continued.

A couple were fornicating in one of the dimmer recesses. The woman was on all fours with the rags of her dress heaped on her back, with a toothless old villain taking station behind, his one good eye pinched shut, the other hidden behind a filthy leather patch. The woman, however, when the light shone upon her, leered at us through her pox-ridden face.

"'Ere, guv," she winked lewdly, "gi' us a quid o' tobacco, an' you can be next!"

We hurried away, leaving them in the dark, with her laughter taunting our backs. Our hasty retreat drove us in the direction from whence came the singing. When the lantern's rays finally found her, this Billingsgate diva seemed oblivious of our presence, but continued with her song, mostly, by the sound of it, through her nose.

As emaciated and unkempt as the rest, she sat in the straw, legs asprawl, with her head thrown back much like a baying hound, tumbling tresses of what might once have been red hair across her shoulders. She sang loudly with little care for holding the tune. It was a voice more used to rising above the noise of a rowdy tavern than the relative quiet of the Yellow House, but she used it with little regard for such discrimination.

"There you are," the gaoler interrupted her with some distaste, holding the lantern high, the better for me to see, "I should have known that it would be you singing that bog Irish trash."

Upon being addressed, the woman abruptly fell silent and opened her eyes, revealing them to be a bright emerald green – the first thing of any beauty I had seen since entering the cell. She must not have been used to the light, for she raised a hand between her face and the lantern.

"Lord t'underin' jayzuz," she cried cheerily, "an' how's yer honours the day?" Then, without pausing for breath, she eagerly leaned forward and said, "Say now, neither of ye foine gentlemen's brought a drop o' the creature with yez, oi don't suppose?"

The gaoler sniffed, his mouth twisting with disgust. "Certainly not!"

"Aw-tut-tut-tut," her head wagged in disappointment, "'tis a sad world, an' sure ye know, here's me parched as a camel's arse!" But when she looked my way, presumably to beseech me in turn, something very curious happened.

"Saints preserve us!" she cried, making the sign of the cross, "'tis himself!" and after much effort, managed to gain her feet, where she swayed on unsteady legs while attempting to brush the more notable stains from her dress.

The bailiff's assistant looked from her to myself, clearly as nonplussed as I.

Curious, I stepped forward, studying her more closely, while she studied me in turn.

She was a tall girl, almost as tall as myself, with a frame large enough, that if it were filled out with muscle, would be a boon to any household where heavy lifting might be required. Her eyes aside, I decided that she was not beautiful, but with a vigorous scrubbing, there was a strong possibility that she might approach handsome. Still it seemed an honest face, and good natured besides, but what attracted most of my attention at the moment was the way she was regarding me. It would be fair to say that she was gaping, as one might at a spectre.

I asked her, "What do you mean, girl?"

She appeared flustered as her mouth opened and closed without a sound until, eventually, she rediscovered her voice.

"Sure, and well ye know, yer honour," and she managed a clumsy curtsy, while her hands made a valiant attempt at arranging her hair into something other than the magpie's nest that it was.

"I am certain that I do not," I told her, more mystified than ever.

"Why," she spoke with conviction, "'tis certain y'ar the Newry Man, The Ramblin' Boy they speak of in song! Have I not dreamed of yourself many a night, with a face like the great Cuchalain hoverin' over me, piercing my soul wit' dose beautiful blue eyes, and coverin' me with that great, brawny chest!"

It was not entirely clear what transpired in her dream, but it was possible to guess when she took me in from head to toe, and gasped, with every appearance of having been happily startled.

"Gosh an' begora!" she cried, "Oh, it *is* yourself! Oi'm dead certain of it now!"

Her behaviour was most curious, to be sure, but there seemed little else to be done but take her from that place. I felt her eyes on my back the whole time that I was counting out the price of her release onto the bailiff's desk from the fishing captain's purse. It was a much lighter purse when the transaction was complete.

Acting on an impulse, when we arrived at Pokeham Path, I purchased a bar of soap and took her down to the wharf.

I was reluctant to have her walk beside me – the smell of her being so strong - but she followed happily enough at a respectful distance, with her belongings tied up in a handkerchief. I continued to feel her eyes on me every step of the way.

Once arrived, I gave her the soap and told her to bathe...*thoroughly.*

She took the brick from my hand, and without any apparent concern for her modesty, slipped from the tatters of her dress and walked, naked, into the water. Once she had reached a depth just past her thighs, she turned to face me – as if she could not bear to tear her eyes away - and dipping the soap into the water, began to scrub as I had asked, paying special attention to her groin, pointedly stating that she was not diseased.

I must confess, that as the layers of grime were slowly peeled away from her body, I felt a certain discomfort with her staring at me so. The reason that I knew she was staring at me was simplicity in itself - I was staring at *her*.

I had said that she was not beautiful, and there was nothing being presented that caused me to change my opinion in that regard. As well as her being slightly bucktoothed, her ribs were far too prominent, as well as her hip bones, while her breasts were over large for my taste and sagged to the recess of her stomach. Still, she was naked and, indeterminate though her age might be, she was far younger than either my mother or Mrs. Dawe.

In time my discomfort grew to such a degree that I began to think of reasons to excuse myself, and was struck with an idea. We had passed a dress shop along the way, and as it would be unthinkable to expect her to wear her own tattered, lice-ridden garment, once she had washed the prison's grime away, I decided to retrace my steps so that I might purchase her a new one. Tess looked about to protest when I turned to leave, but I told her that I would be back shortly, and that in the meantime, she was to make every effort to find which part of her was foul and which part flesh, and to eradicate the former. So resigned, she acceded to my wishes and bent to her task, leaving me free to attend to my own.

The errand took the better part of an hour, as I had little idea about purchasing items of clothing for the opposite sex; but with the good offices of the lady of the establishment (who seemed not to be the least embarrassed about such things as breast size and so forth) we agreed upon a modest homespun item of good quality that was surprisingly affordable. When I returned with the dress draped over one arm, Tess was just stepping out of the water, toweling her hair (which was indeed red) with a tattered piece of sail cloth, donated by one of the several admiring sailors who had taken up station along the beach.

I had to admit that the transformation was quite breathtaking. As if to prove the point, a pinnace sailing close inshore collided with the wharf.

Tess took the dress from me, admiring its quality, and with tear-filled eyes, vowed that it was 'de grandest t'ing ever!' In fact, so profuse was her gratitude that it became

125

embarrassing – doubly so as she spent so much time admiring its many fine points that she neglected to put it on. In the end I had to help her, glaring the sailors away in the process. They left grinning, one or two even knuckling their brow to me, and ran off to help their mates, and, I assume, save the pinnace before it sank.

I finished pulling the dress down over Tess' outstretched arms before stepping back for a look. I had to admit that the proprietress knew her business, for the fit was quite good, and the light grey of the homespun accented both the colours of her eyes and hair far better than I would have imagined.

Tess herself was delighted. She laughed and did a pirouette so that I might admire her all the more. Then, laughing still, she locked her arm in mine as we turned to leave.

It was then that I looked up and noticed, walking toward us along the quay, with a woman who must have been her maidservant - both carrying bundles from shopping - was the captain's daughter.

It must have been Tess's laughter that caught her attention, for the silly girl laughed the way she sang – full bore, without ever a thought to anything else.

She looked up just as the stupid slut was leaning into me, still continuing to drown me with adoration.

I froze, feeling the blood rush into my face. Oblivious, Tess continued to make a confounded nuisance of herself.

The object of my desire stopped to stare – very briefly – those captivating eyes darting from me, and then to Tess, then back to me again without expression. Then before anyone but myself had time to notice, she resumed walking, even managing to smile at some comment her servant had made. As she walked past, it was as though the moment had never been.

Yet we passed quite close, and from the corner of my eye, I saw that once again the colour in her cheeks was a match for my own.

Chapter Seven

I am afraid that I was short with Tess afterward, cowing her into a blessed silence by the time we reached Sally's.

Both women regarded one another with suspicion the moment we walked through the door, and continued to do so even after the introductions were made. Still my mother received her fairly cordially, although she could not completely refrain from the occasional gaze in my direction. Indeed, the atmosphere became so uncomfortable for me that, after only a short while, I left them alone together to become better acquainted, pleading the necessity of finding my own lodgings. As I left, I did my utmost to ignore the sensation of having both their eyes burning into my back.

It was not entirely true that I needed to seek out new lodgings; in fact, it was not true at all. As a gratuity for services rendered, Mrs. Dawe had set me up with my own rooms on Parsons Garden, between the High and Low Path – a much more extravagant dwelling than those on Darkuses…and coincidentally, nearer Dawe Manor than I had been previously. It was that same suffocating closeness experienced this morning that I was now attempting to escape. The difference, however, was that this morning the world had seemed filled with light and beauty; the oncoming evening held only the promise of despair.

The very idea that *she* had seen me with another was enough to send me into the deepest depression. The fact that the occasion had been innocent was of no consequence. The fact that it *appeared* to be guilty as sin was of every consequence conceivable! Never in a thousand years would I have the opportunity of explaining myself – not that I would be believed in any event. It was all too obvious that Tess had been displaying public signs of affection, and she in her *bare feet*, the presumptuous sow! I could have died from shame! It was all too much to accept that Fate could possibly be so cruel. So, gnashing my teeth over the unfairness of it all, I continued down one path after another, wandering aimlessly whilst lashing angrily at inoffensive flaking tables with a stick, unaware of anyone or anything but this new shadow over my heart. Therefore, cloaked in that darkness, I was unaware that dusk had fallen, or that my aimless wandering had carried me once more down to the scene of our meeting on the waterfront.

It was there that I heard a woman scream.

It came from nearby - just around the corner of the Yellowbelly, one of the lower sort of taverns providing service to the common sailors - one from which my mother had often used to conduct business when younger, until an unremunerated rape and one or two beatings from drunken patrons convinced her that it was no longer safe to do so. It was with this thought in mind that I dashed forward, fighting to quell the dread in my heart for any woman so unlucky, or so foolish, to find herself in such a low part of town after dark. For inexperienced whore as she most likely was, few knew better than I how thin was the line between learning from a mistake and the grave.

The waterfront is not well lit at night, but when I rounded the corner of the tavern, there was barely enough illumination coming from its single window to capture a dim view of four men in various states of inebriation surrounding not one but two women, who, even in the poor light, by the richness of their clothing I could see were not common, but ladies of quality. Then, even as I leapt forward with clenched fists, one of the seamen lunged unsteadily at the taller one, who was defiantly shielding the other with her body. He tore at her dress, rending the fabric, causing milk white skin to materialize at her shoulder. The other woman screamed, a shrill cry of pure terror that was identical to that of a moment before.

I was amongst them in seconds. My first blow caught the drunken lout on his temple, crumbling him into a heap without further struggle. Then I was tearing into the next one closest without pause, doubling him over with a fist to the stomach before sending him to join his friend by bringing up my knee to collide with his face.

My assault had been so swift that these first two had no time to react, but now, even while I was turning to face the others, a fist caught my cheekbone a glancing blow causing me to stagger. I swung blindly, and by great good fortune, heard a grunt of pain upon making contact. Then there was a glint of steel, and I twisted away with fire scouring my ribs.

I put a hand to my shirt, then held it up before my eyes, and saw that my fingers were dark with blood. I could feel it now, warm against my skin, as it trickled down my side.

The last man began to circle, stepping warily, the knife held low so that it could be brought up swiftly in a single, killing blow. Shorter than myself by perhaps a head, his frame was lean and muscular with little sign of being impaired by drink. He continued to circle with those same careful steps, his legs bent like coiled springs, ready to leap in when he found an opening.

I turned to match him, step for step, but already my feet were becoming leaden, and knew that it was but a matter of time before he found what he sought.

There was a glimmer of teeth when he smiled a wicked grin, and in a low, hard voice growled, "You need a lesson taught you, boy, about interfering in a man's play."

I laughed just as wickedly, and taunted, trying to bring him to strike while I still possessed the strength to resist. "Play? Is that what you call attacking defenceless women?"

Far off, but fast approaching, I could hear the sound of horses and a carriage. A glance to my left revealed the shorter of the two ladies running off in that direction. Even as I watched, I heard her cry out for aid. Then something moved at my shoulder and I felt the other woman beside me. There was no fear in her voice, merely contempt, when she said to my assailant, "Run, you coward, while you still can!

Then the scene became bathed in light as the tavern door swung open behind me. The altercation had taken so little time that a minute could not have passed since I had responded to that first scream. Now I could hear the sound of feet and the cries of men as they finally succeeded in gathering themselves to come to our assistance, just as my legs gave out, bringing me to my knees.

The villain hesitated, his look of hatred mingling with one of uncertainty. He desired my death greatly, but he desired his own life even more, and could see that to tarry longer would be to his ruin.

He glared at me and promised, "Another day, boy," before turning on his heel and running off into the night.

Then there were feet pounding past me as men from the tavern gave chase, swallowed by the darkness as quickly as my assailant. Others surrounded the lady and myself, milling about - in confusion, mostly - but there was one portly fellow with a balding head and thick spectacles perched on the tip of his bulbous nose who, upon noticing my wound, gently lowered me to the cobblestones, wheezing over the effort, and placed something soft beneath my head. All the while he clucked his tongue disapprovingly, and wondered aloud about what the world was coming to, when drunken brawlers had become commonplace on the streets. My vision was beginning to blur when I heard the lady cut him short, her voice fraught with worry.

"Sir, you need not be so reproachful to your betters. This gentleman has saved my servant and I from a fate worse than death! Why, if it had not been for him, we most certainly would have been attacked by those ruffians, and our honour taken from us! So I will ask you to kindly refrain from your comments, for I shall not listen to them. It is praise that he deserves rather than censure!"

The old man swore, then apologized to the lady for his uncouth tongue, before proceeding to declare, in voluminous tones, that he had never heard the like, 'pon his soul he hadn't. After which he ordered some of the gawkers to look sharp and lay hands on the unconscious villains, and told them that they should be bound and hauled off to the Yellow House for the magistrate to deal with. Then he called for a lantern, and gently peeling my shirt away from my wound, began clucking his tongue all over again.

"How bad is it, Doctor?" asked the fellow holding the light.

"Looks nastier than it is. Slash wound. Ribs prevented it from going too deep, but lost some blood. Needs stitches, that's certain. Hurt like the devil come morning – beg pardon, Miss. You, Samuel," he called out to someone, "move your worthless carcass – beg pardon, Miss – and tell the tavern keeper that I'll need some bandages and boiling water. Boiling mind, not that tepid piss – beg pardon, Miss – he makes his toddies with!"

"Aye aye, Doctor," came the reply followed by the sound of feet rushing away.

"Oh, and Samuel!" the old fellow called after him.

"Doctor?"

"Tell him also that I require a bottle of spirits – brandy will do – and to put it on my tab."

There was a brief pause, then, "I'll tell him, Doctor," Samuel replied doubtfully, "but..."

"Never mind your buts, you indolent scallywag – beg pardon, Miss – just do as I say!"

If Samuel dared a reply, it was left unheard, for the sound of the carriage was much louder now as it rushed onto our street.

A man shouted the horses to a stop over the squeal of the brake, and the clattering of hooves quickly ceased. There followed the sound of the carriage door opening and the cries of a woman in tears. Then for some moments, all was a bedlam of anxious inquiries.

"Miss Elizabeth, are you hurt?" the man asked, his voice grave with concern.

"Oh, Miss!" the woman cried, "thank God you are well! I was so afraid when you bade me leave, I thought I should die!"

"That is enough, Sarah," the lady's voice came from close beside me, stern with rebuke. "Quinn, take her back to the carriage!"

Quinn - the coachman, apparently - was having some difficulty holding his own anxiety in check, but he replied evenly enough, "Yes, Miss!"

"And make a pallet of the rear seat, for it is the more comfortable of the two."

"*Pallet*, Miss?" Quinn's concern was now mingled with a disbelief that he had heard correctly.

"Oh *no*, Miss Elizabeth!" Sarah cried out in shock at the insinuation, "The master would…"

"Your master is not here," Miss Elizabeth replied with some heat, "but I am! You shall do as I say. Is that understood?"

Sufficiently quailed, both servants mumbled their obeisance, and left, but an instant later, their cries of protest were replaced by another.

"'Ere then, what's all this fuss about, Doctor," a man puffed importantly, "an' wot's this I hears about you asking for a bottle of brandy to be put on yore tab, an' it not bein' cleared for nigh on two months gone by?"

"Patience, Smead," the doctor sighed, "all will be explained in time. Suffice it for the moment to say that it is for a medical emergency." Then without pause, he demanded, "Did you bring it?"

"Oh, aye, but…"

"And the water and bandages?"

"Aye, that too."

"*Boiling* water?"

"Of course boiling!" came the offended reply, "Wot do you take me for, then?"

"A sodding pirate – beg pardon, Miss – who waters down the grog, but that's of no importance now. Give it to me."

There was the sound of a cork being unstopped, followed by a gurgle.

"'Ere! I thought you said it was medicinal, like!"

"That was to steady my hand," the doctor replied evenly, "the scientific method that I ascribe to demands it."

Smead scoffed, "Scientific my eye! Why you old charlatan, what do you know about science?"

The doctor's reply was stiff with bruised dignity. "From an obscure text given to me by an old friend, in from Constantinople, if it's anything to you, you swindler! 'Tis said to be the work of Hypocrites, himself – a name, I might add, that I'm sure you wouldn't know from Murphy's sow!" Then, dismissing the tavern keeper with a sniff, he then turned to Elizabeth and said, "You might want to hold him, Miss, naught of these louts has the balls – beg pardon."

"Certainly," she replied, her voice calm and without hesitation. "It is the least that I can do for him, after what he has suffered on my behalf."

"Ready then?"

She leaned across my chest. I could feel the firmness of her breasts as they pressed against me, her face swimming before my eyes.

"Ready." She replied.

I had not foreseen the usage of the spirit. In my lagging consciousness I had thought that it was intended for myself; but while correct on that score, I believed that the dosage was to be taken internally in order to deaden the pain. I was to find, however, that I was wrong – as wrong as a man could be.

Half apologetically, the doctor murmured, "Hold still, you poor bugger – beg pardon, Miss – this is going to hurt like bloody hell – beg pardon again."

There was a generous splash of cool liquid on my wound, and an instant later the tavern keeper's squawk of protest over the waste of good brandy was wiped away by a sudden sheet of the purest pain imaginable. My eyes flew open wide, and I gasped at the unbearable agony burning into my side. Surely the fires of Hell could not burn hotter!

At that moment my mind flexed and my vision cleared. Struggling in torment as I was, I could see the lady's concerned face, bare inches above me. Her eyes sought out my own and held them, openly filled with affectionate concern.

133

"You!" I gasped, and then I was swirling down into a deep pit of darkness, carrying with me, as though etched in my brain, the trauma inflicted upon my person...and the knowledge that the lady I had saved was none other than the captain's daughter herself.

*   *   *

There was a puff of smoke from the casement of the Island Battery's fortifications. Several seconds later the heavy cough of the report reached us from where we watched up on Lighthouse Point, before echoing off the highlands surrounding the harbour.

"Howitzer," Daniel observed with interest, leaning both palms on the handle of his shovel. "Hello, here it comes!"

A small black dot could be seen approaching through the air, growing ever larger as it neared, only to disappear in a cloud of smoke and flame just before cresting the hill, showering us with the din of the explosion, but nothing more.

Daniel snorted his disgust. "They cut the bloody fuse too short! Trust the Frogs for that!"

I peered at him from where I was resting on my own shovel, relishing the downturned corners of his mouth. 'Didn't I tell you that horse wouldn't run?" I chuckled contentedly, and gestured, "Now let us see what mine can do."

A short distance to our front, a gunner finished ramming home the charge into the monster twenty-four-pounder, and two more gingerly carried the cradle containing the heated round shot – red-hot from the furnace – to the muzzle, while a grizzled old sergeant peered down the surface of the barrel before making a minute adjustment to the elevation screw. The two with the cradle held it up to the muzzle and tipped the ball into the bore before skipping nimbly aside. The sergeant took one last look, then, apparently satisfied, unhurriedly put the tip of his smouldering linstock to the touchhole. There was a jet of smoke as the fine grains of powder ignited. In the split-second before they burned their way down into the main charge, he stepped away from the gun, clapping both hands to his ears. Needless to say, we followed his example.

There followed a tremendous roar that shook the ground at our feet, and a great belly of smoke shot out from the muzzle as the gun discharged. A stiff inshore breeze soon cleared the view, however, so we were able to watch the progress of the round as it hurtled toward the horizon before descending in a gradual arc, disappearing against the backdrop of the island guarding the harbour's mouth.

We continued to watch, but there was nothing for what seemed an eternity. Then, just as I was preparing myself for disappointment, a shower of rock suddenly exploded from the breastworks, very near the embrasure from whence the howitzer had just fired. Before the last of the flying debris had settled, a low crump rolled across the divide, attesting to the violence of the concussion.

"Here, that's more like it!" I cried with a satisfied smirk, before turning to my friend with an open palm, demanding, "Pay up, if you please!"

Daniel glared to where the gunners were already busily preparing another round for the twenty-four-pounder, then into the distance at the ruined defence works, before heaving a sigh while rummaging through his pocket for a farthing, and slapped it into my hand.

"Ta very much," I could not help but grin at his annoyance.

"Those fellows mustn't have had much practice," he muttered, referring to *Monsieur's* poor showing.

"Not true," I told him before pointing out the obvious, "They have been busily employed all week." I did not add that we had been their target; nor did I add that they had met with some success, for Daniel was as well aware of the fact as I was myself.

Upon arriving at Lighthouse Point the week previous, we had found it deserted as I had expected, though several lines of French tents were still erect, which was a boon for us as we still lacked our own. Their guns, however, had all been destroyed – their touchholes spiked before being trundled over the face of the cliffs onto the rocks by the water's edge far below. In addition, many of the fortifications had been pulled down, and the furnaces for heating shot destroyed, making it necessary that new ones be built, and guns brought in from the fleet. In the case of the latter, this meant that a road needed to be constructed down to the intended landing place a mile to the east. This, as well as work on the fortifications, all had to be done under continuous accumulated fire from the Island Battery, the French warships anchored in an arc across the middle of the harbour, and the seventeen guns from the battery on Rochefort Point - eleven of which were monster forty-two-pounders. While the range had been extreme, inevitably there had been casualties, including one from our own company, the poor fellow being killed instantly when a cannonball had struck his tent while he slept.

Yet all had been accomplished in good spirits, as the extra pay we received for our labour (two shillings per *diem* to add to our regular twenty a month) as well as increased rations of fresh fish and a gill of rum every day, ensured that the work proceeded with all due alacrity, even though it was still not possible to land any ordinance. In fact, it would be ten days after our fortunate victory at Fresh Water Cove before the seas quieted sufficiently so that the first twenty-four-pounder could be brought ashore. From that point on our labour proceeded much more rapidly, so that now we had a sufficiency of all calibers and makes - howitzers and mortars included – in place to offer a response to the grueling fire to which we had for so long been subjected, with more being brought up every day.

That is not to say that our artillery outnumbered, or even outweighed that of the enemy, for such was certainly not the case. The Island Battery was well prepared to defend the harbour from the largest of warships: its thirty large cannon by far exceeded our own, which at the moment numbered only five. If that were all, the situation would have been desperate enough, but as I had mentioned, there was also the French fleet to contend with. Of the twelve warships facing us, six were ships of the line, two of which were seventy-fours, three being sixty-fours, and one of fifty – a total of three hundred and ninety guns, without counting the frigates of thirty or more, of which there were three - all with lower decks equipped with twenty-four-pounders or heavier. Our position on the heights was unquestionably beneficial as it increased our range, and provided difficulties for those attempting to reach us at extreme elevation. Yet it could also be said that it gave us a superiority in morale, for we could see virtually all of them while they could see but little of us, and it is always unnerving to be fired upon from above. Yet that alone could not account for our having begun to win the artillery duel. Had the French fleet behaved with more aggression and manoeuvred their ships to close with us, it may well have been a completely different story, but they failed to do so. Instead, they remained at a distance and immobile out of fear of the carnage our heated shot might bring to their wooden hulls, all the while blazing away at us to little or no effect. I am by no means an expert on the subject of naval matters in general, nor on the French navy in particular, but it seemed to me that the fighting spirit we had grown to respect in the enemy's land forces was simply not evident in those manning their fleet, with the exception of a single frigate, the *Aréthuse*, whose captain had indeed manoeuvred in close more than once, and had caused us great difficulty.

I turned to Daniel, preparing a comment to this effect, when once again the lightness of the day instantly became shrouded in icy shadow.

Captain Beaumont was not seven paces away, watching the artillery duel, but I thought without much interest.

Daniel noticed my sudden change in mood, and following the direction of my gaze, took note of the captain before turning back to me, concern evident on his face, although for the moment he kept his peace.

As I glared at him, Beaumont turned to me and stared. His face was pale, as though not having slept for some time, and his hand trembled visibly when passing it over his brow.

137

He opened his mouth, I thought, to speak, but then his eyes twitched over to Daniel – who was less concerned with him than myself – and closed it again before stumbling away in a cloud of indecision. I followed him with my eyes, restraining my hatred only with great effort, while my knuckles turned white on the haft of my shovel.

I sensed Daniel stirring uncomfortably, and I knew he was on the verge of speaking, but before any words could be uttered, a new calamity struck in the form of an angry, "You two, there! Back to work! You're not getting extra pay to stand around gawking!"

The ends of Sergeant Bell's moustaches were curled up in a sneer, his eyes reddened from an extra ration of rum, no doubt stolen from our meager stores. Perhaps it made him bold, or perhaps it made him foolish, but it was not an ordinary occasion when confronting Daniel that he chose to put his bravado to the test.

I felt Daniel stiffen, and heard his voice grate when he said, "We've been hard at it all night, Sergeant, *and* off duty at present!" Which was true: advantage had been taken of the full moon, and fortifications for another battery, close inland from the harbour, had been thrown up by volunteers, ourselves included in their number, and had been excused further duty that day.

"What's that!" In his half-inebriated state Bell had been anticipating an easy victory. Now finding his authority challenged, he was instantly quivering with anger. "Stand at attention when I'm addressing you, you horrible man! By God I've had enough of your insolence!"

Daniel stiffened even further - I could feel the heat of his rage – then he formed his massive limbs into a bare resemblance of complying to Bell's order.

Bell, already past the point of caution, allowed himself to become incensed even further by my friend's defiance, and took a step closer…which, unfortunately, was one step too many.

"You will do as I say, Private Hawthorne, and you will do it instanter! Do I make myself clear?"

I sensed trouble, and willed my friend to quell his anger that was abetted by fatigue, but to little avail. Daniel glared his hatred as he might at a snake.

Finding his demand unanswered, Bell screamed, "*Do I?*"

I did not see the blow fall, even though I was watching closely; the situation was as it was, with the very lips on Daniel's face bled white from the strain of holding himself in check, and then Bell was down - bleeding profusely from the mouth – with a faraway look in his eyes as one would have in a daze.

Sensing the world suddenly spinning out of control, I hastened to restrain my friend as best I could, although such an effort was not easily undertaken. Daniel was massively built and nearly unstoppable when aroused.

"Dan, no!" I pleaded, "You will only make matters worse!"

But Daniel pressed forward, intent upon finishing what he had started; the pure savagery written on his face gave proof to the limits to which he had been driven, and his disregard of any consequences that might befall.

I flung my arms around his chest, pinning his own arms to his side. "We shall take this to the general!" I told him.

Where the words had come from I could not say, nor could I say from whence came my conviction.

General Wolfe ruled his division with an iron fist, and was devout in his faith in discipline. Moreover, he demanded that same devotion from those serving under him - any breach of which could be expected to be met with the harshest of punishments. But for all that, he was a man much admired by those of us in the ranks. The alacrity of his aggression toward the enemy had been unwavering, keeping him on the field in conditions that were no better than our own, often sleeping upon the ground while it was said the other generals lived in comparative luxury in their own respective camps. We loved him for that, but even more, we loved him for giving us faith in ourselves, to the point where confidence in ultimate victory welled strong in our hearts. Perhaps it was this faith that I had instinctively turned to in my desperation, even though I could not foresee any assurance for having done so.

The immediate effect, however, *was* reassuring. The force of Daniel's anger became spent as if by magic. His struggles ceased and his body became inert in my arms. He studied my face, even as Jeffers and Harris ran to assist the sergeant, shouting angrily for Daniel to halt even though he had made no further attempt to move.

"He had it coming, Joss," he told me, although there was little passion in his voice, "As God's my witness, no man deserved it more."

"It will be all right," I told him, doing my utmost to look and sound as one who could be believed, "Somehow we will get you through this."

Jeffers and Harris had each taken one of Bell's arms and assisted him to his feet. He stood wavering unsteadily, as if in the face of a gale force wind. His mouth worked in a thoughtful fashion before he raised a palm and spitting into it, deposited two teeth, their roots still covered in gore.

"The general?" Daniel was slowly becoming himself once again. "Do you really think he would help?"

"I will try," I replied.

Bell regarded his teeth with some interest. Unattended, blood covered his face from his mouth to his chin, while dripping from the waxed ends of his moustache. It seemed to me that it took a long while for him to comprehend their meaning, but when it finally reached him, his face transformed into a mask to equal the purest horror that I have ever seen.

"Don't just stand there, you bloody fools!" he cried at his companions through his injured mouth, consonants softened by a lack of dental fullness. He raised his hand, shaking with rage, pointing an accusing finger into Daniel's face. "Arrest him!"

Jeffers and Harris, each with an arm supporting the sergeant, looked uncertain as to the wisdom of leaving him unattended, and even more uncertainly at my friend. It was

140

true that little love was lost between them, yet Daniel's strength was legendary, and serious thought must be given before responding to such a command.

"Are you deaf?" Bell was screaming now, "Arrest him I say!"

They looked from one to the other, each taking a deep breath, and released their supporting grip on Bell so that they might unsling their muskets. Still unsteady, Bell staggered backward as if on the heaving deck of a ship; his hand was now to the traumatized area, trying to minister to the torment brought on by exposed nerve endings, but he never took his eyes off Daniel. "This time you've gone too far, Hawthorne! I'll see the skin off your back before the day's out!" A thought to which I miserably - but in silence - concurred.

Meanwhile Bell's two cronies had leveled their muskets at my friend's breast. "Come along, Hawthorne," Harris said, his voice on edge, though unantagonizing. In that brief moment of violence no one had ever seen my friend so aroused, and they were taking care not to be the cause of a second outburst. "We don't want no more trouble, now do we?"

Daniel was silent, the full weight of his crime having descended upon him, so I answered instead. "There will be no more trouble," I promised before adding, "I shall accompany him."

The two fools looked uncertainly at me, and then just as uncertainly at one another. Finally, unable to decide for themselves, they risked a quick glance back at Bell. The sergeant gestured with angry impatience to show that it was of little consequence to him if I came or stayed, so they turned back to me with relief written all over their faces.

Jeffers gave a short nod, and gestured with his musket. "Right. Fall in, then."

I took Daniel by the elbow and guided him away from where the artillery was still caught up in their duel with the French, totally oblivious to the scene that had transpired.

Harris led us back toward our camp where a stockade had been crudely fashioned from one of a farmer's outbuildings. As we passed through our company's lines - where those not on duty lay about at their ease, drinking their ration of grog and smoking their pipes – several took note of our procession, and quickly surmising what it portended, pointed us out to their fellows. Soon every eye was upon us, mostly in sorrow, for Daniel was well liked by many, and all were aware of the poisonous hatred between him and Bell. The sight of the sergeant's injured mouth, still rimmed with blood, and Daniel's ashen face, combined with his wooden steps, told the tale.

As we passed, Bell recruited perhaps a half dozen others to fall in as well, to eliminate any chance of my friend's rebelling at the last instance. Although this was hardly likely: Daniel was walking as if in a dream, my hand on his elbow his single restraint.

We reached the stockade and my friend was ushered inside. He went meekly, but stopped at the threshold and turned around; Jeffers and Harris quickly stepped between us with crossed muskets in case he chose that moment to attempt to escape. But even at this point, so much was their respect for my friend's strength that they were reluctant to press harder for fear that it might rouse him to press back.

He looked at me; I could see all hope fading from his eyes.

"The general?" he asked.

"I shall try," I repeated.

He nodded once, briefly, then realizing that my promise was all but empty of any real expectation; he turned and went inside, the door slamming shut behind him.

Chapter Eight

My life had been made bearable by Daniel's presence. Now that he had been taken from me, my spirits plummeted as they seldom had before, and I was frantic to save him from the dire peril he was under. For peril there was without question.

Striking a superior was one of the most harshly punished infractions in the King's Regulations, saving only mutiny and dereliction of duty (of which I, myself, had been guilty and duly punished – albeit not according to custom). It would be the cat-o-nine-tails for my friend, almost certainly. Too many had witnessed the incident for it to be a case of one man's word against the other, and even that would have had only the slimmest chance of success. The enmity existing between the two men was not a secret, and Bell's injury was obvious to anyone. It would be his word, along with those vipers, Jeffers and Harris, which would carry the day.

Indeed, there was one factor only that offered the least bit of comfort: the heavy labour required for the assault – the making of roads, and hauling the heavy guns to additional batteries set in place on the heights surrounding the harbour. Our general's impatience for it to be carried out with all due haste allowed no time for a court martial, let alone a punishment parade. One week had passed since Daniel's undoing, yet he still lingered in the stockade with no word of a trial.

It was a comfort, as I have said, but it was of the bleakest sort; it was certain that in due course they would come for him. Then he would be bound to a gun wheel, and the lash would fall.

The cat was no ordinary whip, but a major tool in the army's enforcement of discipline, and much dreaded by us in the ranks. Each of its nine, short leather lashes were weighted with lead to better assist in their cutting into a man's flesh. Virtually all of us had witnessed its effectiveness (it being mandatory to attend punishment parades to encourage our own obedience) and some of us had felt it. None doubted that it was effective in the extreme. I had seen men broken with only a handful of lashes, served for the most minor of misdemeanors. The strongest of men might be able to endure a dozen, perhaps two, and while the severity of the sentence rested purely on the whim of our commanding officer, it was not unusual for someone found guilty of such a serious charge as Daniel's to be awarded as many as a hundred, every one of which would be observed under the watchful eye of an officer to ensure that the utmost force was applied. If such was the case - and it seemed more than likely - it was akin to a sentence of death, as the lashes would cut ever deeper into that unfortunate man's back, flaying away the flesh – one by one revealing the ribs, before biting into his vitals. No more horrible death could ever be imagined.

Hence the end of every day found us staggering back to camp, heavy with fatigue, and my heart sick with the fear of hearing the dreaded roll of the drum, summoning us to the parade, where I would be forced to watch, utterly helpless, as the only friend I possessed in all the world was flayed to death before my eyes. As of yet the summons had not come, but I knew that it could only be a matter of time.

I was engulfed in a fury of impotence, and knew not where to turn. In a moment of desperation I had promised Daniel that I would take his case to the general himself, but both of us knew the unlikelihood of that ever happening, and each passing day seemed only to confirm it.

Men in the ranks did not normally address officers, and on the rare occasions that they did, spoke only when spoken to. True, the army did provide a system where a common private could approach his corporal or sergeant to state his request, and this in *theory*, might be transferred to his superior, and so on up the chain of command; but my sergeant was Bell, and his superior was Captain Beaumont, both of whom were hardly amenable to my plight. Still, in spite of that fact, I had gone to Bell to plead my case – even to beg him, but he had laughed in my face, and was laughing still, even after Harris had shoved me away with taunting words of his own. Therefore, denied

144

even the slimmest glimpse of hope that this avenue had provided, my world was overshadowed with darkness. It seemed that it must drive all reason from my mind, leaving me desperate to find what little solace there was in endless toil, and the knowledge that at the end of every day, thus far at least, the drum had been silent.

Such was my state at midday on the first of July, while we took a brief rest from cutting a road through the forest on the heights above the Royal Battery - an abandoned French emplacement facing the harbour's mouth. As at Lighthouse Point, the ordnance here had also been spiked, rendering them useless, but the battery was poorly placed for our general's purpose at any rate, the high ground to the rear being better suited for our siege guns.

It had been ten days since our first guns had begun to answer the harrying fire of the French, and although scarcely noticed by myself, in that time, as our position became ever more entrenched, events had begun to unfold for the benefit of our cause.

The first, and perhaps most important victory had been the silencing of the Island Battery; for without it's galling fire our work was proceeding much more rapidly, allowing us to bring in guns and supplies in ever increasing numbers. So too did it allow our battery on Lighthouse Point to transfer its attention to the French ships and the walls of the town itself. In addition - and perhaps foremost in the enemy's mind – the mouth of the harbour was now left unguarded, save for the Rochefort Battery, and those guns covering the eastern approach to the town, which were regarded as insufficient for the task alone. If entrance could be gained, the soft underbelly of the fortress would be exposed to eighteen hundred of the Royal Navy's cannon, and almost certainly bring the siege to a swift conclusion.

In answer to this dire threat – and also in accordance with the curious lack of aggression in the enemy's navy – two nights later, under the cloak of darkness, fully a third of their fleet had moved to the harbour mouth, at last...and been scuttled. As a gesture of defiance it was a surprising one, certainly; yet upon reflection, given the otherwise useless participation of those craft afloat, perhaps correct. In truth, it could be said that the most effective ships the French now possessed was that unhappy squadron resting on the North Atlantic seabed, their masts jutting out of the water like a bleak and skeletal forest, effectively denying access to our own ships, threatening close inshore like wolves before a pen of sheep.

As history had taught us to foresee, it was the French army that had gained our respect, meeting us on the open or in ambuscade as the case may be. The Rangers were kept busy in an especially brutal war of their own, keeping the Canadiens and Indians at bay. Blood-chilling tales came to us of a struggle where quarter was neither asked for nor given, and even of scalps taken and lost, as is the custom in this savage country. Yet so efficiently did these few hundred men do their duty that our respect for them grew with every passing day.

Still, it was the forces within the fortress that were our greatest danger. Cannon fire from the walls warned us to keep a watchful eye whenever a shot drew near, often causing delays as we were forced to dive for cover. Then, too, companies of the enemy dashed out in the night, in order to destroy our trenches that were being dug as part of the main attack to the west, delaying our advance even further. Should *Monsieur* be successful to any great degree, the time lost might see us still before the walls with the onset of winter, and our forces woefully unprepared for such an event.

Stories had come to our ears of the other companies of the 51st being caught up in one such desperate struggle, and the light infantry taking casualties before succeeding in driving the enemy away. These tales were discussed amongst ourselves with sober reverence, honouring the bravery of the men on both sides; for none knew better than we the courage it took to stand and fight in the dark, not knowing, in the confusion, who was friend and who was foe.

That had been the way of it for ten days past, yet today all was drudgery and heartache as I fretted over Daniel's fate and did nothing, for there was nothing that I could do. Such were my thoughts during the midday meal, as I sat alone with my back to a stump, and tried to make the most of my ration of fresh cod and stale bread. My spirit suffered from such a malaise that I feared that the task was beyond me.

"God lad, you're looking down in the dumps, you are," Stockingsdale observed, helping himself to a place on the ground by my side without benefit of an invitation. No doubt history had taught him to do so, as such invitations were so seldom offered him. Whatever the case, once seated, he bit into his bread and munched away with evident appetite.

Looking over, I think I envied him at that moment. Benjamin was a creature without any friends and even fewer morals, the lack of which seemed to disturb him not in the least. If only I could look out at the world through eyes such as those, I thought, I need never feel so helpless and inadequate again.

Stockingsdale chewed with gusto, working over the stale crust with the worn stumps of his teeth. Finally, wadding the last bit of cod into his mouth, he turned to me and, with crumbs flying in every direction, asked, "What's wrong, then?"

I looked quickly away, for the sight of Benjamin eating is not pursuant to good digestion; but he must have taken my aversion for reticence, for he pressed even further.

"Summat is awry with you, boy." He said, his mouth still quite full, "Don't try to tell me that it ain't. Why, I've knowd you since you was just a little snot-nose, so don't try to give me the lie."

I do confess that so low were my spirits that any invitation – even one from this vile creature – was enough for me to pour out my misgivings, and so I did. He listened in silence while I told all, speaking to my hands folded around my knee, for I could tell from the revolting sounds that he had not finished chewing. As it happened, I completed my tale just as he swallowed. Feeling it safe to turn to him, I now did so, all the while feeling the weight of the world on my shoulders, and asked him what I should do.

His stare was blank as he idly brushed crumbs from the stubble on his chin. "So what's the problem, then?"

I stared, and with my mouth almost certainly agape, gasped, "What's the problem? Why, you disgusting man! How could you ask such a question? The only friend that I have in the world is about to be flogged to death before my very eyes! That is sufficient, surely!"

But he waved my protests away as if they were of little or no significance. "Nay, nay, lad, all's not so bad!"

Still unmollified, I grated, "How can you say such a thing, you...you unspeakable creature you! Have you never cared for another living being that you could be so unfeeling of my torment?"

Stockingsdale sucked on his teeth, and wiping his palm on his breeches, said, "Aye, unspeakable, that's me, and more besides, for I live as I sees fit, caring naught for God, nor King, nor country, but for my own base nature. Yet as for my ever possessing feelings for another," and here he turned to me, his features stone cold sober, "well ye knows of my yearnings for your ma." But before I could ejaculate upon that presumption, he stated further, "Yet that ain't why I want a word with you."

Nonplussed, I savagely queried, "Then what?"

Benjamin stared out at some bombardiers, struggling with the task of hauling the ponderous weight of a mortar up an incline, yet he had the appearance of one who was disinterested in all that surrounded him. Instead, picking a blade of grass and sticking it into his teeth, he asked, "You would have a word with the captain, then?"

Now puzzled, I stated, "Well you know this to be so."

He continued to pick at his teeth, then asked, "What might be the purpose of such a meetin', then?"

Still puzzled, I managed to stammer, "Why...why to plead on Daniel's behalf, of course!"

Still picking, Stockingsdale waved this away as of no account. "Sure, and well ye knows the chances of ye sprouting wings an' taking flight are about as good as ever that takin' hold." Then, removing the stalk from his mouth, he cursed softly, and turned to me with a look that would brook no nonsense. "Ye must have summat to sweeten the pot, boy!"

If I had thought myself aghast before, it was very little compared to what I was feeling now; for as I felt the flesh creeping over my scalp, there could be little doubt as to his meaning.

"No..." I managed to stammer, "not that! *Certainly* not that!" then shuddered, "Never again!"

His eyes twitched on my own – darting from one to the other – searching.

"Boy," he said with some emphasis, "where's the peril? With you there's naught but a bit of a twinge in yer backside, an' well used to that you should be by now. Would maintainin' yer precious honour be worth riskin' the life of yer precious friend?" He continued before I could reply, which was not difficult, for I was now speechless, "The way I sees it, it comes down to a choice o' which one's the more precious, dunnit?" Then he leaned back against the stump, and replaced the stalk of grass in his mouth. "Mates," he said, wagging his head sadly, "Never cared for 'em myself;" then he seemed to contradict what he had just told me, "Price is always too dear."

When I at last found speech, I was able to venture, "Too dear? But you just said..."

"Aye, but that's me, an' this is you. There's the difference." Then he regarded me once more, and with some significance, asked, "Or is it? Could be that's the question you should be asking yourself."

"But...but you want me to go to him...you want me to..."

"Nothing of the kind," he said with a snort, "It's not what I want that counts, is it? Maybe it's not even about what *you* want, neither. Look," he paused, impulsively reaching out with his hand, but then thought better of the idea and withdrew it – for which I was grateful, "All I'm sayin' is that Sally raised you as best she could. Right or wrong, she gave you the tools to get by in a world that's often more cruel than it's not."

"As a whore!" It was my turn for a derisive snort.

"Aye, as a whore," he agreed, "but an honest one. An' remember, lad, there's something of the whore in all of us – great, or common as dirt, or even the King hisself - *that's* your advantage, boy!"

I was sullen still, yet had no words, so this time he did slap my knee with his palm, leaving a streak of grease in its wake.

"Anyway, think on it, but don't take too long – road's almost built. If you decide you still want to see the captain, find me. It can be arranged."

He paused, considering, then evidently deciding that all had been said that needed saying, rose to his feet, once more wiping his filthy hands on the front of his breeches, and left without another word, leaving me in a greater quandary than ever, but with just the sliver of something else, besides.

I believe that, in some confusing way, it may have been a vestige of hope.

By mid-afternoon I was chopping savagely at the undergrowth with an axe, torn in every conceivable direction. One instant I was cursing Stockingsdale for sticking his nose into my private affairs, the next I was thinking about Daniel, wasting away in the stockade, and fretting that I could not come to his aid. Of course that would remind me of the conversation with Benjamin, and I would actually feel a surge of gratitude for his pointing out to me what I had failed to see for myself, that thanks to the strange quality of my upbringing, there was the wherewithal to save my friend. I had decided to go to Stockingsdale and ask him to arrange an assignation with the captain, but then I was reminded of that time with Beaumont – of the way my very skin crawled when he touched me.

In turn (and this most curious of all) my memories of Elizabeth sprang from the hidden reaches of my mind, and the familiar, bittersweet ache would pierce me all over again, even now, throwing off my aim so that the next blow of the axe came near to striking my foot.

Dearest Elizabeth; sweet memories returned of what it was to live in her world, and for a time, pretend that I did not live in my own. There I drank fine wines from long-stemmed crystal glasses, not rum from a pewter mug. There I smelled perfume from Paris on her lovely neck, and not the sweat from Sally's armpits. But perhaps most of all, in that sphere I was a gentleman, and not a whore, one who would sell his body to anyone, man or woman, if they possessed a sufficiency of funds. In her world I had learned to despise who I was in my own, and swore that I could never be that person again. The very idea of reneging on that vow made my mouth turn sour, for it had been a promise that I had made because of her, and to break it would be to break something that was holy.

It had been a wonderful thing to think of myself as a gentleman, to dress in the finest of clothes, and to be seen about the town. I reveled in the respect of other pedestrians, doffing their hats to me as they would a true man of honour.

I froze, with the axe still poised over my head, even as the thought formed in my mind. I had seemed a man of honour then because people had regarded me so. Where, now, did true honour lie?

In my heart I knew, perhaps I had always known, but it grew heavier with the knowledge.

Slowly, I began to work my way over to where I could see Benjamin straining away, doing his best to lever a boulder aside with a spruce pole. I knew that Sergeant Bell was keeping a close eye on me, and did not wish to arouse his suspicion. Once I had made up my mind as to where the correct course lay, it was as though a veil had been lifted from my eyes, although not the weight from my heart. Daniel's peril demanded that I do my utmost to save him, and so I would, because it was for him, but also because it was the honourable path. It was not even too much of a stretch of my imagination to allow myself to become convinced that it was a path of which Elizabeth would approve, and would forgive the breaking of a vow in order to take it.

Whether or not the feeling that I was walking in a dream was due to my being transported by the nobility of the act I was about to commit, or whether it was because I was resigned to committing it, I could not say, but such was my condition and it grew ever stronger the closer I came to Stockingsdale. My course was set; there could be no turning back. The person I would become in the aftermath was a fear that I could not allow to concern me.

Benjamin managed to move the boulder at last, then stopped to rest, leaning on the pole while wiping the perspiration from his forehead on the sleeve of his shirt. He saw me drawing nearer while in the act of lowering his arm. His expression was a knowing one.

I opened my mouth to speak.

That was when I heard the drum calling us to arms.

*   *   *

Stockingsdale's knowing expression changed to one that was the complete opposite, as I'm sure had mine. We stood where we were, scarcely a few feet apart – I with my axe, and he with his pole - regarding one another for the briefest of moments. I believe that because there had been so much thought and anguish invested in reaching my decision, I was now too committed to leave the situation unresolved. But then the insistency of the call finally penetrated my mind, and my resolve disappeared.

Then both of us were moving as one man, lunging to where our muskets were stacked by the tent lines. It took but seconds to don my tunic, before buckling on the bayonet, and slinging the cross-belt with the ammunition cartouche over my shoulder. I was just in the act of settling my mitre onto my head when the west wind carried the distant sound of thunder to our ears, and was instantly recognized – muskets, perhaps hundreds of them, being fired in a single, disciplined volley. We exchanged significant glances; then, without ever having

152

said a word between us, each took up his musket and raced to join the others.

The company was assembling on the drummer, his sticks a blur as his tattoo continued sounding the alarm. The order came to form in two ranks; then, with hearts beating excitedly in every breast, Captain Beaumont cried, "Forward!" and we were marching with two regular line companies from the 17th over the escarpment, and down the slope in the direction of the fortress, from whence the unceasing crackle of musketry was steadily drawing nearer.

The action soon came into view, and from our vantage on the slopes, we could see it unfolding with startling clarity. The French were out with a vengeance this time, almost a thousand of them, mostly regulars, marching in column along the road bordering the harbour. Already they had passed over the bridge spanning the Barachois, some few hundred yards to the northeast of the Dauphin Bastion, and had covered a good deal of ground since, pushing back our pickets with a screen of Canadien irregular light infantry as they came.

That solid mass of men appeared unstoppable, and indeed, there was many a nervous glance between us, as we knew that our own numbers would be insufficient for the task; still we proceeded with all possible haste through the thick undergrowth when the order for double-time was given, for the enemy's goal could not be more clear.

The battery we were in the process of bringing into position was near to completion, and would command much of the harbour. It was hoped that it would force the enemy's fleet closer to the fortress once it became engaged. It could not be doubted that the enemy was aware of our intentions, and was determined to confound them with a raid, hoping to capture our guns. I ran forward with the rest of my comrades intent on coming to the aid our retreating pickets – who by the colour of their green jackets, I knew to be Rangers. As I ran, a deep anger toward *Monsieur* engulfed me, for wishing to destroy what we had spent so many long hours labouring to build.

However the fortunes of the oncoming battle unfolded, that could not be allowed to take place!

We were still only halfway down the slope when we saw *Monsieur's* column come to a halt and begin to deploy into line, obviously intending to fire a volley into the Rangers, who, although numbering less than fifty, had ceased to retreat and from positions of cover were firing into the enemy in order to delay the advance. The strategy appeared to be working, but I could not help but admire the reckless courage that it took to employ it. When it came, the enemy's volley would be from a range of less than fifty yards, and was certain to be devastating.

The wings of the column continued to unfold while odd puffs of smoke, followed by the reports, indicated that the Rangers were firing as well as they were able. Here and there a single white-coated figure would crumble and fall to the ground, yet the ranks continued to form, the soldiers stepping carefully over their fallen comrades to take their place in the line.

We continued to struggle through the undergrowth, for we were still well out of effective musket range, and the situation was dire. It was inconceivable that the Rangers should absorb the full effect of what *Monsieur* was about to offer, and not be swept away like so much chaff in the wind. The Rangers themselves must have been aware of the peril, yet they calmly continued to fire and reload as fast as was possible, determined to sell their lives dearly to the bitter end.

Finally, we succeeded in clearing the broken ground, yet were still some three hundred yards away, but could only press forward with the certainty that we would arrive too late.

The French line was the customary three ranks deep – the foremost kneeling - spanning the road, and extending well past on either side as their skirmishers retreated to form on the wings, leaving the ground to their front a clear field of fire. When all was ready – even as we were struggling mightily to reach our comrades in time to be of assistance - we heard their commander shout a single command, *"Tirez!"* and a volcano of smoke and fire erupted from all those muzzles, shrouding the enemy, at the same time hurtling a wall of lead into the Rangers' position.

Several of the green jackets spun and fell; one, caught in the act of retreating to better cover, suddenly spread his arms as if meaning to take flight, his face a complete caricature of surprise, as a crimson stain blossomed on his shirt and he was flung, face-down, into the dust. He lay there, feet drumming on the ground while his hands clawed, raking grass and leaves around his head as though the act might somehow save him. Nothing could however, for eventually his struggles waned, and he lay deathly still within the minute.

The French volley had been well-aimed and well-timed, but such is the accuracy of a musket that we could hear the familiar buzzing sound as several balls tore through the air over our heads. One or two actually found a mark, and sent the recipient to the ground – unintentional to be sure, but effective all the same.

I had thought that our line would form some distance to the rear of the Rangers' position, and allow them to retire upon us, but now, with the destruction wrought by the enemy's withering volley staring us in the face, I thought that I was mistaken.

The Ranger's officer, a lieutenant of some senior years, was standing, sword in hand, gazing as at a nightmare at the surrounding carnage. Upwards of a third of his command had fallen. Here, two were down – one lay still, the other was on his hands and knees, coughing blood - over there another, grimacing in pain from a shattered thigh, was being awkwardly dragged behind cover, single-handed, by a fourth whose other arm hung bloody and useless at his side. Everywhere throughout his position the scene was repeated with disheartening regularity. Even as the French wings began to retire back into line of column, confident that their volley had done its work, it did not take a man of unparalleled imagination to read his thoughts: so many of his comrades lay helpless before the oncoming enemy. The prudent action

155

would be to retreat, leaving the dead and the wounded to the mercy of an enemy, which experience had taught him, in the vicious irregular warfare in the woods, was not merciful at all. He turned to us with a look of such appeal – a look that spoke of prudence being a luxury that he could no longer afford.

It begged us to come on.

We did not hesitate. Such was our union of spirit that we surged forward, ever more eager to come to the aid of men we so admired. However, had we succeeded in doing so, it was doubtless that the result of placing our line so close to that of *Monsieur* would have only furthered the attrition in a manner unacceptable to either side. In a trice the officers and sergeants were out in front of their own respective companies, crying for us to halt.

"Damn your eagerness!" Beaumont raged with his back to the enemy, holding his sword aloft as if threatening to cut down the next one of us who dared to take another step; yet his own eyes were bright with excitement, glittering with cruel ferocity, without a shadow visible of the man I detested. "You will obey my command!"

That stopped us, but only just. We stood our ground, white knuckles gripping our muskets, muttering curses, while Bell pushed and shoved us into line. Meanwhile, Beaumont spun an about face, exchanged a meaningful glance with the Ranger lieutenant, then beyond him to the French - who were still proceeding to reform into column - before spinning back to us.

"Right," he cried, "I need volunteers! Who amongst you is willing to bring back the wounded?"

Before there was time to consider, I had shoved my musket into the surprised hands of the man standing next to me, and stepped forward, along with perhaps a dozen others.

Beaumont looked directly into my face, yet, in the heat of the moment, I do not believe that he recognized me. Instead, without further hesitation, he gave a curt nod and said, "Off you go!"

We burst from the line at a dead run, time being of the essence; for the Canadiens had swept in from the wings, and were now sprinting ahead of their main force to renew their role as skirmishers. Soon they would be pressing hard against the Rangers who, given that there were no longer enough of them left standing to both fight and assist their wounded (and also given their reluctance to desert them) were almost certain to be annihilated.

I was amongst the foremost to reach their position, sweeping past their lieutenant – who seemed dazed with surprise – and amidst cries of agony, hoisted the unfortunate man with the broken leg onto my back, while others did the same for his afflicted countrymen, even as a French drum signaled the advance.

The lieutenant could not take his eyes from me as I staggered past, stumbling under the wounded man's weight. When I came near, he seemed to collect himself sufficiently to say with some warmth, "Thank you," and after a brief glance at the badge on my mitre, appended, "the 51st!" Then, seeing that his wounded were being looked to, with inestimable relief, he returned to his duty. In a low, firm voice, he cried to his remaining men, "Hold them!"

Burdened as I was, I was unable to witness the activities behind me as *Monsieur* closed in. Instead I heard, more than saw, the action as it unfolded.

First there was the sound of one, then two muskets being discharged, followed by a fusillade from marksmen acting individually rather than in concert; on the one side were those pushing forward, on the other those, who against vastly superior numbers, were desperately trying to delay that advance so that we might escape..

The air seemed filled with the angry hiss of musket balls, and I seldom felt more naked with my back to the foe; yet although I often felt the heat of their passing, none of those errant missiles found me. I continued to struggle with my burden, concentrating on putting one foot before the other, doing my utmost to ignore the battle raging in the rear, until at long last I felt the presence of others of my company, relieving me of the weight of the wounded man from my back. Then I resumed my place in the line, settling in to await the enemy with my musket loaded and at the ready.

Meanwhile, the Rangers who could still fight were gradually falling back on our flanks. Every so often one or two would stop to send a ball at their pursuers, forcing them to keep their distance, before retiring a few more paces under the covering fire of their comrades. While we waited, still out of effective range, I noted one Ranger, his hat lost somewhere over the ground already covered, queue undone, draping long salt and pepper hair across his shoulders, as the man with whom I had shared the dubious shelter of a tree on the day of our landing. Even as I watched, willing his safe return in a fret-filled silence, he brought his musket to bear, and sent a ball into the chest of one of the Canadiens, a wild-looking fellow dressed in buckskins, with several fringes of scalps tied to his belt. I was filled with a savage elation to see him fall, and renewed the gladness I felt for having been able to rescue the wounded; for it was indeed doubtful that, had they been abandoned, they would have remained unmolested.

After having fired, my erstwhile companion continued to fall back, and by the merest of chances his eyes happened to fall upon me where I waited in the second rank. In the heat of battle, it was inconceivable that he should recognize me, but he offered a cheerful grin, the scar on his face bending awkwardly as he did so. I returned the greeting on the chance that he did see me after all, and then he was gone, retiring further down the line, leaving us a clear field between *Monsieur* and ourselves.

As they neared, the French skirmishers approached with greater caution, yet continued to close, firing independently as they came. This was their function, to do their utmost to disrupt our line, and to allow their main force, coming up from behind, to manoeuvre into unmolested ranks. It was an action that required the spirit of a gambler, as well as precise timing. The gamble was that we would not waste a volley on such a

158

scattered and relatively insignificant foe, but would wait for the main body to come up, in the hope that we would not have time to reload before this was accomplished.

The French lieutenant was very good at his job, coolly pointing out likely looking targets with his sword, before turning to watch while the column to the rear once more hinged at the centre, and began to unfold. He was judging the time until the line would be formed and could effectively close. Apparently considering it to be sufficiently near, he wagered that his men could press forward still further, to within fifty yards, increasing the accuracy of their weapons, and satisfactorily confident that we dare not reply. Had he been faced with regular European infantry, such a gamble would undoubtedly have proved correct. What he had failed to consider in the equation, however, was how quickly a British soldier could reload, and so led his men to their destruction.

The enemy's effectiveness had been galling up to this point, sending round after round at our tightly packed ranks. Most went astray, to be sure, yet, increasingly, as they drew nearer, I could hear the screams of those of my comrades who had been hit, and - with the absence of any bandsmen (to whom such a duty would normally fall), must lie unattended, while the line maintained its front.

The effect of those cries on our nerves was as it might well be imagined, for they could be heard clearly by all. That, combined with the sounds of musket balls passing uncomfortably close around our heads, required the greatest determination for us to hold our ground without wavering. Thus when Captain Beaumont - who had also been gauging time and distance with equal diligence as the enemy – cried "Present!" we obeyed with a sense of relief, and the utmost alacrity.

Too late, the French lieutenant saw his blunder.

"Fire!"

The musket kicked viciously into my shoulder as the volley crashed out in near perfect unison, and the customary cloud of smoke blossomed from the ends of barrels up and down the line.

"Reload!"

Without pause, I set the hammer on half cock, then quickly reached into my cartouche for another cartridge. In one swift motion I brought it to my mouth, tearing one end of the paper away with my teeth and placed a pinch of powder in the frisson, snapped the pan lid shut before upending the musket and poured the remainder down the barrel, followed by the ball still wrapped in paper, ramming it home with the rod. Then it was out and seated in its slot, and the musket was at my shoulder, signaling to Captain Beaumont that I was ready.

"Make ready!"

As one, our muskets shifted and rose as we lifted them to the salute so as to drag our hammers back to full cock.

"Present!"

Again as one, our muskets swung down in a quarter arc as we leveled our pieces at the enemy, and saw that the smoke had cleared from our front, revealing the aftermath of our first volley.

The ground was littered with bodies – both in the white coats of the Bourbon kings, and the homespun or buckskins of the Canadiens - some still, many others rolling on the ground in pain. I glanced to the spot where the young lieutenant had been standing, directing the fire of his men. A motionless form lay on the ground, the gold tassel from a sabre's hilt draped carelessly across one outflung wrist – a hard payment for a single lapse in judgment.

"Steady, men!"

Beaumont's cry rang over the field just as my eye narrowed down the length of my musket's barrel.

The main body of the enemy was advancing through the smoke, and had closed to a distance of some sixty yards. Even as I watched, the order was given to halt and make ready. More than three times our number, we had but one hope – to even the odds before they could deliver that one crashing salvo that could only tear us to pieces.

Then Beaumont's sword slashed down as he screamed: "Fire!"

Chapter Nine

Our volley was as well timed as the first, muskets crashing out in unison as we sent *Monsieur* our greeting.

"Reload!"

I went through the motions of recharging my weapon as if I were a machine, all too aware of the French muskets leveled at us on the other side of the curtain of smoke, but also aware of the cries from the many injured coming from that side of the divide - evidence of our having delivered a telling blow. I was still in the act of pouring the powder down my musket's barrel when there came a glimmer of fire through the fog, followed instantly by an explosion from the French line, and the angry bees were swarming into our ranks again.

Something brushed past my cheek, soft as a breeze, while the man to my left clutched at his breast and fell to the ground. I thrust the ball into the muzzle before ramming it home. Then I was standing at shoulder arms, waiting for the command, praying that I would be alive when it came.

Fortunately, I did not have long to wait.

"Front rank! Make ready!"

The muskets of the men kneeling came up, filling the air with the ratcheting sound of hammers being drawn back.

"Present!"

Along with the others, the man kneeling in front of me leveled his weapon at the enemy, invisible behind the cloud of spent powder, his knuckles white from gripping the stock.

Sword aloft, Beaumont hesitated an instant, looking to the left, and then to the right, making sure that he was in concert with the neighbouring companies, before slashing it to the ground.

"Fire!"

Coming as it did on the heels of the thunderous French volley, that of our front rank was only a distant echo by comparison. This came as no surprise; but my heart would have been gladdened immeasurably if we had been capable of a more defiant roar.

"The front rank will retire with the wounded, to reform on Mr. Greenly!"

Our strategy became clear to me on the instant. I silently approved, for it would have been madness to try to hold our ground. Instead we would fight a delaying action, much as had done the Rangers, giving others of our forces time to come to our aid. Wishing them wings for their feet, I stepped aside to allow the man in front of me to pass.

"Good luck, mate," he murmured, and then was gone from sight at the double.

"Second rank! Make ready! Present! Fire!"

No sooner had the musket crashed into my shoulder than I heard, "The second rank will retire!"

I took a precious moment to stoop over my fallen comrade, but he was already dead, the bullet having pierced his heart, so I raced back with the others to join the first rank, already forming line some thirty paces to the rear, and were frantically reloading. My flight was interrupted when I spied one man struggling with the ponderous weight of Simmons, our company's remaining lieutenant, who had taken a ball in the thigh. Rushing over, I took one of his arms, and slinging it around my neck, ignored his cries of pain as, together, we carried him to safety, jogging heavily under the strain.

We deposited him without ceremony, alongside some six or seven other injured, lying on the ground in various states of distress, all under the care of a corporal's section, whose duty it would be to retire while we delayed the enemy. Soon the wounded would be free to nurse their pain, and to dwell on the surgeon with his knife, preparing to receive them back at camp. With Simmons down, and Forsyth drowned on the day of the landing, for a fleeting moment it occurred to me that our company's compliment of officers had now dwindled to Captain Beaumont, and young Ensign Greenly. In truth, the lieutenants would not be much missed; for Simmons, like Forsyth, had long been with the regiment, serving with neither distinction nor advancement, regarding the North American theatre with almost as much contempt as they regarded their own men. Indeed, it was widely accepted among the ranks, that without Captain Beaumont, and General Wolfe's insistence on relentless drill, we would have been poorly prepared for a campaign where junior officers were to play such an important role.

Just then another volley erupted from the French, much the same as the first. Here and there men fell, although this time not nearly as many, visibility being uncertain, and the distance between us having been increased out of effective range.

I took my place in the line, and was in the act of reloading when I could hear the tread of hundreds of marching feet, and knew that *Monsieur* was coming after us. Moments later, I could see them emerging from the powder cloud like wraiths wandering through the fog, muskets at shoulder arms.

Captain Beaumont's voice rang out, "First rank! Make ready! Present! Fire! The first rank will retire!"

Standing this time, the men in the first line fired their pieces and sped away. On command, those of us in the second took one pace forward, providing cover for our retreating comrades, before offering our own volley for *Monsieur* to sample. Then we were off again to join them.

Twice more the manoeuvre was repeated, but though the ground they captured was dearly bought, the enemy continued to press us back with their overwhelming numbers. The situation was beginning to become desperate, as the numbers of our own wounded continued to mount. If the battle remained as it was, there would not be enough of us left to care for them, and it would become necessary to leave them behind. Every one of us knew that this might become an eventuality, although it was not a thought to dwell upon.

We had retreated all the way to the base of the heights when the French fired another volley, tumbling even more of us to the ground. I had just finished loading, and was bringing my musket to shoulder arms when there came a shouted command from their side of the field. Although the words were foreign, every man of us understood their meaning when we heard the distinctive sound of hundreds of bayonets hissing from their scabbards.

Someone muttered, "Christ, we're in for it now!" and then they were emerging through the smoke as before, although this time they were holding their muskets before them, the lethal tips of their bayonets leveled at our breasts, an officer with a plumed hat urging them forward.

I had not seen the man who had predicted our end, although I silently agreed. This time *Monsieur* meant to finish us, and would not stop until he had reached our position. Further retreat was out of the question, as we would be routed from the field the minute we turned our backs on that bristling hedge of steel. Even so, many a man glanced nervously at his neighbour. If one should falter, others would follow his lead, and the French goal would have been achieved without ever having come to grips with us.

Beaumont cried, "Steady Lads!" and flexed his sabre, his eyes flashing with excitement. "It's time to make a stand and earn your pay!"

We must have been as mad as our captain, for we gave a mighty cheer, bolstering our courage; those who had looked on the verge of breaking only a moment earlier, were now exulting as loud as the rest.

Then came the command.

"Make ready!"

Up and down the line, men growled their defiance as every hammer was brought to full cock.

"Present!"

There was a unity of motion as all brought their muskets to bear.

"Fire!"

Our line exploded in a hail of lead, and sent it on to the enemy. Many fell, perhaps dozens, although all knew that even this was too few.

Then, laughing wildly, Beaumont cried, "Now lads! Fix bayonets and prepare to receive those bastards! Before this day is over, I expect every mother's son of them to be sent straight to hell!"

It was madness, of course, for we remained far outnumbered, but still we gave another lusty cheer as the bayonets sang from our scabbards. I believe that at that moment we were all mad, and felt that the task was one that was not beyond our capabilities!

The French came on, every step measured to the beat of their drums, every face stern with determination, and every heart merciless with the will to succeed. We watched them come, marching in that slow, even tread, willing our own determination to be their equal.

Then, suddenly, Beaumont swore, "Sod this for a farthing, boys! I'll not stand here, content to meet the Frogs at their pleasure! Drummer! Sound the advance!" and then, signaling his intention to the other companies, he waved his sword and cried, "Forward!"

Our drummer, busily attending some of our wounded, was caught by surprise, and we had covered some distance before he could scramble to his instrument. He caught up to us on the run, beating the time as he came, so hard that I believed that I could hear it echoing high in the hills.

Only it was not an echo, and it was then that I realized that it was yet another instrument – or perhaps more than one - drumming men to the advance at double-time.

Both the French commander and ours recognized it, too, for they called their respective forces to a halt on the same instant. Curious, and at the risk of sanction, I glanced back, and could not restrain a gasp of relief.

At first, only the tips of their mitres were visible over the ridge of the escarpment, but then came their heads, then more rapidly, their torsos showing the green facings of the 45th. Then they were to the lip and over the edge, followed by rank after rank of red-coated infantry bearing the distinctive colours of the 35th waving boldly in the wind. In all my life I had seldom seen anything more worthy of rejoicing. What made it all the more pleasing to the eye was that the entire force appeared to be led by a common soldier, uncommonly tall, but which we knew was none other than General Wolfe himself!

Others in our beleaguered force had also witnessed the arrival of our rescuers, and had also recognized the slight figure of our general at their head, waving his sword, and urging the men down the slope with all due haste, for a cheer was sent up almost immediately, which was quelled with great force by the sergeants and corporals, reminding us of our immediate peril.

With my eyes once more to my front, I studied the French commander – a full colonel – as he took stock of the situation. He was quickly calculating the numbers coming down the slope and comparing them with his own, as well as considering the time that it would take before they arrived. Then he returned his attention to us, considered briefly, and barked a command. At once the French muskets were upended as they began to reload.

It was clear what his calculations had surmised: rather than risk being caught in a hand-to-hand struggle, leaving his flanks dangerously exposed, it was best that the fight return to the superiority of his firepower. Therefore, as the gap between our two forces had now become narrowed to within thirty paces, it was decided that there was time to deliver one last, killing volley that would sweep us from the field. Then, unencumbered by our numbers, he would be free to meet this new threat, which, although superior to his own, was not overwhelmingly so, and might yet be defeated.

Our own officers were in a similar quandary. Had the reinforcements heralded their arrival only a few moments earlier, the situation would have been markedly different, and our impetuous advance would almost certainly not have been ordered. Yet here we were, caught within easy musket range, after we had taken such pains to be otherwise, and fatigued from the many retreats in the bargain. A decision had to be made – to attack or retreat – moreover, it needed to be made at once. To stand where we were, to match *Monsieur* volley for volley, was to invite disaster. Yet, which way did disaster not lie?

Beaumont delivered his answer.

With eyes shining more deliriously than ever, he waved his sword and cried, "Come on!" then sprinted off toward the enemy at a run.

We were mad indeed. For in that brief moment, when we realized that help was close to hand, sanity seemed to have found its way again, only to shine a light on our peril; yet when we stood there, watching, as our captain dashed off toward the French alone, the madness reclaimed us, and before any were rightfully aware, we were pelting after him as hard as we could, and the devil take the hindmost! Gone was the stately advance, gone was the discipline of the line. All that was left was a rabid urge to close with *Monsieur* before he had time to reload.

Thirty yards is a short distance, and can be easily covered in a very few seconds when at a dead run; yet the time was sufficient for many things to pass through my mind.

First, I cursed Beaumont for a fool for not retreating, but dismissed the notion even as it was formulating. Fatigued as we were, the French would have pursued and caught us on the tips of their bayonets with our backs painfully exposed.

Second, I cursed him for leading us on this madcap adventure that was beyond anything that we had come to know of civilized warfare! Our ranks had dissolved as the more nimble of foot surged ahead and the lesser fell behind. The discipline that we had come to accept as holy writ had gone by the board, leaving not a single mass formation, but fierce individuals bent on nothing more noble than brute survival! Yet, this too, I was compelled to concede as the wiser choice, as to follow any other course of action would lead to almost certain death.

Thirdly, at this moment of extreme peril, the memory of that desperate night, when I had rescued Elizabeth from those four ruffians, emerged – yet again unbidden, as if my mind had a will of its own. Then, I remembered her smile, and the magic when she had looked so deeply into my eyes.

"I shall love you forever!"

Then I was in amongst the foremost ranks of the enemy, screaming my rage at the top of my lungs and expecting every moment to be my last.

A young French soldier, with the beginnings of a ginger moustache sprouting on his lip, had abandoned his attempt to reload, dropped his cartridge, and taking up his musket, leveled it at my chest. He screamed his own defiance, yet with a countenance so contorted by fear that I was certain it was a match for my own!

So headlong had been our advance that my momentum carried me into him before I could hesitate, and had I not parried his thrust at the critical moment, beyond any shadow of a doubt I would have impaled myself on his bayonet; but then I was past his defence, and could clearly smell the garlic on his breath as I closed in vengefully. There was no time to implement my own bayonet, only to lower my shoulder as I crashed into his chest, sending him hurtling to the ground and leaving me to stagger onward, struggling to maintain my balance, as the second rank rose to meet me.

I felt something bite into the fleshy part of my arm, and I was striking back blindly with the butt of my musket. A face engorged with rage swam before my eyes, then fell away, and I was lunging at the nearest white coat I could see. There was a tug on the tip of my bayonet, then a scream, and it too disappeared. Then I slashed at another but missed, leaving my flank horribly exposed. Had he chosen that moment to strike, I would have been a dead man, and indeed, I braced myself against the agony of cold steel sliding through my ribs. But instead, that was the moment we both heard the French drums beating the recall.

Our eyes met for the briefest of instances, and for the briefest of instances he hesitated, torn between obeying the drums, and a primordial desire to satisfy his own lust for blood. Then quite suddenly he was gone, leaving me with the impression that I was dreaming, for surely he could not have winked at me before he turned and ran back to join his fellows!

Bereft of the immediacy of enemies, as I watched *Monsieur* depart, I could only stand in a stupor, not quite accepting the fact that life continued to course through my veins. My sense of reality was in no way aided upon finding myself next to Stockingsdale. The shameless miscreant was exulting in high spirits, cackling aloud as he undid his flies and exposed himself to the enemy.

Slowly, the exultation passed, and with it his ardour; while re-buttoning, he noticed me and grinned. With a wink he said, "Nothing like bein' alive, eh Josiah?" and, without warning, burst into tears.

I silently agreed. Never had my life been so precious, nor, in spite of all things experienced to the contrary, ever so sweet, but then the exultation was suddenly jarred from my mind.

"After them, men!" a high, reedy voice called out over the sudden stillness, "After them I say, for they will not stand!"

I returned to the present, to see the general sprinting down the road toward us, with solid ranks of redcoats at his heels. He was waving us on with his sword, frantically urging us forward with words and gestures.

"You have them beat, my brave fellows!" cried he, "Just one more push and the day will be ours!"

As clear as I had thought my mind had become, I had difficulty believing what my ears had just heard; nor for the moment could I comprehend their meaning. Surely he could not wish for us to proceed further! Had we not already done enough? But then Beaumont was rasping out orders, and Sergeant Bell was having us form into ranks yet again. I willed myself to drum up my last vestige of courage.

It was true that *Monsieur* had retired, but he was not yet chased from the field. When I saw the running, white-coated figures stop to re-form some small distance from where we stood, his intentions became clear. By retreating, he had merely disengaged himself from what would have been a disastrous hand-to-hand engagement, had the general fallen upon him while he was caught, still in the process of dispatching our own decimated, but still willing to fight, companies. Even as I watched them form into ranks, and begin again the process of recharging their muskets, it was painfully obvious that the French in no way considered themselves defeated, but were determined to meet our reinforced numbers with all the vigour that we had come to respect, if not admire, in so ancient a foe.

What also became clear was Wolfe's urging us to attack. By disrupting the enemy before he could reload, we had gained valuable time for the general to come up with superior force, and a ball in every musket, placing *Monsieur* at a serious disadvantage. Thus far we had succeeded, but it was not yet enough. If we did not act at once, there was still an opportunity for him to even the odds.

The madness had left us, but the urgency had not. So when Captain Beaumont called for the advance, we followed, matching his pace as well as we were able. By the absence of his tattoo, it was clear that, at some point in the fray, our drummer had fallen.

We rushed forward, intent upon catching the enemy with his muskets as empty as our own. Their colonel was a capable officer, for we were within paces of their line, when an order was given and the hindmost rank broke away to prepare a position further to the rear, leaving the foremost to keep us at bay, much as we had ourselves, during our earlier withdrawl.

There was one, glaring difference, however: during our retreat, we had never allowed the enemy to close.

With the absence of half his strength, *Monsieur's* line was more equal to our own, and had we attacked it with the same vigour as our earlier assault, we must have routed it completely; but fatigued as we were from the constant fighting, such an effort was now beyond our capabilities.

Our two lines closed, but not with the ringing clash as before. I eyed my opposite number warily, as he eyed me in return. The tips of our bayonets carved circles in the air as we each searched for an advantage. He lunged and I parried, but he managed to deflect my point from his breast. Then, with the ends of his moustache twitching, he retreated a step. Pressing closely, I advanced one.

Such was the tone of our second close engagement all along the line. In the absence of a berserker's rage, both sides were left with little more than a hard-earned respect for one another…and a desperate will to survive.

There was also another, and perhaps higher reason for our reluctance to slaughter one another, for such was only a secondary consideration. *Monsieur* merely wished to buy time for his line to consolidate and reload to the rear. We, in turn, required the same while the general shortened the distance between us.

My opponent retreated a second step, taking care with his footing. I advanced with him, our bayonets overlapping.

"Keep close, lads!" Captain Beaumont called out as we gradually forced them back, "Don't allow any separation!"

I did not take my eyes from the man facing me. Both of us could hear the rattle of ramrods seating charges in the French muskets behind him. Our bid to prevent the enemy from loading had only partially succeeded, yet had only partially failed, leaving them still greatly disadvantaged against our ever-nearing reinforcements. Even now the drums were drawing closer – perhaps a hundred yards away – and would be caught up to us within the minute.

In the meantime, our engagement was a stalemate, leaving the opposing commanders in a quandary, but more so the French colonel. While continuing to press, we remained safe from the peril of a volley, which coming from such short range, could not have failed to be lethal. The rear rank of the enemy, now loaded and waiting, could not fire for fear of hitting their comrades, even if they were so inclined as to expend that threat on our comparatively few numbers. Had they done so, there would not have been sufficient time to recharge their weapons, forcing them to face our vastly augmented numbers at a complete disadvantage.

172

A further complication for the enemy was that, having bought the time that was required, those in his front rank could no longer break away with any degree of safety. Had they attempted to run, they would have exposed their backs to *our* bayonets. The resultant slaughter would have been frightful.

The situation was untenable for both sides and could not last. Finally, the drums fell silent as the general called a halt.

From behind us came the order, "Make ready!" followed by the sound of well over a thousand hammers being ratcheted to full cock.

Captain Beaumont called out, "That's enough, lads!" and we pressed no further.

Warily, the enemy continued his retreat - first one pace, and then another – finally achieving the separation he desired, although now it was too late.

As if choreographed for a play, at the very same instant the opposing commanders gave the order.

"Run for it boys!" Captain Beaumont shouted, and I was breaking away, even as the corner of my eye caught my opponent doing the same, then I was running back with the rest of my comrades, to form on the left of our line with the grenadiers of the 45th. Before we were halfway there, however, someone shouted, "Down!" and I was flinging myself to the ground, just as our volley roared out over my head.

I spared a moment to glance, and was just in time to see a great number of the French go down. I tried to pick out the man who had been facing me, but could not do so – the back of one Frenchman being much like another. Irrationally, perhaps, I sent out a silent hope that he had survived that killing salvo, and then was on my feet again, pelting toward our line.

I rejoined the ranks just as the drums sounded once more. General Wolfe waved his sword, and in his high, distinctive voice, cried out, "Forward!" and, once more, we advanced in unison, this time not to stop until we had pushed *Monsieur* back across the bridge at the Barachois.

The enemy must have replied to our own volley, as a thin veil of smoke hovered before their line, but in the confusion I had not noticed, and there were no discerning consequences for those of us nearby. Then, with his last precious round discharged, and with no time for another, the French colonel, having lost in his gamble, waved for his men to retreat.

It began as orderly, but as we continued to press forward, became increasingly less so. Panic now seemed to be settling into their ranks, and although I could see none throwing away their weapons, their haste to withdraw seemed precipitate, to the point of becoming a rout.

The faster they withdrew, the faster we pressed on. We fed off the enemy's fear, and became more emboldened. Of all the enemy, it was the Canadiens who fought with the most frantic desperation, as doubtless, for many of them this was their home. They alone gave up their ground with any reluctance, snarling their hatred like savages, but were continually forced back as their numbers were few. Finally, one – a great bearded fellow, dressed entirely in buckskins – became so incensed that he attacked our line single-handed, with nothing more lethal in his hand than a tomahawk. He was the bravest man on the field that day, but was shot down before having covered more than a dozen paces.

We had now chased the enemy to the very bridgehead on the Barachois, and it was anticipated that a telling blow might be inflicted upon him here. The bridge was too narrow to accommodate such a force in full retreat, and must necessarily cause a delay while they milled about, trapped with their backs to the water, allowing us to come to grips; yet scarcely had we begun to descend down a gentle slope in what was hoped to be our final push, when a single cannon from the Dauphin Bastion fired a shot, feeling us out for distance. The ball struck the ground, well short, bounced twice, and rolled to a stop some few yards in front of us. Then the general was waving us back, frantically gesturing toward the harbour. When we looked to the cause of his excitement, it was made immediately clear.

The slope upon which we had been standing gradually led to a declivity as it descended to the shore, leaving a certain amount of low ground that must be traversed in order for us to

174

reach the bridge. It was at the entrance to this terrain that the French frigate, the *Aréthuse*, had taken station, threatening us with her broadside. Even as we watched, her hull disappeared in a wreath of smoke, and a hail of grapeshot scythed across the field, thankfully, to no effect.

Caught in an impasse once again, we stood where we were, watching the last of the French cross the bridge and enter the town, helpless to intervene. We dared not advance any further.

It was much the same as had been the situation upon the first day of our landing, or so it seemed to me – *Monsieur* was bottled up in Loiusbourg, and we unable to get at him. But the general, who happened to be close by, seemed not the least annoyed. To the contrary, his face was alight with excitement when I heard him exclaim.

"This is too good a chance to miss, by god!"

He was not looking at the fleeing backs of the enemy, but instead to the high ground overlooking the inlet, and some few hundreds of yards beyond, to the fortress itself.

Captain Beaumont, still exultant from the day's action, was standing at his elbow, and believed himself to have been addressed. He asked, "Sir?"

Wolfe slapped his thigh with great satisfaction, never taking his eyes from the hill; then finally turning his attention to our captain, he seemed surprised.

"Ah," he cried, smiling affably, "it's you, Beaumont! My sincerest congratulations! That was a damned good showing you..." he raised his eyes, smiling at each and every one of us, "...and your splendid fellows did today, a damned good showing, indeed!"

Flushed with pride, Beaumont stretched ever higher to the attention, as did we all. A general's praise was something that was seldom heard. To have singled us out in front of the army was not an honour to be sniffed at.

"Why, thank you, sir!" Beaumont exclaimed, smiling his own pleasure.

"Many more men would not have been alive to see the sun go down if it were not for your excellent leadership; 'pon my soul, I've seldom seen troops so ably led!"

"Very kind of you to say, sir," said Beaumont, still smiling, before modestly adding, "but it was no great hardship when I have the best men in the army behind..."

He turned as he spoke, so that we all might benefit from his praise, but when his eyes met mine, the smile faltered.

I saw that the excitement was still there – aye, and cruelty, too – the savage elation of the victorious warrior anticipating the spoils; but also there was recognition, followed closely by confusion. But I would not say that the barbarity was diminished; no, rather it became cunningly veiled as he turned back to the general. "That is to say, sir, there's not many that can compare with the 51st!"

Wolfe seemed not to have noticed Beaumont's sudden transformation, for his attention was back on the hill.

"A useful place, wouldn't you say, Captain?"

Beaumont roused himself sufficiently from his thoughts to look up and agree, "Very useful, indeed, sir!"

To which the general nodded before he repeated, musing, as if to himself, "This is too good a chance to miss!"

At which our captain repeated, "Sir?"

"That hill!" he cried, beginning to pace about in his excitement, "I mean to have it!"

Uncertainly, we looked from the high ground, rising ahead, to the frigate waiting in the harbour, as if daring us to make such a move. Then we stared at our general, scarcely able to credit what we were hearing! The heights, which Wolfe had just sworn that he must take, lay on the far side of the declivity, necessitating any storming force to be exposed to the scathing broadside of the frigate.

The silence that greeted his statement pulled the general from his euphoria long enough to sense our doubt.

Gravely he smiled, "Come, have you not often heard me say that the greatness of an object should come into consideration as opposed to the impediments that lie in the way?"

Beaumont answered for us all, "Yes sir, of course," although he appeared to remain uncertain.

In spite of our discipline, we in the ranks began to fidget, as men will when they have given their utmost, and even more is demanded of them. Surely the general did not plan for us to attempt this mad scheme? Why, it was tantamount to suicide! I was sure that every one of us would be cut down before we had reached halfway to our objective!

Beaumont opened his mouth to speak, but whether in agreement or to protest, no one could say; nor would there be any way of ascertaining for some time to come, for fate chose that moment to intervene.

The ground where we stood was close to the place where the buckskin-clad Canadien had fallen. No attention had been paid to this body any more than to the others lying nearby. None suspected that he had been feigning. Therefore all were stunned to immobility when the man suddenly leapt to his feet, and screaming a savage war cry, rushed at the general with the sun glinting off the razor edge of his tomahawk.

I have no recollection of acting - only of one moment being aware of the imminent peril, and the next of standing with my musket, while the smoke from spent powder roiled in the air in front of me. The ball caught the man in the neck, and must have come dangerously close to the general himself as he stood between his assailant and me. Great gouts of blood sprayed from the wound, showering Wolfe and others in crimson. Then, while the man lay dying, I broke from the ranks to step forward and stab him through the body.

The entire incident took less than a heartbeat from start to finish, or so it seemed. When I could finally bring myself to look up, after having made quite certain that this savage man was no more, I found that not another soul had moved, and that all were regarding me with open-mouthed amazement. Of a sudden, feeling unbearably exposed before all of those gaping faces, I shouldered my weapon, and made to step back into line.

"You there," I heard the general say in a voice that was shaking, "fellow!"

I stopped, standing rigid at attention, not daring to look nor to speak to such an exalted person.

Then I heard him ask, not unkindly, "What is your name?"

Yet the moment was too great for me, and my voice refused to answer.

" Private Stubb, sir," Beaumont answered in my stead, and I stood more rigid than ever: for this was the closest I had been to the captain since that fateful day.

"Surely he has a Christian name as well?" the general asked, I thought, with just a hint of amusement.

"J-Josiah," I was so stricken that the 'sir' which should have been appended, remained unspoken – an unforgiveable omission.

Yet if anyone noticed the absence, they did not say, not even the general himself. Instead, speaking ever so softly, he said, "Look at me, Josiah." and somehow I found the courage to obey.

He stared at me, studying my features closely, not so different than when he had studied the hill only moments before. Then, without smiling, he said, "I owe you my life. Anything within my power that you would ask of me I will grant. This I most solemnly promise."

I believe that was when it struck me how far the events of the day had come – from Daniel's plight, and Stockingsdale's suggestion of how I might serve him. I thought of Bell and Beaumont, and while I could find it within me to hate the one, there was a curious emptiness of feeling when it came to the other. I wanted to hate him - indeed, I felt it a duty to - but today I had followed him willingly, placing my life in his hands without reservation. It had to be admitted that Beaumont was a capable officer, perhaps the very best of his kind, and it was confusing to me that I should regard him so.

However, this thought remained unformed, for Daniel's honest face swam before me, the very noblest of friends. If in my place such an invitation had been put before *him*, he would not have hesitated.

Therefore, finding courage within that thought, I looked to the general…and uttered the words that would allow my friend to live.

Chapter Ten

I stood at attention, the ranks formed into a square enclosing a single twenty-four-pounder. We could hear a drum slowly beat out 'The Rogue's March', and Daniel was brought forward under escort, stripped to the waist.

The drummer stopped when the small procession reached the cannon. At this point he put his instrument aside and took up the cat, while the prisoner's escort bound his wrists to the gun carriage wheel.

Daniel looked to the left and then the right, eyes unfocused. I had made sure that his ration of rum had been doubled that morning.

The drummer pulled the strands of the cat through his hand, and looked to Captain Beaumont for the order to proceed. He received a terse nod, while Sergeant Bell struggled to restrain his fury.

I willed myself to bear witness to the scene. Striking a superior was a grievous breach of discipline; the general had told me as much, in words contrary to the kindness he had previously shown.

Upon hearing my request, his mien had slowly transformed into something cold and unspeakably hard, quickly growing to hot anger, cursing and swearing most foul, and, I believe, even going so far as to damn my eyes for me. In a voice choked with rage, he had bellowed that discipline was the backbone of any army, and damned my impertinence when I had agreed. Raging now, he declared, that without discipline, we were nothing more than a mob. It was unthinkable that punishment should ever be curtailed – egregiously unthinkable, in fact - and how dare I possess the impudence even to ask for such a thing? Then, with storm clouds gathering overhead, he had snarled me back into ranks, and had stomped away in a fury.

It was only later, after we had stormed and taken his precious hill, and had dug in under heavy bombardment, that Stockingsdale came to me with the news that Daniel's punishment was to be restricted to twelve lashes, and that the drummer had been ordered not to be excessive in his zeal when applying them. I did not ask where Benjamin had come by this information, nor did I doubt its veracity. A creature as shameless as he was bound to have venues open to him that were not so for men of a more scrupulous nature.

Still, the cat was the cat – one of the most feared instruments for any of us in the ranks of His Majesty's combined services. One lash could break a man's skin, two could scar him for life; twelve was a punishment worthy of respect. So when I heard the leather of the straps reach his back, I felt a twinge from the bandage on my arm, willing my mind away from the unpleasant scene before my eyes, and went, instead, to the evening after the battle.

Stockingsdale had sought me out, and had found me, alone by a fire, with my coat off, nursing a cut on my forearm, most likely received during the course of our madcap bayonet charge. At the time, I had been vaguely aware of the bite of pain piercing through my fear. Although not severe, it required attention all the same.

He pulled up short, the corners of his mouth drawn down with worry when he saw me addressing the injury, but gathered himself after a moment, sufficiently to take stock.

He studied the wound for a moment before declaring, "Not so bad," then uttered a surprised, "Here, what's this?" when he noticed my preparations.

I had gently bathed the area around the wound with a cloth, fished from a kettle of boiling water, settled amongst the ashes of the fire. Then, uncorking a bottle of spirits with my teeth, had yelped with pain as I poured its contents directly onto the wound.

"Something I learned back in St. John's," I told him. "From a capable doctor...when he was sober." Then I motioned with my head to the bandage still boiling in the kettle, and said, "You might offer to help a fellow."

Comprehending my meaning, Stockingsdale said, "Of a certainty, Josiah," before setting aside his musket, and drawing

181

his bayonet, intending to use it to pluck the cloth from the water.

"Wash your hands first," I managed through clenched teeth – for the cut was deeper than I had first thought – then nodded at his bayonet, "and that, too." For there was no telling where it had been.

The perverse creature frowned at his hands, filthy with blood and ground-in dirt, then at myself. "Wash my hands?" he asked, uncertain as to whether or not I was speaking in jest, "Whatever for, lad?"

The fingers of pain were beginning to coil around my stomach, and I had not the wherewithal to explain. "Just do it," I told him, though my jaw was clenched like a vice. I tossed the cloth with which I had cleansed my wound back into the kettle, and managed to add, "with that!"

Perplexed now, Stockingsdale's frown deepened, but when he saw the state of my distress, he acceded to my wishes and gingerly soaked the cloth in the kettle before applying it to the accumulated grime from his hands, all the while gasping over his own discomfort, for the water was thoroughly boiling. At length he attempted to proceed.

"Not yet," I said, holding the bottle out to him, "now this."

Stockingsdale somehow overcame his surprise, and with a great sigh (that spoke volumes of what he thought of my elaborate preparations) reached out his hands and allowed me to pour the spirits over them, scrubbing them together as I did so.

At last ready, he ventured, "Now?"

"Now," I replied, and he took the bandage from the pot, binding my wound with a speed and efficiency that surprised me.

After the ordeal was over, we had shared the rest of the bottle between us, speaking little, both wrapped in our own thoughts. But the day had been a long one and soon both our heads began to nod as we became overcome with exhaustion. I lay upon the ground under the stars, pillowing my head with my coat. I closed my eyes...and dreamed of waking from a different sleep, in a different time...

*   *   *

I awoke to find myself in a large room with heavy curtains of finest velvet drawn over the windows. I lay in a bed of sumptuous comfort, with a mattress and silken coverlet stuffed with expensive goose down, and with surroundings equally as elegant. Yet amid all of this opulence (none of which was recognizable) I believe that it was something so vulgar as the sound of snoring that had lulled me awake.

Blinking myself to full consciousness, I turned my head toward the aggravating noise, at the same time wincing from a sharp pain in my side, warning me to caution.

Through the gloom I beheld the engine of my disturbance, and slowly recognized her as a middle-aged woman slouched asleep in a chair beside the bed. Her head lolled against the back of the chair, her mouth slack and very much agape, issuing that dreadful sound with every breath. As I studied her more closely, it seemed a face that was known to me. When, gradually, and with dawning surprise, I recognized her as the maidservant of the captain's daughter - the object of my devotion - I came awake with a start, followed instantly by a yelp of pain, caused by my re-discovering the extreme tenderness in my side. I must have cried out more loudly than I had realized, for as the memory of the desperate fight outside the tavern returned, of the knife slicing across my ribs, and the tender expression on that beautiful face as the agony transported me into unconsciousness, the woman abruptly ceased her snoring, and her eyes fluttered open with the shock of one who has just been startled awake.

She sat there, regarding me – and I her – for what seemed a very long time, while her sleep-dulled mind struggled to process information. Then, quite suddenly, her eyes opened very wide indeed.

"The Lord be praised!" She was on her feet in an instant, heading to the door, only to stop and turn in a fluster, as if she had found herself with two duties to perform at once, and knew not which held precedence.

She bobbed a small curtsy, and asked, "Would you care for anything, sir?"

I must have gaped at the unfamiliar manner with which she had addressed me, for after further moments had passed without any reply, her expression grew uncertain, and she repeated, "Sir?"

Her confusion spurred me to answer; but when I opened my mouth to speak, all that would issue forth was a dry croak.

The maid's countenance (I recalled that her name was Sarah) instantly softened to a maternal sympathy as she clicked her tongue, and said, "Oh, you poor lamb, sir! Mercy! You would think I'd never nursed anyone before, wouldn't you? Here, I'll get you something that will help." So saying, she went to a basin on the nightstand, and pouring water from the pitcher, soaked a cloth, which she used to moisten my lips.

"I would give you a proper drink, sir," she apologized, "but you might choke lying down, and the coughing could open up your stitches."

Weakly, I managed to ask, "Stitches?"

"Oh, my word!" she cried, "Yes, sir, so many I couldn't count!"

I began to fumble with the bed covers. Sarah must have realized my intention, for she folded them back with her own hand so that I might inspect my wound.

"Not much to see, I'm afraid, sir."

I had to agree, for most of my torso was completely swathed in bandages, covering any sign of my assailant's handiwork.

"The doctor said you was to rest, and remain in bed," she informed me, "You're not to move about, neither. As I said before, sir, the stitches might come undone."

Heeding her warning, I lay back, and she replaced the bed covers; the simple movements proving exhausting for me. Finally, it occurred to ask her where I was.

"Bless you sir!" she told me, "But this is the captain's house, on King's Lower Brook, or rather his sister's house," she amended in a confidential murmur, that suggested that she was much given to gossip, "A lady widowed to a fishing admiral, t'is said, at the moment visiting relatives in England."

I processed this information in silence. King's Lower Brook was an area known to the town's elite. However, I had just enough wit not to say as much; instead, I asked, "The captain?"

Patiently, Sarah replied, "Captain Broadstreet, sir, Miss Elizabeth's father."

"Elizabeth," for the first time I spoke her name aloud, having just remembered her being so referred to the night of the altercation.

Sarah's lips pressed together in prim disapproval of her mistress being referred to so familiarly. "*Miss* Elizabeth insisted on bringing you here, sir."

I remembered that also, and the protests that both she and the coachman had made. I wondered if everything was not as tranquil as it seemed at present, but before I could ask, she said, "But enough of my talking, sir. The doctor said that he would like to see you as soon as you wake."

She made it to the door this time, before stopping and turning to face me.

"I would like to add, if I may, sir," she began with a shyness that was a mystery to me, "that I'm so grateful for what you done - I mean saving Miss Elizabeth and myself from those ruffians and all. It was very brave, and very noble!" And then she was gone, piping at the moistness in her eyes, before I could utter any reply.

I waited, admiring the richness of my surroundings, and marveled at the coincidence of fate – how chance had overcome the formidable obstacles that had barred me from this world, and given me a glimpse of what it was to dwell here – me, Josiah Stubb, born in the gutter, was now, literally, lying in the bed of gentility – King's Lower Brook, no less. Then, too, I thought of the slim figure with those russet tresses and milk-white skin, of her radiant blue eyes, and magical smile. Fate had given me this chance to be near her. Could I dare to hope that it might give me more?

This was answered within the minute, when feet could be heard hurrying down the corridor, and the sound of a man's voice (distantly familiar) loudly protesting.

"You'll forgive me, Miss, it's not my place to say, but this is highly irregular for a young lady, such as yourself, to be in the presence of a man abed – beg pardon for sayin' so."

"You are correct, Doctor," I immediately recognized the low velvet of her voice, and my heart leapt with anticipation, "it is not your place. May I remind you that I am mistress in this house, and it is I who will decide what is, or what is not, proper."

"Of course, Miss – beg pardon – but your father…"

"My father is away on the King's business, but he would expect me to treat charitably the man who saved his only daughter from dishonour, would you not think?"

"Certainly Miss, but…"

"And as my father's duty requires him to be away for the foreseeable future, it falls upon me to be both host and hostess. I would not be so unfeeling as to fail to reward him for his bravery."

The man's voice, which I now recognized as that of the doctor who had first treated my injury, asked with a hint of suspicion, "*Reward*, Miss?"

The velvet faltered only slightly, "Did I say reward? Naturally, I meant to say 'thank' him for his noble deed."

"Naturally, Miss, but…"

Just then, there came the briefest of knocks, and the door swung inward revealing the captain's daughter, even more beautiful than I had remembered. Her hair cascading around her shoulders like molten copper, the blue of her eyes competed with its luster, contributing a deep glow of their own, sending the warmth of her gaze across the space between us, instantly filling my breast with the heat of passion.

Her dress was of bluest silk complimenting her eyes, cut low, revealing the smooth whiteness of her budding cleavage. I cannot think how I managed to breathe in her presence.

"But you must think of your..." The doctor entered after her, his protest trailing away at the sight of me...or perhaps he sensed, correctly, that he was no longer being heeded. "Ah, there you are, sir!" he said, changing tack in mid-sentence, "Awake at last I see; and how are you feeling, may I ask?"

He bustled his girth past Elizabeth, and walked importantly to the bed, placing a hand to my forehead with all the dramatic air of an actor upon a stage.

I tried to speak, but my voice was as of yet unrecognizable as my own. All the while conscious of her presence, I was ashamed that she should see me as an invalid.

The doctor removed his hand from my brow, frowning his disapproval.

"A slight fever!" he declared censoriously, as if the fault were mine, then placed his hand upon my wrist.

I tried to speak a second time, but was forestalled.

"Silence, sir!" he admonished with his head tilted to one side, as though listening, "I must have absolute silence! Medical science demands it!"

I meekly did as he bade me, aware of how foolish I must look to her, yet at the same time, tormented by thirst.

"Hmm," he frowned askance at the ceiling, "Pulse is a little weak, but no more than to be expected. You experienced a severe loss of blood, young man!" he accused, much as he had of my fever.

Now Elizabeth spoke for the first time upon entering. "Doctor, for the love of pity, will you not give him water?" Her voice did not rise: the words, spoken in a listless murmur, were like ripples lapping gently on a well-sanded shore.

The doctor frowned, considering, as though this was an extraordinary request. Finally he took his spectacles from the end of his nose, and producing a linen handkerchief from his sleeve, began to polish the lenses, taking great pains in the process.

"Yes," he decided very seriously, "I believe that would be amenable to the patient's recovery. Liquids, sir!" he wagged a finger in my face, stating it as though the idea was originally his own; "You must drink an abundance of liquids to replenish that which you have lost! It is a fact of science, sir!"

In the end it was Elizabeth who poured water into a glass, then came to the bedside, and propping up my head with her arm, tilted it to my lips.

It was nectar, coursing over my tongue, massaging my throat as it washed its way to my stomach. I forgot myself to the point where I seized the glass from her hand, and began to drink greedily.

The doctor immediately snatched it from my grasp, spilling water onto the sheets. His face was a countenance of horror.

"Moderation, sir!" he cried, "Everything in moderation! You have not partaken of liquids for a considerable space of time, and it would go ill for you to receive a surfeit now! The shock to your stomach might well induce vomiting – beg pardon, Miss – and the muscle contractions tear away my sutures!"

Mindful of appearing more ridiculous than ever, I picked weakly at the sodden linen, and found that, to a greater degree, I had discovered my voice at last.

"You spoke of a considerable space of time, Doctor; how long have I been here?"

It was Elizabeth who answered. "Why, you have been with us for three days, sir, in and out of fever."

"And likely to have perished, too!" the doctor interjected, again with a tone that suggested disapproval, "were it not for an obscure passage from Hippocrates, himself – on the cleansing of wounds, sir - and my enlightened attention thereof!"

He seemed about to postulate further, but Elizabeth murmured, "I am very grateful, Doctor." And before he could reply, she turned her attention back to me, "For it gives me the

188

opportunity to say how truly grateful I also am to you, sir. My fate would have been unthinkable but for your intervention."

The doctor, perhaps feeling on the verge of being left out of the conversation, murmured, "Here! Here! A damned fine act, young fellow – beg pardon, Miss – a damned fine act, indeed, sir!"

Although warming in the glow of her gratitude, I could but think: three days had come and gone. Sally must wonder at my disappearance, and be worried half out of her wits.

I struggled to rise, "I must be away!"

A look of dismay crossed Elizabeth's face, while a renewed sense of horror assembled on the doctor's.

"Impossible!" he cried, "Absolutely out of the question! Why you are in no fit state, sir! No fit state at all!"

"Please, sir," Elizabeth murmured. Not yet entreating me with her eyes, she placed a hand upon my arm, instead. "The doctor is correct. You are in no fit state to travel." Then she did look at me, and in that moment I was helpless to deny her anything. "If there is some other you would wish to get word to…" she hesitated almost as though she had become confused; then blushing slightly, she forced herself to press on, "…a wife, or a lover, perhaps, Quinn would be happy to be of service to you?"

Much belatedly, I remembered our passing on the promenade earlier that fateful day – she on the arm of her maid, and I being mangled by that Irish bitch, Tess. It was but a natural conclusion for her to draw – Tess was either my wife or my lover, and no more common woman could be imagined. As for my mother, my mind quailed at the very idea of Quinn knocking at her door with news of my convalescence, and carrying his impressions of my domestic life back to his mistress.

I lay back on the pillow, and though my heart felt ill at ease, I told her, "No, there is no one."

To which the doctor harrumphed sympathetically, while Elizabeth looked demurely down at her hands, blushing ever more fiercely…and assumed a secretive smile.

I spent a further two weeks as a guest under the Captain's roof (or rather, his sister's) or so I was told; for my state of consciousness was but a temporary interlude before the fever returned with a vengeance.

My head became an inferno, trapping my mind in a cauldron of delirium, where reality became intertwined with nightmare, making it impossible to tell one from the other. I was once more in our little shanty, out on Maggoty Cove, in bed with Sally – she wearing a pig's head mask, asking me, "'Oo's bin a good boy, then?" and plunging something into me with such force as would like to tear my insides apart.

"Please, Sally," I groaned, "Don't, you're hurting me!"

"Saints preserve us," now it was Tess's voice coming from behind the mask, "and is this any way for the great Cuchalain to behave? Take it like a man, and then we'll have some grog!"

Then it was the withered old body of Mrs. Dawe, and her voice complaining, "Buggered, by God! Aye, and when it's Mr. Dawe's gelt what's payin' for the time! Surely he would have wanted me to have a turn!"

"It's a whore's bargain, Josiah," *Mariposa's captain* said philosophically. The coarse hair on his chest was matted, and tangled with sweat, the pig's snout bobbing up and down like an obscene phallus as he rutted away at me.

"Stop!" I cried, "I beg of you! Something has torn loose inside, I can feel it!"

"You have ruptured your sutures!" cried the doctor in a voice filled with wrath, "Confound it, sir! My best work undone! This is a serious blow to medical science, sir! A serious blow! Very well, if that is the way of it, I shall prescribe a posit of finely ground pepper…to be administered anally, of course!"

"Poor man," Elizabeth's voice crooned into my ear, "you are suffering horribly! Yet have no fear, for I shall save you!" I felt the weight of her on my chest, holding me down, and the fire was burning along my ribs again, spreading to encompass

190

my entire being, and then I was screaming, and screaming, begging to be allowed to die and have done with it.

I believe that I did die, plunging into utter darkness, choking on sulfur and brimstone, and a dreadful voice growling from out of nowhere, "Go back, whoreson, there's no need of you here!" And then there was a great boom of laughter, taunting me, as I continued to spiral down, until, at last, loss of consciousness allowed a reprieve.

This time when I awoke, it was to find myself staring into her eyes, lines of worry surrounding them, with tears glistening in the corners. Her face hung suspended above me, then as gladsome relief transformed her, slowly, very slowly, it began to descend. Her skin smelled of honey, her hair of lilac, and when, at last, they brushed against my own, her lips were sweetness itself.

Her smile was tremulous when she said, "I bid you welcome, sir, back to the world of the living."

I attempted to answer, but she intervened a finger between our lips, and still smiling, shook her head.

"You have been most ill."

Feeling very weak, in spite of the swelling in my heart, I gestured for water. Understanding, she took a cloth and tenderly sponged my lips.

"Josiah," I told her, once more with an invalid's croak.

She frowned ever so prettily.

"My name."

"Ah!" The frown disappeared, "And I am Elizabeth."

"Yes."

She seemed to come back to herself, reminded of duty unfulfilled.

"Forgive me," she said, "I must summon the doctor."

I shook my head, feeling disinclined for that worthy's bedside manner, yet even less inclined for the spell of the moment to be broken.

"You are beautiful!" I told her.

She laughed and blushed with pleasure, "I am happy that you think so, Josiah." I had never heard my name more wonderfully spoken. Then she gently pulled away. "I must leave you to rest."

"No. Stay."

She frowned ever so prettily, and said, "You must regain your strength."

Somehow I found the boldness to venture, "Another kiss, then."

Her laughter was not of the girlish sort, not giggles tittered behind clenched fingers, but open and as honest as her face.

She shook her head, and said, "For that you must also forgive me. I was curious and selfish, but it would not do to excite you further. Your stitches could open yet again."

Determined, I replied, "I will open them myself if you won't."

This caused her to pause, uncertain, then she laughed again, and acquiesced.

"Very well then, good sir, as a reward for saving my life."

This time her mouth opened, our tongues caressed, briefly, and then, too soon, with her face blushing pink, she was gone, closing the door softly behind her.

However, when I opened my eyes the next morning, she was there again, patiently waiting.

*   *   *

It is said that the young heal quickly, and so it was in my case, although the fortitude required to overcome both the injury and subsequent fever had left me extremely weak for some time after. Indeed, when the doctor unwound the bandages for the final time, and after carefully sniffing at the wound, before declaring it to be free of putrefaction, and satisfactorily healed, I was still scarcely able to rise from my bed. Thus it was that, upon finally being able to do so, it was necessary to lean upon Elizabeth's arm, heavily at first, but less and less so as my strength returned.

"Exercise, sir!" declared the doctor thunderously, as if I were not doing that very thing, "It is exercise that will invigorate the system back to its former robustness! It has been scientifically proven to do so!"

He glared, as if daring me to deny it, but instead I offered him a weary smile, and meekly replied, "Yes, Doctor."

To which he sniffed dismissively, glowered with disapproving frankness at where my hand rested on Elizabeth's arm, and stalked away, harrumphing loudly.

"The good doctor must be feeling even more liverish than normal," I observed.

Elizabeth showed her dimples. "Perchance he is out of sorts with your recovery."

I frowned, for this remark held no logic, so she explained.

"I had decided to hire him for his services, under certain conditions. For in spite of his surly manner, and oftentimes radical approach to medicine, he is still an accomplished physician – better, so I am told, than the governor's own."

"I will not argue the fact," I replied, "for I am a living testament to his skill, and am duly grateful for it."

We had been taking one of our thrice-daily walks through the garden. What had once taken the better part of an hour - and several stops to rest along the way - could now be done in mere minutes. However, we continued on - the grounds being pleasingly private, and the warmth of her touch infinitely more pleasing still.

She took my arm and squeezed it to her. "I am most happy that such is the case," she smiled, "yet now that it is, the need for the doctor's employment is nearing an end."

With a guilty twinge I cried, "I have been blind!" For I had become so entwined with my own world that I had not spared a thought for another, "I cannot allow him to leave unrewarded!"

"Please, Josiah, there is no need," she assured me, "for he has already been well recompensed."

"But to be leaving this house," I protested, "and all its comforts – it must be hard for him. He cannot have much in the world. I gathered as much from our first meeting."

"Not so hard as one might think," said Elizabeth, with a smile curling at the corners of her lovely mouth, "Staying under this roof was one of the conditions which I had imposed upon him."

Incredulous, I asked, "You *imposed* upon him to stay here?" for it hardly seemed likely.

"Of course," she said, "for I wanted him where I could observe his every move."

Still confused, I asked, "Whatever for?"

"The good doctor has a weakness for spirits," she confided, "and I could not have that interfere with your recovery, Josiah. The second condition I required of him was that he should not touch a drop for the duration of your treatment, and to ensure that he kept his word, I locked all of the strong drink in the house away."

I stared, regarding this fascinating creature with an ever deeper respect.

She laughed, hugging my arm to her once more, "So you see, while he may regret leaving the comforts of this house, he will much less regret returning to the tavern with a heavy purse, for I fear that in the time that has passed he has worked up a goodly thirst!"

I stopped, and taking both of her hands in my own, asked, "How can I ever repay you, Elizabeth? You have saved my life!"

To which she bobbed a curtsy, and laughing, replied, "And you have saved mine, Josiah, so we are even on that score."

I did not return the smile when I said, "No, never that."

Her face grew serious as well, when she agreed, "No, never," yet I felt that her meaning was not the same as my own.

Then she brightened, "But if you feel that you must repay me…"

"I do," I told her fervently, "anything at all!"

"Well," she considered, her dimples showing again, "you may kiss me, if you like."

Now it was my turn to laugh, taken well aback, for this was the first opportunity I was given to do so since the day I had woken from my fever. In that time our friendship had blossomed as though it was the most natural thing in the world. It seemed to be mere hours before I felt as if I had known her for the entirety of my life, and possibly lifetimes before. I wondered, by her easy manner in my presence, if she felt the same? As time went on, this notion grew ever stronger, for the first time in my life rendering me (for lack of a better word) happy. But I had no wish to tempt capricious fate, so refrained from reminding her of those brief, exquisite moments, although it was hardly easy to do so. Elizabeth had not spoken of them either, until now, which was proof that they still lingered in her mind.

In gratitude, I lowered my face to hers, but she stopped me with a hand upon my chest.

"Not here," she cautioned, looking about to see if we were alone, then pointed, "Over there, behind the hedge."

So we took a casual stroll, innocence personified, until we were out of sight of the house. At last, satisfied that we were alone, she turned to me, more eagerly than I thought might have been proper for a lady.

Her lips tasted as sweet as the first time, reassuring me that I had not simply imagined such bliss. When I felt her hand curl onto my neck, I was emboldened to embrace her more closely. Our tongues entwined, and I was pressing my lips against her, she pressing back with enthusiasm. I felt her hands creep to the back of my head, pulling me ever closer. I surrendered to the demand, and was soon crushing her body against my own, caressing her breasts with a fevered hand, all the while marveling that she did not resist me.

I felt such a passion as I had never felt before; the need to possess her was becoming nigh impossible to control!

And yet, that is what I did.

Where I found the willpower I cannot say, but when I pulled away, Elizabeth's eyes were glazed, her breath coming in gasps, with colour high on her cheeks. I abruptly turned away, unable to meet her face.

We stood there, awkward, for my part at least, not knowing what to say. The silence stretched on, until it seemed unbearable, when I felt her hand on my arm.

"Josiah?" Her voice was tentative, as if afraid. "What is it? Have I done something wrong?"

I told her, "No," yet it *was* wrong – everything was – even when it felt so incredibly right. At last I looked at her. Her countenance was worried, her eyes searching, darting back and forth on my own. I forced a smile, coaxing her to do the same.

I told her, "We should get back," and added the feeble explanation, "the good doctor might be looking for me."

Relief fought with disappointment for control of her features. "Yes," she agreed, perhaps reluctantly, "we should."

The moment passed, both of us fidgeting uncomfortably in an awkward silence. At length I gave her my arm, and we strolled back to the house together, without any outward sign of what had taken place, except for the colour on our cheeks.

We continued to say very little. At length I pleaded fatigue, to which she apologized overly profusely for having kept me from my rest. We separated in the parlour without another word.

That night at dinner, I announced to her that I felt well enough to return to my own lodgings.

*   *   *

The reason why I had pulled away at that moment was that, to me, Elizabeth was a jewel of incalculable value, one which I would not see compromised in any way. Her honour, which had been purchased at such a dear price by my own person, I felt should not be something so willingly squandered over so base an instinct as lust; and even though I knew that what I felt for her was singular to my experience, I could not convince myself that I was worthy of it, as indeed, I was not.

However I might ruminate on the subject – however I might interject reason with fancy - it always came down to the same conclusion:

I was a whore.

A reminder of this came the very next afternoon, within the hour of Quinn having delivered me to my apartments.

I gazed around the rooms as I walked through the door, leaning slightly on the cane Elizabeth had pressed upon me as a parting gift. They were spacious and clean, and more to the point, furnished. Modestly, perhaps, yet acceptable for a simple bachelor of limited means, even should he aspire to refer to himself as a gentleman. Not that my means were exceedingly limited: thanks to a demand for my talent, I could deceive everyone that I carried with me the air of respectability. Everyone, that is, except one solitary person: try as I might, I could not deceive myself.

While I could be cleansed of the gutter on the outside, such was not so easily attained inwardly. Thus it was that the evening before, when informing Elizabeth of my desire to leave, she had flashed a smile perhaps too brilliant, hastening to assure me that she understood completely. I took elaborate care to keep my eyes on the plate in front of me, for it was more than I could bear to look at her, seeing only the lips which I had soiled. I owed her my life. The best way to repay such a debt, I knew, was to bow out of hers.

Now, having summarily explored my rooms, I sat on the bed, considering upon whether or not to visit Sally, as I knew that she would be beside herself with worry, and I had left all my personal effects there besides. But the mere thought of entering those too-familiar rooms, so weighted with memory, and of seeing my mother again – looking at me the same way as Elizabeth had only this morning at breakfast, could be considered only as a gross parody of all things decent, and was something that I was not yet certain that I could abide.

It was in this frame of mind, as I wrestled with what the best course of action should be taken, that there came a knock upon the door.

I stayed on the bed, annoyed at having my thoughts disturbed, but the knocking continued, becoming ever more persistent. So at last I rose, and taking up my cane, hobbled through the front room to answer it.

Mrs. Dawe stood on the other side of the threshold, as always, dressed from head to toe in black, ostensibly in mourning her deceased husband.

"Why, Isabelle!" I exclaimed, both shaken from my reverie, as well as taken by surprise, for there remained several hours of sunlight in the day.

"Don't you 'Isabelle' me, cully!" she rasped, and was over the threshold like a rat scurrying down a drainpipe.

Once inside, I hurriedly closed the door, and started anew. "Mrs. Dawe, this is indeed a surprise!"

"Aye, I'm sure it is," she croaked, regarding me balefully, then leapt immediately to the attack, "Where have you been, you black-hearted rascal!"

"Why," I stammered, taken aback, "I have been detained!"

"Like as not," she sneered, "in the arms of another, and me half sick with worry, you mealy-livered son of a whore!"

Then she stopped, eyes wide, as she realized what she had just said. Her expression was so comical that I had to smile.

"I cannot attest to my liver," I told her, "but well you know what I am."

At which her expression softened, as it always did, once the initial broadside had been delivered. She held out her arms and I went to her.

"Oh you big black-hearted villain!" she crooned, caressing my hair, "Have you no thought of decency?"

It seemed a bit hard for my ear, for decency had never been our issue. Apparently, the thought occurred to her, too.

"What I mean is...oh hell, I'm not sure, but I've been worried 'til I'm halfway out of my mind!"

Feeling genuinely contrite, I said, "I must apologize, Isabelle, but it was never my intention to cause you injury."

"Wasn't it though?" she moaned, clinging to me, "It would be just like you to want to see me suffer!"

I pulled away, holding her frail little body at arm's length.

"You know that is not so."

At which she closed her eyes, pinching out tears, while she swung a feeble fist against my chest.

"No," she snuffled, "I know that it's not, but, all the same, you do cause my heart injury, Josiah; as the Lord is my witness, you do – more fool *me* for allowing it!"

"I am sorry, Isabelle." The words sounded meager to my ear, yet they were the only ones I could offer.

They must have been found wanting to her own ear as well, for she struggled free of my arms, suddenly fierce once more.

"What you must think of me! To come here in the middle of the day, for all the wagging tongues to see! To the apartments of a whore," she spat, "because I couldn't stay away! Me! A woman of some respect in the community, must risk all because she couldn't stay away from a lowly *whore*!"

I regarded her in silence, knowing that it was intended for her words to wound, and was curiously relieved that they did not.

"Aye!" she said, eyes flashing, "Did I not recognize the coat of arms on the coach that brought you hither! Do you think me simple, or did you simply not care? It's that Broadstreet bitch, isn't it!" She glowered, as dangerous as I had ever seen her. "A fancy piece, I must say, and would not have thought her the sort to reduce herself to your talents!"

Caught unaware, I was stricken at last.

"She is not," I told her, although I fear my expression gave way to my feelings.

Ever mercurial, Isabelle changed yet again; her anger disappeared on the instant, leaving to my eye a woman haggard and old.

She placed a consoling hand upon my arm, saying, "Oh Josiah, lad, did I not tell you to be careful?"

I knew that, this time, her words were kindly intended, yet it was the kindness that succeeded where her wrath had not; for they merely served to confirm what, in my heart, I longed to refute. I felt trapped – indeed, I *was* trapped – the air suffocating, the very walls of the apartment closing in on me.

"What do you want of me, Isabelle?" I asked, more harshly than intended, suddenly wishing for her to leave.

Sadly, she answered, "Well you know the answer to that, Josiah," and stood on her toes to kiss my lips, but I turned my face away.

"You are aware of my rule," I reminded her, still sullen.

"Aye," she whispered sadly, contenting herself with a peck on my cheek, "I'm aware." She sighed, "I may be a foolish old trot, but at least I know how the game is played…at least I know that." So saying, she produced a fine purse - heavy and bulging by the look - and with delicate care, placed it on the table.

And there it was. The choice was mine; yet there never really had been a choice – whether to maintain my troth to Elizabeth (a troth that had never existed – *could* never exist), or to go on with my life, such as it was. There could only be one answer.

I took her by the hand, and without further ado, led her into my new bedroom.

Perhaps I was more vigorous with her than I would normally have been, in spite of my recently healed wound, for there was an anger in me for having the truth thrust in my face yet again, but she uttered not a word of complaint.

Afterward, I lay on the bed - she beside me, her head on my chest, the coarse grey strands of her hair splayed all around.

"You will be careful, Josiah?" she asked in a tremulous whisper, "Promise me you will."

My anger was now spent, leaving in its wake nothing but a vast and bitter emptiness. What did it matter – what did anything matter any longer? So, with my eyes remaining fixed on the ceiling, I lied.

"I promise, Isabelle."

She did not speak further; yet as the room grew darker, I could feel the heat of her tears on my skin.

Chapter Eleven

Daniel had changed.

I had hoped that it might be otherwise. I wanted – needed – to believe that everything that could be done on his behalf had been carried out as only a faithful comrade might do; yet after punishment had been served, such were not the signs emanating from my friend upon his release.

From that day on, his war was not only with the French – it was with all the world, but with none more so than with himself.

Meanwhile, ever since *Monsieur* had come out of Louisbourg, and been so ignominiously sent back in again, events had begun to gain a momentum of their own.

The very next night, after one of their ships had endured a minor strike from our battery on Lighthouse Point, true to form, instead of striking back, the French squadron had abandoned their positions in the harbour and sought refuge so near the fortress that the great two-deckers were left aground at low tide, for all intents and purposes rendering those priceless floating batteries useless for all future operations. To confirm the suspicion, two days later, it was reported that the vast majority of their crews had been seen leaving the ships altogether, presumably to assist in Louisbourg's defence in a way that had eluded them while still afloat. To witness all of those hundreds of guns, and thousands of sailors so effectively taken out of the fight by a battery of never more than *five guns*, manned by no more than fifty of our artillerymen at any one time, raised our spirits in a way that few things ever could.

However, the exuberance of such occasions now appeared to be hopelessly beyond the reach of my friend.

By my reckoning, it was the fifth day of July when I went to meet him at the hospital, where he had been sent, as was customary after undergoing the cat. He had been given a clean bill of health, and was being released for duty. I was to find, however, that his health was limited to the physical; for something had soured in his spirit, until it could no longer follow him into the sunlight; nor would it ever do so again, for as long as I knew him.

I had asked, and for a wonder received, permission to greet him as he emerged early that morning. I wore a smile of welcome, as there was no reason to believe that anything had altered. Daniel had endured his punishment without a murmur, and as the cat had barely succeeded in breaking his skin, and he being fortified with a double ration of spirit, the entire ceremony bore the essence of the anti-climatic, and was over in, perhaps, less than a minute. But the cat affects us all differently, and none more so than the proud. For a lesser man it is possible to bend to the winds of his fate, but I was to learn that for someone like my friend, who could never bring himself to bend, there was only to endure...or to break.

"Hello, Dan," I smiled, offering my hand.

He did not return my smile, nor would he look at me, but instead looked at his feet, or at the horizon, or anywhere that was not at my face. He grunted a reply, while standing with an inexplicable air of awkwardness, with his own hands jammed firm into his pockets.

Registering the darkness of his mood as of small consequence – for I could not yet accept that it could be anything more – I reached out, meaning to take him by the elbow, to lead him from the hospital's grounds, but he angrily jerked away.

I believe that he sensed my shock, yet he did not deign to acknowledge it. Instead he grated, in a voice so savage that I could not credit that it had come from my friend, "I should have killed the bastard!"

I was taken well aback, so could not keep my own voice from faltering when I asked, "What do you mean, Daniel? Who would you kill?"

Although he continued to avoid my eyes, his lip curled into a lupine snarl, and he spat a single word, "Bell!"

It hung in the air, heavy as rain, yet would not descend. Finally, in an effort to disperse it, I laughed and said, "No you don't, neither! Come along, just let be!"

But it would not disperse, as though there was an agent within him, keeping it poised as a barricade, with my friend on one side, and myself on the other.

Finally, concerned, I asked, "Dan, are you well?"

But he would not answer; instead, in a hard-grained voice he said, "Leave me be!" before brusquely inquiring, "What is to be my duty? For I doubt that I have been released for my leisure!"

There it was again, a barrier I knew not how to pierce, and growing ever stronger, ever deeper, as every moment passed. Too late, I could see that all was not well with my friend, yet knew not how to appease him. In that brief instant (which felt not at all brief, in any way imaginable) I reasoned that I could only hope for an improvement with time.

For the past few days, our company had been employed digging entrenchments on Wolfe's new hill, creating the grounds for a strong redoubt into which would be installed yet another battery, capable of harassing both the fortress and whatever was left of *Monsieur's* fleet, and so I told him.

"Then let me to it," he said, and started off, as if impatient to be away. Whether such impatience was reserved solely for the hospital or for myself, I was becoming increasingly unsure.

"We shall go together," I told him, intending to sound light-hearted, but this unanticipated state of affairs had rendered me so uncertain that my simple statement had very nearly been spoken in the interrogative.

Although Daniel did not readily agree to my company, neither did he demure, but kept on without speaking, all the while emanating a coldness that cast a shadow over what should have been a fine day.

I walked beside him, lost in confusion, for it could not be overstated that this person transformed was not what I had expected - rather the opposite. In fact, at the point of greeting him, I had been silently rehearsing a modest protest, expecting him to begin our reunification with a profusion of gratitude for my efforts on his behalf. Others of our company had congratulated my good fortune, and had praised my having the courage to face the general with my request; for I have said earlier that Daniel was popular amongst us all, and many were dismayed by the peril he had come under. So with such heartfelt sentiments coming from others, I did not think it unnatural that the same might be expected from the recipient of my endeavours, and perhaps even unnatural if it were not. Yet my disappointment on my vanity's behalf was but a shadow of my concern on his. With this in mind, the best course of action seemed to be to accede to his wish for privacy, observe him, and hope that his outburst against Bell was but a symptom of a momentary ill-humour.

At length we came to the declivity where the enemy frigate had forced us to retire after chasing their soldiers back into Louisbourg. The *Aréthuse* was still there, prowling back and forth like a wolf in front of a rabbit den, but the declivity she had commanded had now been masked from her guns with an epaulement, fully nine feet high, sixteen feet wide, and, perhaps, a quarter of a mile long, so that our forces might pass through in safety. The effort taken to construct it had been magnificent, often under heavy bombardment, and the material required had been tremendous as well: the vast supply of fascines that we had laboured so mightily to produce back in Halifax had now been seriously depleted, threatening a shortage for our other fortifications yet to be built. Worse, the need for such a daunting structure was often in question, as passage from one side to the other might be accomplished in relative safety by a minor detour.

Be that as it may, as I had been numbered in those of its construction – frantically toiling for days on end, while quaking fear quickly developed an acute sense of timing for dodging the endless cannon fire – I had hoped that Daniel, who had thus far failed to utter another word, would be driven to remark on the impressive result of our efforts. In truth, he did stop for a brief stare, but though I was watching closely, there was no sign of amazement before we continued on, muttering under his breath, which I, although crestfallen, thought better than to question.

The morning was still young by the time we arrived at the redoubt. Work parties swarmed atop the crest of the hill, digging entrenchments here, gun emplacements there, while others struggled with bringing up heavy timbers and fascines. All was conducted under the watchful eye of an officer of engineers who, between shouting orders at some men reinforcing a breastwork, or damning the eyes of some laggards leaning on their shovels, was busily scribbling out drawings on a pad of paper and handing them to various of his staff, before dispatching them to oversee some of the finer points of the work.

The 51st were toiling away on the earthen walls of the main magazine, even as a train of artillerymen were carefully trundling in barrels of gunpowder, stacking them in rows upon raised pallets, covering the whole with tarpaulins as protection against the damp. The walls were already thick, but the engineer declared that he wanted them thicker still, and threatened that the consequences would be dire if the work was not completed by sundown.

Several hands were raised in greeting upon our arrival, but their ready smiles turned to perplexed frowns as Daniel ignored them with the same cold indifference as he had with myself. In any case, they were soon driven back to work under a blistering barrage of invective from a burly sergeant of engineers, or a more toothless version of the same from Bell.

That worthy regarded my friend with black hatred, but thought better than to force an encounter when, upon being glared at in turn, an even darker fury suddenly enlivened Daniel's face. He clenched his fists, and started toward his enemy, cold vengeance written on every feature, but I, who had anticipated such a moment, was quick to react. Taking up a spade from a stack nearby, I stepped in front of him, holding it across his chest, effectively barring his path, but in a manner suggesting, to any watchful eye, that it was only an offer that he take it.

I pleaded under my breath, "Do not do this, Dan, I beg of you!"

"Bastard!" he seethed through his teeth, although he was not speaking to me, nor was he looking at me, but over my shoulder at Bell's fast receding back.

"Take it, you fool!" I urged, willing him to obey me. Had I been more myself, I am sure that he would not have done so, but I do confess that my patience was wearing thin, and it had the effect of injecting a note of command into my voice. "I will not stand here and see everything I have striven for on your behalf undone in a moment of selfish stupidity!"

Daniel had ceased to surge toward the retreating Bell, but 'though I had hoped that my words might sting him into seeing reason at last, I was to be disappointed.

Now Daniel was looking at me, but this man was someone I did not know. His grey eyes were cold and hard as flint, with nothing in them whatever of friendship. They cut through me, sending a chill down my spine, causing the hair under my queue to rise when the corner of his lip slowly curled into a sneer.

"Selfish stupidity is it, Joss? Aye, you'd know much about that, wouldn't you?" Now both lips curled, "You, with all your fancy airs, pretending you're not trash like the rest of us, thinking you know better, thinking you know what it's like to feel the cat, damn your eyes!" Suddenly he leaned into me, so close I could feel his breath on my face. "Well let me tell you something, my so very clever friend, you don't know anything at all!" He rasped the back of his neck with his palm, "It burns! It burns its way into you, tearing at your innards, until it's all you can think of – until it's everything you are! 'Selfish stupidity' you call it!" His lips stretched into a grin, although his eyes never softened, nor did they waver. Then slowly it faded, and he gave a single, swift nod. "Aye, that's your sort!" Then he snatched the shovel from my hands, and stalked away without a backward glance.

I was left standing alone in a state of shock. It was inconceivable that such a fury, as had just been exhibited by my friend, could have grown so quickly and so completely, yet there were no other conclusions to draw.

I knew that the pain of the cat was not the cause, although it most certainly must have stung, even with the drummer holding back the full force of his arm. I had seen Daniel sit calm as you could ask for, whistling softly through his teeth, while the surgeon probed for a ball embedded in his thigh. The wound had been deep – taken in a skirmish with French insurgents near Halifax over the winter – and the surgeon's old hands not steady, and but for a single hiss when the ball was drawn out, he had suffered through the ordeal without a word of complaint. So, no, I could not believe that it was the pain.

What I was beginning to suspect was that it was the ignominy of the punishment that was so difficult to bear.

There was some truth to what Daniel had said, that I affected the language and the manners of my betters. I had hoped that by presuming to be a gentleman, in time it might prove possible to become one in fact as well as fancy. I had succeeded so well in deceiving myself, that when Beaumont had blackmailed me into returning to my old ways, the effect on my spirit had been shattering.

I picked up another shovel for my own use, and began to dig. Being reminded of that time with the captain was still quite painful, and in spite of myself, caused me to glance over to where he was standing at the edge of the excavation with his hands clasped behind his back.

He was staring directly at me. For how long I did not know, but by the way my flesh began to crawl, I judged it to be for some time. His face was pale, and the corners of his mouth drawn into a wan frown. He seemed about to take a step toward me, but perhaps the hostility on my own face made him change his mind. Then one hand emerged from behind his back, half-forming a gesture before stopping, suspended in the air. Then, forlorn, it dropped to his side and he turned away, leaving me to my thoughts.

All was confusion. It was beyond argument that Beaumont was a fine officer, and I would follow him into battle without hesitation, yet I hated him with all my heart. Perhaps it was the same way that Daniel hated Sergeant Bell for, in his mind, having been the cause of his being flogged, and the humiliation which he could not forgive. What I could not fathom, however, was his hostility toward myself.

Just then my struggle with reason was interrupted by a train of artillerymen, aided by a captured yoke of oxen, dragging a heavy mortar on a carriage with over-sized wheels, especially designed for this role back in Halifax. It had been rumoured that today would mark the beginning of this battery's being put into action, and it would seem that this had now been proven to be correct. A whip cracked over the oxen's ears and the men pulled in unison, inching the mortar ever nearer to where a bed had been prepared. The huge wheels on the carriage gouged through the soft earth, leaving twin furrows in their wake for as far as the eye could see. The sun was not yet high, but already the men were red in the face, sweating in their shirtsleeves, while one of the oxen lowed a patient protest. Finally the officer in charge called the procession to a halt, while others began the process of lowering the mortar onto its bed of timbers. One of the beasts blew softly through his nostrils, then arched his back and stooled in the mud, while his companion dozed where it was standing, with half-lidded eyes.

I set the shovel aside, and took up a mattock in its stead – the heavy clay proving abnormally difficult to work. Some yards away, as far as it was possible to be from the rest of us without risk of rebuke, Daniel did the same. He had set aside his coat in the growing heat, and was throwing himself into the work with a determined desperation; already the back of his shirt was even more sodden than those of the labouring artillerymen.

That was when I finally noticed the small red stain on the back of his breeches...and it was growing even as I stared.

Suddenly the air became frigid, as if through some malevolent sorcery we had been transported into the very heart of winter. It was a mighty effort to tear my eyes away from the dismaying sight, but I had to know.

Beaumont was pacing back and forth near where the bombardiers were busily toiling over the half-seated mortar, head down, his face a mask of misery. As I glared, he turned, with the intention of retracing his steps, but then he happened to raise his head.

There must have been something in the way I stared that made him stop and dart his eyes toward Daniel. It was barely more than a glance, but it was sufficient. For mere glance though it may have been, it was one rife with guilt.

His eyes darted back to me, and I held them, making no attempt to hide the fact that I knew, nor did I try to conceal my contempt, and then my only thought was for my friend.

I acted without thinking. Dismissing Beaumont from my thoughts, I took a step toward Daniel, seeking to give him warning, only to be brought up short by the captain of engineers.

"Stop! You there, that man!"

Obedience had been too well drilled into me not to mind the order, though I turned to face him, with a hurried knuckle to my brow, "But sir..."

"Silence!" his face was purple with rage, "How dare you speak! Get back to your duty!" Then, not satisfied with this outburst, he pointed an accusing finger into my face, and said, "Sergeant! Take that man's name and numbah!"

Bell, who had been hovering nearby, could not restrain a vengeful sneer as he took a notepad from his pocket, and lisped through the gap in his teeth, "It will be a pleasure, sir!"

I was frozen where I stood, helpless to go to the aid of my friend, yet before Bell had a chance to put pencil to paper, help came in the most unforeseen quarter imaginable.

"Hold, Sergeant!" Beaumont cried, then turned to the engineer and, giving a brief nod to show his respect, murmured, "A word with you, Captain, if you please."

The engineer blinked his surprise, clearly annoyed at having his order countermanded, but could scarcely refuse Beaumont's request. All eyes were on the two officers – all that is, except for Daniel's and my own.

Daniel had been labouring with his mind at odds with everything and everyone, caught up in the struggle of dealing with his anger, and, yes, with an illogical sense of shame, as I knew only too well. Yet he had not been so lost to the world, that when the captain accosted me, he did not pause to take notice.

The engineer forced a wolfish smile, fooling no one. He returned the nod, and with scarcely any attempt at civility, and with much stiffness said, "Certainly, Captain!" before following Beaumont a short distance aside, all the while fairly twitching with vexation.

Daniel looked from myself to the two officers, and then back to me, clearly wondering, as must all within earshot. Yet when he took note of my expression, he could not fail to understand that his secret was now known, and how I had made that conclusion. His face reddened with embarrassment and anger, which I ignored, but darted my eyes down to were his coat lay at his feet.

"Right, you lot! Back to work!" Sergeant Bell snapped, and it was the sound of spades and mattocks thudding into the ground once more. As I returned to my duty, it was still possible to see from the corner of my eye, without apparent notice from anyone else, Daniel casually pick up his coat (turned inside out, as per King's regulations while on menial duty) and put it on, the tails at the back effectively maintaining his secret from the others.

Meanwhile, over to the side, the two captains had their heads together, their voices low so as not to be overheard. But the engineer was clearly in a fine taking, and at intermittent periods, the task of keeping his voice out of hearing proved beyond his ability. Words and phrases could be discerned: "How dare you, sir!" "Won't have it, d'ye hear!" "Discipline...essential!"

At one point, in order that he might make himself heard, Beaumont's voice also rose.

"…saved the general's life!"

It was not necessary to look up from my labour to know that both men were staring at me.

Uncomfortably subdued, the engineer cleared his throat and grudgingly allowed that, of course, that made all the difference in the world…and thank God the general had been saved!

With that said, the conversation came to a close, apparently, along with the matter of my being put on report. For the remainder of that morning, I worked as hard as I had ever done, for I knew that I had been fortunate, and did not wish to give reason for the engineer to regret his decision. However, had I given the matter the same thought then as I did later, I would have realized that the captain would hardly risk being put under the light of General Wolfe's displeasure by punishing the man who had saved him, but had he known that the outcome of that encounter had seen that same general thundering off, incoherent with rage, and that, in fact, there was good reason to believe that he would have been *pleased* to see me flogged, the morning might well have ended differently.

Both the blessing and the bane of mindless toil is that one's thoughts were free to go where they will. As I swung the mattock, over and over again, to loosen the hard yellow clay, so it was with myself.

My first thoughts were for Daniel, and the outrage that had been inflicted upon him while in containment. It explained his anger, and it also explained his unfettered bitterness, toward even me; for though I had done much to reduce the pain of his ordeal, it was not enough to save him from the very worst. Had I known – had I the least inclination that that damned sodomite, Beaumont, would play the predator with my friend, something could have been done to prevent it, though I knew not what.

Then, suddenly, with a sinking heart, I *did* now, and it became painfully clear.

I had not told Daniel of my own ordeal with Captain Beaumont – the shame had been too great – but he would have been able to make the deduction once the same had been done to him, as my anger and bitterness was similar to his own. He must regard my omission as a betrayal, and perhaps rightly so. If I had satisfied his concern he would have been forewarned. Instead I had acted on the assumption that Beaumont had used me because of my past, and though coerced, had not been compelled physically by others, but had reluctantly surrendered so that my life might be spared. The same could not be said in Daniel's case, as the consequences of his spurning the advance would in no way be similar...unless, of course, he had not been *told* of what had been achieved on his behalf!

The mattock hung, suspended over my head; then, slowly, I lowered it to my side, thinking. Of course! In all likelihood, Beaumont had withheld the information that I had managed to save his life. In collusion with this silence, he would have presented Daniel with the threat of a false sentence (false, yes, but more believable than the truth), which, without a doubt, would have been severe. It would hardly have been necessary to explain how such a flogging was likely to end, for we in the ranks were ever aware of the results of punishment, even more so than would an officer; for as we were constantly under the threat of its being implemented against us, it was in our best interest to be well informed. Brave and proud though Daniel might be, the thought of being flogged to death would have been enough to quail even the stoutest heart; and when told that there might be an alternative, he would have agreed as readily as I. For such was a straw that any drowning man would have grasped.

Was my silence what he had been so angrily referring to, when he had taken my words and turned them against me? Was this what he meant by '*selfish stupidity*'? If so, it was an accusation that I well deserved.

However, although this change in Daniel was quite sufficient to keep my mind occupied, there was one other item that competed for attention, based purely on its defiance of logic, and that was Beaumont himself.

First, there was the impossibility of juxtaposing the merciless sodomite with the man I had heard in tears that evening of my debasement. Equally impossible to contemplate was the pale figure that was even now pacing listlessly, back and forth, seeming to be more spirit than human, exhibiting every air of hopeless contrition. How was it possible for a monster to be hidden in such a person, and why would he come to my aid – I, who he surely must know, hated him with all my heart?

It was to be admitted that there did lie in this an explanation of sorts: he had been watching, and had also seen the evidence of his crime on Daniel's breeches, and guessed at my intention to warn him. It was possible that he had not been helping us, but himself. Once the evidence had been revealed, it would have been inevitable that questions would arise. Although the possibility of anything being proven was by no means guaranteed (for neither of us could testify without drawing disgrace upon ourselves), there would be suspicions as well as talk, and a close scrutiny he could ill afford. It was possible that this was the explanation for why he had acted as he had done, and indeed, there was some logic to it. Yet even though that might well have been part of the reason, there was an indefinable notion within me that it was not all – that he had acted more out of decency rather than self-preservation. It was the decency that I found so at odds with a beast that had shown so effectively that he held neither kindness nor mercy in his heart.

Finally, perhaps the most perplexing of all, was myself. How was it possible that I could hate this man so, and yet give him my allegiance without the least hesitation, or, come to that, animosity? There was always discipline to consider, of course, yet it was not unheard of for hated officers of even the best disciplined troops to be found upon the field after a battle with a bullet in their back. I knew that I was capable of such an action, as I had killed before, but although Beaumont was an enemy if ever there was, to my complete consternation, he also was not.

I recalled the skirmish of this past week, of how I had obeyed without question – yes, because of discipline, but also because I had willingly put my faith in the man, even when I knew of the monstrosities of which he was capable. There had never been any thought of putting a bullet in his back: rather the hatred I felt seemed to be for someone else. What I felt for him, during those moments, was completely the opposite.

I swung the mattock with such force – and such fury – that there was a sharp crack, and the handle snapped in two. Unseeing, I stared at the jagged splinters of hickory in my hands, my breast heaving from the exertion. The mere thought that I could love such a monster had reduced me to a rage that left me trembling with self-loathing.

Angrily, I threw the broken haft to the ground. Still trembling, I did my utmost to ward away the notion, yet it persevered. I looked up and saw him regarding me still, his face a twisted mixture of shame and compassion, as if he were capable of reading my thoughts. The very air between us seemed heavy with unuttered words – words that I had no wish to speak, or to hear. What he had done to me had taken away everything that I had strived so mightily to become. By a single, detestable act he had retrieved a past that was to have remained forgotten, effectively destroying any fanciful notions that I had contrived to build. At that moment of penetration, he had taken away the comforting shroud, and in the unforgiving glare of truth, had revealed to me the person of my reality that I could never escape.

So it was with some relief that I felt the heat of my anger for him reawaken, expelling any further notions as if they had never been. Strangely comforted, I dismissed him from my mind, and picking up my shovel, returned to work.

Come the midday meal, I sought out Daniel, sitting gingerly on a half-finished parapet, chewing on his bread ration, watching with feigned interest as the bombardiers put the finishing touches on the mortar's placement.

He studiously ignored my approach, though he was well aware of it. Instead, without taking his eyes from the artillerymen he took up the pewter mug at his feet and helped himself to a healthy draft.

I decided to forego the formalities.

"Forgive me. I did not know."

Finally satisfied with its placement, the bombardiers where fastening the mortar in place by hammering heavy pins into the timbers, even as others began to roll barrels of powder forward, and still others issued from the magazine, carrying the bombs in their cradles.

Daniel seemed to find the process most interesting, for he refused to take his eyes from the proceedings.

Finally he relented enough to say, "Forgiveness is what you want now, is it, Joss?" He took another swallow of rum before tearing into the loaf with his teeth. He chewed slowly as he watched powder being measured into the mortar's chamber.

"I understand now what you meant by selfish stupidity. I was wrong not to tell you. You were right, it was selfish of me, to remain silent I mean."

He did not speak while considering my words. Slowly, the hardness faded from his face, although it never quite left his eyes.

"It's not something a man wishes to talk about," he allowed grudgingly.

"If I had told you..."

"If you had told me, nothing would have changed. Do you really think I wouldn't have knocked Bell's teeth out for him if I knew what I was in for? They were going to flog me to death, remember? And we saw what a deterrent that was."

Quietly, I told him, "No, they weren't."

Daniel laughed bitterly. "Oh, aye! I know that now, but not beforetime."

"They refused permission for me to visit."

"I figured as much."

"The bastard!" I swore.

An artillery lieutenant rested a foot on the parapet, staring out at the fortress. He raised a brass telescope to his eye, and then took it away again, still staring, while he gauged the range. Finally he turned to a sergeant waiting patiently by one of the bombs, holding a fuse in one hand, and a knife in the other. The lieutenant snapped an order, and the sergeant cut perhaps a quarter of the fuse away, before inserting it in the bomb's touchhole.

"Aye, he's a bastard, all right," Daniel savagely agreed, "with or without his bloody teeth!"

Two artillerymen carried the bomb over to where the mortar crouched, waiting. With great care, they ladled it into the squat ugly snout, before spinning away with their hands over their ears. The sergeant touched a match to the charge, and there was a tremendous explosion, followed by a vast column of smoke racing skyward, only to be carried away by the wind, blanketing the hill behind us in fog.

The bomb soared impossibly high until it was nothing but a speck against the washed blue of the sky. It seemed to rise forever, before lazily rolling into an arc as it plummeted, screaming, toward the city. Then came a mighty flash of smoke and flame, perhaps a hundred feet in the air, and perhaps as many yards from the Dauphin Bastion. Seconds later, the report came to our ears like rolling thunder.

I turned away from the sight to stare at my friend, instead. "You are referring to Sergeant Bell?"

"Of course," he replied, "who else?"

"Why, to Captain Beaumont, naturally!"

Daniel gave a grimace, then nodded as he watched the bombardiers struggle with crowbars, adjusting the range. The lieutenant cursed and told the sergeant to lengthen the fuse by a quarter of an inch.

"I hate him, too, never fear, or I hate who he was when he…" he hesitated, "…when he did what he did!"

Gently, I inquired, "Yet you hate Bell more?"

217

His head snapped around to face me, his eyes burning pits of sulfur.

"It's always been that bastard, right from the beginning! Why, he had to get drunk before he figured himself enough of a man to face me!"

"Yes, but it was Beaumont..."

"Beaumont did what he did," he repeated, this time without wavering, "but he can't help being what he is anymore than you or I being what we are!" He carried on, unaware that I had flushed and looked away in my own turn. "It's Bell who's nothing but pure evil, not because he can't help it, but because he *likes* it!"

Astonished, I could only stare, and marvel that he could, if not *forgive* Captain Beaumont for his transgression, at least make an effort toward understanding him, and succeeding far better than I had myself.

He continued in a hard, grating voice, "It was Bell who came to my cell after I'd been with Beaumont; it was him that told me what you done...how you saved the general and all. He told me with that bloody sneer on his face; then he laughed, and said what a bloody pity it was that I hadn't known sooner! And there was me, lying on the straw, sicker than a dog, unable to defend myself, when he saw fit to continue his taunt by laying into me with his boots until I was nigh unconscious!" I thought that there was no possibility for him to look any more poisonous, but now his face was a picture of pure hatred as he continued with, "But I was still aware enough to see him standing over me, still with that bloody sneer, and unbutton his...and take it out...and *piss* on my face!"

I had known that he had been mistreated, but this was even worse than I had imagined! A rum business to be sure, there was no mistaking that, but neither would any good come from his thirst for revenge, and I told him as much, with all the sympathy I could muster. I argued that it was best to put it from his mind, that time would heal all, and that he would be the better man for it. I continued along the same vein for several more minutes; Daniel heard me out, mostly in silence, but the hardness never left his eyes, and when the call came to return to duty, he seemed more relieved than anything.

Meanwhile, the rest of that day was quite eventful, our redoubt being a major hive of activity, perhaps the greatest anywhere thus far in the siege. More and more guns were brought up, and soon had the range, raking the walls of the fortress, all the way from the Dauphin Bastion to the Citadel, as well as damaging ships in the harbour and setting fires in the town.

The French guns enthusiastically returned our fire, but soon found that they could not easily reach us, as our elevation was too great. All the while rounds from our twenty-four-pounders and mortars continued to sweep the walls of the enemy, and to carry away great slabs of stone and mortar with every hit, sending piles of rubble cascading down into the moat. In time it would be filled, and a practicable breach achieved. Then it would be the turn of the infantry to make our assault. We would put away our shovels, and the desperate work would finally begin.

It was impossible not to be caught up in the excitement, even after Bell ordered us back to work with a withering stream of blasphemy. We reluctantly obeyed, but our hearts continued to grow lighter with every cheer we heard coming from the guns, heralding some small success. As the day wore on, the cheers steadily increased as the gunners' accuracy improved.

My own enthusiasm seemed boundless – so much so that thoughts of Beaumont and Bell, and even Daniel, were put aside when at last the day ended and we were ordered back to camp, whispering amongst ourselves like excited children, while each ventured to anticipate how long *Monsieur* could resist such punishment.

Yet the day had been long, and we over-weary. I sought out my blanket early and fell into a deep sleep at once, awaking hours later to the sound of reveille, and the grey light of dawn.

I stretched and yawned, reluctant to come out from under the warmth of my blanket, but when I noticed that the space across from me where Daniel slept was empty, an unpleasant premonition settled in the pit of my stomach. I was on my feet at once, just as a hue and a cry arose from outside. I stuck my head out through the tent flap, and saw a group of our fellows crowded together a short distance away with their backs to me, talking nervously amongst themselves. I hurried into my coat and rushed outside, fighting to ignore the dread closing over my heart.

I thrust my way through the crowd and was soon standing over the spot where Sergeant Bell lay in a careless sprawl amongst a pool of blood, his eyes staring but sightless, his mouth half open, frozen in a silent cry, revealing the gap where his front teeth had been weeks before. His throat had been sliced from ear to ear, the wound gaping like a laughing mouth, already attracting the attention of early morning flies.

Horrified, I struggled to keep it at bay, but the thought crept into my mind, forcing its way through denial, until, trembling with sorrow, I was left with no other choice but to pay heed:

'Oh Daniel, what have you done?'

Chapter Twelve

A search was launched, and it was soon discovered that a picket (a sound man by all accounts) had reported possibly seeing a shadowy figure making for the fortress shortly before dawn. The morning's roll call revealed that Daniel was the only man in our company unaccounted for.

"That does not prove a thing," I vowed to Stockingsdale when the news came out, "Anyone of us could have committed the murder, even someone from another regiment, or even the French, or a raiding band of Indians!"

Stockingsdale did not reply, for we both knew that I was grasping at straws.

"Why, Bell was the most hated man in the company, a drunkard and a viper who created enemies simply by walking across the parade square! Every one of us had motive to do him in!"

"Aye," Stockingsdale rubbed his chin, "Bell will go unlamented, that's certain; it's doubtful even his own mother would care a fig, provided the bastard ever had one, but you know as well as I, Josiah, that murder is only part of this sorry business."

Crestfallen, I allowed that his argument had weight: for whether or not he was responsible for the sergeant's death, it was incontrovertible that Daniel was absent without leave. Furthermore, inquiries to neighbouring units in the sector had revealed that no other men had gone missing during the night; therefore (barring the picket's shadowy figure not being a French spy) unthinkable though it may be, the possibility that Daniel had deserted to the enemy seemed very real.

Unbidden, a memory resurfaced from the day of the landing – Daniel and I discussing my transgression, and the limited options available to me.

"You could run," Daniel had suggested, indicating the fortress, *"you could run there!"*

The workings of the mind are oftentimes an enigma, yet the consternation I felt over the night's proceedings knew no bounds. Had the question been posed earlier, about the possibility of Daniel turning murderer as well as traitor, I would have thought it a jest in poor taste, but I was now forced to consider precisely those circumstances in all seriousness.

The memory of him from the previous day was the next to reassert itself: the anger, the bitterness, the alienating hostility in his eyes, all indicated a mind that had been pushed past the point of accepting the unacceptable. Given a mind such as Daniel's – so proud and unbending – the wisdom of forcing him to such a degree, of Bell's taunting as he lay injured in body and spirit, must be brought into question. It had been Daniel's spirit that Bell had sought to break, the same spirit that he had always regarded as a threat to his authority; and while he may well have succeeded, the result was that it had rendered Daniel unpredictable, or rather, given the rage he had exhibited at the mere sight of his enemy, very predictable indeed. For now, with the benefit of hindsight, I had to admit that, after having been submitted to such a horrendous train of mortal insults, it was beyond my friend's ability not to react. But was he capable of murder? I had only to visualize a meeting of the two in the dead of night to admit that he was: there was no scene of such a circumstance taking place I could imagine that would leave Bell standing.

It was shear agony for me to reach such a conclusion, for having reached it, I was forced to recall how I had tried to convince him that the best course of action would be to accept what had been done and to put it behind him. I, of all people, should have known that such a course was beyond Daniel's capabilities. That, in turn, caused me to ask myself what I should have told him instead, but received no answer.

As to desertion, once it could be accepted that my friend had been capable of murder, that same set of circumstances would have left him with little choice to act otherwise. There was no recourse to an appeal to authority, for in its twisted form, it was authority that had been his foe; so too, it could be argued, was it my own. The difference being, of course, that I was not the same man as Daniel, and this had been my salvation.

It was my past that had saved me. As much as it had been my intention to let it be forgotten, in the end my acceptance of who I was (bitter and angry though it left me) had allowed my mind to bend to the winds of fortune, and to endure. Daniel had had no such resources to draw upon, and so it was that those same winds had broken him.

I am not suggesting that this was a conclusion that I was able to realize as quickly as it took the time to write it, for it would take many months before I could come to terms with his betrayal; and make no mistake, it was the sting of betrayal, of his having gone over to the enemy, that left the deepest wound. It was not that he had turned his coat against his king that so poisoned me against him, but that he had turned it against his comrades, and even more so, against myself. Of course such had never been the case at the time, not when considered to the degree to which I have just written, but such consideration was a luxury I did not then possess, nor even if I had, would it have been accepted. Regardless of the circumstances, regardless of the evil that had taken place, regardless of the torment that ruled him, the choices that he had made had transgressed the code that ruled a soldier in the ranks.

I do not refer to the discipline that comes from authority, but the deeply seated loyalty we had to one another: that when standing in the face of the enemy, is all there is between a line that will hold and one that will break. It was our unwillingness to falter, even in the face of death, because the comrades on either side of us did not falter. It was our great leveler, where the pettiness that oftentimes existed amongst us was cast aside so that the whole might achieve cohesion. When all was said, the root of the matter was that it was our pillar of strength, and the lack of it was our greatest weakness. In one night's work Daniel had dishonoured that code; indeed, he had cast doubts upon that in which absolute faith is a necessity, and in so doing, had placed himself irrevocably outside the bounds of our sympathy.

I had earlier inferred that he was selfishly stupid, and while I had since reached the conclusion that I was wrong, had now come to see that I was equally right; for it was his pride and selfish stupidity in depriving Bell of his teeth that had removed him from the ranks in the first instance, and on the very eve of battle at that, depleting our numbers at a time when every man must count to his utmost. Now, with this new turn of events, it was impossible to say what the outcome of his absence would mean.

All of this was going through my mind as I joined the others in our next endeavour. Parties had been sent out to comb the area, searching for Daniel, but thankfully I was not included in their number; for such was my confusion that I had no wish to come face to face with him, however unlikely the possibility, because I was by no means sure of what my reaction might be. Instead, duty led me back to the shovel, although this time in a different sector.

Keeping to the heights, we left Wolfe's new battery behind, outflanking the Barachois, circling the town, until we came to a position well to the west, where we met up with units from other divisions, and engineers waiting with instructions for the continuation of an approach: a series of parallels and saps – those great, saw-toothed trenches that were intended to be the means of our closing to the fortress. Painstakingly dug, inch by inch, never in a straight line, but always in a series of serrated angles so as to offer the maximum protection, saps were the time-proven method of attack in siege warfare, from whence, once heavy artillery had affected a practicable breach, the infantry would debouch to take the city.

These particular trenches had been started some weeks earlier, starting at a slight edifice, perhaps a mile from the fortress, known by us as Green Hill. It was a place which our Chief Engineer, Bastide, had chosen as the point for the main thrust toward the Dauphin Bastion, although 'thrust' is, perhaps, not the appropriate word.

In that month's time, progress had been even slower than the usual snail's pace that approaches often took, for worse ground for digging could not be imagined, consisting, it seemed, almost entirely of rocks and bog. Yet Bastide was insistent that this was to be our main effort, in spite of the difficulties, or in spite of the fact that not a single cannon under his command had yet to be fired in anger, let alone to create a breach. Instead, they lingered in the rear, out of effective range, unable to move forward until roads could be built to carry their ponderous weight, and judging by the progress being made in that quarter, looked to remain so for the foreseeable future. All this obstinately in the face of the fact that Wolfe, the most junior of the three brigadiers, had already succeeded in opening a bombardment of the town weeks earlier from artillery placed above the old Royal Battery, and attacking the walls from his new position just the previous day, and had inflicted significant damage. It seemed remarkable that his successes (which at any given time, had been achieved with fewer than two thousand men) continued to be overlooked by his superiors, and were regarded rather as a harassing fire, while hundreds of guns under *their* commands remained silent and useless, and thousands of men expended their energy to so little result. As sick at heart as I was over Daniel's plight, it was not possible to be unaware of the croaking in our ranks, for it had become apparent that our company was to assist in what was generally regarded by the common soldiery as a fool's errand, and were not pleased by the decision. Indeed, Stockingsdale made an effort to illicit some opinion from me on the issue, but when I proved unresponsive, eventually left me to myself.

At the time, it seemed to be the height of madness for Daniel to seek asylum within the walls of the town. Anyone could see that the French were hemmed in, and the noose was growing ever more taut with each successive day. Why then would he choose to place himself in such a trap, which could only delay his capture, and nothing more? At that point, the only conclusion left to the unknown would be whether he

225

should be shot for desertion, or hanged for murder, for there could be no other alternative. It seemed that the only explanation was that his were simply the actions of a desperate mind.

However, once we took up our shovels and proceeded down into the parallel (judging the distance remaining to that thus far achieved) faith in our eventual success began to become shadowed with doubt.

To stay the present course could only succeed in consuming valuable time (weeks, certainly, but more probably months) bringing the point at which a siege could be brought to a successful conclusion perilously close to winter. If the French should prove effective in delaying us further, there would be very little choice but to abandon the field. Given that, although the enemy's ships had been driven close in to the town, the harbour was still denied our fleet; and ignoring Wolfe's successes in favour of supporting the very nearly non-existent efforts of the more senior generals, it would seem that *Monsieur* had reason to take heart. Should the siege be lifted, it could only be viewed as yet another in a long list of defeats. The effect that this would have on our nation's spirits would be incalculable; the notion that some in Whitehall might feel driven to go so far as to sue for an unfavourable peace was not at all out of the question.

Helpless to do otherwise, I sank the blade of my shovel into the ankle-deep mud, wrestling with the suction as it struggled to resist me, and at length, piled my pitiful offering onto other offerings equally as pitiful, slowly forming a protective breastwork from the constant barrage from the fortress.

The purely menial nature of the task demanded that my mind should go elsewhere for sustenance, yet when mine did so, it instantly began to roil around thoughts of Daniel, vainly seeking to pierce through the insoluble problems, serving only to add to my burden. So it was with a tremendous effort of will that I put him aside, only to be confronted by conflicting thoughts of Beaumont, so in confused desperation, my mind escaped where it would, and although hardly less burdensome to my heart, in the end would not be denied...

*   *   *

Sally had aged in the time I had been away. Her hair, never lustrous, now leaned toward grey at the temples, accenting the wrinkles at the corners of her eyes, and around the down-turned edges of her mouth. So too did a shocking loss of weight fail to reveal a show of health, but rather the opposite. Skin hung in fleshless folds from her arms, neck and cheeks, virtually everywhere, sapping the colour from her eyes and the glow of life from her face.

It was the day following the taking of my leave from the Broadstreet home. Heavy in heart, I had walked across town to Sally's as I still had only the clothes upon my back and very little else.

Tess answered when, after some hesitation, I decided to knock on the door; it being necessary to remind myself that this was no longer my home.

Her eyes fluttering wide at the sight of me, she joyously cried, "Gosh and begora! 'Tis himself, and us fearin' he'd gone to the shades!" Then she flung her arms around my neck, and began covering my face with kisses and the rank fumes of rum.

Taken by surprise, I struggled to extricate myself, but the woman was strong, and I may have been struggling there still, had there not come a familiar voice from inside.

"'Oo's at the door, Tess dear?" The words were weak, and somewhat slurred, but had a desirable effect.

Slowly, the Irish girl allowed me to unfold her from my body, until finally she stood before me, with her head bowed, though her hands continued to press against my chest, trembling.

Once more the question issued forth, now impatient, "Tess? Where the bloody 'ell are you, girl?"

Stung into action, she spun her head to the open door, and cried, "Mum! 'Tis the master, your son!" and then, just as swiftly, she spun back to me, green eyes blazing, and

227

whispered, "But I knows better! For sure y'ar the Ramblin' Boy, the Newry Highwayman, and the ghost of the great Cuchalain, all rolled into one!" at which point she swung the door wide, bobbed a curtsy, and in a gladsome voice said, "Please come in, young sir!"

I entered, hat in hand, to find my mother in the condition described, staring, much as had Tess but a moment before. A pot of rum was perched on the arm of her chair, now forgotten. Then with an oath she was on her feet, crossing the room toward me. I rushed to meet her with my arms open wide, for I was stricken with guilt at the sight of her, and could not doubt that it had been on my account; but just as I was about to embrace her, she pulled up short a step away, and with eyes blazing, delivered a massive blow to the side of my face.

Taken by surprise for the second time in as many minutes, my head exploded in a blinding light, and I staggered back, catching my heel on a table leg, and was sent sprawling to the floor.

"Now then, you young villain!" Sally advanced, rolling up her sleeves, her features once more flush with colour. "Where the bloody 'ell 'ave you been, then? Too good to call on yore mother now, is that it? Too good to let 'er know yore awright? Well, my fine young rascal, we shall see about that, won't we?"

Instinctively, I flung up my arms as a means of protection, fully expecting her to savage me further, but by now she had overcome her short burst of fury, and with some effort, regained a modicum of control. Finally, although still struggling to suppress the heat of her passion, she stooped over to help me rise. I allowed her an uncertain hand, yet when I had risen no further than to my knees, she was smothering me in her arms, and once more I suffered my face to be awash with kisses and fumes, although this time there was an addition of tears.

"Ow Josiah!" she sobbed, "My dear, sweet boy! An' 'ere's me thinkin' all along you was dead!"

"I am sorry, Mother," I told her as we assisted one another to our feet, "but I was unavoidably detained."

At which she threw up her hands in misery, crying shrilly, "Detained is it? Ow! My poor boy's bin rotting in the Yellow 'ouse!"

I protested, "No, Sally!" and, eventually, was able to calm her to the point where it was possible to relate my story.

Both women listened, mostly in silence, but as I recounted my struggle with Elizabeth's assailants, Tess suddenly cried, "Pearls before swine!" and with eyes flashing she said, "I can see it all now! You wadin' into those vile ruffians just like the great Cuchalain rushing the hordes of Connacht with nothing but his bare hands!" She would have gone further in her rapture, but Sally bid her be quiet pretty sharp, quailing her to silence, yet she continued to watch me as I carried on with my tale, all too aware of being regarded by eyes naked with adoration.

I was once more interrupted when I told them of my wound, for nothing would do but that Sally, bursting with concern, vowed that she must inspect it immediately. Therefore, wincing with embarrassment, I raised my shirt and did my utmost to appear disinterested while both women closed in for a look.

The scar, once so livid, was now a healthy pink, meandering down the length of my torso, and had been of little bother for days now. Entranced, Tess reached out her hand, I think to caress it, only to have Sally slap it irritably away.

"Oright, enough o'that!" she hissed, as if forbidding the touch of a prized possession.

After an uncomfortable pause, I continued on without further interruption until, feeling the blood rush to my face, I revealed the identity of who it was that I had saved. Sally's hand fluttered to her throat as she gasped, "Ow! My stars!" and when I was finished, regarded me with great shrewdness, while Tess, her bosom heaving with every breath, was ever more worshipful.

At last, her features carefully composed, and in a tone unnaturally casual, Sally bid her, "Tess, dear, why don't you make us all a nice cup of tea, then, eh? There's a good girl."

Clearly, the girl did not wish to be absent from the room, but knew better than to defy my mother. So she dipped her a curtsy and shuffled disconsolately away to the kitchen, leaving the door ajar.

Sally watched her go with a curious mixture of imperious affection, and when we were alone, took me by the arm and led me to the far end of the room.

"She is a good girl," she allowed, "keeps yore old mum company, an is a 'elp around the place, an' don't mind the occasional tipple, every now and then," here she paused to sigh, "but she's a deranged sort when it comes to men, and loses her mind completely when yore name's mentioned, an' you can imagine how often that might be: claimin', all glamorous-like, that you come to her in dreams, only it's not you, but this Coo-mathingy fellow, and that he rogers her silly, night after night, until she's fair besotted," she sniffed, "the bog-trotting slut! Still, you can't expect any better from those people, now can you?"

From the kitchen there came a frightful crash, as if a teacup had just been hurled to the floor.

Sally regarded the kitchen door through narrowed eyes, and with another spiteful sniff, said, "That ort'a keep her mind on her duty!" and then turned back to me, gently pulling me down to a chair. I allowed myself to be seated while she took another opposite me; then taking a moment for composure, she began.

"This Broadstreet girl," she asked, with the sudden return of that shrewd look, "wot's she like, then?"

I was ready for the question, for I knew my mother, yet still I struggled. I longed to tell her that she was the sun and the earth and the stars, and even the very sky itself; that her tears were gentle rain, and her smiles golden rays; that her touch was joy, and her embrace was heaven; but I knew that this would not serve, so I told her, "Why, she is very nice!" Yet in spite of myself, I could not hold her gaze for long.

"Ow," she moaned sadly, caressing my arm with a maternal hand, "just as I thort." She continued to caress, but as I felt nothing carnal in the act, did not pull away. "Do you remember, Josiah, wot I told you about love, when you was just a wee lad?"

"Yes, Sally, of course I do." I murmured uncomfortably, still unable meet her eyes, for it had been on that very same night that my mother had robbed me of my childhood.

"It's evil!" she hissed suddenly, eyes flashing with the violence of a lioness springing from her lair, "It's vile and it's cruel! It's bitter dregs of wine from a foul barrel, that will creep up on you in the guise of the pure and innocent only to…"

Gently as I could, I placed two fingers over her mouth.

"I know, Sally," I told her, struggling to put light in my smile, yet I fear that it was bitter, "I know."

Still unmollified, she flared, "Remember who you are!"

"How can I forget?" I asked, more bitterly than ever. "I am a whore, who is the son of a whore, who is possibly the daughter of a whore before her!"

The caressing hand clamped onto my arm like a claw. Suddenly cold and hard, she said, "Now you just listen to me, my oh-so hoity-toity son! An' you better listen 'ard, if you know wot's good for you!" My eyes came up to challenge her, but I could not stand the ferocity of her gaze for long. "You are wot you are! Ain't no use wishin' it was otherwise, 'cause it ain't! Yes, yore a whore! An' yes, so am I! An' yes, so may well have been my mother - whoever she was – but that's our strength, don't you see?" She was clinging to my arm with both hands now, beseeching me to understand. "Yore 'eart must ever be cold, an' any thoughts of love cast forever away! With talents such as yores, why, you'll 'ave the world at yore feet in no time at all, you'll see! All you 'ave to do is keep yore bleedin' 'ead on straight!"

231

There had been a time when the promise of having the world at my feet had held a great attraction for me, but now, with thoughts of Elizabeth whirling through my mind, what good was any of that if she was not to play a part? I felt trapped between my past and what I longed to be my future, but I could only answer Sally – equally as bitterly, equally as hard, "Yes, Mother, I know!"

Even as ardent as she was, my mother recoiled from my vehemence, only to close in again with a still worried, "Josiah, are you sure?"

I spat, "Yes, of course I am!"

She continued to regard me with doubt, but unwilling to challenge the veracity of the stance I had taken. Finally, thoughtfully, she ventured, "The Broadstreets are gentry. It couldn't 'urt to be on friendly terms with the likes of them." Never one to turn away from the speculation of coin, was Sally.

I gave my head a firm shake, and told her, "No, Mother," and I believe that I meant it…at the time I was almost certain that I did.

*   *   *

Tess accompanied me back to my apartments on Parson's Garden, helping to transport my valuables to my new lodgings, with Sally's stern admonishment to her that that was *all* that was to be transported during the course of her duties.

"I'll 'ave none of yore sluttish ways around my son," she had told her matter-of-factly, yet still with that same possessiveness that I had noted earlier.

Sometime during the course of my packing she had disappeared into her room, later re-emerging with her cheeks garishly rouged and in her finest dress, which hung from her sunken frame like a sack.

Ordinarily bold of face, Tess kept her eyes modestly to the floor, and without the least protestation of being accused of having 'sluttish ways', murmured, "Yes, mum."

For myself, I found the statement a trifle hard – more like a case of the pot calling the kettle black than anything –

but if my mother was aware of the hypocrisy, she kept it well hidden.

All my belongings were packed and waiting at the door – clothing mostly, and books, with here and there the odd trinket that had been a gift from someone or other. There had been a moment of some tension earlier, when I had refused Sally's invitation to stay for dinner. Her possessive tone had returned, and when she approached me with the invitation, placing a hand on my arm, I sensed nothing maternal in the gesture, noting too, that she had doused herself with scent: all the effect of which had me recoiling in discomfort. So I made an excuse that I was anxious to be set up in my new lodgings, although not with much conviction.

Her eyes had hardened, as they often did whenever she could not have her way with me, yet there must have been something equally as cold in my own eyes, for eventually the hardness melted away, and with a resigned sigh and a trembling jowl, she sniffed and said, that if I was of such a mind then she would have Tess lend a hand, as she was a strapping girl and could easily carry as much as I.

Now, as we walked along the street, wending our way through the traffic, I asked how things were set between my mother and her.

"Not so bad," she smiled contentedly, " your mother can be a caution at times, and she's a wee bit miserly with the rum, so she is, but we get along." By being 'a wee bit miserly', no doubt Tess was referring to the fact that strong drink ran not so freely as in a tavern, but I knew that Sally liked company while partaking, and that she partook often, but would insist upon a degree of sobriety from the girl in the performance of her duties.

"And money?"

She flapped a dismissive hand, "Not to worry, young sir. We make enough to get by, an' that was even before the sojers started comin' in."

I took it that she was referring to the military buildup that had begun taking place in our settlement. For months now

233

there had been nothing but the talk of war with our ancient enemy, the French, and these numbers appeared to be the proof in the pudding.

I stopped and stared at her, and to her look of enquiry asked, "'We'? Do you mean to say that *you*...and..." I stammered, not knowing how to proceed further.

Understanding settled onto her ruddy complexion, followed by a snort of laughter. "Faith! An' what would you have me? Sure an' I cleans up after the mess, an' serves the grog, an' tends to other needs as well, but they're such darlin' lads, an' I don't mind thumpin' the mattress with one or two a night. Besides," and the bold look was back in her eyes, challenging me, "how should I not? For who should you say was the more comely of the two?"

If it was possible to preen under the weight of several bales of luggage, she was doing so now, daring me to deny that she was my mother's superior in both looks and figure.

"Sure, an' what young bull would chose an old cow when there's a willin' heifer to hand?"

I could not argue with her logic, nor, overly, with the bovine comparison, in either case. Both had hard years behind them, and 'beauty' was not a word to be used in the same sentence with either of their names. If Tess was correct in her assertion that she was the more desirable of the two, it was only by degrees, and had as much to do with the separation of their years as anything.

She continued to regard me with that same bold stare; the same as she wore whilst bathing in the harbour those few weeks earlier. In truth that had been *all* that she wore.

I could not suppress a smile, and warned her, "Have a care, girl, remember what Sally told you."

She returned the smile, yet dismissed my mother's direction as of little concern. "Sure, and how could she blame me if I was to have a romp with you? For it would be her choice, too, if you'd but let her, so it would!"

Startled, I glanced quickly around to make sure that we had not been overheard. Feeling the blood rushing to my face,

234

I lowered my voice and hissed, "Do you mean to say that she...she...actually *told* you about...that?"

Wearily, Tess rolled her eyes, "Aw! It's tired of hearin' it that I am! For 'tis always 'Josiah this' or 'Josiah that', an' Josiah's wonderful knob, so it is, an' how it never failed to please her to perfection, an' how she yearns for it still! True, 'tis while the poor dear's in her cups, yet 'tis selfish of her to go on so, an' not expect to rouse my curiosity, now isn't it?" Her eyes grew languid as she dipped me a wink, "Not that my curiosity ever needed arousin', you understand."

I was scandalized and could only stare, mute with disbelief that my mother should have so easily disclosed such a thing: yet here was this great Irish sot, giving it the lie by absolutely trumpeting it to the world!

Still hissing, I did my best to glare, and said, "Will you not be quiet!"

She offered me a look of amusement, any sign of the meek and obedient servant long since brushed away. Then she shrugged, and at last was blessedly silent.

We continued on without speaking, leaving each to their own thoughts, until by the time we arrived at my door, I could not help asking, "You do not mind?"

She walked past me over the threshold, and set the packages down with a relieved sigh. I thought that she had not heard me, for she answered not a word until, with one hand massaging her lower back, she straightened up and said, "And how should I mind? I knows what hard times is, do I not? Aye, I've done that an' worse in my time, just to get by," then she looked me full in the face, "An' we all have to get by, now don't we, young sir?" Then, without waiting for a reply (for which I was grateful, as I had none ready to hand) she took a turn around the place spinning on her toes. "Aw, 'tis grand, so it is! So big and so clean!" Then, with all the innocence of a girl, suddenly asked, "And where might you be keepin' the bed?"

I could not help but laugh, although I made no move to show her. Instead, I remained by the door, holding it wider as an invitation for her to leave.

Dejected, her arms fell to her sides as a sullen pout replaced her smile, but she did not disobey. When she reached my side, I pressed a shilling into her hand. Startled, she protested that it was not necessary, but after much arguing, surrendered to my insistence. She stood there a moment, regarding the coin, turning it over and over, expertly, through her fingers.

"Well you know, darlin' man," she whispered, every inch of her wistful sadness and longing, "what a shilling will buy you."

I closed her hand gently around the coin, and said with genuine warmth (for she had refused to judge my mother), "Perhaps it has bought me a friend?"

Still sad, she offered a half-smile while a tear overflowed onto her cheek. Then, suddenly bracing herself, she seemed to gain stature before my very eyes.

"Aye," she said knowingly, "you will not have me now, but you will in the night, so you will - creeping into my room on wings of stealth, as always. The Ramblin' Boy come for his reward!"

"Perhaps," I smiled to indulge her.

"Aw, but you will!" she insisted, "All that I must do is close my eyes, then 'tis *my* will that's to be obeyed, not yours!" and before I could stop her, she darted forward, kissing me full upon the mouth, then was gone, soon lost among the busy traffic of the day.

Chapter Thirteen

I managed to settle into my new lodgings with very little effort, and soon life took on the mask of normalcy. I say 'mask' for all was pretense, and nothing could ever be the same again.

I will admit that it was gratifying to be welcomed back into my world with the open arms (and even more open purses) of a clientele distressed by my mysterious disappearance. Their relief took many forms: everything from an impetuous burst of anger from Sally and Mrs. Dawe, to open joy, as exhibited by Tess, and everything else in between. Some, I suspect, were merely happy for the return of my services, yet I fancy that most had been genuinely concerned for my safety, and made much of the scar across my torso, questioning me in depth about the ordeal. Although I spoke freely about the battle with the ruffians outside the tavern when asked, whenever there was an inquiry as to the identity of the women I had saved, I always pretended ignorance, for reasons which I was not entirely sure.

It was possible, I suppose, that I was protecting Elizabeth's reputation, as it was deemed unseemly for a lady to be found in those parts after nightfall. There would always be those who would appear to accept the explanation - that it was due to her having been so newly arrived and ignorant of the danger - with a wink and a nod, but who would waste little time wagging their tongues to others with a different story of their own making; one that would not see her character go unblemished. Yet I believe that it was also that the very act of speaking her name was a chore to me. My chest would tighten, and my throat constrict until I thought that I must suffocate. Such a reaction could not help but display my feelings, which would only lead to embarrassment for us both.

After a time, when my tale had become well known, interest receded, as will always be the case over such things, and the questions with it. If any still wondered as to the ladies' identities, they kept it to themselves.

So I resumed contributing to society in the only way that I knew, often entertaining in my rooms well into the early hours of the morning as, one by one, gentlemen of some substance, or an ancient dowager, longing for the touch of a man, with nothing to offer in return but her wealth, would steal up to my door and scratch at the panels to be let in, terrified lest they should be seen, yet unable to stay away. All this was carried on with the tacit approval of Mrs. Dawe, who although not enthusiastically supportive, was willing to tolerate the others on the proviso that the relationship was professional…and that she be given every Thursday evening. In turn, I was able to discretely conduct my affairs, and pay a rent that was more than generous on her behalf.

The arrangement suited all parties so well that it could be said, with some degree of truth, that I began to prosper.

I dined out most evenings at one or the other of the town's better taverns: *The Oak* was quite respectable, *The London*, at the top of Hill o' Chips, showed promise as it was frequented by gentlemen from the garrison, but proved to be a disappointment. I was to arrive at the impression that the army regarded St. John's as a dreary backwater, and worse, were subject to the command of the Royal Navy. Consequently, as a rule only the most incorrigible officers were posted there – those given too much to drink and other vices. The result of which was that *The London's* quality of diner was what one might imagine. Undeterred however, I continued to seek out the better establishments, drinking some of the finer wines in their cellars, while conversing with people of varying degrees of gentility. Many, who knew me professionally, were at first nervous of my presence, yet when they saw that I meant no harm, would speak to me without fear of being exposed, for they were by no means singular to my acquaintance. Often there would be men of some influence, who knew me only as a gentleman, and would converse with me on matters of commerce, or politics, or what have you. In time I would be able to venture an opinion upon virtually any subject, and soon became known as someone to be sought out for sound reason and impeccable judgment, one of the results of which was that the gratuities, left later by grateful clients, began to climb steeply; and through it all I hardened my heart as my mother had warned me to do, taking in wealth for honest service, but never affection. For although I prospered, I could by no means say that I was happy nor even content, no matter how much I tried to convince myself that it was otherwise.

For of course Elizabeth still weighed heavily on my mind: the memories of her smile, the clear blue of her eyes, the gentleness of her voice, all radiated within my breast, filling me with a glow as warm as the sun, rising ever higher as I recalled the taste of her lips and the feel of her skin under my hand during that so very brief time, only to grow cold and empty with dismay after a moment's reflection.

She and I were from two different worlds: to entertain any notion that was contrary to this conviction could only bring ruin to us both. I knew it was best to forget her, and I prayed that it might happen; yet such strong emotions did not so easily fade. For hard as my heart was now, and as impervious as I was to others, Elizabeth had already been inside before the doors had slammed shut, and I could not get her out. None was allowed to pass through those portals, not even myself. So it was, that while I appeared a success in every way possible, unhappiness was ever my constant companion.

Such was the state of my life one evening, several months later, after dining at *The Britannia* – across from the naval yard, and therefore well-frequented by officers from that branch of the service. It was a place, I might add, which I found quite amenable to my tastes. For whereas the army chose to see our little settlement as the back-of-beyond, fit only for their most worthless officers, our harbour was strategically situated, and was regarded as an important hub in the navy's chain of possessions, the result of which we were often visited by the finest minds they possessed, and their numbers were by no means few, creating an ambience altogether more pleasing to my mind.

So it was that I was enjoined in conversation with a major of marines that evening. I believe that the topic we were discussing was the likelihood of diplomacy having any effect with the French before hostilities were declared, when the outer door opened, and in walked Captain Broadstreet.

"Don't see that it makes a damned bit of difference if hostilities are declared, or if they are not," the major was saying in his usual quarrelsome tone, "They have already begun! Why, just look at the events this summer past, in the Ohio Valley. That young whipper-snapper, Washington – good god, sir! Are you ill? Why, you look as pale as a ghost!"

In truth, I did feel faint, as the captain stood just inside the door, the empty sleeve of his coat pinned to his breast, while he critically surveyed the room with his piercing blue eyes. It were as if he were still standing on his quarterdeck, searching for signs of lubberly seamanship, and was ready to eradicate it at a moment's notice.

Puzzled, the major naturally followed the direction I was staring, for I was suddenly aware of his satisfied, "Ah! Good evening to you, sir!" and then he was standing, offering the chair next to him. "Would you care to join us? The claret is passable, and the conversation even better!"

The captain's eyes settled on the major, registering instant recognition. The scar on his face bent upwards as he broke into a warm smile. He took a step forward, offering his hand.

"Good to see you, John! Keeping on the leeside of trouble, I hope!" He laughed good-naturedly at his own jest, and gave the major's hand a hearty shake before turning to me, his smile of welcome already half-formed while he waited for the major to make the introductions.

I do not recall rising to my feet, but suddenly I was standing, and offering him a stiff bow.

"Captain Broadstreet," The major gestured grandly toward me, "may I present to you my good friend, young Master Stubb!"

The captain was in the act of offering me his hand, and somehow I was in the act of taking it, when he stopped, a frown wrinkling his brow, reminding me achingly of his daughter.

"'Stubb', did you say?" His voice should have been roughened from years of shouting into the wind, or over the roar of cannon, but it was soft and low, scarcely above a whisper, like velvet caressing my ear. "Not *Josiah* Stubb, surely?" Although there could be no mistaking his urgency, his tone had not risen in inflection.

My mouth opened, but I could not speak, only gape and flounder, helpless as a newborn.

Seemingly cursed to being forever puzzled, the major frowned and said, "Why, the very same. Damn me, sir, are you acquainted?"

Never taking his eyes from me, the captain told him, "Only by reputation, I think." And then to me, taking hold at last, "Allow me to shake your hand, sir! I would deem it a very great honour!"

My voice was not as steady as I would have liked; still, I managed to reply, "The honour is all mine, sir."

We regained our chairs and nothing would do but that the captain should summon the barmaid to bring us their best bottle (no, it didn't matter which, but the very best, d'ye hear!) and turn to the major, who, by now, was eager for an explanation.

"It was the bravest thing ever I heard, John!" the captain's words rushed together like a soft, silken wind, "The very bravest thing!"

Of course the major, all agog, demanded enlightenment, and the captain was happy to oblige.

" The story was told to me by my daughter..."

The major's perpetual frown deepened, "Your daughter? What, d'you mean Elizabeth?"

"Yes, of course Elizabeth. Well you know that I have no other."

"Last I saw of her she was just a wee chit of a girl!"

Patiently the captain replied, "Alas, that is no longer the case; she is a young woman of sixteen years now."

To which the major arched an eyebrow, "Stunner, is she?"

"The very picture of her mother," the captain agreed, his patience coming to an end, "Now, if I may?"

"What's she got to do with young Stubb here?" the major demanded, twitching his chin in my direction, "It all seems damned odd to me!"

The captain paused to retain his composure. "If you will listen, John, I shall tell you." Then he proceeded with the story, which, if in Elizabeth's words, as he claimed, set me up as a hero I would never have recognized, had I not been present at the time.

The major was able to remain silent throughout, but for the odd, "Damn me, sir!" or, "God rot him, he had it coming!" in regard to the second assailant, or, "The finest thing I've ever heard!" with regard to myself, finally grasped my hand, when the captain had finished, and as he had done before him, gasped, "An honour, sir! Be damned if it isn't!"

"When I think…" in the grip of emotion, the captain continued. "When I think of what might have befallen her – my dear sweet Elizabeth," but words failed him, so he took up my hand once more, and said simply, " My dear fellow!" and then again, "My dear, dear fellow! I have been searching for you, ever since returning to port, so that I might offer you my gratitude!"

In a flash of memory, I had a brief glimpse of Sally speculatively saying, *The Broadstreets are gentry…"* And almost felt the thrust from behind as she urged me on, but I was capable only of saying, "Sir, I am grateful that I had the opportunity to be of service, that is all."

"Hear! Hear! Well said, sir!" quoth the major, "Well said, indeed!" not realizing that he was being ignored.

"From this moment forward," the captain continued, his hand enveloping my own - his eyes all but piercing the tempest within me – "my home shall be your home, and all within it shall be yours."

Unthinking, I pulled away from his grasp, and in a whirlwind of confusion, stammered, "Truly, sir, that is not necessary!"

Unfazed by my impropriety, the captain calmly regained my hand, and then assured me, "Nonetheless, young man, it is so." When I failed to respond, he continued on in a somewhat lighter tone, "I am having a dinner engagement, on the morrow evening – a tedious affair perhaps, but necessary, so my people tell me." Then as those blue eyes, reminding me so much of another's, bore into me, he said, "I would be deeply obliged to you, sir, if you would attend as my guest of honour."

The major gasped and gargled, but for once articulated nothing. As for myself, I found I was not much his superior. For in a voice that haunts me still, I bowed and heard myself reply, "Sir, I am at your service."

*   *   *

The hour was late when I let Mrs. Dawe out the door. The weather being clement lately, and as her rheumatism was somewhat in abeyance, she felt it convenient to visit me twice that week. As the *Mariposa* had had to catch the tide, thereby forcing a cancellation of its captain's appointment, I was able to oblige her.

The rooms were dimly lit as she adjusted her dress and put the finishing touches to her wig, yet the colour on her cheeks was plainly visible, outshining the rouge that she had painted on before coming to call. I could not help but reflect that our meetings might be having a beneficial effect for her.

Indeed, Mrs. Dawe seemed in high good spirits when at last she draped her shawl over her head and came to where I waited by the door. I do confess that it was gratifying to see her so, as I fear that I had not been up to my usual service, being distracted as I was.

She paused to cup my cheek in her small, brittle hand. "Oh, but you're a bonny lad!"

"Why thank you, Isabelle," I told her without much thought, "and may I say that you are a bonny lass?" at which she simpered horribly, but only for a moment before those shrewd old eyes suddenly narrowed with concern.

"What is it, boy? Something's wrong!"

Dismayed that I had not been able to conceal my worry from her, I attempted to tell her that it was nothing but the lateness of the hour.

"Don't give me the lie, cully," she snapped impatiently, eyes more narrow than ever, "you're hiding something from me, and I would know what it is!"

It is frequently necessary for a whore to be a liar, and I believe that, at sixteen years, I had succeeded in becoming one of some accomplishment, yet Mrs. Dawe had always been my Achilles heel in that regard, and though I continued in my attempt to dissuade her, she would have none of it, but became more impatient with me by the minute. So at last, perhaps because the hour was becoming exceedingly late, and I sensed that she would not leave uninformed, I told her the truth.

She heard me out in silence, but the colour began to drain from her cheeks, while her lips slowly pressed together, until they formed a single, grim streak across her face.

"What did I tell you?" she grated when I had finished, "Did I not say to have a care?" There was heat coming from her eyes that had little to do with the results of my labour.

Miserably, I told her, "It was unavoidable."

"Aye! *'Unavoidable'*, says you!" she spat, scorching my face with her glare, "But *irresponsible*, says I! You have been reckless, boy! Reckless and stupid!"

"Isabelle!" I cried out in some anguish, "I must protest!"

"'*Protest*' is it?" Her lips scarcely moved when she hissed, "Well *protest* this, my fine young fool! It's your high and mighty airs that was the cause! It was your constantly seeking out the company of your betters, instead of staying in the gutter where you belong! Why, if God had given you the brains of a sheep, you would have seen that it would have come to this one day!"

I could feel the blood rushing to my face as my temper rose.

"The gutter, you say!" I replied stiffly, "May I remind you, *Mrs. Dawe*, that I am no longer the street urchin you once knew!"

"Oh, *aren't* you now?" Her mouth dripped sarcasm, "Aye, you may think that you've risen high," then, with a curt gesture encompassing the comfort of my rooms, she continued to hiss, ever more dangerous, "but make no mistake, boy, this is still the gutter, and you're still the brat you've always been! Nothing will ever change that!" Before the sting of her words had fully settled, she continued in a voice so low and fierce I could hardly credit that it should come from that frail, little figure. "I give you warning: don't forget who gave you all this, and don't forget who could just as easily take it away!"

Ordinarily I would have accepted her rebuke without demur, but there was something in me that was stung by her words, and had roused me to defiance. So there was coldness in my own voice, as I felt the sneer curl onto my lip.

"Yes, you could take it away," I told her, "but you won't, Isabelle; we both know that, do we not? You have an uncommon craving, and it will not go away, even if I do!"

She glared her anger, and I thought that she might fling herself upon me in an effort to claw out my eyes; but eventually, when she made no attempt to deny what I had stated, I saw that the anger was mingled with something that might have been fear.

"Oh you have become hard, Josiah – hard and cruel!" she gasped, unconsciously bringing her hand to her throat, and then in a voice that was more than half pleading, she asked, "What made you so?"

Without flinching, I felt my sneer broaden when I told her, "Why Isabelle, the gutter that you speak of so freely!" and suddenly, feeling the weight of my fatigue descend upon my shoulders as if it were the weight of the world, I said, "I wish you a good evening," and began to close the door on her.

Her eyes registering alarm, she cried, "You will not go tomorrow, Josiah! I forbid it! Promise me that you will stay away!"

The door slammed shut, blocking anything further from my ears.

I longed for sleep, but my spirit was now restless from indecisive anger. Mrs. Dawe was partial to Madeira, and always made sure that I had a bottle or two to hand. Her glass sat on the table, scarcely touched, for she had seemed especially eager this evening. I took it up and tossed back the contents in a single swallow before pouring myself another.

I knew that much of what Isabelle had said was true, but the knowledge had not been sweetened by her flinging it in my face. A rebellion was raging inside me, and would not dissipate until a further two drafts had been consumed.

Finally, I set the glass back on the table, and there I left it. She was right, as always: I had been a fool to think that I could aspire to be someone I was not. It was my vanity that had driven me, but a moment's reflection would have told me that a whore had no business being vain. Pride was a luxury reserved for the privileged classes, its price impossibly high for those living in the gutter – and she had been right about that, too: wherever I went, the gutter would follow.

I resolved to do as I was bidden, and would not attend Captain Broadstreet's dinner after all. At last, sure in my decision, I made my way to the bedroom, feeling the call of sleep as seldom before.

That was when there came a knock on the door – scarcely more than the scratch of a bird.

Thinking that it could only be Isabelle, returned to remonstrate further, I hastened back to answer the summons in order to reassure her that we were in agreement, and so to mend the rift that had grown between us. Words to that effect were already verging on my lips as I grasped the latch and pulled open the door.

But it was not Mrs. Dawe.

Light from the dying embers of the fire spilled out onto the street, revealing a slight figure of a woman standing across from me, cowled in a hooded cloak of rich velvet, the royal blue seeming black where the light failed to reach.

She appeared to be waiting, uncertain how to proceed. In truth, I had no wish to proceed at all: the night having already been long, with more than its share of disappointments, I felt it beyond me to endure any further.

"It is late," I said, doing my best not to speak unkindly, but in my fatigue it was difficult to be sure.

But the figure did not move – apparently unwilling to enter uninvited, yet equally unwilling to leave, as if once arrived, knew not what her next course of action might be.

Curious, I peered into those hooded depths, trying to discern the occupant's features, but its folds were deep, and the shadow deeper still, so I was denied that satisfaction.

"Come back tomorrow," I told her.

Still she did not move, but stood before me as if sculpted from marble, with only a slight tremor in the fringe of her robe to indicate otherwise.

It was the trembling that vanquished my obstinence, and perhaps also the very lateness of the hour that had caused it in the first instance, for I forgot myself so much as to take pity. I opened the door further and stood aside, gesturing her inward. "Very well, come inside; there is nothing to fear."

For another long moment she still refused to move, as if she were a wraith forever doomed to haunt the street outside my home; then suddenly, apparently having reached a decision, she lurched forward, walking past me to the fire, on legs that seemed fashioned of wood. There she took station, still trembling, with her back facing me.

Closing the door behind her, I maintained the distance between us, for newcomers were often nervous, and did not wish to feel threatened.

"May I offer you a refreshment?" I asked, "A glass of wine, perhaps?"

In response, her hands emerged from the cloak as she raised them to her cowl, slowly, as if filled with every reluctance to do so. I could not help but notice that they were white and smooth, not veined or covered in liverish spots, as was usual.

Slowly, ever so hesitantly, the hood began to recede. When I saw the first traces of the rich, red glow of her hair, I could not speak for sheer amazement. When Elizabeth finally turned to face me, it was as though the world had been placed in a trance - so divorced from what was possible, that I was certain I was dreaming.

I passed a hand before my eyes, reeling in confusion, yet when I took it away, she was there still, standing by the fire in the room that doubled as both kitchen and parlour. Her dress was of russet silk, matching her hair, the bodice cut low. A sapphire, fastened tight to her throat with a broad band of ribbon, glimmered in the firelight, twinkling as it bobbed when she swallowed. It twinkled now as she struggled for courage.

Still it was she who was the first to find her voice, as soft and low as I remembered.

Eyes over-bright, she gazed about, taking note of the bed through the open door, before quickly turning away. "Your rooms are as I had imagined."

She stood close by the fire, but her arms were folded over her breasts as if chilled. The sapphire continued to twinkle while I struggled to collect my wits.

The moment grew long until finally she gave a nervous laugh, and said, "Will you not ask me to sit?"

But instead of offering her hospitality, I was at last able to stammer, "Elizabeth, you should not have come!"

"Forgive me," she spoke as if lacking in breath, rushing her words as she continued to embrace herself, "I forced Quinn to show me where you live."

"You should not have come," I repeated, still unconvinced that she had. Perhaps if I touched her, perhaps if I should caress her hair I could believe; but I remained rooted to the spot, overwhelmed with happiness…and wretched with dismay.

"I had to come," the words still rushed and breathless, "Oh Josiah, can you not see? I had to!"

"It is unseemly!"

As a preliminary to answering, she let the cloak slip from her shoulders, and I saw that they were bare – the milk-white of her skin flushed and glowing. "I know," she said, "but you would not come to me. What else was I to do?"

I was gripped by torment, and spoke more harshly than intended.

"Forget about me! Put me from your life!"

She replied simply, "I cannot."

"You must!"

"Never!"

I had to tell her. She was giving me no alternative.

"Elizabeth, all is not as it seems!"

"I know."

I swung toward her in a single, swift motion, seeking out her eyes; but she was already regarding me directly.

"I know," she reaffirmed, her gaze never wavering.

I was cast into ever deeper confusion. I could remember standing at the open door with Isabelle - words exchanged in anger – '*Make no mistake, boy, this is still the gutter, and you're still the brat you always were! Nothing will ever change that!*'

"You saw?"

"Yes, I saw," she kept her eyes riveted on me, "and I heard…every word."

I felt myself wilting under her unflinching gaze, and had to look away. "Then you know everything."

"Dearest Josiah," she chided gently, "I already did."

The heat from the fire was suffocating me. Over in the corner, a mouse tacked its claws on the floorboards, nose twitching, searching for food; while, dimly, out on the street, a horse's hooves clopped along the packed earth as a late night reveller wended his way home.

"You already knew?" I could not believe my ears. "But when...how?"

Sadly, she smiled, "You should never underestimate a woman's curiosity," she told me, "especially if she has means." Then she admitted, "I knew within the week after you left."

I felt naked before her, so many of my secrets revealed, while the heat from the fire grew ever more intense.

I gasped, "How you must despise me!"

Her voice was reflective, "In truth I wanted to, or so I thought." She laughed a bitter laugh, "Although a woman's mind does not always know what it is that she wants!" Then the laughter stopped abruptly when she looked at me. "I wanted to blame you for not being who you seemed. I wanted it to be your fault for your being who you are." Her heels clicked on the floor as she approached me. Her scent was of lilac and roses. Gently, she placed a hand on my arm. "Then through the course of time I realized that none of us are to blame, myself no more than you. All we can change is who we will become."

I pulled my arm away, accusing harshly, "You would not say that, had it been *you* born to the gutter!"

She made no further attempt to come near, yet neither did she retreat. Instead, speaking quietly, she said, "Perhaps you are right, and yet, were not those who assailed my maid and I also from the gutter? You made a *choice,* Josiah! You are still the same man who rescued me!"

"Is that why you came here tonight?" I asked, even then knowing I was being unreasonably bitter, "To tell the guttersnipe what a good boy he's become? Very well, you have said it; now leave!"

But she did not leave, even though I could sense her anxiety return. I could hear it in her voice when, tremulously, she said, "That is not the reason!"

Concerned, I looked at her, already repentant for the violence with which I had spoken.

She stood before me simply as a woman, every gesture a confirmation. Her hands rested at her side, a simple motion drew attention to her dress, the nakedness of her shoulders, and the daring, low cut of her bodice. On that slender throat, the sapphire bobbed like a thing alive as, finally, her nerve faltered and she looked away, whispering, breathless once more:

"You know that is not so!"

No longer forced to suffer her attention, she was now submitting to mine; and as I looked upon her, I realized how impossible it was to do otherwise.

But it was all wrong!

"Then why?" I asked. "Elizabeth, is this out of gratitude? If so, it is not necessary, I assure you!"

With her cheeks well flushed; she spoke into her shoulder, "Not gratitude! Love! You are also the boy who kissed me!"

"One kiss is not love!"

"Is it not?" she asked, then gave an imperceptible shrug, "I have loved you from the moment I first saw you on the pier, upon the day of my arrival."

I felt the heat consuming me; I was sure that she could feel it too, as her shoulders continued to redden, and her lips slightly parted, as if she were struggling for breath.

But nothing had changed...nothing ever could!

"Elizabeth," I told her, my voice trembling from the strain, "I am a *whore*!"

"Say you so, Josiah?" and remarkably she smiled, even as her anxiety grew. Then, hesitantly, she put her hand into a pocket of her dress, and drew out a purse. "I confess that I have little knowledge of such proceedings," she said, and turning to face me, I could see her lower lip trembling. She held up the purse, willing her smile not to falter, and asked, "Is this enough?"

I do not remember dashing it from her hand, but there were her eyes fluttering in startled surprise, and the sound as the purse struck the floor, bursting open, followed by the ringing sound of coins rolling to every corner of the room.

251

Just for an instant we were face to face, both of our breasts heaving, her eyes reflecting the flames from the fire, then my arm dashed around her waist, drawing her to me, and I was crushing my mouth to her lips. She clung to me, as I was clinging to her, overcome with the knowledge that I was holding her, something I had thought never to do again. Now, against every point of reason, I could feel her, and smell her, and taste her as if the intervening weeks had never been...and, surrendering to the madness, so I did.

The sapphire was the first item to go. I longed to kiss the sweetness of her throat, yet it barred my path, so I tore it from her, and flung it I do not know where. Then I was at her shoulders: kissing, nibbling, biting, unaware that she was biting me in turn. All the world was my passion, and no obstacle could be tolerated. There was the rend of fabric, and her dress was laid bare to her waist. With the last vestige of my sanity, I had just enough presence of mind to sweep her up in my arms, and with her still clinging to me, carry her through into the bedroom...

Much later, we lay entwined in the sheets, side by side, drenched in perspiration, staring at – but not seeing - the wooden beams on the ceiling.

"I had no idea!" she gasped, her eyes still unfocused, her stomach still rapidly undulating, as - sobbing now - she repeated to the room at large, "Oh Josiah! Verily, I had no idea!"

Suddenly, she coiled away, with her back to me; her hands clasped to her face in what I thought might be horror. There was a thin trickle of blood tracing across the back of her thigh, and more staining the sheet, yet before I could fully comprehend its meaning, she flung herself onto her back once more, laughing to the ceiling.

"Oh Josiah!" she exulted, "It was *magnificent!*"

Chapter Fourteen

I escorted her all the way to King's Lower Brook shortly thereafter, as there was very little time before the sun arose, and it would not do for her to be recognized on the street, returning at such an uncommon hour with her bodice rent in twain. She had taken incredible risks to come to me, and so had set a whirlwind in motion: whatever that outcome should be, bringing her safely home (for no honest men were yet abroad) was one event, at least, that was still within my power with which I might exercise a degree of control.

In any case, our route was uneventful, and we were able to attain her home without hindrance.

We paused for a moment, outside the hedge which had been the very same place of our last private meeting.

She was radiant, even in the waning moonlight.

"You will come – this evening?" and she once again kissed my lips, which I eagerly returned, "Say you will come!"

"I will come," I told her, even though I was struggling with conflicting emotions. Yet the madness had settled in me, and I was at a loss to say otherwise.

"Promise me!"

"I promise."

"Promise me that you promise!" and then she laughed and kissed me again, long and lingering. "Oh Josiah, my heart trembles at the very mention of your name!" and then, suddenly terribly serious, she demanded, "You *will* come…to dinner? You must! My father thinks highly of you!"

"I will come," I repeated, maintaining as steady a gaze as I was able, "I will be there." Somewhere in the town a cockerel crowed, anticipating the dawn. "Quickly now; you must go!"

She rose on her toes, caressing my mouth with her tongue, and then with a glowing smile she was gone, skipping across the lawn to the door. There came a rattle of a key in the lock and she disappeared from sight, the echo of her laughter dissipating virtually at the same instant as a light came on in the servants' quarters to signal the beginning of a new day.

Relieved for her safety, I now turned for home, my thoughts deeply troubled, yet equally rejoicing. Nothing had changed, I remained a prisoner of my life, and yet, miraculously, *everything* had changed!

What had happened had been wrong in its entirety: it had been wrong of her to come, and equally wrong for me to surrender to her advances. In her naivety, in an amazing act of regard, she had chosen to put my secret aside as of no consequence, believing that we could sail unmolested through the shoals of public sanction simply by ignoring it. Yet I, who knew better, had succumbed to desire. I had been incapable of denying her what she had taken such obvious risks to attain, nor had I been capable of refusing myself when every other instinct had told me that it could only lead to ruin. But my greatest failure lay in that I could not help my burning desire to believe that she was right, and I wrong.

And yet! And yet! I stopped on the street, spinning a pirouette of purest joy.

She *had* come to me! She had cut through the barriers, even the unvarnished truth, with such courage and determination that it was impossible to doubt the depth of her regard! She saw in me a person that Mrs. Dawe and the others never could – not even my own mother, nor even Tess, who worshipped in me someone I plainly was not. It was Elizabeth's vision of who I was that challenged me to see it for myself, so casting a new light on my life, and suddenly making all things seem possible. In that single, brave act a hardened heart had melted under the heat of her passion – under the warmth of her…love.

Startled, I stopped to consider, placing a hand over my mouth, lest inadvertently I spoke the word aloud. Even so much as thinking it was an item of such luxury as not to be considered, like a crown, or travelling to a distant star, and yet here I was.

"I am in love."

I had allowed no more than a whisper to escape, to let it hang in the air, fearful, yet needing to feel how it resonated in my ear. To my great, dawning joy, I, Josiah Stubb, little more than trash from the gutter, who had hitherto believed himself denied access to the greater beauty of the world, discovered that it resonated astonishingly well.

Accordingly I lay back my head, and filling my lungs, emptied them with all my might to the sky:

"I am hopelessly in love!"

Then, laughing, amidst a sudden onslaught of barking dogs, of oaths, curses and catcalls of those suddenly awakened, I ran the remaining distance to my home.

*   *   *

In order to be fair, my mind had put up a token of resistance to the idea of my going to dinner, for it sourly reminded me, that in spite of my foolish joy, the world was still the same, and that all the barriers remained solidly in place. What I was considering, even as I arose, refreshed from a long restful sleep, and began to dress in my finest evening clothes, was surely madness without parallel. I did not disagree, yet continued to make my preparations without hesitation; for cold reasoning and sound judgment were but poor defences against that which ruled my heart, and therefore were easily swept aside as of very little consequence.

So it was, that at eight of the clock that evening (dressed in blue coat and breeches of fine wool, silver buckled shoes, yellow silk waistcoat, white stockings and linen shirt, with ruffles of lace at both throat and cuffs) I knocked upon the broad oak panels of the Broadstreet door with my ebony cane, looking and feeling every inch a gentleman.

The door was answered by a liveried servant. I announced myself, and had the gratification of seeing his welcoming smile before bowing me in with deference. And there was the captain himself come to greet me. I doffed my tricorne, and we exchanged bows before he came forward, smiling, and once again enveloped my hand. A warmer welcome I had never received...save only for one.

"So good of you to come!" he murmured in that soft velvet voice, as if I had done him the greatest of honours, "My daughter is quite beside herself at the expectation of seeing you again!"

I returned his smile with all the warmth that was in me, and replied, "Sir, it can be but a shadow of my own excitement."

He nodded his approval, and I noted, with relief, that he had not deigned to wear a wig, but had his hair clubbed in the back, as was my own. It had not occurred to me until the last instant that I might appear coarse and provincial if not so adorned, yet it would seem that my host was a practical man of modern ideas, which dovetailed nicely with my own.

Without relinquishing my hand, he led me into the dining salon saying, "Come, I would be honoured if you would meet our guests."

We entered side by side, my hand still held prisoner in his grasp.

The dining table, aglitter with candles, silver, cut glass and fine china, was quite beyond anything of my experience; yet what most commanded my attention was that the murmur of conversation stopped abruptly the instant I crossed over the threshold, before suddenly bursting into applause.

Astonished, I could only stare, gaping like a fool!

The gathering was small, a mere four others. The first was a man, generous of girth, and equally flushed of face, and adorned in a monstrous wig that draped to his stomach. His corpulent figure was clothed entirely in gold silk brocade, rendering a light unto himself. His smile was not warm, nor were the black beads of his eyes. His hands came together again and again, as, uncomfortably, I felt anew what it was to be viewed as a commodity – of weight and counterweight, and of a chattel whose worth was yet to be determined.

The second was his entire opposite in physique: tall and thin, nose protruding on an equal scale as to his chin's receding, he was dressed completely in black but for a clerical collar, his smile polite rather than warm, and so too was his applause, as if he were judging my worth also.

The third was the marine major, heartily pounding his hands together, while a ghastly smile took up residence on his red, beefy face, and he thundered, "Bravo!" and, "Here! Here!" at the top of his lungs.

However, even though such a welcome was so agreeable to one so lowly born, it was the fourth guest that most captured my attention. For there, dressed entirely in red silk, with a heavily powdered face and wig (the wig carefully coifed to aspire toward the ceiling, supporting a tiara that matched the priceless necklace at her throat) was Mrs. Dawe.

Her face was a grimacing mask intended as a smile that would not have fooled a child; her applause was far too voluble to be real.

At length, Captain Broadstreet held up his hand, bringing quiet to the room. Such was necessary, as he spoke with that same velvet smoothness, scarcely higher than that of a whisper.

"Gentlemen...and lady," he bowed in deference to Mrs. Dawe, who, in spite of her discomfort at seeing me here, made much of the attention, "may I introduce to all of you this most excellent young man who, by his singular act of bravery, is responsible for my dear Elizabeth's safety on that terrible night of which most of you have heard me speak, and at no small cost to his own health – Mr. Josiah Stubb!"

I stood, blushing furiously, while the gathering broke into further applause, and another bellowed, "Here! Here!" from the major. After which point the captain made the round of introductions, although I remembered not a single name other than those already known to me. The golden man of wide girth, however, I was given to understand was one of our settlement's leading merchants, and he of the clerical collar the local representative of the Church of England. All else was lost to me, even as I murmured polite replies to individual greetings, as Isabelle's presence had unnerved me as much as I had her.

I had known that she commanded some stature, naturally, and given that she was the widow of not only the

257

local magistrate, but also one of the settlement's wealthiest merchants in living memory, perhaps my surprise that her social status rose so high was not warranted, yet she was the last person I expected to see in Captain Broadstreet's dining room, barring my own mother, or indeed, myself.

With my wits scattered to the four winds, when introduced, I could only bow as though I were a machine hinged at the waist, offer her my hand, and with a smile that must surely have seemed utterly as false as her own, cry, "Isabelle! How wonderful to see you again!"

It was only when I saw Mrs. Dawe's eyes grow round with panic, and dart nervous glances left and right, that I realized just how great was my blunder.

Captain Broadstreet's brow knit quizzically when he asked, "Why, are both of you previously acquainted?"

At which point Mrs. Dawe compounded my error by stating rather too quickly, in a shrill nervous voice, "Certainly not!"

The silence was as heavy as it was absolute. The man of gold coughed politely into his lace handkerchief, while the major frowned, first at Isabelle, then at myself, and the reverend made a great show of studying his nails. To deny my acquaintance mere seconds after I had greeted her, not only by name, but by her Christian name (clearly indicating that we were of some intimacy) instead of quelling any further interest, she had succeeded in provoking it to the highest degree. Obviously an explanation was called for, but in my confusion, I was at a loss to give it. Judging by the look of utter horror written upon her face, Mrs. Dawe was as well.

The evening was in imminent danger of coming to ruin before ever it had the opportunity to start, and yet I was helpless in the face of this impending disaster, fearing that both of us were doomed to disgrace, when suddenly, behind me I heard sweet laughter, then:

"Oh Mrs. Dawe!" Elizabeth cried, entering the room, and embracing the older woman affectionately by the arm, "I vow, you are such a stickler for convention!" turning to the captain, she asked, "Is she not, Father?" and then to myself, a warm, "A good evening to you, sir!"

She was more beautiful than ever I had seen her. Without powder, or make-up of any kind, she looked ravishing in a green satin dress, a string of pearls adorning her neck while others depended from her ears. Her hair shone with luster, and was once more done up in ringlets, capturing the eyes of all in the room.

Captain Broadstreet looked from his daughter to Isabelle, uncommitted, before allowing that Mrs. Dawe was a proper lady…if that was what she had intended to imply.

"Precisely, Papa!" Elizabeth smiled impishly, "For she would sooner die than to admit acquaintance to anyone without proper introduction!" She turned back to the elder woman, chucking her arm, "Would you not, my dear?"

Isabelle could only gaze at her, stupefied, the events having quite outpaced her capabilities of comprehension. I, on the other hand, had begun to collect my wits, and with gratitude, took the opening that Elizabeth had shown me.

"Dear Mrs. Dawe," I bowed once more, my face showing red, "forgive my forwardness, I beg of you! My only excuse is that I am overwhelmed by the reception given me by all these good people." I paused to send a warm smile about the room, "It wounds me to see that I have offered offence, unwitting though it was."

"And yet you do know her?" Captain Broadstreet asked, to my relief not as an inquisitor, but more as a bemused observer.

It was Elizabeth who answered for me, and I swear there was a twinkle in her eye when she said, "Only professionally, Father. That is to say, through matters of business."

It was said so innocently, yet Isabelle stared her a dagger, and seemed on the verge of an angry retort. However, her instinct for survival prevailed, and she found herself forced, reluctantly, to agree.

"Indeed," she grated, "Mr. Stubb and I are merely acquainted on a professional basis."

"You are a merchant, sir?" the corpulent man in gold inquired, "Forgive me, but I make it my business to keep myself informed of such things, yet your name has been heretofore unknown to me."

"Only in a manner of speaking, sir," I admitted. "I supply a commodity."

"A very *rare* commodity!" Elizabeth appended, with a touch of colour to her cheeks.

"Indeed!" Isabelle repeated, darting her another glare...to which Elizabeth responded with her sweetest smile.

The major harrumphed. "All sounds damned mysterious to me!" Then realizing in whose company he kept, flushed and bowed. "I beg your pardon, ladies."

"And yet I must agree," quoth the merchant, attempting not to sound over-eager, "perhaps, sir, you could enlighten us as to which commodity you supply?"

"Alas, sir, I must decline," I replied gravely, "For as a purveyor of goods yourself, surely you must understand the value of discretion."

Here the man of the cloth ponderously interjected, with his eyes cast upward to the ceiling, "Great and mysterious are the ways of the Lord, and all of His creation!" and with the good-natured laughter that followed, all tension ceased, bringing the ordeal to a satisfactory conclusion.

As guest of honour, I was seated to the right of my host throughout dinner. Elizabeth, filling the station of hostess in place of her deceased mother, should have sat on the captain's left, but, apparently to the surprise of none but myself, murmured that as the chair to my right would be more convenient to direct the servants, took post there, without the least demure from her father. Instead, he sat in his chair, in spite of his empty sleeve, looking elegant in his uniform of fine broadcloth, bedecked with the gold braid of his rank, and idly fingered his napkin ring, while wearing a secretive half-smile, taking care to look in every direction but our own.

The dinner itself was unremarkable but for the excellent food and warm conversation, and also the warmth of

Elizabeth's hand upon my thigh under the tablecloth. The wine was also decidedly superior, and Isabelle, seated across the table, made abundant use of it, favouring me with sour looks, and Elizabeth with a mixture of pure hatred, covetous envy, and grudging respect. Indeed, by the time dessert was served, she was so under its influence that her wig slipped, spilling her tiara into the *blanc mange*, while the others pretended not to notice.

Shortly after, Elizabeth released my thigh and arose. With a warm smile to myself, and a slightly more worried one to her father (exchanging signals unspoken) she announced that the ladies would retire, leaving the men to their brandy and tobacco.

Two footmen were required to assist Mrs. Dawe to her feet, who in words strongly slurred, announced that she would prefer her carriage instead, then left without bidding her host a good evening…at which he appeared decidedly relieved.

Once both ladies had left, the captain called for brandy, but instead of leading the conversation, taking my arm, he said, "Forgive me, gentlemen, but I would have a word in private with this young man," and led me out of the room by a different door than the ladies had used, leaving the clergyman with a congregation of two, and the mystery of our leaving a topic for discussion.

Although puzzled and not a little worried, I complied with his wish, and followed him down a corridor to another door opening to his study. It would seem that our arrival had been anticipated: the place was well-lit with candles, displaying bookshelves crammed to bursting with leather-bound tomes, comfortable furnishings, and a great desk of polished oak. Resting upon a side table was an ornate model of a two-decker with guns run out, steering under topsails, while above the mantelpiece was hung a heavy sword with a pearl-inlaid hilt; the several nicks in the blade giving testament of much hard service.

The captain poured brandy from a decanter, managing gracefully with only one hand. Then, offering me a glass, there followed a pause while he arranged his thoughts. Finally, he looked at me and asked, "May I call you by your Christian name?"

"Most assuredly, sir," I replied, trying to withhold my surprise; for this was the very first time anyone had troubled themselves to ask such a question.

He nodded, admiring the candlelight through his glass. Then he said, "Josiah, tell me of your family."

I had known it was a question that would be asked of me eventually; the quality of one's family being of the utmost importance in society. Now that the moment had come, I was sorely tempted to lie, yet Captain Broadstreet had treated me with every kindness, and as I admired him, settled for a half-truth instead.

"Sir," I began, forcing my eyes to meet his, even now marveling at how closely they resembled those of his daughter, "I come from humble origins, so humble, I fear, you can scarcely imagine."

I was vastly relieved when he shrugged. "That is not of importance," he said evenly. "Why, I myself was the younger son of a weaver. What matters," he continued, taking me in at a glance, "is that you seem to have made something of yourself. You dress well, your manners are impeccable, and you speak like a gentleman. I take all these as signs in your favour, Josiah, perhaps even more so as your common beginning indicates that the distance you have come is not inconsiderable. But tell me, have you family in St. John's?"

I paused to take breath, for I was about to utter the lie to the half-truth. "Sir, I was raised in an orphanage, they tell me, in London. I came to St. John's as an indentured servant, and those are my earliest recollections."

An expression of pain crossed his face, and his eyes glistened when, in a voice grown husky with sorrow, he said, "Just a child, and to be treated so! Oh Josiah, my boy, you have risen high, indeed!"

I did not reply – I could not – for I was racked with guilt, first from having lied to a man I so respected, and to an equal degree, because this was the second time under this roof that I had denied my mother's existence; but there was no other recourse open to me. The lie was out; there was nothing left but to live it.

However, Captain Broadstreet now changed tack, and with it his mood became lighter, as if the subject gladdened his heart.

"My daughter is the world to me, and is all that I have left of her mother, ever since she died giving birth, all those years ago." He turned away, his finger idly running up and down the rigging on the ship. "I was away when she died; did Elizabeth tell you?"

I replied, "No, sir, she did not," and waited, for there was nothing else I could say.

Grimly the captain nodded, "Duty," he told me, "it has kept me away for long years at a time, and always when I return, I marvel at how much she has changed…how much she has grown, until came the day when I returned to find she was a child no longer, but a beautiful young lady." He paused, his smile growing more whimsical, "It is a wonderful thing to watch your child grow, it is what a parent longs for: to watch as she materializes into this astonishing person, with her own sense of reason and ideas, ready to take her place in the world; yet it is also what we fear, for that day arrives far too soon, with far too little warning."

He sighed heavily, took his hand away from the ship's rigging, and turned once more to face me. "I can sense that Elizabeth will soon spread her wings, and leave this house and my protection. It is a thought that saddens me utterly, yet even greater, it induces fear." Again he paused, as if unsure how to proceed; then with another sigh, choosing his words carefully, he carried on. "In the course of my duty, I have seen much of the world, many things wondrous, yet for every one of beauty, there are ten-fold that are dangerous pitfalls, each capable of ruining the life of the young and unworldly. A parent worries," his smile became rueful, "it is their duty to worry, but even if it were not, it is something which we cannot help. I would fain see Elizabeth safe, and even more, see her happy. It would break a father's heart if it were not so."

Now he pulled himself to his full, impressive height, with his hand tucked carefully behind his back, though his eyes were warm when he looked at me and he said, "I have seen the way you regard my daughter, and I have seen how she looks at you - the very picture of her mother on the day of our wedding - yet even if I had not seen it, she has made her wishes known to me, and I cannot help but approve. If it is no longer to be myself, her choice of protector could not have been more sound than the one who has proven himself so eminently capable of the task."

I felt the heat rise in the room, even as it started to spin, requiring me to lay a steadying hand upon the surface of the desk, while the other passed over my brow.

"What I am trying to say, Josiah," the captain continued, almost shyly, while colour rose on his own cheeks, "is that...should you feel inclined to call on Elizabeth, I shall raise no objection."

*   *   *

I took my leave shortly thereafter, the world continuing to spin as the captain escorted me to the door, and saw me off with yet another warm clasp of my hand. The hour being late, I had thought that Elizabeth must have long since retired, but when a shadow darted out from the side of the house, I knew on the instant that it was she.

I seized her to my breast, still incapable of believing my good fortune. Willingly, she allowed herself to be so embraced.

"Did he tell you?" she asked.

"Yes," I told her, though my voice sounded far away.

"And what did you reply?"

I found myself laughing, even while squeezing her ever closer. "In truth, I know not!"

"But you will come?"

I leaned down, gently taking her chin between thumb and forefinger, turning that lovely face up to my own.

"Most assuredly," I said, with my breast on the very verge of bursting; and then, fulfilling a burning need, I kissed her.

*   *   *

When I arrived at my home there was a light on in the window, no less than what I might have expected. Bracing myself, I opened the door and stepped inside.

There was a purse of gold on the kitchen table; Mrs. Dawe was waiting on the bed, naked, with a glass of Madeira in her hand, and the bottle half-empty beside her.

"Whore!" she leered, "come closer, fer I'za itch what needs scratchin'!" then she chortled at her wit, spilling wine onto the shriveled dugs of her breasts.

Suddenly weary, I told her, "Isabelle, you must leave."

"Come here I say!" she insisted, slapping the mattress, "An' bring yer knob with you!" When I did not move, her face suddenly grew even more ugly as she spat, "So, it's that way, is it? You think that the game's over now do you? Well cully, there's somethin' you best unnerstan' – s'over when I sez s'over!"

"Please," I said, "it is late…"

"Wouldn't listen to me,' she took a long slurp from the glass, "wouldn't stay away from that Broadstreet bitch, would you, not like I told you to. Oh no, not you, my fine d'lectable whore, you thought you knew better'n me, admit it! Well, ducky," she said in a low dangerous growl, "you'll dance to the tune, so now's time t'pay the piper!" She lay back on the bed, cackling like a slattern, and beckoned with a solitary finger.

Grimacing, I asked, "And should I refuse?"

Abruptly, she ceased her laughter, and sat up once again. Then with furtive cunning, she said, "Oh, you don't wanna do that, cully! No, not never! Why, t'would be Queer Street for you, my lad, an' well you knows it, too!" When I still did not move, she pointed out the obvious, "An' then where'd you be, eh? Back to your fat bitch of a mother, I reckon," she gulped

265

some more wine before speculating, "Wunner what that high an' mighty Broadstreet slut'd think of you then, eh?"

"Elizabeth already knows the worst," I informed her, suddenly finding myself fighting to stay awake, "and what is more to the point, she knows about you as well." Now it was my turn to speculate, "I wonder what the town would think if it was known that you were in the habit of visiting the home of such a low person as myself?"

Isabelle gargled her indignation, for if there was one thing of more worth to her than my slavish subjugation, it was her reputation within the town's society.

Eyes suddenly showing fear, she declared, "You wouldn't dare!"

"Oh would I not?" It was a gauntlet thrown at her feet, one that she dare not pick up. Still, she had to try.

"T'would be your own undoing!"

"Isabelle," I answered as patiently as was possible, "you must ask yourself if the undoing of a whore is the equivalent to the disgrace of a lady; one has much farther to fall, you know." I could tell that she had already asked herself that very same question, for it was written on her face, plain as day…as well as the conclusion she had come to.

She glared at me for a long moment, then, remarkably, those hard wrinkled old features collapsed into tears, rendering what had been unbearably plain, into something unbearably ugly. Also remarkably, I thought, she sobbed, "Oh Josiah, you are cruel!"

"Am I?" I asked, mildly surprised, but after a moment's reflection, admitted, "Perhaps you are right, perhaps I am cruel…although I have no wish to be; but if cruelty is the substance required to win back my life, I shall use it without hesitation."

"Your *life*!" she spat at me, suddenly enraged again, "Boy, you'd best get it through yer skull that ye *have* no life – an' the sooner the lesson's learned, the better it'll be! Why yer nuthin' but a fancy-dressed *whore*, subject to the beck and call of yer betters, an' that's all you'll ever be!"

266

Diverting as it was, I could endure the conversation no longer. So I passed a weary hand over my eyes, and said, "I am going to leave for one hour, when I return, I shall expect to find you gone."

So saying, I turned and left without another word, ignoring the taunts she screamed at my back. As promised, I stumbled about in the dark for the stated period of time, too tired to think or indeed, to remember the places where I had been.

When I returned she had gone...and with her the purse that had sat on the table.

*   *   *

I visited Lower King's Brook often after that - every day, in fact every moment that was available. Many times Elizabeth was in the company of her father, and we would talk of worldly affairs: subjects in which I had thought myself well-schooled, yet I was to discover that the captain was quite my superior. Elizabeth herself, far from being the foolish woman that she had so apologetically claimed to be, proved to have a mind that was at least my equal, and did not restrict herself to topics traditionally set aside for the fairer sex, nor was she discouraged from doing so by her sire. Rather, the captain seemed to take pleasure in his daughter's thoughts, as I did myself, placing value on her education, which was as delightful as it was contrary to established form.

As much as I took joy in them, however, usually these times did not last over long, as the captain inevitably claimed to be called away by his duty, and would solemnly excuse himself from the room, leaving Elizabeth and I to plan our day together, with only her maidservant, Sarah, our solitary chaperone.

Yet even this last line of honour's defence was outflanked with ridiculous ease. The Broadstreets possessed a stable, and Sarah did not ride. It was here, after suffering many a tumble that I succeeded in learning the bare rudiments of the art. Elizabeth, who sat a horse very well and rode like a Cossack, could control the most mettlesome charger with ease;

yet she raised no objection, nor thought the less of me, when my own choice would invariably be a gentle, doe-eyed mare of advanced years and girth, who saw greater virtue in placid grazing than exerting herself to a gallop.

I do not doubt that we made a ridiculous spectacle on the streets, to any eye knowledgeable in horseflesh– with her effortlessly curbing a fine Arab stallion, and myself mounted upon a docile creature that some might have reckoned as more suited to a plow, but this was endured with good humour, as the town limits were soon left behind, and the wide open countryside beckoned.

It was during one of these excursions that an event took place which has stayed with me over the years. But what am I saying? It has *all* stayed with me, even though not a day goes by that I try to forget. It is simply that this instance stands well above the others in its clarity, as well as in the fondness of my remembering, and is quite beyond the bounds of my imagination to suppose that it might be otherwise to the end of my days.

We broke into a canter as soon as we reached the Barrens, and the traffic had thinned sufficiently to allow us to proceed with greater haste. Soon we were alone, setting off down Freshwater Road, but when she impatiently quirted her mount to a gallop, I failed to follow suit, as my experience of a canter was already sufficiently terrifying to imagine anything greater, and I was already gripping onto the saddle for dear life.

Elizabeth had raced well ahead before realizing that I had been left behind. Whereupon she reined in, rearing the stallion back on his haunches, and returned at the trot to where I was, if not exactly riding, at least not suffering another tumble. It was a warm August afternoon, and she removed the scarf from her hair, and laughing, shook it free. It struck me that I had never seen anything more beautiful…nor anyone more alive.

"Forgive me, Josiah!" she laughed, tucking her scarf into the front of her riding coat, "I am consumed with impatience!"

There was no need for me to inquire as to the form of her impatience, as she had made her wishes well known the night before.

The captain had excused himself immediately after dinner to work in his study. Sarah had dropped off to sleep in the sitting room within the hour, leaving us alone to discuss idle matters; and when the sound of her snores had become too insufferable and, as the evening was more than usually clement, we decided upon a stroll under the moonlight.

It was all so much of a guise, of course: the ardency of youth seldom slumbers. I, for one, had been keen for this moment ever since arising from my bed that morning. It was always a delight to be in the company of Elizabeth and her father, although the conventions weighed heavily, having her so near (so close as to smell the enticement of her perfume) yet so far away as to be untouchable, and of course it was her touch that I craved. The wonder of that milk-white skin and her beautiful, firm young body, combined with the blissful memory of that night she had come to me, were never far from the forefront of my thoughts. Yet as day followed day, and night followed night, without another such opportunity, I was becoming consumed with frustration. Given the high colour of her cheeks, and the half-parted, wanton twist to her lips whenever we were near (and we were in constant company) it would seem that Elizabeth was of the same mind. Thus it was that the moon was given but scant attention, and we were enthralled with one another before ever reaching the hedges.

I felt her surrender on her lips, willing me to place my hands where I would, and my mouth to consume her amidst the heady aroma of her scent, while her moans urged me ever further. All the while I felt the stars spinning overhead, pulling us toward consummation.

But then, suddenly I was seized by a suffocating constriction in my throat, commanding that I stop, and I was pushing her from me, so violent that we both gasped with surprise at what I had done. We stood for a moment, without speech, eyes flashing, while our breasts heaved, facing one another like adversaries in a ring.

"I am sorry," I told her at last, my thoughts in turmoil, "I cannot, not here...your father..." It was as far as reason would allow me: the close proximity of a kind and gentle man I so admired, it would somehow be as treason, the breaking of a solemn oath. He had entrusted me with his daughter's honour, the first instance that anyone had entrusted me with anything, and his being so near, I felt the gravity of the moment weigh heavy on my shoulders.

Unable to articulate further, I turned in ever greater frustration, with the intention of returning to my home.

"Josiah! Wait!"

The similarity of her own emotions was abundantly clear, the words spoken in a breathless rush.

I stopped, still tormented by opposing wills. She had not moved, perhaps she could not, yet I heard her clearly when she said, in that same, low, breathless whisper, "Tomorrow...we could ride into the country...to the glade." The moon was bright; I could see her eyes, shining with a longing that was close to madness. "That first time...in your room...I cannot stop myself from thinking...from remembering...*please*, I must have more!"

She understood the reason for my reticence, yet her voice was filled with entreaty. Even had it not been, this compromise was all that was needed for my fledgling sense of honour to be vanquished.

"Tomorrow," I answered, "in the glade."

Then she rushed to me, reaching up and pulling my lips down to hers. I felt the heat of her breath as she whispered in my ear:

"Until then!" and she broke away, once more laughing and skipping across the lawn. She reached the door and opened it, her figure stark in silhouette. She laughed again, then blew me a kiss, and cried, "Oh! I cannot wait!" Suddenly the heaviness was gone, and I could laugh also, and blow her a kiss in return. Then I was alone in the night, left to dream about the very next afternoon.

And now it had come.

We rode on, side by side, walking the horses. To the eye of a casual observer, we might appear companionable, and at our ease; yet the Arab was not fooled, and was infected by our excitement, tossing his head, jingling the halter chains, even offering a suggestive whinny to my mare – a suggestion to which that aged dowager showed not the slightest bit of interest in responding.

At last we came to the banks of a Fresh Water Brook, bordering a thicket of brush, and murmuring drowsily in the afternoon sun. Here and there a trout would leap from its surface to catch an unwary fly, droplets of water dancing in the light, then would be gone again with a faint splash, tiny rills eddying outward. It was a secret place of our own.

She was off the Arab in an instant, producing a blanket from her saddlebag while I tethered the horses. Then she was running across the green to where an imposing thicket of pincherries drowsed in the still of the day. Without pause, she swept into the brush with myself hard on her heels, until we burst through into a secretive glade, stumbled upon earlier, on a day when Sarah had accompanied us to pick berries. Neither of us spoke of it then or since, until the previous night, but both had recognized that it was perfect for a tryst, for when Elizabeth finally did mention the place, there had been no need for clarification.

She stopped in the very middle, spreading the blanket upon the soft and heavy loam. I thought that she might suddenly be taken with shyness, but she had shirked off her dress in all eagerness, and was supine in the twinkling of an eye.

I spared a moment to gaze down at her upturned, laughing face, and another to take in the perfection of her body, while her hair splayed over the blanket, outlining her face in its flame.

271

Then I was on the ground beside her, with one arm draped across her stomach. Her hands reached out, fingers curling to the back of my neck.

I was relieved to be freed of last night's burden, and was only now realizing how stupid I had been. The captain was not a fool, yet I thought he would not deny us such moments, perhaps even approve. If evidence was required, I had only to look upon Elizabeth's eagerly smiling face – the most dutiful of daughters lay in my arms with no outward feelings of remorse.

I had thought to kiss her, indeed, had lowered my head to do so, when she forestalled me, the blue of her eyes soft and glowing.

"I love you, Josiah," she told me, "and I shall love you forever and ever!"

Such a feeling welled inside of me that I was helpless to answer. Instead, foolishly, I reached out and picked a flower, and prompted her to giggle as I sprinkled its petals across her breasts. Then suddenly the laughter stopped, and she had both her hands to the sides of my face. I had never seen her look so fierce.

"Nothing shall ever come between us, I swear it!"

Then she pulled me down…and I dwelled with her there, as I had on the night when she first came to me.

Much later we lay still, while the warm summer's sun began to dry the sweat clinging to our skin. Every so often I could feel her shudder…and then again…and yet again, at first with some violence, but every time more receding, like the ripples on a pond, until at last she was still.

I rolled away, and she gasped for air, and then suddenly laughed aloud.

"Oh Josiah!" her laughter was interspersed with more gasps, her lungs demanding a return of what had been so recklessly spent. "I thought…I thought that I must have been mistaken, that the first time could not have been so wonderful, that my memory had been deceiving me, but I was *wrong*!" She turned to me, tenderly cupping my cheek in the palm of her hand, still laughing when she said, "Oh, Josiah, I was so *wonderfully* wrong!" Then, with her laughter subsiding, she curled into me, resting her head upon my shoulder before repeating contentedly, "I swear that I will love you forever and ever, for the rest of my life!"

I lay beside her, but it was Sally's face that swam before my eyes. I was once more a child of thirteen years, and she was lecturing me on the evils of love; I could even hear the coarse, tobacco-ridden rasp of her voice – '*There are those wot would steal your 'eart, an' use it against you when you least expect it! That is love, my son, an' it is wicked and terrible!*'

They had ever been words that I had lived by, and could not, in truth, say that I had not prospered by them. However, it was not until that moment that I finally understood the full depth of their meaning. This girl beside me held my heart in her hand, it was useless to deny it, and should she so desire, she could dash it to pieces, utterly destroy me, and I would be helpless to oppose her. The power she held over me was like that of a goddess, and so, thrusting Sally's vision from my mind, like a goddess I worshipped her, and whispered:

"And I love you."

Dearest Elizabeth.

Chapter Fifteen

The work on the parallel had been proceeding at its usual snail's pace in the uncooperative ground. Let it not be said that it was due to lack of effort, however, for we worked, ate and slept in that trench, burrowing like moles, one shovelful at a time, each day a reminder that in the end such a desperate effort might not be enough. It was the ninth day of July, and it was even odds that our main attack would be launched before the onset of winter.

That being said, however, in other areas events were far more satisfying: the battery on Wolfe's hill continued to cause significant damage, from the Dauphin Gate to the King's Bastion, striking guns from their mountings and forcing the defenders to seek shelter. Mortars and howitzers had taken to bombarding the town, draining *Monsieur's* will to resist, and it is said that another battery had finally driven the *Aréthuse* from her moorings, where she had hitherto commanded the roads.

On the very first day of our arrival at the parallel, a truce had been called by a party of the enemy, smartly dressed in white and gold, with ostrich plumes in their hats. Word went round our ranks that one of them was Drucour, the French commander, although it was not possible to be certain.

It was said that the delegation had come to complain that a bomb had struck their hospital, killing a surgeon and wounding others. General Amherst suggested placing their sick and wounded on one of their ships and sailing further up the harbour, out of the line of fire, or to place itself amongst our fleet to heighten its safety. The meeting ended without a conclusion however, for as useless as they had proven to be up until this point, *Monsieur* appeared reluctant to give up one of his few remaining ships for the mere purpose of saving lives. So the truce ended inconclusively, and the bombardment continued.

Now, as we toiled away, with the dull 'thump' of cannonballs from the fortress striking the earthworks we had just thrown up the night before, the plight of those within the walls made me think of Daniel, and I wondered how he fared. He must know that his life was forfeit should the fortunes of war go against him, for there could be no escape, not for him, nor for any of the others who had thought fit to desert our ranks. His Majesty would seek his revenge.

The thought rendered me sick to my heart, not for the faceless others, but for the man who had become my close companion even before the day I had first walked into barracks. Try as I might, I could not reconcile that laughing, friendly face with that of a murderer, even though I knew it to be true, and that his motive had been so dire as to unsettle any man's brain – anyone, that is, except for those who were most hardened to the darker side of the world. There might be some who would suggest that all soldiers were made from this mould, but they would be wrong. For the ranks were filled with all sorts: high and low, from every walk of life, and for whatever reason: we were people – neighbours and friends, sons and fathers - nothing more, nothing less.

Just then my thoughts were interrupted when Company Sergeant Major Balfur cried, "Stubb!"

Immediately, I grounded my spade, coming to attention in my shirtsleeves.

"Sergeant Major!"

Ever since his death, Balfur had assumed Bell's duties along with his own, and while the lads knew him as a likeable sort, it was thought best to keep on his good side, for his tongue was quite capable of cutting equally as deep as the cat.

Unhurried, he walked up to me, making a great show of inspecting my appearance. Finally he said, "You're out of uniform, Stubb!" pointedly ignoring the fact that several hundred of my comrades were similarly attired.

Mystified, but with eyes front, I explained, "Fatigue duty, Sergeant Major! King's Regulations state…"

"So you would quote King's Regulations to me, would you?" he interrupted in a mild tone – one we knew that could

275

turn cold as ice in a heartbeat. "There are some who might consider that as insolence."

There came a great 'wump' from the other side of the earthworks as a ball from the fortress struck home, sending torrents of clay and soil tumbling into the trench, undoing hours of backbreaking toil. Ordinarily this would have been sufficient cause for much soldierly cursing and invective flung toward the enemy, but now the workings were silent. Not a man had ducked or even winced. The counter bombardment went unnoticed as I felt all eyes upon myself.

I was perplexed, and could think of nothing to say in reply. Indeed, I thought it best not to do so at any rate.

Meanwhile, Balfur warmed to the subject he had chosen.

"You think you're high and mighty, don't you Stubb?"

Surprised, I could only stammer, "No, Sergeant Major!"

"Better than the rest of us in the common herd?"

To which I immediately repeated, "*No,* Sergeant Major!" with all the emphasis that I dared.

All of which Balfur summarily ignored. Instead, with his lip curling into a sneer, he continued, "You believe that you have friends in high places, don't you? You believe that they will somehow help you with a leg up, isn't that so?"

I could feel my legs trembling, and although I knew not what the nature was of my transgression, nor the reason for such extraordinary accusations, I could feel it all suspended above my head, like a violent storm, poised to descend and destroy me. Fearful, I looked into the sergeant's eyes, seeking a kernel of what was to be my fate. Yet his face remained as unreadable as granite, suspending my doom for a moment longer…and then, with an, "I expect you're right!" broke into a broad grin, and tossed something against my chest.

Instinctively, my hand clutched at the object; then after delivering an enquiring look for an explanation, and receiving none, stared down to see for myself.

Entwined in my fingers was a swatch of silver-gilt lace.

I looked from it to him, uncomprehending.

Balfur winked, and his face suddenly wreathed into a warm smile. "As soon as you sew that on your cuffs, perhaps I shall be allowed to return to my proper duties, and leave you to make a balls-up of this lot," and then he was shaking my hand, "Let me be the first to congratulate you, Sergeant. In my view there could have been no finer choice."

Stupidly, I wondered to myself, as comrades came to offer similar congratulations:

'Sergeant? But how? Why?'

But before any meaning could be properly absorbed, Balfur lowered his head, whispering, so as not to be overheard, "There is one other thing."

I could only gape at him, hopelessly out of my depth.

"The captain wishes to see you."

Slowly, as the implication dawned on me, my blood began to run cold.

Why? Why at this very instant? Why, when the last he had spoken directly to me had been in a cabin, upon ground newly taken, after he had buggered me? 'Get out!' he had said, as if speaking to something unspeakably low, like dirt...or a whore. Since that time there had been confusing and inexplicable looks of what could have been sorrowful entreaty from his side, and those of naked hatred from mine. Compounded with that were the sins that had been done to Daniel, and all that had followed. If ever I were in the presence of an enemy, it would be on the moment when he and I stood face to face...and now Balfur was telling me that the moment was at hand.

So much had happened so quickly, and with so little warning. Only moments earlier there had been the monotonous work in the trench, endless toil with mattock and spade, day after grueling day. Now I was being told that I had been promoted, and there was not the time to wonder if it was even an advancement that I desired, before being summoned into the presence of my enemy. I could not recall ever feeling less prepared.

Balfur cleared his throat, and murmured, "The captain said at once, Josiah." Ever the sharp one, Balfur had sensed early on that there was something between Beaumont and myself, and although he had never asked, was considerate enough to understand that I would not welcome the news. Yet in truth, there was little that I could do but gird myself as best I could, and obey the command, hoping that I was equal to the task.

I found Beaumont a short distance to the rear. There was little enough to keep officers occupied on work details, but the captain had managed to make himself useful supervising a party placing fascines to fill in a ditch. Still, the men were working lively, and there was little for him to do but pace up and down, with his hands clasped behind his back in a manner that had become familiar to us all. He appeared deep in thought, the corners of his mouth drawn into a frown, and lines of worry creasing his brow. He did not witness my approach, so stopped short with surprise when I came to attention, snapped a salute, and announced myself.

"Private Stubb reporting as ordered, sir!"

He unclasped his hands long enough to pass one of them over his brow. He seemed momentarily confused, but with a visible effort soon managed to bring his mind back to the present.

"Ah yes, Stubb," and then, with the barest wisp of a smile, murmured in that soft, cultured voice, "Although I believe that it is 'Private' no longer, is it? I offer you my congratulations."

I remained at attention, eyes front, with my face set in a mask, and made no reply. It must have been no more than what he expected of me, for there was but a short interval before he continued.

"I have summoned you to inform you that this was not my decision."

I flinched, ever so slightly. So much had happened in so little time that it had yet to occur to me to wonder who it was that had authorized my promotion. Nor had I considered the

278

unlikelihood of one ever being presented to me in the first place; a fact that was confirmed a moment later.

Glancing briefly to left and right, in order to be sure that there was no one in close proximity, he lowered his voice still further, until it was very nearly a whisper. "You must know that I would be the last man on earth to approve something that would put you so much in my company."

Over at the ditch, two men struggled up to the lip, rolling an over-sized fascine before them. Reaching the edge, they toppled it in without ceremony, cursing under their breath as they wiped the sweat from their foreheads on the dirt-encrusted sleeves of their shirts. One of them looked over incuriously to where the captain was addressing a common soldier. Perhaps he wondered briefly what on earth an officer would have to say to an enlisted man; probably he would have thought that I was an especially egregious disciplinary case that required a proper dressing down by his commander. Whatever the reason, his interest was fleeting, as he turned and walked away without ever a backward glance.

Still at attention, I rasped, "Permission to speak, sir."

"Yes, of course, by all means," Beaumont replied courteously, although he sounded cautious, as if he were bracing himself for what might come.

"I respectfully decline the promotion, sir."

There followed a long astonished silence. Even the sound of the cannon became muted, as if more distant than reality suggested. Somewhere out of my line of sight, a sergeant barked out the cadence to men hauling on ropes, sweating, as they pulled the ponderous weight of a gun across the uneven ground. It was a heavy silence, heavy and cold at the same instant.

Then the captain laughed, but there was very little humour in it.

"I fear you cannot," he said, explaining, "It came from the general himself!"

My face still a mask, I allowed myself a moment to absorb this information. So the general was still insisting on meddling with my life! It beggared belief! The last I had seen of him, he had just finished berating me in front of the army for my appeal for leniency on Daniel's behalf; much good it had done me in the end, too. Now Bell was dead, and Daniel might well follow, in spite of all that I had exerted for it to be otherwise.

"I must insist, sir."

The captain gasped his astonishment. "You will do nothing of the sort, is that clear! It is unthinkable for you to decline such an honour, simply unheard of!" then he continued, his tone more conciliatory, "Now see here, Stubb, I know that it will be difficult, after…after what has happened, but you must see reason, man! It will not be as bad as all that, you know. We will be able to get on, I should think." Then, uttering another short bark of laughter, he exclaimed, "Why, if the general should hear that you…" Suddenly Beaumont stopped; for a brief instant his face showed fear, and then it was gone, but it was all that was required to enable me to come to an understanding.

"He will want to know why, won't he, sir?" I asked, feeling new energy growing within me. "He will start asking questions, and the more he asks, the more he will unearth about what you and Sergeant Bell, and the rest of the scum have been doing to the men under your care!"

I felt the energy continue to grow, even as I saw it wane in him. Naked fear possessed him now, fear of exposure and disgrace, for without question there would be a scandal. He would be ruined, certainly ejected from the army, possibly even disowned and imprisoned. There would be no place left for him, no family…nothing at all.

Casually, I put my hand in my pocket and pulled out the handful of lace. Without a word, I tossed it to the ground at his feet. Then, without waiting to be dismissed, I turned on my heel and walked away.

*   *   *

It was our company's turn in the rotation to stand picket duty that night. I had drawn the first watch, alone in the dark,

280

far from the comfort of the cheerful fire that my comrades sat around even as I stared nervously at the shadows, wondering if each was a rock, or a bush, or an Indian bent upon relieving me of my scalp. I gripped my musket across my chest, bayonet already fixed, and not for the first time checked the priming in the pan.

I had been left to myself upon my return from speaking to Beaumont. To be sure, to begin with there had been frowns and sidelong glances, enough to make my skin twitch; but when I failed to sew the lace to my cuffs, the looks became interchanged amongst themselves, inevitably followed by indifferent shrugs before life carried on in the same old way.

Now, as I strained my ears, translating the slightest sound into the stealthy approach of boots or moccasins stealing upon me in the darkness – there was much that I would have given for the company of a friend.

A twig snapped from close behind me. Quick as lightning, I spun on my heel, pulling back on the hammer while raising my musket to my shoulder.

Nerves taught as a bowstring, I whispered, "Halt! Who goes there?" my finger already taking up the slack on the trigger.

Captain Beaumont's voice replied, "A friend. Put up your weapon."

For a moment I remained frozen where I stood, staring down the barrel, trying to discern which shadow he might be. In that brief instant I transformed from a nerve-ridden sentry to a calculating assassin. In that frame of mind it occurred to me that cases of the unwary being shot while approaching a nervous picket were not unknown. There would be punishment, of course, possibly even a flogging, but few questions asked, and the captain would be sent to Hell, as he so richly deserved.

And there he was, stepping out of the shadows, not five feet from the tip of my bayonet. It was a gift from heaven, impossible to miss at such close range.

Trembling with the effort, I raised the musket's muzzle toward the stars, putting the hammer at rest. The night was not particularly warm, yet sweat pebbled my brow beneath the mitre's band. I was disgusted with my weakness, yet oddly relieved.

If Beaumont was aware of my struggle, he did not let on. Instead, he seemed preoccupied with a struggle of his own. I knew him for a brave man; even in the depths of my hatred, I had to admit that he was brave, yet tonight he appeared nervous, fidgeting with his cuffs, fingers never still, like spirits unable to rest. He came directly to the point without delay.

"Josiah, I must speak with you."

If proof was needed that he was nervous, it was supplied in abundance when he addressed me with such familiarity. My reply was equally informal.

"God damn your eyes! What do you want?"

It was here that I realized that I was mistaken: he was neither nervous nor frightened, but a man caught up in the torment of his own conscience.

"Please Josiah," his eyes shone unnaturally bright in the moonlight, "I...I...know that I have wronged you..."

"*Wronged* me?" I could not believe my ears, "Why, you bloody sodomite! What do *you* know about being wronged? Power is all you understand - the power of the entitled over the unentitled, of the strong over the weak. Wronged? The notion never occurred to you until you suddenly realized there might be a price to pay! Well, God rot your soul, you are going to discover what it is to suffer, and be damned to you!" I felt such a savage anger that I feared that I might strike him where he stood. It was while I struggled with the notion that it might just possibly be acceptable to strike him that he managed to reply.

He bowed his head, a groaning, clutching sob escaping from deep inside his chest as his shoulders began to shake, as would a woman or a child in utter sorrow; but at the last instant, with a mountainous effort, he was able to choke it back and regain at least a portion of his composure.

With a flash of spirit, he said, "You are mistaken! I *do* know what it is to be wronged! For it is as you say: God *has* damned me!" Then his courage failed him, leaving in its place a man so forlorn as I had never thought to see. He continued in a voice so low that it was scarcely more than a sigh, "You cannot imagine that I care for the creature that I have become. You cannot imagine that I *approve*! For most assuredly, Josiah, I do not!"

I was both piqued and perplexed at the same instant, but I do not think that I felt pity for him...no, not yet. I wanted to think of him as purely evil, my rage demanded it. I wanted to be free to hate him with all of my heart and soul. Even he had admitted to having wronged me, and honour demanded revenge. I had earned the right to hate him (by God I had!) and yet...whether it was weakness, or curiosity, or whether I harboured a kernel of uncertainty, I required an explanation for his deeds.

"Talk sense, damn you!"

His reply was a bitter hiss, "I told you, I am damned! *God* has damned me! It was He who put the demon within me, to make me want..." he paused, searching for words, "...*unnatural* things. Is that not being wronged? Is that not omnipotence over the powerless? Do you think that I would not wish it otherwise, that I might be as others? I would! With all my heart I would, but I am not!"

He paused, perhaps to allow me to interject more invective, perhaps because he felt that it was no less than what he deserved - this man who seemed to be asking my forgiveness, yet who seemed unable to forgive himself, who longed for kindness, yet invited my spite. I possessed enough bitterness and anger for two men, but though I felt the time for me to share that with him drawing close, I decided first to give him the chance to say his piece.

When I did not reply, he continued.

"I fight it!" he said, "The demon! I fight it constantly, just as Elijah fought the dark angel! Every day is a struggle, every night a torment! You cannot know what it is like, for you have not been *cursed*!"

Here there was a question which I thought obvious, so, presented it:

"Then why did you allow yourself to fail me?"

"You ask 'why'? Why the demon succeeded in your exception..." and with bowed head, appended, "...and with others, when night after night, it was I who prevailed instead? How might I answer such a question? How best to tell you how the heat of battle infects me!"

He paused, searching for a way to explain the unexplainable; but something was already stirring within me. It was not forgiveness, but perhaps it was the first ray of understanding.

I understood the heat of battle, as I equally understood the heat of my *own* blood. On such occasions passion consistently overcame virtue – consistently provided for the baser functions over who we believed ourselves to be.

God only knew that I was not a stranger to base desire, to the animal in every one of us. Nor was I a stranger to passion, to the evocative appeal of those desired, or to the feeling of helplessness in the face of the torrent – of the unleashing of the experience of life in the face of death. Had I an outlet, would I have sought it without regard for what was deemed acceptable, or what was not? Perhaps. I could not, in truth, say no.

It was not a contemplation that I welcomed, nor was it one I could ignore once it had made itself known. Was it possible that I was not so different from this man after all?

However, I could not as yet put these thoughts into words, even had my mind been clear. My desire to hate was too strong; it had been nursed and cosseted too long to be so easily vanquished. It controlled my reason as assuredly as *Monsieur* still controlled the great bastions of Louisbourg, and with as little sign of surrender. Yet it might be said that this was the first indication that it was being placed under siege, and already there were cracks in the defences.

However, my voice remained harsh when I told him, "You are a fool!"

Plainly, Beaumont had been expecting much from me, for much there was to say, yet he had not expected this, as I could clearly see his face register surprise, even in the wan light of the moon. Still, so great was his need for self-loathing that he would not deny it. Instead, he merely inquired:

"A fool?"

"Aye, a fool! You believe yourself possessed of a demon. In all certainty a demon there is, yet it is not one inflicted by God, but by yourself!"

"But that is not so," he protested, "I have told you of my struggle…"

I cut him short and spat, "Your struggle *is* the demon!"

He was caught, as if someone had stolen his capacity for speech, which indeed I had; so the field was left uncontested for me to continue.

"Beaumont, you have used my past against me, and I shall hate you for it until my dying breath! Yet, it is my past of which I shall now speak.

"Yes, I was a whore, and as a whore I knew many like you – far too *many* like you…but not like you at all. Those men accepted what they were, and were not foolish enough to deny it, at least not to themselves. When denial is taken away, a sodomite is merely that – precisely what he is, and nothing more; for a certainty he is not a demon.

"Were you aware that it was my mother who tutored me to be a whore? Did you know that it was my tutor in all other fields who acted as my very first client, or that my mother stole my virginity when I was still very young? No, you would not know that, nor would I expect you to know, yet it was so all the same.

"It was necessary for me to accept that life was many things, Beaumont. It was necessary for me to accept that my mother was not only a whore, but a licentious whore, guilty of incest, and inciting an unknowing child to incest as well. Yet it was she who showed me my talent – that I was fair of face and

285

figure, an allure to gentlemen of a certain taste. I must confess to you that I did not enjoy their attentions, nor did I ever seek them; yet they kept us from starvation, and I could accept that they were not evil men. Not only from their kindness, but because *they* could accept that they were not evil as well.

"What it comes down to, Beaumont, is that you are what you believe yourself to be. Perhaps all those other men could not admit as much to the world, but at least, unlike you, they could admit it to themselves!"

He found his voice at last, and stubbornly persisted, "But it is a sickness…an affliction!"

I told him, "It is but a simple truth, and that is all."

I suppose, in its way, this was the strangest conversation of my experience: I, a common soldier, lecturing an officer, a man who had done me a great wrong, on how to be more kind, more accepting of his nature, and of himself. I do not know whether that reflected good on me or ill, but at some point during the proceedings my rage had dissipated into the night air. I could never like this man; too much had transpired for me to even consider forgiveness, and yet…

"In battle," I told him, "the lads will follow you anywhere, into Hell itself, if need be. We entrust our lives to you gladly, because you care. That is not the mark of a man possessed of a demon."

He stared at me, his features still twisted with pain and self-loathing, yet I do not believe that it was merely my imagination that told me that they were now less so, nor that the glimmer in his eyes was the beginning of something that might have been gratitude.

Finally, he opened his mouth to speak, but before he could do so, he was interrupted by a distant scream, and then another, and then another after that, piercing the still night air like the eldritch cry of the demon I had just so recently, and hotly, denied the existence of.

Yet it was no demon, not of the otherworld. We froze for an instant, but an instant only before springing into action, for it was a sound that we both well recognized:

The blood curdling screams of men dying.

Chapter Sixteen

All that had so recently passed was forgotten on the instant. Seized in the grip of apprehension, our heads swiveled toward the dreadful sounds. I turned to Beaumont and saw that he was already looking at me, his eyes wide with excitement. Then I was filling my lungs to their utmost and crying, "Alarm!" and again, "Alarm!" as loud as I was able before firing my musket into the air, the report thunderous in the still of the night.

We knew only too well that the screams had come from an observation post, set at the head of a sap between our lines and the town, its role being to give advanced warning should *Monsieur* see fit to come out. In that regard it had succeeded but, alas, not as intended. Those men must have been taken by surprise. No shots had been fired, which could only mean that they had been slain with cold steel.

Now the menace from the shadows was real as, straining my eyes into the darkness, I could just see what must have been hundreds of the enemy advancing rapidly on our position, with here and there moonlight glimmering off their weapons.

Captain Beaumont touched my sleeve. "Quickly! We must rejoin the company!" then led off at a run.

For him, as well as myself, everything that had transpired earlier had now been swept away. I could sense his excitement growing and realized, even as I fought to keep my own panic at bay, that he was laughing wildly, as if a different person had suddenly awoken within him, and was being let loose for the purpose that it existed, to fight, for no reason more noble than the exhilarating pleasure it gave him.

We came thundering into the picket, shouting out our presence so as not to be mistaken for the enemy. The men had been alerted, and the fire doused in order that we not offer too perfect a target to the approaching foe. I could hear the reassuring voice of Balfur, growling curses as he shoved and jostled the lads into line.

My lungs were rasping in great, ragged breaths, the cool night air transformed into burning coals, scouring my lungs as I thrust my way between two of my comrades. Both were nervously squinting into the darkness, cursing their lack of vision, for there had not been enough time for their sight to adjust.

"Is all in readiness, Sergeant Major?" I could still hear the excitement in Beaumont's voice; it was a force that he must fight to contain. Yet it was a strange paradox that he spoke with a calm and boundless confidence, settling our nerves.

Balfur stiffened to attention, and barked, "Sir!"

"Excellent," the captain replied. I could see his teeth flash in the moonlight as his exhilaration continued to grow. It was as though he was aware that he was the perfect man, at the perfect time, and at the perfect place. There was a beauty to him, an allure; we were drawn to it, holding it in our minds like a talisman that we illogically believed would see us safely through the coming clash of arms. It was perhaps foolish of us to feel so, for there were scarcely seventy of us to face odds that must be overwelming.

Beaumont called out, "Check your priming, lads! *Monsieur* is coming to call, and it would be impolite for us not to offer him a warm greeting upon his arrival!"

There was laughter, some confident, some nervous. Balfur roared for silence while I struggled to reload.

Already we could hear the menacing tread of French boots as they crept ever closer. They had slowed their advance, organized their ranks, and were coming on with greater caution, for they knew not our numbers.

"Wait for my command!" Beamont cried. It was a needless order, for it had not occurred to any one of us to do otherwise, but we could sense that the captain was already struggling with anticipation, and must say something, anything, to relieve the pressure, so was forgiven.

I had just reseated my ramrod back into its slot beneath the barrel when I heard:

"Make ready!"

Our muskets stabbed at the sky, each of us dragging his hammer back to full cock.

"Present!"

I leveled my weapon, my eye straining down the length of the barrel. Already the shadows were transforming into shapes of men, the white of their coats increasingly visible.

"Fire!"

I squeezed the trigger; there was a flash as the priming ignited, briefly illuminating the man next to me, and then the crash of our discharge, bright flashes stabbing into the darkness as the butt of my weapon kicked into my shoulder.

Before the effect of our volley could be learned, the captain shouted, "Fall back, at the double!"

We broke ranks, sprinting to the rear as fast as our feet could carry us, the devil taking the hindmost - each man intent upon vacating what was soon to become a killing ground, and then it came.

"*Tirez!*"

A line four times that of our own, and thrice as deep, was illuminated in crashing thunder, sending a curtain of lead scything across the short distance, piercing the darkness to seek us out.

The air filled with the familiar sounds of balls rushing past our ears. There were screams and cries as men were hit, but not so many as if we had attempted to hold our ground. Had such been the case, there could not have been a man left standing. Yet I could see Balfur running a short distance in front of me, moonlight glinting off the gilt on his cuffs. Suddenly he threw up his arms, and was flung forward, his mitre tumbling off into the night, as he fell face-first to the ground. He made no sound – no cry of pain. His death must have come on the instant.

I was by him without another glance, for there was no time. I sprinted toward our lines where I prayed that they were forming up to receive the attack.

Hard on the heels of their volley came a great shout from the French, immediately followed by the sound of them advancing at a run. They had witnessed the size of our own volley, and knew they had little to fear. I could hear their boots drumming the ground behind me, and imagined the evil glint of their bayonets as they pressed in for the kill. To tarry even for a second was to invite death. In truth, my back was a million nerve endings, each anticipating the imminent bite of steel. I was strong, and fleet of foot, but I had already seen much hard running ever since sounding the alarm. The confidence of only a moment earlier had vanished without a trace. Fear ruled me now; it spurred me onward, yet flesh and bone have their limit, as every dead soldier knows.

My life flashed before me – a cliché perhaps, but true. It was Elizabeth that I saw: smiling on the quay, holding me, concerned as I lost consciousness outside the tavern; our first kiss; her tremulous smile on that night she came to me; and later in the glade, offering herself without hesitation, crying out my name over and over, my mind reeling with the struggle to accept that this was me, and that this was her, and that the moment truly existed.

And afterward, those clear blue eyes holding me with their spell: "I shall love you forever and ever!"

Elizabeth...

Then we were approaching our lines, but even at a dead run I could tell that something was wrong. There were no orderly commands, or men arranged in ranks preparing to receive the assault. Even the fires had not been extinguished, but continued to burn, outlining the bedlam of a world of confusion, of people shouting, with none listening, and chaos reigning all around. It took only an instant to realize that they were on the verge of panic - the reason all too clear.

Monsieur had succeeded with his surprise. The alarm had been raised too late. It took time to assemble several hundred men into line, and time was a luxury that they did not have. If our observation post had been alert, if our own picket had been able to stand for a second volley, precious seconds

291

would have been bought. Now those seconds were lost, and disaster was closing to the brink.

Captain Beaumont saw it, too; for suddenly from close by I heard him shout, his voice ringing out over the din.

"To me the 51st! Come on, lads! Charge!"

He could see that they would not stand against a determined onslaught; their only hope was to advance, to make a desperate assault of their own into *Monsieur* before he had a chance to form into line.

I turned; Beaumont stood not two paces away, bareheaded, his sabre drawn, eyes flashing, near wild with excitement - the man, place and time all matched to perfection. It had been necessary for him to cease running, to fill his lungs so that he might be heard.

It had taken but a moment.

Then I saw his eyes fly open the same instant that the tip of a bayonet sprang from his breast.

It must have happened in a second, but to me it seemed very much longer.

He stared at the needle-sharp point with utter fascination, and then I fancy that he looked at me, and it seemed as though it were with the same old entreaty. He appeared to reach out as if continuing to seek forgiveness, but lacked the strength to complete the gesture. Then his sword fell from his hand as his knees gave out, and he crumpled to the ground. I saw the Frenchman put his boot upon his back, tugging at his musket to pull the blade free.

I do not remember the rage settling upon me; I do not remember covering the ground between us, only the sight of my own bayonet in his neck, and the dark spray of his blood as he fell. Then I was parrying a thrust and stabbing blindly, hearing a scream as another fell away, groping at his stomach. There was an instant of savage elation, knowing that his death would not be an easy one. Then I parried another thrust and smashed the butt of my musket into a snarling face, only now realizing that I was desperately shouting out to my comrades to come on, to charge before it was too late, without realizing that I was fulfilling my captain's last wishes.

Another Frenchman raced toward me, musket leveled. Unthinking, I knocked his barrel aside with my own and bowled into his chest with my shoulder, sending him sprawling. He must have landed on a rock, for as I plunged my bayonet into his body, I could feel it grate onto something ungiving, snapping it off at the lock-ring.

And then I heard them, thin and plaintive, yet rising above the general din, not a great roar of unified intention, but here and there single voices taking up the call, crying for the others to press forward to our aid.

Two more Frenchmen came out of the night, one on either flank. There was barely time for me to shift my grip on my musket to the muzzle before one was lunging at me. I swung my weapon like a club, feeling it connect with his skull and turned to meet the other without waiting to see him fall.

Behind me, the cries of 'Forward!" continued to rise. In their dozens, and then their scores, men were hastening to check *Monsieur's* advance. Already the clash of arms had grown to a tumult, the cries of the wounded and dying adding to the melee.

My adversary hesitated, unsure in the face of this crazed *anglais*, who was begging him to draw near so that he might join his friends in Hell. He took a hesitant step backward, but regained his courage when two more of his fellows came out of the night.

Warily, I stood watching them with my musket gripped in both hands, poised over my head, ready to strike.

Grim-faced, they stepped forward, determined to make a swift end of me.

Using the brief moment given me, once more I filled my lungs and cried, "To me! The 51st! Forward!"

Then one was lunging at my chest, and I sent him to join the others at my feet. Something bit deep into my shoulder. I spun to face this new foe only to find that my arm would no longer answer. Seeing this, the remaining two gained heart, rushing in for the kill. Desperately, I swung my musket single-handed, feeling it connect with the barrel of one of their muskets, glancing the blow to one side. Then I let go my weapon, and lowering my shoulder, careened into his chest, sending him to the ground, both of us crying out in pain. Savagely, I stomped on his face, and turned to meet the last man with nothing but my bare hands, feeling the warm blood dripping down the inside of my sleeve with my shoulder throbbing agony with every beat of my heart. But before I could complete my turn, fire tore through my side, and I was falling, screaming, onto Captain Beaumont's body. In vain I made a frantic attempt to twist around, holding up my good arm to ward off the killing blow that I was sure must come.

It never did; for at last the miracle had arrived.

It came heralded by the sound of cheering – *British* cheering! The Frenchman hovered above me, his bayonet leveled at my breast, poised to strike. But he, too, could hear our cries, and it caused him to pause. Then he turned and was gone a mere moment before our lads were swarming all around me, and past without stopping as they chased after him and his fellows, leaving me alone to nurse my wounds. Soon more redcoats appeared, rushing past to join my comrades, their facings unreadable in the dark. Then there were hundreds more, as if the entire army was converging on the point of danger, none stopping, but all hurrying into the night, leaving me to my fate.

I fumbled my scarf from my neck, and lay back, pressing it to the wound in my side.

I was vaguely aware of the crackle of musketry in the distance, and it registered that *Monsieur* had turned to make a stand. He might hold his ground for a while, perhaps even for an hour, but certainly no longer. Every minute more and more of our infantry were racing past, running toward the sound of battle, determined to force him back into his cage.

The fighting madness had left me; that and loss of blood rendering me so weak as to be unable to rise. I possessed the presence of mind to wonder at the seriousness of my wounds, but had the capacity for little more. Soon there was not enough strength to hold the cloth to my side, and once more the blood began to flow freely. My head lolled until I could feel the coarseness of the grass beneath my cheek, and I found myself face to face with Captain Beaumont, desperate entreaty forever frozen on his face.

With the last of my strength I reached out with my good hand, fumbling to close the lids of his eyes, and wondered with a disembodied interest if I were destined to follow him one final time.

Still wondering, I lost consciousness.

*   *   *

Somehow they found me before I bled to death. I was taken to the hospital, still unconscious, where a surgeon plugged my wounds with tobacco, and bound them with strips torn from a dirty sheet, pronouncing, that although my liver must have had an almighty scare, nothing vital had been touched, and if it were the will of God, I would live.

Stockingsdale was the first to visit me, shortly after I had regained consciousness.

His musket was slung over his shoulder, and his mitre tucked under his arm. Although his face was much grimed by powder, and he seemed weary beyond words, he managed to smile at the sight of me.

"Well then, young Josiah," he said softly, so as not to disturb the others, "how are we feeling then, eh?"

It was still dark outside, and a lantern hung on the tent pole, casting shadows across his face. I plucked feebly at the bandages, dismayed by their uncleanliness.

"Please Benjamin, you must take these away."

Stockingsdale risked a surreptitious glance at the surgeon in his blood-spattered apron through the open door of the operating theater, while he performed an amputation on some poor lad's arm. Muffled screams through teeth clenched on a plug of leather mingled with the surgeon cursing at the orderly to hold the man still.

Satisfied, Benjamin turned back to me and winked.

"Never fret, lad," from inside his coat he produced rolls of clean bandages. In sharp contrast to his face, his hands looked recently washed. "I haven't forgotten. We'll see ye right as rain in no time at all." So saying, he cut away the filthy strips of linen with a knife, clucked his tongue disapprovingly over the tobacco plugs, and plucked them from my wounds with visible signs of disgust, muttering, "Bloody witch doctors!" under his breath. Then producing a flask, and a swatch of cloth, he gently sponged around my wounds, the alcohol feeling cool against my skin. When this was done to his satisfaction, he hesitated, then offered the flask to me.

He advised, "Best have a swig 'fore we begin."

I accepted with gratitude, and brought it to my lips. The liquor burned its way to the pit of my stomach, dulling the pain. I handed it back and said, "Pray continue."

"Aye," Benjamin replied, taking a stick from his pocket and holding it to my mouth. I took it in my teeth, clenching down for all I was worth.

"Are ye ready, lad?"

I managed a brief nod; an instant later there was the cool trickle of the brandy on the open wound, and the world exploded once more into excruciating pain.

I felt the stick snap in two, just as I lost consciousness for the second time in as many hours.

*   *   *

It was late afternoon when I awoke to find the general standing over my pallet, his face grim with typical disapproval.

"You!" he accused.

I stiffened to attention where I lay, gasping at the pain caused by the sudden movement.

Wolfe never let on that he noticed. Instead he turned to his aide, a young lieutenant from the 45th, and snapped, "Are you quite sure this is the man?"

The lieutenant produced a sheet of paper, studied it for a moment, and then politely asked of me, "Stubb, is it?"

Bewildered, I could only reply, "Yes sir."

"Private *Josiah* Stubb?"

Again I replied to the affirmative, but Wolfe interjected with an angry, "Belay that! It's Sergeant Stubb, or was anyway! Promoted him myself!"

"But sir," I protested, "I respectfully…"

"Damn your impudence, hold your tongue!" he snarled, his face suddenly a mass of storm; "How dare you address your commanding general without being spoken to!"

"But sir…"

"Silence, I say, or I shall have you flogged!"

So I fell into a reluctant silence, wondering, not for the first time, how the Almighty could possibly have endowed such a pacific featured man with so fierce a temperament.

"But sir," the lieutenant said with an uncertain frown, "he seems to have some objection."

"Must I argue with everyone this day?" Wolfe hissed impatiently, "It is *Sergeant*, I tell you!"

"But sir, if he has declined?"

Wolfe fixed the unfortunate man with a glare of pure ice. "*Declined*?" Too late, the lieutenant realized his blunder, and began to wither under that stare. "Are you suggesting that an enlisted man of *mine* would be so foolish as to decline a promotion given to him by his commanding officer – by *me*? Are you suggesting, sir, that my men are *fools*?"

Utterly routed, the lieutenant lapsed into a silence as complete as my own.

The general offered a surly harrumph, then looking ever less pleased, suddenly barked, "Pray, what are you waiting for, sir? Proceed!"

The lieutenant jumped, then nervously cleared his throat. Once more referring to the paper, he began: "On the night of the ninth day of July, in the year of our Lord seventeen hundred and fifty-eight, at the siege of the French fortress of Louisbourg, on the island of Ile Royal of the Americas, which doth command the straights of the River Saint Lawrence, in His Most Christian Majesty's colony of New France, when the enemy did come out in force, and our lines caught unprepared, Pr…" the lieutenant gulped before correcting himself,

"*Sergeant* Stubb, of the grenadier company of the 51st regiment of the line, then on picket duty, guarding the western approaches, did personally and alone, without regard to his own safety, and in the highest traditions of His Majesty's Armed Services..."

"Yes, quite," the general rasped impatiently, "That will do, I think," then turning the full brunt of his disapproval on me, said, "You are to receive a field commission, effective immediately. Lieutenant!"

Once more the poor young man jumped as if he had been stuck by a pin. Reaching into a pocket, he produced a crescent of silver attached to a chain, somewhat less than the size of my hand. With great care, he placed the chain around my neck, explaining, "Your badge of rank."

I accepted it without a word, for in truth there were no words in me, while I felt the weight of the device on my chest.

It was a gorget, an officer's insignia. For a moment I stared, bemused, at the royal coat of arms engraved upon its surface, until the very vigour in the air reminded me that I was not alone.

I glanced up, perhaps thinking to seek an explanation, and found the general regarding me in turn, up and down. Apparently finding the image wanting, he abruptly tore the lace from his cuff, and hissed, "Take this man, and stitch it to your collar." Then, apparently believing that more clarity was required, he snapped, "That is an *order*!" So saying, he gave a last, curt nod, and with a rasped, "Come along, Lieutenant!" spun on his heel and stalked off, carrying an aura of pure force of will before him.

The young officer hesitated, nervously darting his eyes from the general's receding back to my own weak and pathetic form.

Without turning, Wolfe thundered impatiently, "Lieutenant!"

The harried younger man came to a decision, and darting out his hand, grasped my own, murmuring, "Congratulations...*Lieutenant*!" and then he was off, scampering after our commander, at the same time attempting to maintain some semblance of the dignity that his office required, with, I fear, little success.

I was left alone to stare at these items: their significance, along with the words the aide had spoken, were far beyond my comprehension, while I struggled with my memory of that brief, abrasive meeting.

Unlike the navy, the army operated on a system of officers purchasing their commissions, and had done so since the time of its creation. Britain's class society was mirrored in her regiments of foot, and it was said even more so in her cavalry. That such practice was not followed in the navy, or in the recently created services of the artillery and engineers (where a grasp of science was preferred over social rank) was ignored with ease by the peers of the realm, who virtually alone had sufficient funds for advancement.

There were few exceptions to this rule, although they did exist. It was possible for a commoner of wealth to purchase a commission, but they were seldom warmly received in the blue-blooded officers' mess, and were often regarded as inferior. With that being said, it was doubly hard for those of the second exception: for those who possessed neither social standing nor money, who were presented with a commission on the field.

Such cases were exceedingly rare, in which a single act of bravery, witnessed on the field of battle, might suddenly raise a humble private to the lofty heights of an officer.

It was generally thought to be a bag of mixed blessings by those of us in the ranks, however. For, as I have said, such an individual might well be shunned by his fellow officers, which was quite bad enough; but by far the worst was the separation from his erstwhile comrades. He would be forced to exchange the familiarity of the barracks for the cold hostility of an officer's billet, but even more, he would be regarded with jealousy and suspicion by those he had once thought of as his mates. They might well regard him as an ambitious upstart undeserving of his questionable good fortune: for all would know that there were many acts of courage on the battlefield, and that it was only due to his exploits having been witnessed by an officer that he was now in a position to lord it over those who were no less brave.

All of these things went through my mind while I dandled the swatch of lace in my hand; that and how General Wolfe, in spite of all of his evident hostility, still continued to insist upon meddling in my life. I had never considered myself as an officer, never once in all my time in the army. Surely there were others more qualified; certainly there were others more senior. Was the fool not aware of the folly he was committing? Two promotions in one campaign was beyond belief, and sure to cause problems in the end. Why, it was irresponsible! Not only that, it was the most flagrant act of incompetence from a general in the history of the British army – in the history of *any* army, anywhere in the world!

I seethed and fumed some more in a similar vein, while one hand grasped the gorget until my fingers were numb, and the other twisted the scrap of lace into knots until it was scarcely recognizable. At last, when I had fretted myself into exhaustion (a state easily achieved, given my already weakened condition) I slumped back onto the mattress, pillowing my head with my good arm, and stared at the roof of the tent with unseeing eyes.

Only a fool would say that Wolfe was predictable, yet only a fool would turn a blind eye to his successes. Many of those had been caused by the bravery of the men under him; much had been luck and pure energy, combined with a modicum of skill; but (and I could not deny it) much of it had been caused by the greatest military mind of our day.

Where other generals lumbered, Wolfe soared; where they balked at obstacles, he conquered them, again and again, with a mind that was incapable of contemplating defeat. Where they hesitated to act, he acted without hesitation, the pure boldness of his movements astonishing everyone, most especially the enemy. He was our best: the keenest sense of tactics, the best mind for strategy, the darling of the army in fact. It was said that even General Amherst placed value to his opinion...

...and his *opinion* was to choose me.

It struck me like a blow to the stomach.

Our best general had chosen me, not because I had saved his life, nor from any other idea of bestowing favour felt owed to an underling, but because he was a fighting general, and he saw in me a weapon with which he could defeat the enemy...with which he could *win*! If one word could be used to describe Wolfe it was that one, his desire to win. In order to achieve that end, he would use every tool at his disposal, including myself. That he deemed me worthy was humbling beyond measure.

Now it remained to be seen if I could prove as much to myself.

That moment would have to wait, however, for the battle to defend the parallel – that useless ditch that had taken so much time and labour, as well as lives – was to be my last during the Louisbourg campaign. My wounds required time to heal, more time than Louisbourg had herself.

I awoke early in the pre-dawn of the next morning, surprised to find Stockingsdale and a few of the lads come to fetch me from the hospital while everyone, including the orderlies, lay sleeping. Cautioning me to silence with exorbitant gestures, they picked me up, pallet and all, and carried me out of the tent on tip-toes, and set off across our lines to where the 51st was camped.

"Colonel's orders," Stockingsdale explained, looking grim as ever I saw him, "You'll not have to worry about yon poxy bastard of a surgeon getting his filthy paws on you again, not while Benjamin Stockingsdale has a word on it! We'll get you home and take care of you proper." By '*home*' Benjamin, of course, meant the regiment. Few in the army had much faith in the hospitals, and for good reason, considering it a place where one went to die rather than to recover. Therefore it was reassuring to know that I was leaving this one while there was still breath in my lungs.

Compared to the hospital, the night air smelled amazingly fresh and clean, even though it contained the usual stench of camp life: unwashed humanity, the choking fog of wood smoke and spent powder, and of course, the ever present latrines. It had rained some time earlier, and the mud had been churned to a soupy gruel through which the lads slid and slithered in the dark as they struggled under my weight, apologizing with surprising tenderness whenever an especially galling jolt caused me to groan. Walking alongside my pallet carrying a burning faggot to light the way, Stockingsdale hissed at them to take greater care, before assuring me that there was not far to go.

It occurred to me that there was something about him that might be different. Was it in his bearing? Perhaps, although it was difficult to be sure. His coat, although faded, was freshly brushed, and the pompom on his mitre freshly combed, giving him a jaunty air that I had never seen in the man before, but it was not until I saw the gilt lace stitched to his cuff that it finally came home to me.

"They have made you sergeant!" I exclaimed, perhaps more incredulous than intended. I could only surmise that it was my preoccupation with my own affairs that had kept me from noticing earlier.

He managed an apologetic grin.

"Aye," he said modestly, flourishing his sleeve, "scrapin' the bottom of the barrel, I expect."

"Nothing of the sort!" I told him, and meant it.

He made a dismissive gesture, although looking pleased. Then, pausing to consider, the smile vanished, and very serious, he replied, "Thank you, sir."

Sir? I felt as though I was an imposter in a dream, and doubted that I would ever become used to being so addressed.

To my great surprise, the colonel greeted me quite affably when he came to visit later that morning, after I had rested. He was often thought cold and aloof by the men, but this time he was all beaming smiles. It was not until he

302

divulged, that after personally witnessing my part in turning the tide of the battle, that his purpose was to show gratitude.

"It was a jolly good show!" he said, enthusiastically pumping my hand up and down, not noticing me wince, fearing that my wounds might re-open from so much abuse. Without releasing his grip on me, he turned to the adjutant: a tall elegant man with a hooked nose, and steel pellets for eyes, "It was the damnedest thing, eh Major? The damnedest thing I ever saw, 'pon my soul t'was!"

The major allowed the wisp of a smile to crease the pale features of his face, before murmuring something polite. The colonel, by contrast, a short, rotund, grey-haired, grandfatherly figure, with a large unfashionable walrus moustache, and an ill-fitting uniform, was undaunted, as he was easily voluble enough for them both, going on in the same vein until my hand was wrung dry, and I was blushing quite furiously from the praise. Then at last, perhaps realizing that he was merely using different words to say the same thing over and over, he abruptly ceased, and turned to the adjutant.

"The sword, if you please, Major."

The adjutant stepped forward, cradling a sheathed hangar in both his hands. I could not suppress a gasp, for I recognized the gold thread woven into the hilt. The last time I had seen it was when it fell from Captain Beaumont's lifeless fingers.

"Cost me twenty guineas at the auction," the colonel confided, "Couldn't purchase it meself, of course, had to use a proxy. Money well spent, though. Couldn't conceive of a better purpose." He bowed his head, his tone softening, "Beaumont was a good officer. Only fitting that you should have his sword."

The major leaned over the pallet, presenting the weapon, then realizing that my strength might still be insufficient to take it from him, he hesitated a moment before laying it across my thighs.

Slowly, I reached out and with the tips of my fingers, tracing the silver fastenings on the scabbard's burnished steel.

It was a fine sword, an officer's weapon, and I felt its weight upon my shoulders even though it lay across my legs.

"Thank you, sir," I told him, but I could not raise my head, nor could my voice be as steady as I would have liked. "I swear to bring it no dishonour."

"Indeed," the colonel answered kindly, and then at last sensing my need for solitude, he cleared his throat before wishing me a swift recovery, summoned the major, and left without further ado.

For a long moment I lay there, my good hand on the scabbard, then entwining around the hilt, struggling to understand what I was feeling.

I had hated Beaumont with all my heart, and for good reason. He had taken an image of who I was away from me, a theft which I could never forgive; and yet he had been a man living in continual suffering because his own identity - his perception of what an honourable man should be had been stolen by fate. He had been a paradox: a soul so tortured that it could only find joy in the face of death. His sins against me insured that he was a man that I must hate; yet his actions on the field were such that I would have followed him anywhere.

I had regained my image of myself. Although the cost had been high, and had been paid for in blood, my own as well as that of others. I wondered if, after we had spoken, in the last few moments of his life, his had been regained also, if only by degrees. I was aware of no contradiction in my feelings about him when I found myself hoping that it had.

Bowing my head, I sent out a wish that wherever his soul had passed on to, to whatever world awaited, it was now, at long last, at peace.

*   *   *

A week passed in my convalescence, kept abed by my wounds, with Benjamin somehow contriving to stay by my side to see to my needs. Although we were well behind the front lines, we were exposed to the usual sounds of an ongoing siege, but with an intensity that seemed gradually to increase during that span of time. Wolfe now had batteries installed at regular intervals all along the heights from above the Grand Battery to the Barachois, harassing the remaining French ships, the walls of the fortress, and the town itself, in a continuous hail of artillery, step by step, wearing away *Monsieur's* desire to resist.

Then that very evening just after darkness fell, a new cannonade suddenly exploded all along Louisbourg's walls, awaking those who had been lulled by the monotonous rhythm of our own guns. I summoned Benjamin for an explanation, but he was unable to supply one. Obviously something of great portent was taking place, but we knew not what it was. As no alarm had been sounded in our camp, and no call to stand to arms, it stood to reason that the cannonade was not in support of some desperate endeavour by the French, but rather an attempt to repel an assault by our own forces. Remaining in ignorance of where that might be, while witnessing the fury of *Monsieur's* barrage, we could only wait, and tremble for the success of our effort.

Unable to rest through such a din, I insisted Stockingsdale help me to a camp chair by the tent's entrance, so that I might witness the proceedings with my own eyes. There we maintained our vigil all through that long night, transfixed with excitement, while waiting for news of what was transpiring.

Meanwhile, tongues of flame were flashing from *Monsieur's* cannon all along the walls, stabbing into the darkness toward the north, answered just as fiercely by lights twinkling in a great semi-circle from the surrounding heights, where the guns from our own batteries were dug-in. The terrible duel continued without abating, each side hurling waves of destruction every which way, and so it continued, hour after hour, until the gray light of dawn. When the sun finally broke the horizon, we were just able to make out the top of a hill - less than a mile from our position, and scarcely a few hundred yards from the Dauphin Bastion - swarming with small red-coated figures frantically digging entrenchments. Already the green of the hill was scarred by long dark lines as the sod was peeled away, and hundreds of spades and mattocks did their work burrowing ever deeper like so many badgers. It was apparent that our boys had been so employed for hours, for their work appeared to be on the verge of completion.

Eventually, it being seen by *Monsieur* that our entrenchments had become effective, the French cannon began to wane - as if in despair over this latest change in events. Gradually, this was answered by a tremendous cheer along our entire line – at first a ripple, but growing until it drowned out the booming of the guns, and became a river of joy, a veritable sea of exultation!

Our people were everywhere shouting themselves hoarse. Stockingsdale forgot himself so much as to throw his mitre into the air and cry, "By God! That's our Jimmy! Damned if it ain't!" gnashing his gums as only Stockingsdale could, with myself doing my utmost to join in, overcoming my weakness for a brief spell as exhilaration soared within me.

So it was that I bore witness to the events of the sixteenth day of July, when, on the night previous, General Wolfe led an attack on Gallows Hill, taking the French completely by surprise in a move so audaciously close to the fortress walls that it could only be described in words that would one day resound throughout the world: so simple in their simplicity, and yet so poignant – 'Wolfe's luck'.

It is often said that soldiers value luck, and there is truth to it. For those who stand face to face against the enemy, with nothing more than fickle Chance deciding who should remain standing, and who should fall, they will place higher credit on a general with good fortune over one with skill. Wolfe, it should be said, had both.

Now, with Gallows Hill in his possession, it could not be doubted that very little time would be lost before he had yet another battery set in place on its summit, pounding the Dauphin Bastion to rubble, silencing the guns on the walls and inflicting even more damage to the town.

It would not be for another two days until the cannon from the main attack would finally commence firing on the formidable walls of the Queen's Bastion, and at a distance three times greater than the battery on Gallows Hill, over ground so broken, that even had a practicable breach ever been achieved, would never have presented a realistic opportunity to a storming party.

By and large, the common soldiery were not fools, nor were they blind to the comparison of Lawrence's and Whitmore's lack of achievements to those accomplished by our lucky general, accordingly placing him high in their esteem, severe task master though he was. He demanded of us our utmost, and we gave it gladly, for we knew that our efforts would bring results that were both immediate and tangible, things that appeal to a soldier's mind. We believed in him, and perhaps just as importantly, he believed in us, because, in a war that had been dragging on for three long years, largely with only catastrophe and defeat to show for it, we felt more ready to believe in ourselves. If a commander has success in accomplishing that, he will have forged a weapon of such invincibility that might, in the end, go forth and conquer an entire continent…if only for him.

With the guns still raging, I allowed Stockingsdale to help me back to my pallet. With such valuable ground in his possession, surely Amherst must now turn away from the council of his more senior generals and make Gallows Hill the focus of our main attack, just as those very same generals must now, at long last, concede their error. There was still much to do: a new parallel would have to be dug, and a practicable breach achieved before the final, terrible storming could occur. Perhaps the major struggle still lay before us, and many more would have to die. But from that day forward, there could not be a soul still breathing on the Louisbourg peninsula who, if convinced of no other thing, was at the very least convinced of this:

The endgame was at hand.

Chapter Seventeen

One week later found me on my feet at last, able to make my way gingerly about camp with the aid of a stick whenever exhaustion overtook me. Little by little my strength was returning, but by no means could I lay any claim to being fully recovered, so had as of yet no duties assigned me.

Over on Gallows Hill, as predicted, a new parallel had been started, and reinforcements rushed in to secure the position. As I had anticipated, the senior generals could no longer turn a blind eye to the value of Wolfe's accomplishments. Now work was proceeding under continuous close range fire from the fortress; although given that our vast superiority in artillery was constantly sweeping the battlements, there were now very few cannon with which *Monsieur* could answer. For the most part, he could only watch as the saps crept in ever closer until their earthen ramparts were very nearly within extreme musket range. At the same time our heavier guns battered the walls into rubble, affecting a breach much sooner than any would have thought possible only a short time earlier.

Much of the regiment had been transferred to this new area of engagement, but as a convalescent I was free to remain in camp unburdened with anything more arduous than regaining my strength. It was with some relief, I must admit, for as predicted, several of my now fellow officers had given me a cool if not hostile, reception, while not so predictably perhaps, others had been extremely kind, even effusively so, praising my exploit so highly that I finally became discomforted in the presence of both. Consequently, my separation from them came as a relief.

In contrast, I was feeling the separation from the lads far more keenly, and often found myself wishing for a return to the security of their ranks. It was not easy to pass by a campfire where men were talking (men with whom I had used to sit until very recently) yarning about home, women, or the war, knowing that I was no longer welcome there, and knowing that I would not be hailed in any form of camaraderie, as that too had vanished as surely as if it had been physically taken from me.

So it was, that being largely unwelcome in both camps, I found myself isolated, a man of neither world, and was left with much time to my thoughts.

It was during these days that I all the more keenly felt Daniel's absence, and wondered how he fared. Was he on the walls even now, staring out at me, feeling anything akin to thoughts of my own? No. That would not be likely. Then where? And what was it like for him, and for the others inside, with shot and shell raining down around them, one grueling day after the other, knowing that we were coming? Word had spread around the army that the French frigate, *Aréthuse* (that which had so often succeeded in being a thorn in our side, the single enemy ship of any consequence at all) had slipped from the harbour, and had successfully eluded our fleet. Had Daniel been aboard her? One could only hope, but it seemed pointless to speculate further.

And with that, with the heaviness that filled my spirit whenever left to dwell on current affairs alone, my thoughts would not be dissuaded, but turned of their own volition back to Elizabeth…

*   *   *

She and I had tarried for much of that warm summer afternoon in the glade; dallying in the shade of boughs heavy with fruit, while butterflies danced with the flowers, and bullfrogs croaked at the winking droplets left by the leaping trout. Overhead, lost in a forest of murmuring leaves, an oriole sang high and sweet, countered by the chittering of a squirrel scolding our behaviour. In all of my life there had never been such moments as idyllic as these.

Now that I had been able to overcome a lifetime of reticence, I spoke to her of love as if my words had been water pent up too long behind a dam, and upon that barrier being sundered, were flowing from me like a river, like a flood of adoration that swept her up and carried her away. In truth, I

309

was surprised when she burst into tears, and clung to me as she had clung but moments before, the difference being her love of my words rather than the love of my body.

At first concerned and bewildered, I could not countenance such behaviour, and told her so. Shyly, she revealed that what I had just spoken was more than she had ever allowed herself to dream; that she had come to me with no other thought but that she should be free to express her own love, never imagining that it could ever be returned; that what I sold to others, I would give freely to her. Then even more shyly, she reached over to where her dress lay on the ground beside us. Rummaging through a pocket, she produced yet another purse.

She dandled it in her hand, blushing crimson, as she confessed through her tears, "My own love I have freely given, yet it was my understanding that this was your profession, and that you should be reimbursed accordingly." She pressed it into my hand, saying, "This is rightly so, as you have given to me more than I can ever repay."

"How say you that, love?" Although thunderstruck with the implication, my tone remained tender, for I was not capable of feeling anger toward her.

"I had not sought to be anything to you other than an equal to the others," she confessed, "all I asked was to have you near as much as you were willing, and that I should be free to love you with all my heart." Gesturing to the purse, she said, "I would give this and more to continue as we are."

Slowly, with much deliberation, I reached out and returned the purse to her dress. Then cupping her lovely face in both my hands I tenderly kissed her, and said, "As would I."

Much later, we at last lay spent, she curled in my arms, and lying in this manner, soon fell into sleep.

Something woke me. The first thing I sensed, through sleep-dulled eyes, was that the sun had begun to fall, with only hours left in the day. The second was that we were no longer alone.

In a trice I was fully awake and on my feet. every nerve alert to danger, and was greeted by a dark, mirthless chuckle.

"A pretty sight, wouldn't you say, Ned? Aye, a very pretty sight, indeed!"

I whirled around to see two men standing just inside our glade. Their ragged clothing and grizzled mien proclaimed them to be riff-raff from the shanties down by the quay...the one on the right distantly familiar.

It was he who had spoken, so my mind was delving into memory even before I saw him. I had heard that hard, grating voice before, but where?

Shorter than myself by a head, he was stockier built, but stepping carefully on the balls of his feet at a crouch, like a cat; and I felt the scar across my ribs give a twinge as the memory returned. Yes, I had seen this man before: on an evil night outside a tavern, when there had been murder in the air. It had followed him then, and I knew that it was with us now.

"Hello, boy," this villain greeted me with a wicked grin, "didn't I warn you not to interfere with men while they're at their play?" Slowly, he drew a dagger from the soiled depths of his shirt and brandished it, still grinning, "I told you there'd be a reckoning, didn't I? That night's work cost me three of my mates, thanks to you; they was all hung only a fortnight ago, and they're still rotting up on Gibbet Hill. Losing mates is a bitter business, boy, that's why this'll be all the sweeter for me."

The one on my left (evidently answering to 'Ned') - a big, burly brute, with a mangy beard, and wisps of straggly hair clinging to the fringes of a bald and flaking scalp - chortled in anticipation of the fun. I spared him a quick glance, and saw that his front teeth were missing, the others yellow with decay.

I sensed Elizabeth stirring at my feet.

"Josiah?" she called out in a voice drugged with sleep, and then I heard her gasp as she came fully awake.

The first offered her a leer that made my skin crawl, and said, "Well rested are you, dearie? I hope so. I likes'em to put

311

up a struggle." Then his eyes swiveled back to me, and hardened, "but first there's business to attend."

Slowly, I reached down and pulled her to her feet, never taking my eyes from the two assassins. She scrambled behind me without a word, while I reached over to where my clothing lay on the ground. I inserted a hand in my boot, and pulled out my dagger. Ever since that night outside the tavern, I had taken the precaution of carrying it with me for my own defence.

I heard Ned growl a warning, "Watch it, Jeb, he's armed!"

Jeb's eyes glittered as he chuckled, "I'm not blind, Ned." And then to me, "Right then, boy, this is going to be even more fun than I thought!"

At that they began to close in, Ned circling around until he was lost from the corner of my eye. To compensate, I retreated until he once more came into view. All the while my mind was desperately wrestling with the situation, trying to think of a way to even the odds. I needed time to consider, but I could see that it would be mere moments before they made their move, and then it would be too late for thinking. I needed to act, but knew not what form that should take. Here we were, naked, and all but defenceless. If I should fall, Elizabeth's fate would be unspeakable. The knowledge emboldened my spirit.

"How came you here?" I demanded, "How is it that quayside scum find themselves so far from the gutter?"

Ned growled in anger, and I hoped that he might lunge for me so that I might take him out of the fight early, but Jeb forestalled him with a word. He was relaxed, in total control. It was apparent that my wielding a knife did not worry him overly, nor should it have. I was a novice in his world, and he knew it. In fact, I believe that he felt such confidence as to indulge an inclination to gloat. My taunt had not excited him to anger; instead he chose to interpret it as an honest question.

"Well might you ask," he grinned smugly, his teeth even more decayed than his companion's, "although the knowledge will do you little good."

Ned continued slowly to circle. Guiding Elizabeth with my left hand, still presenting the knife with my right, together we took another step back.

"Yet it would do you no harm," I reasoned.

My answer pleased him, for he paused to laugh, a great, evil guffaw. Then he tilted his head to one side and nodded, "Aye," he said, "you're right enough there, for dead men tell no tales," glancing over my shoulder, he added, "nor women, neither." He took another pause to consider, then, "Very well. It's not often that I get to mix business with pleasure, so I shall tell you, and you can take the knowledge with you to Hell." He took a final pause for effect, and said, "'twas the Dawe crone."

For a dangerous moment I was shocked to immobility, and if they had chosen that time to strike, we would have been done for. What he was suggesting scarcely seemed possible! In many ways Isabelle had become my strongest ally, allowing me to escape from my mother's attention by setting me up in rooms of my own. Why, it had been she who had given me Tess's name so that Sally's life should not be too arduous in my absence. I knew that she was fond of me; it was not difficult to recall her cupping my cheek in her bony, liver-spotted hand, with a look that passed for tenderness on those severe old features. Yet hard on that notion I thought, aye, she was fond of me, the same as she was fond of a favourite hound, until the moment I had become disobedient. It had always been her intention that I should know my place, and had severely discouraged any attempt I had made to rise above it. In the end I had proven too unruly to control, and it must have displeased her to the extreme. But to come to this? It hardly seemed likely.

I told Jeb, "I do not believe you."

He grinned ever wider, and shrugged. "I care not a shite what you believe, boy! But ask yourself this; why should I lie?"

I had to concede that there was truth in that. Why should he? Still it lacked credulity.

I said, "But I do not understand. She would have you murder me? For whatever reason?"

Jeb's laughter was derisive when he replied, "How should I know, and why should I care? But I will tell you this: you are not the first murder she's contracted me for; the first was her husband, that pox-ridden magistrate, may he rot in Hell! His death was a pleasure, as will be yours." Here he offered a slight shrug, "Otherwise, all I care for is the colour of her gold, and that she was willing to pay right handsomely, so that neither you nor your little slut live to see another day."

Behind me, I could feel Elizabeth's hands resting lightly on my waist, ready to react to any direction that I might give. I was aware of a curious sense of gratitude when I realized that she was not trembling. It was as though, while aware of the moment's gravity, she believed herself safe under my protection.

Meanwhile, Jeb's last words were mulling through my mind. Isabelle had not been above murder to rid herself of an unwanted husband (and I was shocked at how unsurprised I was when given knowledge of it); now, if this villain were to be believed, she had specifically stated that both Elizabeth and myself were to die, and though her reasoning horrified me to the point of making my flesh crawl, her motive for doing so became clearer.

She had been fond of me, true, and had been willing to share my attentions with others as long as our interaction remained based purely on my profession. Now, realizing that this was no longer the case, she had reacted out of jealousy for Elizabeth's vast superiority in beauty and youth, and out of spite for my having refused her – for what she was now denied. I had little trouble envisioning that mind, filled with supreme arrogance and craving, vowing that no other would have what she herself could not. It made the blood run cold in my veins, but in truth, I wondered at my folly that I had not foreseen such a situation approaching, but had been blinded by the wonder of my transformation under the warmth of Elizabeth's regard.

314

Now it was evident that Jeb had grown tired of our parley, and wished to see an end to it. Once more his knife came up and he continued to close, all humour gone from his face. What replaced it was cold determination.

Strangely, as dire as the situation was, I was filled with a reflective glow as my own knife came up to counter. Elizabeth saw me as something wonderful, a vision of myself that I had not previously foreseen. Yet in a measure, because of the strength of her belief, had I not become that person? Had I not grown before my own eyes, as well as hers? I felt her hands resting lightly upon my waist, transmitting her emotions; I knew that she was alert to the danger and aware of her fate should I fail, yet I sensed very little fear, but much of faith that I would somehow prevail. It was that faith that made me twice the man that I was. She believed in me, and it was unthinkable that I could ever disappoint her.

Still it would seem that death was entirely likely, until a vision passed through my mind, of my lying on the ground, already forgotten, with my life's blood flowing from my wounds, and these unspeakable creatures closing in on my beloved.

I became consumed with a grim determination.

Suddenly, with a shout, I lunged forward, feinting at Jeb, freezing him on the defensive, then spinning, leapt into the air without taking the time for proper aim, and flung the knife with all my strength at the spot where I judged Ned to be.

It was a desperate gamble, to be sure. Chances were excellent that my judgment would be off and the knife would sail harmlessly past its target, and our defence would be reduced to my bare hands. However, our situation was already desperate, and to act otherwise would be merely to accept the inevitable - a reasoning which was not to be contemplated.

As fortune would have it, my judgment was sound and my hand steady. I had a protracted vision of the moment. It must have been slowed in my mind to a much greater length than the mere flash of a second that it actually was, for I could see Ned lunging toward Elizabeth, his face contorted with lecherous rage, and then my knife was twirling past her ear (so close as to fan tendrils of her hair in its passing) to embed itself in the middle of the birthmark on the brute's forehead, even as his filthy hands were reaching out like talons to seize her.

There was an instant of the utmost surprise registering on his face, as his eyes flew wide before life deserted them. As I had said, he was a big man, and with a girth to match, yet the force of my throw, aided by blind desperation, had been so great as to stop him in his tracks and fling him backward.

Even as I completed my spin and returned to the earth, my momentum carried me, full-tilt, to where Jeb awaited with his dagger, braced four-square to skewer me. I could hear the sound of his friend's body crash to the ground and begin the loud process of dying.

So there I was, with the situation having changed drastically in scarcely more than a blink of an eye. Now there was only one assailant to face, but I was literally naked and without a weapon, careening headlong into an opponent who not only still possessed his knife, but had shown in the past that he was proficient in its use. So while it could be said that the situation had changed, it could not in any way be said that the odds had been evened.

By the time I had completed my manoeuvre, there was only half a step between us, and then I was crashing into him with my eyes glued to his blade, and both hands desperately groping for his wrist.

I was only partially successful. Jeb had been taken by surprise, frozen in uncertainty for the briefest of moments, which could be the only reason why I succeeded in grasping his wrist and closing with him, but not before I felt the bite of steel sear across my forearm. Then I was crashing into him like a battering ram, and I could hear him grunt in pain as we both went sprawling. I landed on top, feeling the rush of foul air from his lungs brush by my face. But the impact had jarred loose my brief hold on his wrist, and he was the first to react, spinning out from under me with feline speed, and leapt to his feet. My reactions were far too slow; I expected to feel his dagger plunging into my back every moment as I struggled to stand. I had gambled and lost; the advantage was still his. Even if I managed to regain my feet, he would be poised and ready. Unarmed as I was, he could cut me up at his leisure…and then he would be free to do his worst to Elizabeth.

The horror of the thought lent a sudden surge of energy to my limbs, and I was on my feet, every fiber of my body poised and alert, ready to sell my life dearly.

He stood facing me, crouched as always, ready to spring, like the predatory cat that he was. He brought up the hand that had held the knife, and for the first time we both noticed that it was no longer there. A look of almost comic puzzlement passed over his face as he stared stupidly at his empty hand.

And then, still wondering, we both looked at his chest.

A crimson flower was blossoming onto the filthy grey of his shirt, the haft of the dagger protruding from the center. Raising his eyes from the wound, he gave me a look of such comic stupidity - of such an appeal to my humanity - that I could think of nothing to answer but a short bark of laughter.

The front of his shirt became saturated; then he coughed, and dark crimson erupted from his mouth onto his chin.

Slowly, like a faltering monolith, he sank to his knees, his lips all the while silently mouthing that there must be some mistake, that the moment should be returned to him, and a better conclusion achieved. I made no effort to oblige him, nor would it have done any good if I had. He continued to look upset with this unexpected state of affairs, until as a final supplication, he reached out to me, at the same moment that he fell forward to the ground.

Almost immediately, the oriole rejoiced in high, sweet notes over the stillness of the moment, the squirrel chittering away in imperfect harmony.

I looked to Elizabeth.

She was staring at the bodies of our assailants – from one to the other – disbelief registering on her face as the blood pooled around their wounds. When finally she looked at me, I saw that her face was ghostly pale, her eyes unnaturally bright.

Awkwardly, as if her voice was not her own, she stammered, "Josiah?" with an interrogative inflection, as though the world had suddenly become a single daunting question.

"All is well," I told her. When I opened my arms, hesitantly, she came into them…and then burst into tears.

*   *   *

It was late when we returned to town, with the first pale stars just visible above the high rooftops in a cloudless evening sky. We had returned on foot, leading our horses, with the bodies of Jeb and his cohort slung across the saddles. It was my intention to deliver them to the magistrate, but it was first incumbent upon me to deliver Elizabeth safely to her home.

She had been largely silent during the hour it had taken for us to return, still pale and shaken from our ordeal. It was my intention to recite a story to the magistrate that I had been set upon by these ruffians alone, and that their sole purpose had been banditry. To tell the truth was not to be contemplated; it was vital that Elizabeth's reputation be protected at all costs, and it was not inconceivable that this could still be maintained. It would do little good to reveal my plan to her, for she would almost certainly protest, but I was firm in my resolve, that whatever unwanted publicity should arise from this day's work, none should attend to her.

There was also the not inconsiderable issue of Mrs. Dawe. Here I had toyed with the idea of telling the magistrate the truth, but decided not to on two counts. First, the truth was far more likely to come out - that is to say that truth which must remain secret, the secret of my life for one thing, but certainly Elizabeth's and my relationship, and that would not do. Second, Isabelle Dawe circulated in high circles, bringing her to account for her crime would by no means be an easy task, all the more so in that her filthy hirelings had breathed their last. In the eyes of the law, it would be my word against hers – a whore against a lady of influence – without any evidence to speak of. For it had been Jeb who had stated it

318

himself, dead men tell no tales, which effectively put the both of them out of reach of any questioning from the magistrate.

When all had been considered, it was without a doubt that the story I had invented was best for all parties concerned. Isabelle had shown her hand, and forwarned is forearmed, as the saying goes; whatever transpired from this moment on would be conducted in private between her and myself. No good could come of it being otherwise.

Elizabeth did come out of her state until moments before we arrived at her door. I had feared that the shock of the encounter had rendered her speechless, and I was happy to be proven wrong, for she was merely heavily engaged with her thoughts.

"I have never seen a man die before." Her eyes were on the ground, but I knew that was not what she was seeing. The reins from the halter trailed listlessly through her fingers, and my heart was wrenched with sorrow when she said, "It was horrible!"

Quietly, I told her, "I would give anything for this day not to happen."

But here she surprised me, for without lifting her eyes, or changing her manner in any way, she replied, "Oh, but I cannot agree!"

I was not aware that I had stopped until the mare began to nuzzle my back.

Stupidly I asked, "Elizabeth, are you well?"

"Quite well, thank you," she answered with the ghost of a smile.

"But…"

"Dearest Josiah, can you not see?" She cut me off without a change in inflection, her voice so soft that I had mistaken it for melancholy, "Without this day I would not have had those wonderful moments with you! I might never have known what it was to feel so alive! You have opened my eyes, and allowed me to see a universe far different than I could ever have imagined!"

I was gratified, to be sure, but equally puzzled. I confess that it was in order to prompt a reply that I quietly said, "And yet it ended so badly."

"Oh, but you are wrong!" she replied, still with that same half-smile. "True, it was horrible to watch those men die, and yet it was magnificent!"

Frowning, I stammered, "Elizabeth, I..."

Now she looked up at me, her face set in gravest sobriety. "Those were evil men," she said, "one of whom had caused you injury before," she motioned toward my bandaged forearm, "and another today. It is fitting that they will no longer trouble the world." She continued without pause, "What I mean, Josiah, is that this is the second occasion that I have watched you fight for my honour, nay, for my very life! The first time was in darkness, but today you were in the full light of the sun, and quite terrible to behold." Here she paused a moment before continuing with, "And yet, at the same time, so like a god that I cannot find the words to describe it!"

I could only stare, mouthing like a fool, at which she laughed merrily and kissed me.

"I would reward your gallantry, sir, at the earliest date that you care to be so disposed."

That moment shall remain forever frozen in my memory, for it was the last of a life I had dared to dream.

We had just walked the horses into the courtyard, and I was in the process of kissing her adieu, when suddenly a procession of torches erupted from the house and stables, bathing us in a circle of their baleful glare.

Shading my eyes with the flat of my hand, I thought that I recognized Quinn as the foremost. Grim-featured, he reached out and snatched Elizabeth from my grasp, where she was taken by others, disappearing from sight with little more than a cry of astonishment, cut short as she was whisked away into the confines of the house.

Completely at a loss I asked, "Quinn? What is the meaning of this?"

In reply, I received a fist to the side of my head, bringing me to my knees. Before I could protest, a boot caught me in the ribs, sending me sprawling to the ground. I lay there winded, too dazed to move.

"Enough!" I heard a voice roar, one that was used to being heard above the most fierce of gales, or over the thunderous crash of broadsides.

I was aware that the forest of masculine legs crowding around me (with every indication of doing me even more injury) had frozen at the command, and were now parting, standing aside, as another approached. The courtyard had fallen deathly silent, and the sound of his heels, loud and distinct upon the paving stones, was that of impending doom.

"I never commanded this!" Having seen order returned, Captain Broadstreet's voice was once more reduced to a soothing caress, and yet with a nuance of an ice-clad hiss to show his dissatisfaction.

Quinn must have been in a rare taking, for he dared to protest, "But, your honour…" and was cut short for his pains.

"Silence, I say! You were to remove my daughter, and nothing more! Now stand aside!"

The coachman's stump-like legs abruptly took a step backward into the crowd, to be replaced by the silk stockings and white linen breeches of the captain.

I wiped the back of my hand across the corner of my mouth, seeing the blood that came away on my knuckles with a curious sense of a resigned calm. I turned my face up to him, not knowing what to expect. He gazed down at me, his eyes cold and merciless in the torchlight, in a way I had never before seen; yet I did not look away.

Unsmiling, he regarded me for a few moments more; and though to be held in such a cold stare could not help but make me feel very small, I continued to regard him with calm dispassion, until suddenly, he bent down, offering his hand.

Hesitantly, I accepted, and was drawn to my feet, feeling the strength in his arm, but could sense from him no wish to offer violence.

We stood facing one another, a world apart from the sea of hostile faces surrounding us, and I knew what had happened. Word had gotten out, and as always, as such things go, an ear to the door had spread the news throughout the servants' quarters like wildfire, most likely before the informer had properly finished with her tale.

We continued to regard one another: he coldly distant, and myself resigned and waiting. But it had already been a trying day, and I found myself suddenly anxious for the unpleasant scene to be over. So it was that I was the first to speak.

"Who told you, sir?"

I thought his eyes showed surprise, quickly followed by what might have been an irritated annoyance.

"Damn you man! Will you not even attempt to deny it?" There was anger to be sure, yet perhaps also a deep disappointment that I had not offered to do so.

"To what end?" I replied, "It would appear that a verdict has already been achieved."

I could see that he had an even angrier retort verging on his lips, but before he could utter a word of it, I heard Quinn's voice coming from behind me.

"Sir?"

"What is it?" The hard blue of his eyes tore away from me, bearing a promise of wrath for the interruption…only to blossom wide with surprise.

I turned, knowing what I was going to find.

As was his habit, Quinn was the first to see to the horses, and when the halo from his torch pushed back the darkness, it was to reveal the both of them standing, patiently waiting to be relieved of their grizzly burdens.

Astonished gasps escaped from many a manly throat; someone whispered, "Murder!"

The captain strode past me without a word. He studied the corpses, bending their faces toward him, each in turn, with Quinn holding his torch low so that he might study them the better. Then, without pause, he straightened and turning to me,

322

snapped, "What happened?" but before I could answer, he thought better of it, and held up a hand to forestall me. Instead he turned to Quinn: "Take them away. Put them in the root cellar until you hear from me. Have cook prepare coffee - enough for everyone. I fear that the night is on a long tack." Then, gesturing to me, he said, "Come!" and led the way back to the house, his hand tucked into the small of his back. For the first time I thought the empty sleeve on his coat rendered an appearance of loss.

I followed without a word, through the front door and down the corridor to his study. As I went, I found myself gazing around me, attempting to preserve every last item to memory. There had been so much happiness here, but now I feared that I should never again set foot under this roof.

He held the door for me, so I preceded him into the room, a single candle casting its pale light as before. There was no offer for me to sit, so I remained standing, as did he.

Finally he pierced me with his cold blue eyes, and said, "Now, tell me."

Chapter Eighteen

I had mentioned earlier the story that I had intended on telling the magistrate, but it was clear that such would hardly do here. It was known to all in this house that I had been out riding with Elizabeth, and returned very late with two dead men in tow. Further, it was to the benefit of Elizabeth's safety that I retain as much of the truth as was possible. I had placed myself beyond any claim to Captain Broadstreet's friendship, but at least, on this one instance, it was to be hoped that we might still be allied.

So I told him that we had gone further than intended, and were waylaid by the two cutthroats.

"Those men were known to the authorities." In spite of his preoccupation concerning his daughter and myself, the captain was still able to reason. "Back alleys and nightfall are their tools of trade. They have seldom been seen out of the gutter. But what reason would they have to be out in the country?"

I could have lied, and told him that I did not know, but of course there was Elizabeth's safety to think of.

"Sir," I told him, "they had followed us, and waited in ambush for our return."

He studied me as I had never felt myself studied before. Much of my will went toward returning that look with all implacability.

Without changing his expression, he asked, "What think you the reason? Was it robbery?"

Slowly, I shook my head and replied, "No sir. It was murder."

Perhaps it was my very bluntness that caused him to gasp and grow pale.

Badly shaken, he demanded, "How came you by this knowledge?"

I stared hard into him, so that there could be no doubting my word. "One of them told me, sir. A confident fellow, he thought to taunt me with the information, as he felt that I would not live to relate it."

"But why? Whatever could be the reason? Do you..." he paused, struggling to regain control of himself, before asking, "...do you believe that they had designs upon my daughter's honour?"

"I am certain of it, sir," I told him, my tone steady and uncompromising, the room suddenly close, "but only as an amusement before murdering her as well."

Captain Broadstreet turned white as a sheet, appearing utterly at a loss. Some few moments passed before he could gather enough of himself to say, "I must ask you again, were you informed of the reason?"

"I was sir; they were hirelings."

"Hirelings? But who...?"

Now his eyes registered open astonishment, coming to the same conclusion even as I told him.

"I believe it to be the same person who has informed on me, sir - Isabelle Dawe."

Once out, her name hung in the air like a physical entity. I could see that my daring to mention her had offended him - that at some level of his mind this was information that he did not wish to know, so he attempted to stare me down with an angry glare; but eventually, as the long moments passed, his eyes were the first to turn away.

"Yes, it was she. She came to me this very afternoon, to warn me away from you. It had come to her attention that you were providing a...*service* to one or two of her maids in return for money." The corners of his mouth were drawn sharply down, and I thought he was about to be ill. Then he spun on me, eyes flashing, "Dammit, Josiah! Is it true?"

I felt my face redden, but I believe that I was steady enough when I replied, "Sir, it is true what she suggests. Being a whore is all that I have ever known. It is not true, however, that this was a case of knowing one or two of her maids; it was the lady herself."

325

He barked a short, mirthless laugh, "But that is preposterous! Isabelle Dawe is a leading member of our society! Do you take me for a fool?"

"Sir, I beg you to consider. You have known me for many months now..."

"Fie!" he interrupted, suddenly all in a rage, "I did not know you at all, it seems!"

I bowed my head, "It grieves me to hear you say so; although I confess that I can hardly blame you, and for that I am filled with regret, more than words can ever say." I was wreathed in misery, yet forced myself to press on, "I fear very much that what I am about to tell you will cause you offense, and for that I am also most heartily sorry, but I must ask you to put it aside for the sake of your daughter."

His rage was still very real, so much so that I thought he might strike me. I braced myself to accept the blow; but although the tension was still very high, the moment passed until he managed to regain control of himself, albeit with a visible effort.

"Very well," he rasped, "pray proceed!"

Once he had given his permission, there was no recourse but to continue, although I wished very much for it to be otherwise. So I took a deep breath to steady myself, and thought of Elizabeth.

"Sir, I have been a whore ever since I was a child, and in that time have succeeded in gaining some small talent, enough that I can command the highest price for my service. You have seen for yourself that I might pass as a man of affluence, in a way that is quite beyond the reach of a maid's income to support." I paused to gauge his reaction, but although quite pale, he kept his thoughts to himself. So I took a fresh breath, and continued, "Again, I shall ask you to consider: who but the lady herself would be in a position to afford me?"

He allowed himself some passion when he cried, "But this is ridiculous! You cannot think me such a fool as to believe her so morally corrupt!"

To which I replied, "All of my life I have heard of this morality, and I thought how wonderful it would be to have such a luxury. Still, I can claim no expertise on the subject of what is corrupt and what is not. All I can do is observe that she has been a widow of faded charms for more than a year. I might add," I ventured pointedly, "that if our assailant is to be believed, that her widowhood was a contrived affair with the aid of his office.' Before he could interject, I pressed on. "Surely, sir, in spite of her plainness, you must acknowledge the possibility that she might still harbour a lust for connubial desires? What creature among us does not? In that light, where else should she come to satisfy her need, but to a place where her money atones for what she lacks in beauty and gentle demeanour?"

Now, grievously agitated, he began to pace back and forth, cursing quietly beneath his breath, waving his hand as if warding away an unpleasant notion. Then, stopping abruptly, he rounded on me again.

"What proof do you have?"

"Sir," I replied, "I have none."

"Then it is your word against hers?" he demanded angrily.

"It is," I acknowledged.

My answer seemed to irritate him more than ever, for he took to pacing again, pausing only to give the bell-pull a sharp tug before continuing, back and forth, across the floor, the sound of his shoes loud even through the thick Persian carpet.

Presently there came a quiet knock at the door.

The captain cried, "Come!"

The door opened, and Elizabeth's maidservant, Sarah, entered, obviously distressed and wringing her hands, her eyes reddened from tears as she curtsied.

"Well?" the captain demanded impatiently, "Did you ask her?"

She sniffled and replied, "Yes sir," before delivering a dark glance in my direction.

"And?"

327

But she hesitated to continue, looking significantly at myself before returning to her master. Her meaning was not lost on the captain.

"Very well," he turned to me, and though the chill remained, his words were civil, "I must ask you to excuse us," and led her from the room, closing the door firmly behind him.

I was left to pace about the captain's study, trying not to dwell on events beyond my control. I did not doubt that Elizabeth would corroborate my story, yet the knowledge gave me no pleasure. This calamity was largely of my doing, and it pained me that she should be drawn into it. But now it was out of my hands. There was very little that I could do but try to protect her as best I could. In the meantime, all that was left to me was to pace back and forth, and curse my impotence.

The clock on the mantel struck the half-hour before the captain returned, very pale and evidently disturbed even greater than before. I braced myself, and waited.

He seemed distracted, and could no longer meet my eye.

Finally, he began:

"Elizabeth has confirmed what you have told me, as I am sure that you must have known she would."

I said nothing, and he fidgeted nervously with the inkwell on his desk. A good while passed before he spoke again.

"She also told us a good deal more than what you have thus far revealed."

I had not thought it possible, but I felt my spirits plummet even further, for I had feared as much.

"She has made clear to me what Madam Dawe's motive was for attempting this heinous crime – that it was in a fit of jealous rage for my daughter having supplanted her in..." there was an unhappy pause while he struggled, and then rushed the last words as if they were painful to him, "...in your *bed*!"

I hurried to reply, but he held up his hand before a syllable could be uttered. He still would not look at me.

"She goes even further: she tells of how you had attempted to end it, and that it was she who came to you in the night, and...*begged*," he spat the word, "and how it was she who had begged yet again, for *today's* assignation!"

Misery consumed me. It gave me no pleasure to see this man I held in such regard brought to this by my doing.

"How you must hate me," I said, steeped in my own unhappiness.

He gasped something that might have been bitter laughter or a sob, and turned to me at last, eyes brimming with tears.

"Verily I wanted to," he agreed, "perhaps there is a part of me that wants to still – to take a horsewhip and thrash you to within an inch of your life, or," he gestured abruptly to the mantelpiece, "to take that sword from its pegs and cut you down where you stand!" Then, incredibly, even as the tears overflowed, unnoticed, down the sides of his face, he broke into the ghost of a smile, and said, "but I cannot."

"If you could," I told him, "if you would, you need only voice your inclination, and I shall fetch the whip, or even the sword, and gladly submit myself to your justice."

The captain regarded me gravely, as if considering, then shook his head. Instead, he went to the window, leaning his hand upon the sill. Everything was utter darkness beyond the pane, but still he looked.

"I have found that life bears many burdens," he said, for the first time his voice was more his own. "For myself, the foremost of these is duty, the placing of others before myself: duty to my king, duty to my country, duty to the navy, duty to my ship and her crew - all bear a ponderous weight. Yet there is another duty: one that a father owes to his child, which in its way, is more ponderous than all others combined.

"I see in Elizabeth much of her mother, God be praised: a beautiful, strong-willed creature who is difficult to deny when her mind is set...as who should know better than myself?" I watched as a wan smile appeared in the window's reflection, "It is my duty to see to her upbringing, and I cannot say that I am sorry for the person she has become. It is my duty to see to her safety, and in that regard, I have twice to thank you for her life, so no, Josiah, I cannot hate you." Now he pushed himself away from the window to face me again. The smile was gone, and in its place was a sad determination to bring our conversation to an end.

"I have also a duty to see to her happiness and well-being," he said, "and I have found that the two do not always go hand in hand." He continued without pause, "I am told that she loves you."

"And I her," I replied, for it was a simple enough truth.

He nodded thoughtfully, but otherwise carried on as if I had not spoken.

"If it had been any other young lady, I would have told her that she knew nothing of love, that she was naught but a foolish child, and then confine her to her rooms until she saw reason; but she is, as I have said, her mother's daughter, and knows her own heart as very few others. So you see, any appeal to her would go unheeded."

There was an uncomfortable pause while he struggled with his pride. In the end, I said the words for him.

"So you are appealing to me instead."

He did not deny it but replied, "Josiah, surely you can see that it would never do?"

I could, of course, in fact, I could see little else. It had finally come to the point where I must stop pretending. I bowed my head in acceptance, willing my heart to maintain an even rhythm, and my tears to stand at bay.

The moments passed, and then he came forward, placing a fatherly hand upon my shoulder.

"What will you do?"

It was a question to which I had not applied myself, yet at least part of the answer was obvious.

"I shall leave Saint John's," I told him.

It was the only reasonable choice left open to me. I could not remain here, for either of our sakes, so needs must leave behind all that I had ever known. The world suddenly loomed very large and I very small, totally unprepared to take my place in it.

He nodded his agreement, his hand still upon my shoulder. "It is possible that I might be of service; would you think a position in the navy agreeable to you?"

But I knew nothing of the sea, and perhaps there was something else that made me shake my head; I wondered if it was not pride.

"You have been kind to me, sir, in spite of all the grief I have caused you, and I am deeply indebted to you for it. Please, do not ask of me that I become more indebted still."

The captain studied me yet again. Perhaps he was gauging the veracity with which I spoke, wondering if a gentle encouragement was all that was needed for me to accept his offer. What he saw I cannot say, but eventually he replied:

"You are an enigma, Josiah; born of the gutter, and in many ways dwelling there still, but you carry it with a dignity I have seldom seen in those far more privileged, with every advantage in their favour, and virtually no obstacles to overcome." So saying, he offered me his hand, "You have my admiration, sir, as well as my gratitude that you have not made this any more difficult than circumstances require."

With that, the meeting concluded, and with it everything that I had come to know of the world in which they lived.

I turned to go, my head spinning, only half-believing that the sum of the day's events had come to this. Yet I had the presence of mind to pause at the door.

"Sir?"

Captain Broadstrett had not moved from where he was standing by his desk, regarding me with a mixture of wariness, and what I dared to hope was affection.

"Yes, Josiah?"

"What will become of Mrs. Dawe?"

Gently, he replied, "Leave her to me, lad."

But I persisted, "Will she be brought to trial?"

It was clear that he did not wish to discuss the subject, for he regarded me through half-closed lids, yet I stood my ground, and at last he relented.

"Questions will be asked," he told me. "Depending on the answers, an investigation may follow. There is no evidence, as you know. All that the magistrate will have is your word, as well as my daughter's, with which to bring a powerful member of society to justice. Your word will carry very little weight," he added, though not unkindly, "Elizabeth's considerably more."

"May I see her?" I asked.

Again, not unkindly, he replied, "Please understand, I think it best that I refuse."

In fact I did understand, yet I had to ask. So in the stead of pleading further, I thrust the subject from my mind, and returned to the matter of Isabelle Dawe.

"If your investigation proves inconclusive, will you continue to allow Elizabeth to stand as a witness in the event of a prosecution?"

He said evenly, "I am certain that my daughter shall do what is right."

I gave a thoughtful nod, and bade him a good evening before walking out the door for the last time.

As I made my way through the darkness, heavy at heart and lost in spirit, I thought of the direction that the process of an official investigation might take, unearthing much about Elizabeth and myself, and in all likelihood, very little about Isabelle. Then, disarmed of evidence, Elizabeth would insist upon prosecuting, pitting her word against that evil old harridan's for my sake alone. What neither the captain nor myself had ventured to admit was that it would not be enough.

Tongues would wag, that was a certainty. Much would fall upon Isabelle, to be sure, but at least as much would fall upon Elizabeth for standing by me, even if it meant her ruin.

I could not allow that to happen.

My first steps into exile had brought me, unerringly, to Jobs Cove, to the kitchen entrance of the yellow ochre house that Captain Dawe had bequeathed to his wife. I reached into my boot and brought out the knife. The day had already seen it used in much hard service, but there remained one more task to hand.

I slid the blade between the door and frame, guessing that any lock in the servants' wing would not be overly imposing. In truth, I felt the bolt slide silently back with very little effort.

Quickly, I stepped inside, so far unobserved. Pausing only to take off my shoes, I proceeded through the parlour, soundless in my stocking feet, and up the wide, balustraded stairs, freezing near the top when a soft creak emanated from a tread as I placed my weight upon it; but the house was deep in slumber, and I was able to make my way to the top without further hindrance.

More than once, I had been summoned to Isabelle's bed. Those occasions had been in the beginning, until she decided that the arrangement would not do. In order that the servants should be given no food for gossip, she had begun to come to my apartments instead. Yet the memories of those earlier visits had not left me.

Three doors down the corridor, I grasped the knob and turned, pushing silently inward.

I was immediately greeted by the sound of irregular snoring coming from the canopied bed by the window; moonlight streaming through the panes bathed the rumpled coverlet in a silver hue.

I crept across the room, only to freeze when the snoring abruptly stopped, and I heard her say, "Josiah?" followed by much incoherent mumbling, then once more, "Josiah lad!" and more mumbling.

I realized that she was speaking in dreams, so continued silently forward until I arrived at her side. She opened her eyes when I placed a hand over her mouth. I believe that the dream still held her, for she did not start when she saw my face, but gently reached out for me instead, reminding me of a different time – of a different world, before I had dared to have dreams of my own.

Softly, I whispered, "Hush, my dear," at the same instant sliding the knife into her heart.

She obliged pleasingly well – the first and only time I have ever known her to do so.

*   *   *

The door to Sally's apartments swung open of its own accord as soon as my hand touched the latch. I stepped inside, and was greeted by perhaps a dozen sullen masculine faces in various states of inebriation, sitting here and there, or standing with their backs to the wall, to a man looking like so many children playing soldier in their freshly-dyed red woolen tunics.

One of them swore, "Christ, not another one!" a lanky-haired lad of about my own age, with a growth on the side of his face, and the beginnings of a moustache sprouting amongst the pimples on his upper lip.

"Nothing to me," another slurred, "long's he knows I's next."

To which, glaring angrily in his general direction, the first replied, "Sod that! I'm next!"

"Not!"

"Bloody well am!"

Their voices continued to rise, to be joined by others protesting that both were wrong and it was their turn just as soon as those sodding bastards, in with the girls at the present, stopped being pigs and remembered that they had mates waiting with money to hand, until general mayhem threatened to fill the room.

Then from behind one of the doors, I heard my mother call, "Quiet down out there, you boys! The night's still young, isn't it? Everyone'll get a turn, you'll see!"

I strode across the room, stepping carefully over a sleeping form on the floor with what looked and smelled like vomit stains down the front of his shirt.

"Here," a blond giant growled, regarding me with drunken menace, "just where the bloody hell do you think you're goin', boy?"

The door to the second bedroom was half ajar. Looking through it, I caught a glimpse of Tess on her back, her legs spread like the trunks of trees, while a freckle-faced youth, eyes tightly clenched, rutted away at their conjunction, and two others suckled at each of her ample breasts.

"Not to worry," I reassured him, "It is not my intention to jump the queue. I have simply come to have a word with my mother." Then, ignoring his amazed gape, I opened the door and stepped inside.

Sally was on the bed, hunched on her hands and knees, the folds of her belly brushing against the mattress, while the planks groaned in protest. Positioned behind her, near invisible in the midst of her massive buttocks, the stick-like form of Benjamin Stockingsdale was bulling into her with ecstatic energy, the boney cheeks of his own insignificant buttocks pistoning away while he drank deeply from a pewter mug. If anything, the smell of rum was even stronger in here than without.

Softly, I called, "Hello Sally."

Both turned their heads without a break in rhythm, a gratifying look of joyous welcome written on both their faces.

"Ow!" Sally cried, ripples of flesh rolling up and down her back, "Look 'oo's come to see his dear old mum, then! Come 'ere, lad an' give us a kiss!"

As I dutifully obliged her, Stockingsdale called out, "Josiah lad! It's been a while, so it has!"

I offered him a nod as Sally craned her neck, and said, "'E-don't come by so much anymore, not like it was at all, really. Now let's 'ave that kiss, shall we?" I lowered my face and suffered her to slobber on my cheek, turning away only when she put a hand behind my head and tried to pull my face to her lips. As I feared, the wanton look had returned as of old. She stared at me with a deep hunger, while Benjamin grinned and winked at me, at the same time passing her the mug.

Without taking her eyes off me, she accepted the cup and drank deeply before wiping her lips with the back of a meaty hand. Soon, however, she began to look thoughtful, and her eyes to glaze. In a tremulous whisper, she called, "Mr. Stockingsdale?"

Smiling wickedly, Benjamin inquired, "Aye ma'am?"

"I believe that I am about to arrive, if you can oblige me with an increase in tempo, please!"

"Anything for you, Sally," Benjamin sang out happily, and immediately began to apply himself with a special vigour, while my mother, still without taking her eyes from me, impatiently pushed aside her stomach, and began to knead between her legs.

"Ow!" she moaned.

"That's a luv!" Stockingsdale cried encouragement, "come on, old girl, you can do it!"

"Ow!" Sally moaned again, and then again, "Ow! Ow! Gammon!"

Unsmiling now, Stockingsdale began in earnest as his own arrival was heralded by a deep groan. Then, while they were approaching their throes, I pulled a rough-hewn stool from the corner and seated myself, waiting patiently until they were finished.

At last Benjamin's eyes rolled up into his head, and he gave a long, drawn-out shudder, while Sally finally began to emit a high-pitched keening that built to a crescendo seconds before she pitched face first onto the mattress amidst the sound of ecstatic cries, splintering slats, and one or two drunken cheers from the other side of the door.

My mother lay panting for a few seconds more; then abruptly thrusting an exhausted Benjamin from between her buttocks, she heaved herself onto her side to face me.

"That was lovely," she sighed, smiling drowsily. "It always 'elps when I know yore near."

"I am glad, Mother," I told her, and for once I meant it, "Remember me that way."

Ever sensitive to my moods, the drowsiness was gone from her eyes in an instant, and she was sitting up, grasping my arm in both her own, so that it had disappeared to the elbow.

"Wot's this, Josiah?"

Stockingsdale's head popped up from the far side of the bed, from where he had so recently, and unceremoniously, been ejected.

"Yes, Joss, what do you mean?" he asked, "Where are you going?"

"Away," I told them; then suddenly weary, I tipped from the stool onto my knees, and lay my head upon Sally's bosom. "Mother," I told her, "I have been foolish."

*   *

*

Half an hour later there was an insistent pounding on the door by the time I had finished relating my story.

"Come on Stockingsdale!" I recognized the blond giant bellowing, "Out of it, for the love of god, man! Or did you get stuck in there?" A single, drunken chortle greeted this wit, and then he was pounding on the door again with his fists, growling threats through the planks if Benjamin failed to exit at once.

Sally had long since collapsed into a torrent of frantic tears, bewailing a cruel fate that could allow such a thing as my leaving come to pass. Stockingsdale, however, was more thoughtful, and soon had things in hand.

"There, Sally," he soothed, "there, there, lass. No need to be down in the dumps; it's not as if the boy will be gone forever, now is it?"

But it would seem that just the thought was sufficient cause for her to burst into another round of tears. "Ow Josiah, luv, I tried to warn you!" Then she clasped me to her so tightly that breathing was not possible, and she threatened to smother me in her bosom.

"Oh dear-oh-dear," Benjamin frowned. "This will never do!"

"Ow! I could just die, I swear!" Sally wailed.

"Nothing of the sort!" his frown deepened. "Now see here, there's nothing else for it; nothing cheers you up like a little tumble, is there my dove? So just stay here and jolly the

337

lads along, and I'll take young Josiah out to have a few words, heh? How does that sound?"

Sally hiccoughed, and wiped at a stream from the end of her nose, mumbling in sorrow. But gradually, as Benjamin's words sank in, her expression grew more speculative.

Then, hesitantly, she asked, "You would do that for me, Mr. Stockingsdale?"

"Aye ma'am," he assured her warmly, "that and more!" He gave her buttock a playful slap, and said, "Now you just have a grapple with that young Hawthorne, what's primed and ready just outside the door, and see if he can't put a smile on your face! Master Josiah and I shall retire to see what's to be done."

When summoned, Hawthorne, the blond giant, came boiling into the bedroom with such impatience that both Benjamin and myself were brushed aside with very little ceremony.

Ever the professional, Sally greeted him with an "'Allo then, dearie. Oo, my stars, yew are a big one, aren't you! That'll be six and tuppence, please."

Even before we had reached the door, he had taken station and was inserted, and by my mother's cries, was well on her way to healing the wound of my absence.

Benjamin escorted me into the kitchen, and sat me down. Even amidst the muddle of my thoughts, it occurred to me how familiar he had become with the place. He went to a cupboard, and rummaging around, came up with an earthenware jar; plunking it down on the table, he invited me to help myself.

As there were no cups provided, I unstopped the cork and drank from the bottle, the neat rum coursing fire through my veins, holding my dejection at bay. Benjamin accepted the jar when offered, and drank deeply in turn.

"Ah!" he said wiping his lips, "That hit the spot!" Then, without relinquishing his grip on the flask, he said, "Now tell me what this is all about."

Up to the present, I had revealed only the base facts: that Elizabeth and I had been found out by her father, and in order

338

to avoid persecution, I thought it best to leave St. John's until the danger had passed. I thought it sufficient reason to explain my course of action, and so it was; yet Stockingsdale sat across the table from me, sipping rum with a knowing look in his eye. And too, there might have been something else to his mien, something so utterly foreign to my experience that it left me fumbling awkwardly for a word to describe it. In the end, much to my surprise, I settled on *'fatherly'*.

I regarded him thoughtfully, perhaps for the first time considering what he was to me. One of my mother's most loyal customers, certainly, but aside from that, he and I had never been close. We would exchange greetings, and perhaps a few words more, but not many. It was at that moment that I realized that it had been I who had always shied away whenever he had made any attempt at friendship; and I saw now, that over the years, those attempts had been often made. He was not, however, the sort one warmed to instinctively: there was too much of the ferret about him for one thing, and the affection he seemed eager to show to my mother and I was hard to accept at face value without at least some suspicion. Certainly much of that was our living in a world where real affection was seldom given, and then only between myself and my mother, and even that proving twisted and unhealthy. It was suspicion that ruled our every day – aye, suspicion and distrust, more's the pity, yet I had seldom felt more vulnerable in my life, and found myself reaching out to that paternal smile.

In the end I told him everything, even about the murder I had committed but a short while before. I spoke long into the night, and when finished, seldom felt so weary, or acutely aware that my life was in his hands.

Without hesitation, those hands now reached across the table to clasp my own; they were warm and dry, and yes...still fatherly.

Just then the kitchen door burst open, and the blond giant stood at the threshold, filling it as completely as had the door itself. I remember that Benjamin had referred to him as

Hawthorne. It had not occurred to me how much time had passed until I saw him there. Six and tuppence was my mother's fee for one hour.

"Christ," he said, rubbing his stomach, "I'm famished. Anything to eat?"

I had never heard Stockingsdale more sober. Quietly he said, "It'll have to wait, Daniel; there's work to be done."

*   *   *

Within the hour, Daniel was once more standing in my mother's kitchen with word from the street.

"There's a hue and a cry, no error," he said, "and an almighty one at that, but no names mentioned, at least not as yet, anyway."

I found myself studying him more closely, too - this second person that I had entrusted my life to in as many hours, with as little to go on but Stockingsdale's word that he was a good sort, and could be relied upon. It was all very foreign to me, this sense of trust, which seemed to come so naturally between these two men, as if it were a palpable entity. As heartsick as I was over the loss of my beloved, I felt drawn toward this new realization as I had seldom been drawn to anything. Perhaps, in a way, I saw instinctively that the huge void I felt by the severing of one bond might only be filled by the forging of another; in any case, given the circumstances it was something I took to surprisingly well.

As I studied him, his clear blue eyes and his handsome, forthright face, that seemed so incapable of deception, I found him studying me in turn. When at length he offered me a wink and a smile, I found myself to be so illogically reassured that I was able to return the gesture, and felt at least part of the burden lift from my heart.

Meanwhile, Stockingsdale was assessing the situation.

"Aye, mayhap the authorities are blind men beating about in the dark for the moment, but t'would be foolish to think that it will remain so. The toffs don't like it when one of their own is done in, and around these parts they don't come any higher than that Dawe bitch. Questions will be asked,

340

that's certain; mayhap your name will arise, Josiah, or mayhap it won't, but it's a chancy business to remain incautious. In that light, I agree with you: you must go. The questions to be answered are where, when and how."

I remained largely silent as Benjamin and Daniel became engaged in a lively discussion over my future: Daniel suggesting that I sign on as a hand in the next fishing vessel ready to set sail with the tide, and Benjamin thinking that I might book passage to some far-off land, perhaps one of the Indies, where it was said that opportunities were rich for a man of the world.

I felt a curious sense of being humbled, by the sheer nonchalance of the conversation. Here were the only two souls in the entire world who as yet knew of my crime, and I had received not one word of censure from either, only support, merely because I was something to Benjamin, and therefore accepted without question as a friend by Daniel. So it was in that same spirit that I felt the beginning of a plan unfold.

I interrupted them both in heated mid-sentence when at last I ventured to speak.

"Perhaps the army?"

All conversation stopped as they paused to stare, first at me, and then at one another in frank astonishment…then turning more thoughtful as the merit of my idea settled upon them.

"I was thinking of anonymity among the masses," I explained.

"It could work, you know," Daniel said, "For weeks now there's been naught but talk of making an attempt on Beauséjour."

"Aye, we'll be going, sure enough," Stockingsdale said thoughtfully, at the same time absently reaching for the rum, before thinking better of it and withdrawing his hand. "There's soldiering to be done in Annapolis Royal, and no error. Soon we'll get a bellyful, maybe more than we bargained for; there's war clouds on the horizon, lads, mark my words."

"War!" Daniel breathed the word as if it were a cherished talisman.

"Aye, war," Benjamin agreed sourly, "and you need not be so happy about it, you young pup! For it little enough resembles what you're thinking."

"It's all I've ever dreamed of ever since running away from the orphanage," Daniel replied, unconvinced, "the excitement, the glory!"

"Mayhap there'll be some of that," Benjamin allowed, "but little enough. More likely you'll find an early grave; for if a Frog's bayonet don't get you, some form of disease will."

Undeterred, Daniel laughed, "That's your sort, Stockingsdale, always looking on the sunny side, you are!"

In spite of his foreboding, Benjamin allowed himself a good-natured grin before returning his attention to me.

"Look you, Josiah," he said, "are you sure that this is what you want? I mean, there's every likelihood of what I've just recited coming to pass. 'Tis a hard life, to be sure, and like as not an unmarked grave in some distant corner of the world your only reward. True, there are all those things that Hawthorne says, but for every man that covers himself in glory, there's a hundred more that fail, leavin' their bones for the kites to pick clean."

In truth, I had not considered battle or glory, just the camaraderie that I had witnessed between these two men, and how something in me craved to become part of that.

I told him, "I am convinced, Benjamin."

He sighed, "So be it, then, and heaven help me if anything should happen to you, for Sally would have my guts for garters!" Then, before I could offer a comment, he said, "Very well, Daniel and I must return to barracks. Spend the night here, 'tis safe enough, I think, and we shall come for you in the morning to collect the King's shilling."

When I protested that I could make the journey on my own, he shook his head sadly over my poor ignorance.

"If your mind is indeed set on this folly," he told me, "then it would be even more foolish of me to forego the extra shilling that is my due for bringing you to the recruiting sergeant."

Chastened, I could only reply, "I see," and feel my face redden under Daniel's laughter.

Our plan seen to, and the hour being late, the two soldiers took themselves away, collecting as they went any of their comrades that still remained, sprawled asleep in various nooks and crannies of the place, leaving me alone at last.

I thought to have a word with my mother, but when I looked through her door, I saw that a combination of rum, excess and violent emotion had carried her away. She lay spent, flat on her back, snoring fit to shake the rafters, the wattles under her chins vibrating like a flurry of feathers. I decided not to wake her, but contented myself with a kiss to her forehead instead. Then, with the day's events catching up with me, I spread a blanket on the parlour floor and lay down to sleep.

I dreamed of Elizabeth.

"I love you, Josiah, and I shall love you forever and ever," she told me, smiling, with the flower petals strewn across her breasts, shadows inside the glade dancing all around.

"Nothing shall ever come between us, I swear it!"

Irrevocably, the hand of fate had interceded and parted us with as little effort as it would take to pluck a flower from the earth. Elizabeth was gone from me, and not for the last time did I feel the dreadful pang of my loss, waking me on the brink of a vast and terrible abyss.

All was darkness when I opened my eyes, and I thought myself still dreaming; for I could still feel Elizabeth's warmth enfolding me, caressing me toward release, yet her body was absent as though I were making love to a ghost. Overwhelmed with grief, I sobbed aloud even as I shuddered violently, spending myself into a wraith. Elizabeth was gone from me, and somehow I must endure.

Then Tess's voice was whispering into my ear.

"Sure, an' I was listenin' at kitchen door, and knows yer goin' away, young master," she said, and I could hear the back of her hand swipe across her mouth, "'twas only a little something for you to remember me by, so it was," and then she kissed me tenderly on the cheek and was gone.

I slept undisturbed until dawn, more peacefully than I would ever have imagined.

There was another tearful scene with my mother the next morning, causing the rum bottle to be uncorked earlier than what was normal, even for her. In light of that, I was grateful when Stockingsdale arrived to escort me away, before the situation became too unbearable. The last I saw of her, she was at the door, bottle in hand, looking the saddest and most disheveled as I had ever seen.

And so began my military career.

I was issued kit and musket, taught how to load and fire same, and to treat it better than I would treat myself. I was given a uniform, and was drilled and drilled and drilled until I swore I was marching in my sleep. I learned to arise in the dark, and stand to before dawn, to salute my betters, and somehow to digest the food. And too, I began to feel that easy comradeship with the others that I so longed for, at some point crossing over from my past life into the life of a soldier, until, on the verge of our departure, the transformation was all but complete.

For the word had come as was anticipated - we were bound for Annapolis Royal - not from above, for in the interest of security, our officers seldom told us more than we needed to know, but through the offices of that strange system of communication that I was to become so familiar with – the gossip of the lads themselves.

Throughout all of this, of course, Elizabeth loomed large in my imagination: her laughter, the blue of her eyes, the touch of her caress, and the heat of her passion, all fading into the shadows as the softness of her voice declared that she would love me forevermore.

The night before we were to board the transports, I contrived to slip away.

Silently, I stole through the streets, steering carefully around foot patrols on the lookout for deserters, until I came once more to King's Lower Brook.

I stood in the shadow of the hedge, peering through the branches to her window. With relief, I saw that it was open, but the room itself was in darkness. Carefully, I removed the letter from my tunic and bound it around a stone with a piece of string. Then, gently, I tossed it underhand, up and through the opening, and was rewarded with a muffled sound as it struck the thick rug on the floor.

I allowed myself to whisper a silent farewell; then, feeling as if I were being rent into a thousand pieces, somehow forced myself to turn away, and retrace my steps back to barracks.

It was impossible to leave her without a word of what had become of me or where I was going. I knew that I must accept that she was destined for another, yet I loved her more dearly than I loved my life, and it was more than I could bear to think that she should be left in ignorance of my fate.

*   *   *

We boarded the transports the next morning, lingering in the stifling heat below decks until well into afternoon. Then with the coming of the tide, we could hear the naval officers shouting orders through their speaking trumpets, and the bare feet of the tars running to obey. At length came the loud clank of the anchor chain rumbling through the hawser, and the hull heeling over as the unfurled sails caught the wind.

To a man, we crowded to the portals to look out upon the harbour as it passed, for we knew not if we would ever see it again in this lifetime. Many called out to the crowd standing on the quay: wives and sweethearts, even children, all waving tearful farewells, all wondering when and where they should be reunited again. For all knew that this could be but the first day of a separation that might span many years, or possibly forever.

345

Though I strained my eyes to tears, I could not see her.

The ship weighed anchor, and left the town behind as we made our way down the length of the harbour to the Narrows before heading out to sea. One by one my comrades returned to their hammocks or to their games of dice as the case may be. Some fighting to hold back tears, some silent and thoughtful, while others – we younger ones, mostly – spoke in hushed tones of excitement of what lay in the future. I, myself, stayed at the portal, breathing the fresh sea air in an attempt to lighten the burden from my heart.

When we turned to approach The Narrows and my portal came to bear, I fancied that I could see, high upon Flagstaff, the figure of a black horse, being held with some difficulty by a soldier. He was tossing his head in high spirits, as might a mettlesome charger. I told myself, that beyond doubt this was the property of an officer, although even at such a distance, even I could tell that this was a beast of quality, and knew of only one such in all the settlement.

It was not for another quarter hour, as our ship's sails fought to catch the breeze, muted by the surrounding hills, and we beat our way to The Narrows, that my hopes were realized.

The figure of a woman stood alone on the very eastern limit of North Head, towering above me from the brink of the cliff.

I stared as if my very life depended upon it…which in many ways it did.

How she had managed to reach such a vantage point, and with what determination, I could not say, but it must have been very great. The ground was wild and broken there, and the face of The Lookout was steep – a place where no horse could ever venture, and only overcome by the most resolute of spirits.

The wind, unfettered from that height, seemed to resent her intrusion into a world where it was king. It buffeted her with merciless rage, tugging her cloak out behind her in a fan of purest blue. I saw that she had mended the bodice of her russet dress. She was wearing it now, the same that she wore on the night she had risked everything to come to me, offering herself and her love. I did not need the cowl to be removed to recognize her, but she did so anyway, the wind catching her hair, sending it streaming after her cloak - ribbons of lustrous red against the brilliance of the blue.

Neither of us called out. Neither of us waved.

Both remained as we were until lost from sight.

Epilogue

Mitre in hand, I stood at the foot of Captain Beaumont's grave, the crude wooden cross already seeming old and faded on the windswept knoll.

Louisbourg had fallen at last, and now it was time for the living to take stock.

The end had come, not in a murderous hail of grapeshot and blood, as most had feared, but in a quiet parley under a flag of truce, amidst much bowing and politeness between dignified generals – a much preferred ending for all concerned...or for most at least.

It was required that *Monsieur* lay down his arms, and to be taken back to England as prisoners of war, and *Monsieur* did not like it. Not for him was a grand march out the fortress under fife and drum, with flags flying, proudly bearing his musket back to France as a free man. Memories of the massacre at Fort William Henry were still a fresh scar in our minds, too fresh to accord our ancient enemy the honours of war. It was said that, contrary to the terms of surrender, a French regiment had burned their muskets, along with their banners, in disgust rather than to lay them at the victorious feet of their conquerors. We did not protest too heatedly; a few muskets and strips of silk were no longer worth dying for. Louisbourg was ours.

The last days leading to the surrender had seen our proud regiments assume a lesser role to the siege guns, and ultimately, to the navy. The very same day that we had begun the new parallel on Gallows Hill, a bomb from a mortar had exploded on the *Célèbre*, one of the five remaining warships in the harbour, starting a fire that quickly spread to *Entrepenant* and *Capricieux* in the crowded anchorage. At two o'clock in the morning the flames on *Entrepenant* pierced through to the magazine, the resultant explosion turning night into day, the smoke so thick that it forced women and children from casements within the citadel. British onlookers from the high ground could see them as they ran about in panic, gradually

348

joining other citizens of the town crowding onto the pier to watch, horrified, as the flames reached the guns of *Capricieux*, and battery after battery had discharged into them at point-blank range.

The next morning found all three ships burned to the waterline.

Four more days of increasingly heavy bombardment followed, setting fires in both the King's and Queen's Bastions as well as penetrating the walls in more than one location, widening the breaches with every round. Eventually the fire from our guns became so intense that only four French cannon were left on the walls still capable of answering, even as our trench drew close enough so that parties of sharpshooters could enfilade the embrasures under cover of its earthen berms.

Life must have been difficult within the fortress during those days. House after house was burned to the ground, or pulled down purposely to prevent fires from spreading. I thought of Daniel, and hoped with all my heart that he had been aboard the French frigate, *Aréthuse*, that had escaped some weeks earlier. The noose was tightening, and it could only be a matter of time before it sought him out in earnest.

The end came on the night of the twenty-fifth day of July.

In its way, it was typical of the entire campaign from start to finish, although hitherto unheard of: through the close cooperation of both services, army and navy. In this instance, it was a joint operation as usual, but with the novel difference being that now our role was to act in support while the navy delivered the hammer blow, not with the massive batteries of her ships of the line, but with a fleet of sixty small boats stealing past *Monsieur's* sunken ships guarding the harbour's mouth, and into the harbour itself. At the same time we amassed our regiments with scaling ladders in the trenches, and increased our cannonade in a feint that drew the town's defenders to the western walls to repel what he supposed was an imminent attack. Invisible in the dark, the small boats closed on *Bienfaisant* and *Prudent*, the two remaining French men-o-war lying, unsuspecting, as close to the fortress as they were able. The small skeleton crews left on board stood no chance and were overwhelmed without serious difficulty; *Bienfaisant* was cut out and captured, *Prudent* ran aground and was burned - the morning finding her little more than a blackened hulk stranded in the mud - leaving the harbour open to attack by all eighteen hundred and forty-two of our fleet's heavy cannon.

The fortress held out for one more day, during which the last of her guns were silenced, and a breach achieved, which the engineers now declared practicable. *Monsieur* had engineers of his own and knew that, although his regiments were still willing to fight the hated *anglais* to the bitter end, resistance was hopeless. In addition, after several weeks of constant bombardment, the town's citizenry had had enough, and could not be subjugated to the horrors that would follow the storming of a fortress. In such a case soldiers (those who survived) maddened by the death and destruction that would undoubtedly be suffered while penetrating the breach, would be set free to debouch upon the town, lusting for blood, to rape and murder as they would. There was nothing to be gained pretending that this would not be so: even the best disciplined troops behaved as animals once a breakthrough was achieved, their sense of rage only increased by what they regarded, perhaps rightly, as an overly stubborn enemy who had made such a sacrifice in blood necessary.

That afternoon a French legation could be seen issuing from the Dauphin gate under a flag of truce. The negotiations had proceeded along the lines stated earlier, but had eventually reached a conclusion of unconditional surrender; for in all humanity, there was no other decision that could have been made.

Now, with the guns at last silent, and *Monsieur* safely stowed aboard the transports, I had thought to come to this lonely hilltop where the 51st had buried her dead, searching for answers that could not be found amongst the living.

What had it all been for?

Oh, it was clear enough when viewed from the world stage. In one fell swoop a troublesome haven for French warships and privateers, that had preyed upon our fishing vessels and merchantmen since time out of mind, had been brought low at last. At the same time it had opened the approaches to the St Lawrence and the very heart of Canada at the French strongholds of Montreal, and the prize of all prizes, Quebec. Yes, it was simple enough to understand.

Yet what of the individuals? An army, after all, was made of many thousands of them. What would they take away, those who survived, when the time came to leave this place?

And what of those who had not survived?

I looked from Beaumont's grave over to young Greenley's: scarcely more than a child, cut down on that same terrible night as Beaumont, never to realize his inheritance of one of England's oldest baronetcies. Would he rejoice, knowing that we had prevailed? Would he deem that his own death had been worth the prize? Or what about Sergeant Bell in the section set aside for enlisted men, or Todsmuir lying next to him? Poor Todsmuir, the pimply-faced youth that night at my mother's, trying so hard to grow something so simple as a moustache – to become a man. He had fared as expected under the surgeon's knife. Would either he or Bell deem this summer's work as worthwhile? Given a chance to do it all over again, would they?

I turned back to Beaumont, that tortured soul, who could only find his place in the world at the head of his men during the heat of battle. He, at least, might decide that his death had been worthwhile, for it was death that he had been seeking all along, to his tortured mind the only thing that could give his life meaning.

And what of Daniel? What did he think? It would seem that he had been aboard the Aréthruse after all; for he had not been numbered among the deserters captured at the surrender. Most likely he would spend the rest of his life a penniless exile. Would he believe that this painting from history's stage

351

had been worth the price he had paid? I felt a pang, as I knew the answer all too well.

What of Amherst? Of Wolfe? Of Stockingsdale? Of myself?

Louisbourg had changed us, perhaps myself most of all.

No doubt Amherst and Wolfe would have honours and promotion heaped upon them by a grateful nation. They were, after all, the lions of the moment, giving the king his first important victory in a war that had stretched on for more than three long years, and covered every point of the globe. In England's eyes they must become as gods.

Stockingsdale had won promotion as well, and perhaps had also won another step closer to my mother's hand. Therein lay his ambition of setting himself up as a man of business, and with his extra sergeant's pay might bring more to the bargaining table by way of improving Sally's establishment. Both she and Tess being past their prime, more and younger girls would need to be purchased for the stable. It was not a lofty vision, nor was it respectable by any means; but after a fashion, it was an honest one.

Then, finally, I came to myself.

Had I found what I had come seeking in Louisbourg? Promotion and glory I had in abundance; but I had not come for glory, nor for the heat of battle, nor to drive *Monsieur* from the Americas, nor for riches. I had come because my comrades had come, for their fraternity, and where were they now?

No doubt Daniel would be begging for alms on the filthy streets of Toulouse, sleeping in the gutters, dreaming of home, and wondering how it had all come to such a sorry state of affairs. I wondered if he would ever pause to think of me in some kind way, but the thought brought me no comfort.

As for the others, my promotion had placed them beyond my reach, as surely as if an invisible wall had sprung up between us. Communication now must be restricted through the offices of Stockingsdale, and then only as an officer to an enlisted man. In short, what I had come for had been taken away from me, and in its place I was a pariah among my fellow officers - an outcast in both worlds. That was all to the negative side of the coin.

To the positive, I had been singled out by General Wolfe himself, as a man deserving of leadership, and if my luck held, my star might continue to rise with his, and who knew where that might lead?

I turned away from the little cemetery with a silent farewell, fingering the silver gorget on my chest, and began the trek back to the Fortress.

Against all odds I, Josiah Stubb, whore and whoreson, blackguard and murderer, the lowliest of the low, had succeeded in becoming an officer, and in some measure, a gentleman. In doing so, an entirely new world had opened its doors to me, one where I had yet to see the horizon. The price that I had paid had been staggeringly high, and if asked tomorrow, I might well say that I reckoned it as too high for what I had received in return. Yet a seed had been planted, a tiny mote that I carried with me in my heart, and its name was '*hope*'. Many doors had been opened, and I would carry this kernel with me through each and every one, nurturing it whenever possible, and protecting it whenever it was not. For within its heart lay but a word…one single solitary thought to carry me forward into the future:

Elizabeth!

The End

Bibliography

Boscawen, Hugh. *The Capture of Louisbourg 1758.* Norman, Ok: University of Oklahoma Press, 2013.

Brumwell, Stephen. *Paths of Glory: The Life and Death of General James Wolfe.* Montreal, PQ: McGill-Queens University Press, 2006.

Chartrand, Rene. *Louisbourg 1758: Wolfe's First Siege.* Oxford: Osprey Publishing, Ltd., 2000

Fowler, William. *Empires at War: The Seven Years' War and the Struggle For North America, 1754-1763.* Vancouver: Douglas & McIntyre, 2005.

Johnston, A.J.B. *Endgame 1758: The Promise, The Glory And The Despair of Louisbourg's Last Decade.* Lincoln, NB: University of Nebraska Press, 2007.

Landry, Peter. *The Lion and The Lily.* Bloomington, IN: Trafford Publishing, 2007.

McLennan, John Stewart. *Louisbourg, From Its Foundation To Its Fall 1713-1758.* Halifax NS: Nimbus Publishing, 2011.

Moore, Christopher. *Louisbourg Portraits: Life In An Eighteenth-Century Garrison Town.* Toronto: McClelland & Stewart, 2000

O'Neill, Paul. *The Oldest City: The Story of St. John's Newfoundland.* Portugal Cove, NF: Older Publications, 2008

Young De Biagi, Susan. *Louisbourg: A Living History.* Halifax, NS: Formac Publishing Company, 1997.

Biography

CW Lovatt, is the award-winning author of numerous short stories, as well as the best-selling novel, *The Adventures of Charlie Smithers*. He lives in Canada, and is the self-appointed Writer-in-Residence of Carroll, Manitoba (population +/- 20).

www.ingramcontent.com/pod-product-compliance
Lightning Source LLC
Chambersburg PA
CBHW032204030726
47494CB00020B/453